St. Helens Libraries

Please return / renew this item by the last date shown. Items may be renewed by phone and Internet.

Telephone: (01744) 676954 or 677822
Email: centrallibrary@sthelens.gov.uk
Online: sthelens.gov.uk/librarycatalogue

P

D1 - - NOV 2018
D7 - - APR 2019

THE SECOND CHANCE

CATHERINE MANN

A TEXAN FOR CHRISTMAS

JULES BENNETT

MILLS & BOON

First Published in Great Britain 2018
by Mills & Boon, an imprint of HarperCollinsPublishers,
1 London Bridge Street, London, SE1 9GF

The Second Chance © 2018 Catherine Mann
A Texan for Christmas © 2018 Jules Bennett

ISBN: 978-0-263-93626-1

1118

MIX
Paper from
responsible sources
FSC
www.fsc.org
FSC™ C007454

This book is produced from independently certified FSC™ paper to ensure responsible forest management.

For more information visit: www.harpercollins.co.uk/green

Printed and bound in Spain
by CPI, Barcelona

THE SECOND CHANCE

CATHERINE MANN

To my gifted and delightful editor, Stacy Boyd.

"Write to communicate to the hearts and minds of others what's burning inside ... edit to let the fire show through the smoke." (Arthur Plotnik)

Prologue

Shana had once thought Chuck was the love of her life.

She'd have bet their marriage would last forever.

But today, Shana Mikkelson had to accept that she and Chuck were finished.

Now she just wanted peace, but peace was in short supply as she threw her husband's jeans into a suitcase on their bed. The musky scent of him wafted up from the denim, filling her every breath like a drug she could only quit cold turkey.

Her grief was too deep for tears. Truth be told, there weren't any tears left to shed. She'd just about cried herself into dehydration over this man. She tugged open his dresser drawer, scooped out an armful of socks and strode over to the bed again to dump them into his open luggage.

She kept her eyes on her task and off the bed where

they'd made love so often—although not as much lately. She definitely kept her gaze away from her handsome husband, his strong jaw jutting as he threw gear into his shaving kit. Too easily, she could be drawn into the sensual lure of the bristle on his face or the temptation to stroke his perpetually mussed sandy-brown hair. His headful of cowlicks refused to fall in line with the rest of his traditional good looks in a way that somehow made him all the more appealing.

He was like his home state of Alaska, majestic and untamed. Commanding the eye, and yet opaque as a dense forest trailing up a mountainside.

His footsteps sounded along the hardwood floor as he approached her. The storm in his green eyes broadcast his silent protest to her edict that he move out. He was leaving under duress. Well, tough. She'd given him chance after chance. He would cut back at work only to plunge into the office twice as hard again. He wasn't interested in significant change, and over time, that had diluted their love until there was nothing left.

Even their marriage counselor wore a defeated look the last time they'd seen him together.

Every weekly appointment since then? Chuck had canceled. Citing work conflicts—his standard reason for missed dinner dates, too. She'd stopped trusting his word long before that. Trust was already difficult for her, after the way her father had betrayed her and her mother. She didn't think she would ever recover from the blow of finding out her dad had a secret second family.

Chuck's extended absences wore on her. Deeply.

Shana swallowed back the painful past and focused on the present. The heartbreaking present.

They were finally expecting a baby.

After failed fertility treatments and three miscarriages, she'd gotten pregnant by surprise. Very much by surprise as their sex life had been on the rocks along with their marriage.

Their communication was at an all-time low. She needed the controlled setting of their counselor's office to tell her husband about the baby. But since Chuck was a consistent no-show, he still didn't know.

Sitting alone in the counselor's office earlier that day, she'd reached the end of her rope. She was done. She would tell him about the baby once their separation was official. She couldn't afford another emotional breakdown, bad for the health of the baby when Shana was already in such a stressful environment.

She stormed into his closet, wrapped her arms around four of his suits and lifted them from the rack. "This should get you through work until we can set aside a time for you to pick up the rest of your things."

She slammed the bulk of designer suits into his open case on the bed.

"Shana, I'm sorry for missing the appointment." He paced barefoot, faded jeans hugging his muscular thighs, his long-sleeved tee stretching across his broad shoulders. His hair was still damp from the shower he'd taken after work. "You have to understand the business merger comes with extra hours. I've bowed out of as many things as I can."

Since the Mikkelson matriarch had married the Steele patriarch, the two former rival oil families were merging their families' companies into Alaska Oil Barons, Inc. The lengthy process had siblings from both sides making power grabs at a time when stockholders needed to see unity.

"And yet you're still secluded in the study every night."

They did nothing together except sleep and eat. No more days spent horseback riding, snowmobiling and traveling. And as much as she wanted to trust Chuck that it was only work and that things would change, she could only bury her head in the sand for so long before she smothered to death.

"I'm doing my best, Shana. Things will get better as the merger takes root."

"So you keep saying." She tossed a handful of silk ties into the suitcase. "Every deadline you give for this magical easing at work just gets pushed back. I feel like a fool for believing you."

"Damn it, Shana, you've got to see the effort." He forked his hand through his hair. "I even had my antisocial brother stand in for me at that wildlife preservation fund-raiser. There aren't as many Mikkelsons as there are Steeles. And with Mom and Glenna both married to Steeles, their loyalties are split in a way mine aren't. I'm a Mikkelson. Period."

As was the baby he knew nothing about.

Thinking about raising their child alone made her heart and head ache. Chuck would want to be a part of the child's life. She didn't doubt that. She just wasn't sure how much time he would make for the baby.

Her ability to trust him had been eroded on so many levels.

Resolve strengthened, she faced him. "It's quite clear where your heart lies."

"That's not fair, Shana. These are extreme times. If

I scale back too much, the Steele family could eclipse our vision and our power," he said, sitting on the edge of the bed. Their bed. Nearly four years ago, when they'd married and built their dream home in Anchorage, she'd decorated their bedroom with such romantic hope in each detail of the modern French provincial decor.

They'd spent a lot of hours in this room—making love, sharing dreams. Until the third miscarriage had taken too much of a toll on both of them.

"Then by all means, don't let me hold you back. *Dig in*." She closed his suitcase with a decisive click and spun away hard and fast.

Too fast. The room spun and she gripped the footboard of the bed to keep from stumbling.

"Shana?"

She blinked fast to clear the spots dancing in front of her eyes, to quell the nausea from her blossoming headache.

If she could just get Chuck to leave so she could lie down and breathe…

"Please. Go." She pushed free the two words, a mammoth undertaking with her stress headache spiking.

Why was he walking so slowly? She saw his mouth moving, but nothing was coming out. That didn't make sense. And then he tipped.

Except no.

The whole room tipped because…

Her hand slid from the bed on her way to the floor.

One

Thirty-six hours later

Until today, Charles "Chuck" Mikkelson had run out of ideas for a second chance with his wife. Admitting defeat had never been an option for him, professionally or personally.

But amnesia as a do-over with Shana was extreme, even for him.

Surely he'd heard the neurologist wrong. Chuck's gut knotted. "Do you mean Shana is disoriented? Fuzzy on things like the time or date? Forgot what she had for dinner?"

After all, she'd suffered a minor aneurysm that had left her unconscious for just over thirty-six hours. The longest day and a half of his life. But finally, she was awake. Alive.

Two physicians occupied the secluded sitting area

where Chuck had been brought after a staffer located him grabbing a bite in the cafeteria while a privately hired nurse sat with Shana. Chuck couldn't believe his wife had actually woken up the one time he'd stepped away from her hospital room. The neurologist—Dr. Harris—sat beside Chuck. Another of Shana's physicians stood at the window. Snow was coming down in thick sheets of white, as if the hospital sterility was outside as well as indoors.

"Shana *is* disoriented, but it's more than that," Dr. Harris explained slowly from the chrome-and-leather chair he'd pulled around to face Chuck. "You need to accept that she has lost her memory."

Amnesia. The word still ricocheted around in Chuck's brain. "She doesn't know who she is?"

Dr. Harris closed the tablet that he'd used earlier to show the part of her brain that was affected. "Actually, she does know her name. She recalls details about herself. The memory loss focuses on more recent events."

"How recent?" Chuck asked, unease creeping up his spine.

"She has the month correct. But five years prior."

Five years ago? That meant… "She doesn't remember anything about me."

Much less about being married to him. There were some times between them lately he wouldn't mind forgetting. But the thought of losing memories of the good times with Shana?

Unthinkable.

The two doctors exchanged somber looks before Shana's other doctor took a seat in the other wingback. Dr. Gibson was young, but tops when it came to fertility specialists. It meant a lot to Chuck that the man had shown up to weigh in on Shana's condition even though they weren't trying for another baby.

"Chuck, I'm sorry to say, she does not remember you," Dr. Gibson said in the quietly comforting tone he'd used during Chuck and Shana's failed in vitro and three miscarriages. A phantom sucker punch to the gut wracked Chuck.

It had been bittersweet when Dr. Gibson had assisted in caring for Chuck's stepsister two months ago, after she delivered twins in a car. Pretending nothing was wrong had been hard as hell for Chuck, and Shana hadn't wanted his comfort.

"We were having trouble. Do you think this memory loss is more psychological than physical?"

He'd blamed himself repeatedly for this aneurysm. If they hadn't been fighting, if intense emotions hadn't raised her blood pressure, maybe this wouldn't have happened.

"There's no question she's had an aneurysm, and she's incredibly lucky to have come through it so well. But that's not to say there aren't psychological aspects in play. The body and mind work in tandem."

Staring at the tablet in the doctor's hand, Chuck moved toward a planter, something to rest on. "How do we proceed from here? What do we tell her, and what's her prognosis?"

"I realize that you need answers, but it's too early to project the long term. For now, the counselor on staff here suggests we answer questions as she asks them, no additional information," Dr. Harris warned. "A psychiatrist will be consulting. Things are still so very new."

The obstetrician leaned forward, elbows on his knees. "Let's focus on the positives. Shana's awake and physically fine. The baby's heartbeat is strong. That's news to celebrate."

Chuck frowned, certain he'd misunderstood. Gibson had to be confusing patients after a late shift.

Dr. Harris straightened. "The baby?"

"What baby?" Chuck said precisely. Because no way could Shana be pregnant now of all times. The dark irony of that would be too much to entertain.

Dr. Gibson's eyebrows shot up before he schooled his face back into an alarmingly blank expression. "She didn't tell you about the pregnancy?"

Chuck shook his head slowly, stunned, half-certain there was an error. Fate couldn't be this twisted.

"Shana is expecting," he said baldly. "Two months along. And from your reaction, Chuck, she hadn't told you yet."

Chuck sifted through the hell of the past day and a half. There hadn't been any need to call Dr. Gibson in on the case on a weekend. Chuck had said no to the possibility of pregnancy when the admission staff had asked.

Now he realized the truth of it. Shana had gotten pregnant without an in vitro procedure.

The reality slammed into Chuck like a ton of bricks. Against all odds, they were expecting a child.

Now.

He couldn't even sort through the layers of "stunned" to feel anything but shock.

Chuck's mind winged back to their attending the baptism for his sister Glenna's daughter. He and Shana had actually spent a week getting along, drawn into their hopes for the future, loving their niece and considering adoption. Glenna clearly loved Fleur, no biological bond needed.

Emotions running high, Chuck and Shana had spent a week in bed together. A week that had apparently defied their odds and borne fruit. He had to be there for Shana and their child.

Dr. Harris opened his tablet again, scrolling through his notes. "While I wish we had known so we could have monitored the fetus, none of the medications she's received should present a risk to the baby's development. We'll keep Shana another night for monitoring."

Dr. Gibson said, "We'll also do an ultrasound and start her on progesterone given her prior miscarriages."

Chuck nodded, still reeling. A baby. She was two months along. She'd known and she hadn't told him. Worse yet, she'd thrown him out without telling him she carried his child.

She'd probably realized that if she told him about the baby, it would have taken a force of nature to budge him from their house. He didn't have the luxury of anger right now.

Dr. Gibson tilted his head, placing a hand on Chuck's shoulder. "I realize this is difficult for you, too. You've both been waiting for this baby for so long, and these aren't the circumstances anyone could have foreseen." He gestured toward the door. "Perhaps seeing you will jog her memory."

And therein lay his problem.

He didn't want her to remember.

Because if she did?

Shana would walk, taking their baby with her.

Shana pushed herself up on the hospital bed, taking her time to be sure the room didn't spin as it had the last time she'd tried. People were acting strange around her, and she wanted answers. Instead, she was stuck lying here alone with only a view of snow slamming down on the mountains.

Well, alone except for a nurse who'd been there since she'd woken up and hadn't left her side, even when the doctors stopped by, doctors who'd been short of answers as to why she was here. Even her phone was missing and the remote control for the TV wasn't working. The nurse said it would be fixed soon.

Shana touched her head, exploring her hairline. A small bandage was located just behind her ear. She'd been assured her long hair covered the shaved patch. The doctor had only told her she'd suffered a minor aneurysm, but that otherwise she was physically fine. Beyond that, they'd been cagey.

Thinking back, she tried to remember what had happened before she'd come to the hospital. The last thing she recalled was an argument with her mother over Shana's refusal to reconcile with her father. Even thinking about the fight and her dad made her headache worse.

She knew avoidance when she heard it. Her work as a private detective had taught her all the signs. She also had a sixth sense for these things and trusted her gut.

Something was going on beyond what they'd told her.

Turning to the nurse, who was making updates on the dry-erase board in her room, Shana asked, "Excuse me? When will the doctor be back? I have questions."

Being in limbo was scary. Her imagination was working overtime.

Just as the nurse opened her mouth to answer, a

knock sounded and the door opened to admit a man. Not the doctor who'd been by to check her out when she'd woken. And even though it felt like a slew of staff had come through her room in the past half hour, she would have remembered this guy. He had an unforgettable face, movie-star quality in a rough-around-the-edges way. His light brown hair was just long enough to be mussed by a woman's fingers, coarse hair that would rasp the skin.

A doctor? He didn't have on a white coat. In fact, he was dressed more casually than any doctor she knew. He wore jeans and a long-sleeved T-shirt that bore the wrinkles of someone who'd pulled a long shift. But his sea green eyes were what held her attention in an unbreakable grip. The colors shifted with the icy intensity of a winter sea.

What crazy thoughts to be having right now, but the tug of attraction made her feel normal on a day that was entirely too abnormal.

"I appreciate that you're all being thorough, but I need to get in touch with my mother. I just want to call her, and no one will give me a phone."

Or a remote control. Or a mirror. Or answers.

Okay, this was getting really weird.

Strangely, the nurse left the room. Physicians usually kept a nurse with them for exams. Although the door had been left open.

"Your mother is on her way. She should be here tomorrow." He stopped by the bed, large hands grasping the bedrail.

Before she could help herself, she checked his ring finger and found...

A wedding band.

Disappointment cooled the attraction. So much for drooling over Mr. Cover Model. She pressed her fingers to her forehead. She should be focused on more serious matters rather than this sexy distraction.

"Which doctor are you?" She settled on the reasonable question, a thousand more zipping around in her fuzzy brain.

"You should rest," he said evasively. "You've been through a lot. Your body needs to recharge."

"Aren't you a doctor?" She massaged her temple. "Or an occupational therapist? I can't recall. There were so many people in the room when I woke up."

"I'm not your doctor."

A nervous skitter started up her spine, like something shifting behind a mist, just out of reach. "Remind me who you are?"

"My name is Chuck, and I'm going to get your doctor." He backed up a step. "Things are…complicated."

"Well, Chuck, I've had people checking me and asking questions, but no one has been answering mine." Panic rose inside her. "Tell me what's going on, or give me a phone to speak to my mother. Why are you keeping her from me?"

"Your mother is flying in." He held up a calming, reassuring hand that somehow only made things worse. "She's not available to talk yet."

A pit formed deep in her belly. The walls bore down on her.

Nothing was as it seemed.

This place was starting to feel like a jail, except the private room full of high-tech equipment and flowers was far too posh for incarceration. She needed to get her life in order, call her mom, check in with her boss

about her caseload and an upcoming court case she
would be testifying in.

"Then I guess that leaves you or the doctor to tell
me, because lying here waiting is most definitely
stressing me out." She swung her legs out from under
the sheet.

The room spun.

Chuck rushed forward and clasped her arm. His
touch was at once both steadying and unsettling.

Her gaze went back to that glinting wedding band.
The spark of awareness made her feel ill. Married
cheaters were the worst. Her father's deceit had left a
wake of devastation. The room started spinning again
but in a different way from having wobbly legs.

Something was wrong here. Very wrong.

"I need to know what's going on and if you won't
tell me—" she reached for the call button "—then I'm
going to find someone who will."

He released her arm. "Okay, we'll talk. There's no
agenda here other than looking out for your health. Any
question you have, I will answer honestly."

Alarms went off in her mind. When people said
words like *honestly* and *truthfully*, that usually meant
they had something to lie about. "I want to know why
everyone is acting so strange around me."

"The aneurysm has affected your memory," he said
slowly, carefully.

Her *memory*? The weight of that word hit her hard.
"How so?"

"You've forgotten the past five years."

His words slammed into her, adding a push to that
merry-go-round feel in her head. "Five years? Gone.
And we know each other?"

Even as her world spiraled, the confusion faded as the logical answer came together—his lack of a medical coat, his familiarity…and the wedding band.

Face somber, Chuck rested his hands on her shoulders, holding her gaze with his. "We more than know each other. I'm your husband."

The horrified expression on Shana's face was damn near insulting. Her gaze shot to his wedding band, then back up to his eyes.

Color drained from her already pale face. She sagged back down into the hospital bed, her blond hair splashing across the pillow. He wanted to protect her, to find some way to wrestle their problems into submission. Not that he'd ever had much luck with that. He needed to put aside his own feelings and focus on her. Focus on keeping her calm—and making the most of this time to heal the rift between them.

Shana thumbed her own bare ring finger. "Married? To each other?"

"For almost four years. Your jewelry was taken off when you were admitted to the hospital." He tapped her ring finger lightly, the softness of her skin so familiar—and seductive. Even in the middle of the worst crisis of his life.

She had a beauty and fire that rocked even a hospital gown.

"You're my husband? I… Why… What happened? This is, um, overwhelming."

"I realize it's a lot to absorb." He pulled a chair closer and sat, taking both of her hands in his. "The doctor said the memory loss could be temporary."

"Or it could be permanent." She didn't pull away,

but she did look at their clasped hands with confusion. "How long have we known each other?"

Those soft blue eyes turned hawkish, reading him like an X-ray machine. He nodded, clearing his throat. Determined to deliver objective facts. To not make this worse.

"We met nearly five years ago." He watched her closely to gauge her reaction. He felt like he knew her so well, but also not at all.

How much of the essence of Shana would still exist with the memory loss?

Questions flooded his mind with too many potential futures to absorb at once.

"So my amnesia starts from right before I met you?" she said slowly, suspicion filling her eyes.

She was too astute. It seemed her private investigator skills were as honed as ever.

"It appears so," he said, treading carefully through this discussion that was full of land mines. "I don't expect you to take my word for anything. Talk to my family, talk to your mother, whatever you need to do to feel reassured."

"You have family nearby?"

"I do. A large family. My mother and some of my siblings live in Anchorage, except for my brother, who's closer to Juneau." He shared the details carefully, watching for signs of recollection. Her amnesia could disappear at any moment and she would go back to tossing him out on his ass. "My mother recently remarried and her new husband has an even larger family, mostly local, too."

"A big family is a blessing." Her blue eyes shone with a pain he recognized.

Learning of her father's hidden second family had wounded Shana deeply as a teen. She had three half siblings she'd never met. Her father's betrayal had cut so deeply that Shana still had trouble trusting. Chuck knew he needed to keep that in mind now more than ever. If he made a misstep, this could go so very wrong.

But he couldn't let her go, especially not now.

He would do what was necessary to protect Shana, and their unborn baby.

There'd been a time when they talked of having at least four children. Life had a different plan for them.

"Considering my family and Mom's new husband's family have been business enemies for decades, we weren't sure about the blessing part at first. Family reunions are dicey, but it's starting to shake out."

"So you and I are happily married?"

Now, there was a loaded question. "We had our problems like any other couple," he hedged.

The last thing he wanted to lead with was their hellish fight right before her aneurysm, a fight that had her hauling his clothes from the closet as she told him to move out. But the doctor had said to answer honestly. He could offer up part of their issues without tipping his hand. "We had been going through fertility treatments to start a family, and that put a strain on us."

"But we were committed enough that we wanted a child together."

"*Want* a child. Present tense." He very much intended to be a full-time father to their child. If this pregnancy went well, Chuck would do everything in his power to be there for his kid.

"You have to realize I'm overwhelmed by all of this." She threaded her fingers through her long, honeyed hair, over her ear, her eyes widening. "Amnesia? It's something we all know about, but I never imagined it could actually happen to me."

"Of course. It's a lot. Take your time. I'm here for you, whatever you need, and I'm not going anywhere."

"Thank you—" She frowned, pressing her temples.

"People call me Chuck," he reminded her. "Or Charles."

"What did I call you?"

The last time they'd been together, she'd called him a list of names better left unsaid right now. "You called me Chuck."

"Thank you, Chuck."

The way her voice wrapped around his name sounded as familiar as ever.

A tap sounded on the door. "Hello?"

A recognizable voice called out an instant before the door opened to the youngest of his siblings—Alayna.

The shiest of them all, she entered hesitantly. There'd been a time as a child when she was as talkative as the rest of them, but then she'd changed. Withdrawn. Telling her to leave would be like plucking wings off a butterfly.

But he'd hoped to keep his family out of this situation a little while longer until he could explain the amnesia to them. Alayna had a quiet way of slipping past people's defenses. While the family probably hadn't noticed she'd left, the staff here likely had been charmed and unaware she was supposed to be anywhere but here.

Hell, even he couldn't find it in himself to be mad at her for caring so much.

Alayna rushed to Shana's bedside and hugged her

gently. "Thank goodness you're awake. I've been so worried."

Shana stared over his sister's shoulder with wide, surprised eyes. "Uh, hello, thank you."

Stepping back, Alayna sank into a chair. "I'm so relieved you're awake, and healthy, and the baby's okay. It's a miracle."

How the hell had she heard the news? And damn, he needed to say something quickly before—

Shana's surprised look shifted to outright stunned. "The baby?"

Two

A baby?

Panic and confusion rocked Shana, the young woman's voice still ringing in her ears. She had a child as well as a husband? Her hand slid to her stomach, still flat. Surely there must be some kind of mistake.

Unless they meant a child that had already been born.

"We have a child?" Shana asked, her mind spinning. "How old? You say the child's okay. Did something happen when I had the aneurysm? Was I driving a car or holding—?"

"Nothing like that." He looked sideways at Alayna, who appeared even more confused than Shana felt.

Slack-jawed, the young woman—late teens, perhaps?—glanced back and forth between them. "I don't understand—"

Chuck placed a silencing hand on the girl's shoulder. "Shana, I'd hoped to share this more carefully, but here goes. You're eight weeks pregnant."

Air whooshed from her lungs. Her ears rang. She could barely wrap her brain around this latest shock. "It's... I...um, I don't know what to say."

The young woman tugged on her overlong sweater nervously, tears welling in her eyes. "I'm sorry. I didn't mean to... Well, I'm just so sorry."

Chuck slung an arm around her shoulders and gave her a comforting squeeze even though his eyes broadcast frustration. "Meet my sister." He turned to the younger woman. "Alayna, Shana's suffering from temporary amnesia and has forgotten about the past five years. You couldn't have known. Although I'm curious as hell how you heard about the pregnancy."

Alayna chewed her already short fingernails. "I thought... Oh my. I'm sorry. I was walking by the nurses' station and overheard them talking about things for shift change... I'm really sorry."

Chuck pulled a tight smile. "It's going to be okay, kiddo. Shana just has some gaps in her memory. It'll all sort out."

Shana wished she could be as confident about that. She'd thought about being a mom someday, but this was too much too fast. Not that it seemed she had any choice in the matter. Her life was on warp speed.

Her father had wrecked her mother's life. Shana had always known when it was her time to be a parent, the decision would have to be made slowly and carefully. If she and Chuck had been trying for a child, then their marriage must have been solid.

So why didn't she feel like the love-at-first-sight lightning bolt had hit her? Lust maybe, but not love.

"Shana, I'm really sorry to have confused you or made things more difficult." Fidgeting, Alayna ducked out from under her brother's arm and stood. "I'll just leave, and we can talk another time when things are less, well, confusing. I'm so sorry."

"It's okay."

Or rather, she hoped it would be. Shana exhaled hard, unsure how she felt about carrying a child she couldn't recall conceiving versus there being a child already in the picture, a child she also wouldn't have remembered giving birth to.

Alayna held up a hand. "I really do apologize." She backed away. "I love you to pieces, Shana."

Standing, Chuck cupped Alayna's shoulder. "If you could get coffee for me I would appreciate it." He pulled a twenty out of his wallet. "Get something for yourself, too. Thanks, kiddo."

Once the door closed, Shana pushed herself up to sit straighter in the bed, unsure when she'd sunk into a slouch.

Chuck rubbed the back of his neck, frustration in his eyes. "I apologize for not managing the news better."

"How could you have predicted any of this? No one could." An understatement.

"You're being too understanding." He sank back in the chair by her bed.

"Well, I do have some questions." Even thinking about the possibilities sent a fresh wave of panic through her, but not knowing was worse. "The child is yours, right?"

"Absolutely yes," he said without hesitation. "The baby is mine. And no, we don't have any other children."

She hadn't even considered that. But what else didn't she know? Five years was a long time to make significant memories. Life-changing memories.

"You said we'd struggled with fertility." She chewed her fingernail. "There's just so much to learn about what's happened over the past five years."

And her brain was on overload, weighing every nugget of information before she trusted the latest revelation. Even well-meaning people had private agendas. And she also knew how easily a person could be misled by someone smooth at lying. Her father had taught her that lesson too painfully.

"Then we won't press any further today." He covered her hand with his and held tight. "I would really feel more comfortable if we called the doctors back in and let them check you over or give us more guidance."

His touch felt…familiar somehow. Strong, yet careful all at once.

She couldn't deny the wisdom in his words. "I just want to know one more thing for now."

He grinned—the first time she'd seen him smile, or remembered seeing him smile—and it shone from his eyes, setting her senses buzzing.

He was sheer magnetism personified.

"Like I have the option of arguing with you?"

She couldn't help but smile back. "Apparently you do know me well. Better than I know myself at the moment, which brings me to my question. What's my last name? Or rather, what's your last name? Did I keep my maiden name?"

His smile faded and he clasped her hand, the left one without a wedding ring. "You took my surname. It's Mikkelson."

Surprise spread through her. "As in the oil family Mikkelsons?"

"Yes, the same." He nodded.

There was a wariness to him she couldn't quite understand. Maybe people befriended him for his money. That would have never crossed her mind. Still, a lot of things made more sense now.

"No wonder I have this private room. Your parents own Mikkelson Oil." She pressed her fingers to the headache starting again.

"It's not Mikkelson Oil anymore. My father passed away nearly three years ago. My mother recently married the head of Steele Oil—widower Jack Steele—merging the two companies into Alaska Oil Barons, Inc."

For what should be big news, he didn't look all that happy about it.

"I'm sorry about your father." She squeezed his hand and a shiver of electricity passed between them, like static popping through her.

His thumb stroked along the inside of her wrist over her speeding pulse. "Thank you. He was fond of you."

"I wish I remembered that."

"Me too."

Awareness increased until the static between them was like a meteor shower. Beautiful…but something she feared could leave her scorched.

The door opened again with a call at the same time. "Dr. Gibson here."

Chuck cleared his throat and stepped back. "He's your ob-gyn."

Dr. Gibson entered, wheeling a machine of some

sort, with a nurse trailing behind. "I hear the two of you were going to have a discussion."

Chuck nodded. "I've told Shana I'm her husband, and she knows about the baby."

"How are you feeling?" Dr. Gibson stopped beside her bed.

"Overwhelmed. A little woozy. But mostly just confused."

"That's understandable," he said with a kind bedside manner that must have been reassuring during all the fertility treatments Chuck had mentioned. "The nurse is going to check your blood pressure, and then we're going to do an ultrasound. We'll go as slowly as you need us to."

Shana's heart skipped a beat. So much was happening so quickly she wanted to tell them all to slow down, to stop altogether. But life didn't work that way. She had to face the present. "No need to wait. I want to know as much as I can."

"Ask anything you like, and I'll do my best to answer," Dr. Gibson said. "Are you all right with Mr. Mikkelson staying in the room? I understand these are rather unusual circumstances."

Shana looked at Chuck. He was her husband. Everyone here knew that. And this was his child. As strange as it felt to have him in the room, he had a right to be here. The past day must have been hellish for him with her health scare. "Of course he can stay."

"Thank you." Chuck took her hand in his, his touch strong and confident.

Those green eyes of his held her, reminding her again of a changeable rolling sea. She could so easily dive in, immerse herself in him.

Lose herself.

And that made him dangerous.

Her first priority right now was deciphering who she was.

She couldn't afford to let down her guard around the one man she should be able to trust with her life.

The next day, as Chuck checked Shana out of the hospital, he was still reeling from seeing that ultrasound.

Snow gathered on the ground. The blacktop parking lot looked more like a field than a place for cars. But he, too, felt like he'd fallen away from the present moment.

He recalled instead a different moment. The first time Shana had announced a pregnancy. The promise and hope of that moment. So different than this one.

He had fantasized about a future with Shana and a kid on the way, but in no realm had his fantasies played out this way. They'd watched ultrasounds together in the past, but they had given up on ever seeing one again.

And now, Chuck was preparing to take his pregnant wife home.

A wife who didn't remember him.

He stepped out of the hospital and into the crisp morning air, an orderly wheeling Shana beside Chuck. His personal staffer had brought around his Escalade, the exhaust puffing clouds into the cold. The snow was pristine after yesterday's storm, piles on the side of the roads from snowplows clearing the way.

As the driver opened the passenger door and left the

engine running for Chuck to drive, Chuck held out his hand for his wife. His pregnant wife.

The ultrasound had made this so real.

There was a baby in the mix of this insane time in his life—the merger, the long hours, the amnesia, and a second chance with Shana he didn't want to waste.

Growing up, he'd dreamed of having a perfect marriage like his parents. That wasn't going to happen. He and Shana had too much water under the bridge, and for too long.

But Chuck had never failed at anything in his life. He didn't want his marriage to be the first. Which meant he needed to use this time together to win over his wife.

Shana spent much of the drive back home in a state of shock, mixed with wary hope that surely her memory would be jogged by something. Soon.

So far, no luck.

The streets leading away from the hospital had markers of familiarity, but her mind whirred. Her memory of the main highway was five years out of date.

Five years.

Such a significant amount of time. She tried to conjure up a holiday, an image of her wedding day. Tried to imagine where she might have tied the knot. Wondered who her best friend was.

But no memories pounded against her mind's eye. Just an ultrasound image and a cyclone of questions.

Questions that hammered harder at her chest as they pulled up to their house. Her home. The home she shared with Chuck, heir to an oil empire and sexy as hell in a Stetson. Chuck had told her that her mother would be going straight from the airport to their house. There had been some delays with her flight.

And as they turned the corner, Shana took in the mammoth structure, eyes moving past the snow-covered arbor to the chimney puffing gray smoke rings against the iced sky. So many rooms, so many memories that refused to materialize. Had they picked this place out together? Had she determined which trees should be placed where?

The automatic security gate slid back to reveal a clear view of the massive two-story house with a French country charm. More of that wary hope filled her as she studied the home and grounds. Would she recognize any of it? Whitewashed brick and porches. So many porches on every floor, enclosed and open, as if there was enough space to accommodate any season.

Beautiful, but unfamiliar.

She'd grown up with security, in a cute ranch-style home made of brick. Her mother had worked at the local air force base as a nurse. Her father had always claimed he was short of money. She'd heard her parents fight about it. Sometimes the words were distinguishable, most of the time not. But in the words that had trickled through, her mom had accused him of having a drinking problem. Another time she'd questioned him about a gambling addiction, even other women. The possibility of him supporting a whole second family had never come up, so far as Shana had known.

Who would suspect that?

God, trust was tough, but right now she wasn't in

a position to walk away. She didn't even know who she was.

And if this pregnancy lasted, she wanted to give her child a chance at a loving home and family.

She shook off the past. She hated dwelling on such negative notions and letting her father have real estate in her brain. He didn't deserve so much as a passing thought. Instead, she focused on the house where, according to Chuck, she'd lived for nearly four years.

The property seemed to be about five acres. In addition to the mansion, the grounds had a small barn and a five-car garage. High-end cars lined the driveway, snow billowing down on them. The counselor had encouraged her to have a controlled meeting of the family as early as Shana could agree to it. Shana had replied that the tension of wondering was worse.

So Chuck's family was here, waiting for her arrival.

If only the curtain would rise, revealing her past. This was a magnificent place set against the mountain range. Would she feel more at peace when she saw the decor? Would she recognize her influence in the home?

Modern French provincial was her style. A promising omen.

"Did we decorate together, or did you leave it all to me?"

"We chose artwork together, but the rest is all you." His face was angular in the glow from the dash. With the sun setting early, the headlights cast stripes ahead as he neared their home, passing a frozen pond.

"Were you okay with that?"

"Completely. We blended both of our tastes where it mattered to me. For example, I had some antlers from a hunting trip with my father that I wanted to keep, and you honored that wish in a thoughtful way."

"How so?"

He parked under a portico, the vehicle still running, heat pumping. "You incorporated them into a massive chandelier with candles over our dining room table. It's a great tribute to my dad."

The nostalgia in his voice drew her closer.

"I wish I could remember having met him." Or remember any of the past five years with Chuck. She swallowed, frustrated at the void. The not knowing.

Chuck stroked her hair back from her face. "Losing him was hard on all of us. For you, too."

Her hand gravitated to his jaw and she let herself test the bristly feel of him under the guise of offering comfort. "You're named for him."

"You remember?" He looked up sharply, those attentive eyes causing her cheeks to heat.

"Not the way you mean. It's more of a guess that feels right." She couldn't miss the wariness in his eyes, something that hinted he would rather she didn't remember. A shiver rippled through her and she pulled her hand away. "Although I don't have a clue who each of those cars belongs to."

He pointed to the first car. "That's my mother's. She wanted to see you in the hospital, but I didn't want you overwhelmed with new faces."

Was that true? Or did his family not like her and that's why only his younger sister had been around?

Either way, he'd been right to keep them away from the hospital, because with Shana's memory of the past five years still a no-show, she was starting to panic over going into her house emotionally blind to re-meet so many people who already knew her.

Maybe having them come over hadn't been such a great idea after all.

But now it was too late to go back.

As the thick door swung open and she stepped through, a sheer mass of humanity greeted her. When Chuck said he had a big family, she hadn't fully comprehended what that meant.

Her eyes flicked as she tried to take in all these new—and yet not new—people and this house at the same time. A tall blonde woman with a baby on her hip leaned against the iron railing of the staircase, her smile warm and welcoming. A cluster of people stood on the white-and-brown-dappled fur rug, crowding around the plush chairs.

Chuck pronounced their names as they moved, but Shana's head throbbed at all the information. She tried to imagine picking out the furniture with the man who held her steady as she pushed through a barrage of people.

People who seemed genuinely concerned for her. People who felt like strangers.

They moved further into the house, her hand reaching out to touch the wall as they turned from the entry hall into the dining room. Her eyes scanned the long wooden table flanked by eight large chairs. It held a table setting for two.

A snapshot of daily life.

Bouquets of fresh flowers and tall candles ran down the table's spine. A familiar touch—a tradition from her mother. She'd brought that here, to her life as a married woman.

A small comfort. But a comfort she embraced, the kind of nod from the universe that something made sense. It gave her the strength to meet even more people.

It helped to divide them into two family trees rather than take them in as one mass of blended family. Chuck's mother, Jeannie, was head of the Mikkelson clan with two sons and two daughters. Jack Steele— Jeannie's new husband—had five adult children, three sons and two daughters. His oldest son was married to Chuck's oldest sister, and the couple had a baby girl. The oldest Steele daughter was married to a scientist and they had twin baby girls.

Shana's heart tugged at the sight of those little ones, reminding her of the child she'd only just learned she carried but that she already loved. Somewhere in the back of her mind, she recalled hearing that Jack had lost his wife and another daughter in a plane crash over fifteen years ago. It had probably been big news across the state at the time, given the prominence of this family.

"It's kind of you all to come greet me." She sank into one of the chairs in the living room, Chuck staying close behind her. His presence, the touch of his hand to her shoulder, stirred something in her. A feeling. A pull. A recognition.

But the touch couldn't assuage her frustration or the dizzying impact of re-meeting five years' worth of connections. She glanced up at Chuck, his sandy-brown hair tousled upward. It caught the light reflecting off the mirror that hung above the mantel.

A mirror world indeed.

She struggled to force that memory of ordering the

piece to her mind's eye. Even as she studied the antlers in front of her, she failed to locate the story from her perspective. All that Shana had was the retelling of a memory that Chuck had shared with her.

As if he knew her distress, Chuck gave her shoulder a quick squeeze.

The smile lines on Jeannie's face deepened. A warm smile. One Shana wanted to take comfort in. The older woman gave a knowing nod. "I can tell by Chuck's face that he thinks we're overwhelming you. But when we heard your mother's flight was delayed for snow, we wanted to bring you something to welcome you home. We're here just to lay eyes on you, bring you food, then be on our way."

"You're hoping that if I see you, it'll jog my memory. I'm sorry, but it doesn't. I may never remember. Thank you for trying, though. For caring." She swallowed, hard. Leaned back into the wooden chair. Looked at the faces of the Mikkelsons and the Steeles. Noted how comfortable they seemed around the long dining room table. Knew their appearance here to be motivated by love.

Somehow that recognition pained her.

"I'm just glad you're alive and well," Jeannie said. "And know we're all only a phone call away if you have any questions."

"I appreciate it. Please stay for dinner." Shana bit her lip. Wishing she had something more to say. Wishing this whole meeting could somehow miraculously deliver up the memories she sought, for herself and for her child. And for this sexy man at her side? For the love she must have lost?

Why was it so difficult to wrap her brain around?

Disappointment swamped her.

In spite of Chuck's family's warm welcome, Shana still couldn't shake an unsettled feeling.

She couldn't stop searching for a reason why she was so certain there was trouble in paradise.

Three

Chuck leaned on the door frame, hand up in a static wave as darkness flooded the horizon. The light from his sister's car blinded him ever so briefly as she threw her SUV into Reverse. He was still unsure how the events of the last several hours had gone.

Running a hand through his thick hair, he stretched, his neck popping. Releasing some of the tension he'd carried.

The night had been an exercise in dodging one land mine after another, worrying about what his family might reveal. He appreciated their concern, and Shana had been emphatic about seeing them, hoping somehow that their appearance would break the dam to release her memories.

All the more reason for him to hustle them out the door. If only he'd managed to dissuade Shana from inviting them in the first place. But to push her to wait would have made her suspicious. He needed her calm. He needed to gain time with Shana, time enough to forge a connection strong enough that she wouldn't leave.

All the more reason he was glad to see his family off. Finally, the last of them had left. Exhaling hard, Chuck closed the door and armed the security system.

Shana should be resting. She was fresh out of the hospital, pregnant and disoriented. Although she'd seemed to welcome the distraction of other people in the house, most likely to keep from being alone with him.

At least his family had been sensitive enough not to mention their marital problems. However, his mother had pulled out photo albums in an attempt to help jog Shana's memories—including his and Shana's wedding pictures, none of which had sparked the least bit of re-membrance. A relief. And strangely irksome as well.

Chuck scrubbed a hand over his jaw, striding past the dining room, cleared by extra staff he'd hired to help during Shana's recovery. Even though he now em-ployed a chef, his family had left behind enough food for an army even though they'd all eaten their fill until the candles had burned down in the silver candelabras. Even as he'd wished them gone, he'd been grateful for the positive spin they'd put on his marriage. Their pres-ence had given off a happy family vibe he needed to stress with his wife.

As much as he told himself to take one day at a time, Chuck found he needed to have this settled, to know Shana would be staying with him. There was no room for compromise on this matter.

A few steps farther down the corridor, he discov-ered Shana in the study, reading on the sofa, a mug of hot cocoa on the coffee table. A blaze roared in the fireplace. Above, snow piled on the skylights, hiding nearly all of the inky night sky. Her hair was loose down her back, her legs curled up under her.

So many times, he'd found her like this in the past. In the early days of their marriage, he wouldn't have thought twice about joining her there, skimming his hands up her lovely legs. Kissing her senseless. Peeling her clothes away until they were both naked, the firelight licking shadows over their skin.

At one time, he'd thought they had a future. Now...

He had to ensure that her future—his child's future—included him.

Perhaps he could recover some ease with her in this room, in a space where they'd been happy. So often they'd shared time in the study, both of them in here while he'd worked from home. Even a year ago, they had still been close enough that he could distract her from her work with a neck massage, or an impromptu dance when her favorite song popped into the speakers from her playlist. Hopefully, those moments would happen again someday soon.

Because no matter what the past had held for them, or what the future promised, he still desired her.

He knelt on one knee by the sofa. "How are you feeling?"

"Exhausted, but cared for." She bit her lip before continuing, "I'd hoped meeting your family would spark memories, but no luck."

Guilt pinched, but it was best for all of them if she didn't remember right away.

Or ever.

He picked up her hand and held it loosely, keeping

himself in check. How easy it would be to sit on the sofa and pull her into his lap. "Shana, I know this has to be awkward for you."

It had been so long since they'd shared that kind of ease.

"That's an understatement." Her eyes held his for a moment before she eased her hand away. She searched the room, her gaze never lingering long on any one spot. He followed her frenzied survey, taking in the bookshelves that arched high to the ceiling. Those shelves had been one of the things she'd loved most about this place, along with the greenhouse. He remembered how her face had lit up at the thought of a ladder leading to books wrapped around the room.

She showed no signs of remembrance on her face.

Giving her space—for now—he pushed to his feet. "I want you to know I'll be sleeping in the guest room."

"Thank you. I realize this is tough for you, too."

"That's an understatement." He repeated her words, except for his own reasons. "But I know it's far worse for you. I want you to take your time, take care of yourself, and the baby."

"Thank you for understanding."

He was walking a tightrope, needing to give her space, but working with a ticking time bomb that meant she could remember their past at any moment.

For now, though, there was peace.

Since she was settled, this would be a neutral time to check on work without worrying about her getting angry at him.

He slid behind the desk and fired up his laptop, watching Shana out of the corner of his eye.

She shifted on the sofa and hugged a throw pillow

over her stomach where their child was nestled, growing. "What are you working on?"

"Clearing away paperwork so I'll have more days off to spend with you."

"I'm not an invalid. And my mother will be here for a week." She tipped her head to the side. "Are you one of those guys who can't stand his mother-in-law?"

He weighed his words carefully as the truth could be tricky on this one. Her mom—Louise—had never seemed to warm to him. But then, she didn't trust many people. Life had left her overcautious.

"About four years ago your mother took a job in California." Louise was a civilian employed nurse at a military installation. "Most of the time, you visited her rather than having her coming back here."

"Hmm…" Shana seemed to digest the information, glancing around the library, her gaze lingering on the laptop and the stack of files. "I'm sorry to keep you from the office."

The words felt like a blow.

They'd had so many arguments over him being a workaholic. He didn't think of his work that way since he loved his job. He'd been groomed to take over for his parents once they retired, except retirement hadn't come. His father had died. His mother had doubled down, working to numb her grief. Only recently had she stepped back, since she'd fallen for her business rival. But now they were merging the oil companies.

It was a dangerous time for Chuck to take personal leave, but he didn't have much of a choice. His wife needed him, and he needed to win her back. For his own sake, and for the sake of their child.

Their family's future depended on it.

He felt the weight of her gaze on him and looked up.

Shana closed her book and reached for the mug of hot cocoa. "What's going on?"

"Why do you ask?" He clamshelled his laptop, looking directly at her.

She set aside her mug and hugged her knees to her chest. "You look worried. I hate that I'm putting more stress on you. I know this has to feel even more awkward for you than it does for me."

He shook his head dismissively. "What makes you say that? You're the one who's lost five years."

"But I'm not the one whose spouse doesn't remember me. I know that has to hurt, and I'm so sorry."

She hugged her knees tighter, eyes locking with his. The heat rose between them in an undeniable connection, building like the crackling fire.

"I'm focused on what's best for you."

"Then what's got you so worried? I don't have to be a private detective to read the tension in you."

He creaked back in the office chair, deciding to share. "We've been struggling with data leaks for a while, trying to follow the trails in email exchanges."

"A mole in the company?" She uncrossed her legs and pushed herself off the couch. As she moved through the white room, her hands lingered on stray books on the coffee table. She walked to the fireplace and picked up a heavy crystal photo frame off the mantel—a picture of the two of them from a romantic train getaway, from Anchorage to the Arctic Circle. He'd been trying to cheer her up after a failed in vitro attempt.

"Seems so. We hired a new employee who, as it turns out, had a vendetta against us and the Steeles."

"What does the spy have to say?" She set the frame

down and drew closer. Lithe as ever. Hot as hell. She sank back into the sofa, curling up.

"She's disappeared somewhere in Canada." He righted his chair, then stood and walked toward her.

"And you've hired private investigators."

"Of course." He sat on the sofa, close enough that her toes grazed his thigh and the scent of her perfume tempted him to bury his face in her neck and inhale deeper. He recalled well how she always preferred floral scents in perfume, shampoo, even essential oils, all carrying through her love of flowers.

As much as he hated the unanswered questions at work, he welcomed the ease of being with Shana this way, without the anger of the past year that had torn their marriage apart.

"What do the investigators have to say about the data trails from her email exchanges?" she asked.

"Nothing."

"Nothing at all?" She shook her head. "That's strange."

"And you think you could do better."

"I surely couldn't do any worse."

He snorted on a laugh. "Fair enough. What are you proposing?"

"I don't know how I used to spend my time while we were married, but I will go stir-crazy just sitting around. Let me do my part and take a stab at finding this woman." She tapped his mouth before he could talk.

The feel of her fingers on him made him ache to clasp her wrist and pull her onto his lap. Seal his mouth to hers and lose themselves in the way they connected best.

But pushing too far, too fast would only harm his cause. So he simply took her arm and pressed a kiss to her palm before lowering her hand. Her throat moved in a long swallow that sent a surge of victory through him.

"So, Shana, how do you want to proceed?"

"Have the human resources department send me her application and any other information on her. I'll start by digging around on the internet to see what I can find."

He wanted to wrap her in a cocoon, keep her close to protect her. Shana was strong-willed, and her fire had attracted him to her from the first.

But her fire, her determination, also made things tough right now. If he wasn't careful, she'd apply those investigative skills to their past.

Perhaps internet research would distract her from the amnesia, keep her from digging too deep into how things had been between them.

The last thing he wanted was for her to find out that on the day of her aneurysm, they'd decided to separate.

For the first time since waking up disoriented in the hospital room, Shana could finally breathe.

The warm shower sluicing down her back eased her tensed muscles. The stress came as much from her too-sexy husband as it did from any medical issues.

If only she could hide in the shower forever, just let the water wash away all tensions, all concerns. She would pretend for just a moment her life was simple and uncomplicated as the scent of her shampoo mingled with the aroma from the floral-scented candle she'd lit.

How could she have forgotten her marriage? Had the aneurysm wiped five years from her mind for life? Or was the loss stress-related, not coincidental that the memory loss started at the time she'd met her husband?

Trust was difficult enough for her under normal circumstances. She slid her hand over her stomach.

There was no room for error. The stakes were too high. And she needed to take care of her health, which included rest.

She turned off the shower and stepped out onto the heated floor. A sigh of pleasure slipped free. She definitely didn't remember these, or any of the other luxuries from this life with Chuck Mega-Wealthy Mikkelson.

Except she was a Mikkelson now, too.

This was all too much to think about.

She should be relaxing. She tugged a towel free and dried off, then wrapped the fluffy cotton around her body. She squeezed water from her hair, making her way into the dressing area.

And slamming into a warm wall of hunky man.

Chuck.

Heat from the floor radiated up to send a flush of awareness through her body. Maybe it had been a bad idea moving in here with him as she waited for a cure for the amnesia. This kind of intimacy, the magnitude of their attraction, all of it so fast was…unsettling.

"Excuse me," he said, clasping her shoulders, his broad hands launching a tingle of excitement through her breasts. "I was just coming in to get some clothes from our closet."

Our closet.

She drew in a couple of steadying breaths. "I, uh…" Her mouth went dry. She clutched the towel in a fist between her breasts. She should step away.

Should.

"I'll leave you to it, then."

His thumbs moved along her collarbone. "I thought you were still downstairs in the kitchen."

The touch scrambled her thoughts and stole her breath.

"I feel bad kicking you out of your bedroom," she said, her eyes drawn to the vibrant green of his. "I can sleep in the guest room. It's not like I'll miss this space since I don't remember it being mine."

Theirs. Together.

Her gaze slid past him into the bedroom. How had they spent their time here before she'd become ill?

She looked up to the tray ceiling and toward the black fan. She felt disoriented, spinning and spinning, like the blades circulating heated air. She wondered if she'd ever stop circling around this awareness, this nagging feeling at the back of her mind.

She hated how she looked at the plush bed, with its overstuffed white pillows pressed against a headboard that practically went to the ceiling, and remembered...nothing.

This place felt foreign.

Even the pieces of her life that she recognized—like the antique perfume bottle from her grandmother on the mirrored bedside table—felt out of place. Familiar but not enough to comfort her.

She realized Chuck hadn't responded. His eyes had been tracking hers as she struggled to deal with this attraction to a man she barely knew.

"I feel bad that things are so awkward between us," she said.

"There's no instruction manual for how to deal with this."

She closed her eyes. Breathed in a hint of his aftershave, which sent a shiver through her that had nothing to do with the chilly day. She opened her eyes. "I've turned your life upside down."

"More like you're turning me inside out in that towel."

"Oh. Right. Sorry." Heat stung her face.

"You have nothing to apologize for. It's not your fault." His hands slid down her arms and then away from her body as he stepped back. "Good night, beautiful. Sleep well."

After the way his touch had felt?

Doubtful her night would be at all restful.

Chuck stretched back into the stiff off-white chair. He blinked his eyes clear, gearing up for another late night in his home office. The yellow light from the desk lamp dully illuminated the study.

He stacked Shana's things on the desk, putting her paperwork off to the left side, adjacent to the floral arrangements she'd picked out only four days ago.

Might as well have been in another lifetime.

The prospect of divorce rattled him.

Mikkelsons didn't fail.

He'd been unable to sleep after walking in on Shana coming out of the shower. Only a couple of days ago they'd been at each other's throats. Now, desire lit up the room every time they were near.

But he saw the wariness in her eyes. And truth be told, he wasn't interested in launching himself into the emotional shredder with her. He needed to save their marriage, but he also needed to keep things lighter between them. Surely they could enjoy the chemistry they shared and get back on an even footing in their relationship. Eventually, if this pregnancy came to term, they could also bring up their child.

Chuck shook his head, needing to focus. And not on Shana for the moment. For now, he needed to pay attention to the numbers on the chart in front of him and prepare for his late-night meeting.

He highlighted a few lines and scribbled thoughts off to the side. His messy handwriting populated the second page of the document. His eyes slid from the chart to his watch. 11:30 p.m.

Sure, it was an unconventional meeting time. But everything lately seemed mighty damn unconventional. He fired up his laptop and turned on another light in the office. He looked around at the space—his shared space with Shana—and could see all the memories. How she'd arranged the bookshelf first by genre, then by author. She loved reading. And he'd been happy to help her locate the perfect ladder, the perfect carpenter for the recessed bookshelves, the perfect table desk. A lifetime ago.

A lifetime he might have another shot at.

The ding of Broderick's conference call interrupted Chuck. Right. Business. Broderick's uncle Conrad was a night owl, too, so the late time didn't faze him, either. As for Chuck, he welcomed the chance to throw himself into work for a while, no matter the time. Broderick had set the time for after his daughter was asleep.

The video feed lurched to life, pixels turning smooth. Conrad and Broderick sat in the conference room at the Alaska Oil Barons, Inc., office, clean-cut and ready.

No Jack Steele this go-around. Just his second-in-command, Broderick, Jack's eldest son. And Jack's brother Conrad stepping in to consult.

Conrad Steele leaned forward, deep blue eyes a stark contrast to his thick salt-and-pepper hair. In his deadpan way, no emotions entering his expression, Conrad asked, "How're things with Shana?"

"Still no recollection of the past. But we're settling into a new routine." One full of desire that left Chuck aching. He wouldn't mention that. "I appreciate your accommodating my working from home."

Broderick nodded, brow tense as he leaned forward, too, setting a pen down on the dark wood conference table. "If you need time off, just say the word."

Chuck barked a laugh. Time off was the furthest thing from his mind. "Last time I took a month for personal reasons, my brother threatened to break my legs."

Conrad smiled tightly. "Trystan handled himself well with the press and at the fund-raiser."

Trystan was the younger Mikkelson brother, who had been adopted by Jeannie and her first husband after his mother, Jeannie's sister, had become addicted to drugs. He was as much a part of the family as all the other Mikkelson siblings.

"Other than punching the paparazzi." Broderick shot his uncle a look.

The older man shrugged. "Some would say the situation warranted a fist to the face."

Grinning, Chuck said, "And some would say you're siding with my brother to cause trouble."

Conrad steepled his fingers along his nose. "Trust between our families isn't going to happen in a day."

Hell yeah on that point. "Especially when people

like Milla Jones are throwing around accusations about my family."

Chuck wondered what Shana might find once she dug into the former employee's files. Shana might have turned his life upside down, demanding more of Chuck than he knew how to give, but there was no denying she was all aces at her job. He wondered why he hadn't asked her to take this on before her accident. Maybe because she'd seemed to have given up on her career as an investigator to make time for her fertility treatments.

Maybe that was one of the mistakes they'd made as a couple.

Conrad creaked back in his chair. "You said it. Not me."

Silence descended. All three men exchanged looks, but no one spoke.

After what seemed like an eternity, Chuck shifted his weight forward, ready to make this conversation productive. "Shana's feeling at loose ends sitting around the house. I've asked her to look into Milla Jones's disappearance." As well as the woman's accusations about the Mikkelson family possibly being involved in the crash that killed Jack Steele's wife and daughter. Chuck hadn't shared the depth of the accusations with Shana yet. It had felt like too much to pile on her tonight.

And he hadn't wanted to taint her feelings about his family. About him.

Broderick crossed his arms over his chest, annoyance written all over his body. "We've dedicated unlimited resources to company investigators looking for Ms. Jones."

And they hadn't turned up a thing. "It doesn't hurt

to have more eyes on the lookout. Shana is good at what she does. I should have thought to ask her earlier."

More than once, Shana had accused him of not supporting her work. In the early days of their marriage, he'd traveled so much on business it had started to take a toll on their relationship. He'd persuaded her to take a hiatus to travel with him. A few months had turned into a year and her position had been filled once she discussed returning. And then they'd turned their attention to starting a family.

Conrad spread his arms in surrender. "Well, by all means, if she can find Milla Jones, then I'm in. Whatever we can do to help her, we will."

"Thank you," Chuck said. "She'll need something to take her mind off losing her memory."

Conrad leaned forward on his elbows. "How are you?"

"Concerned," he admitted. "She's so damn stubborn."

A rustle from across the room caught his attention. A little noise, the sound of footfalls, the creak of a door hinge. He looked up and over, past the computer screen and into the depths of the ill-lit room.

Shana.

She stood at the door frame, blond hair loose.

But those eyes.

After being married to Shana for nearly four years, he knew that look all too well.

He was in the doghouse.

Four

Shana held herself in check by sheer force of will.

How. Dare. He.

Appease her? Placate her?

Lingering in the threshold to the home office—her *shared* home office—her blood boiled.

Did this man know her at all after five years together? And while she might still be locked out of her memories, she couldn't imagine that she had changed so much that any man—let alone her husband—would think she needed to be thrown a pity case to work on.

As if that would solve a damn thing.

Gripping the door frame, she felt her cheeks heat even more as she locked eyes with Chuck. The glow from the computer screen somehow made this broad-shouldered man seem impossibly Viking-like, with that squared jaw and stubble.

Her righteous anger at being thrown a case as a *distraction* was paralleled only by her anger at finding him so damn sexy.

She'd come downstairs for a snack in an attempt to feed her emotions that were still too tingly from their encounter outside the shower. Of course, that could also have something to do with why she couldn't keep herself from following the intoxicating timbre of his voice.

Too bad his words hadn't matched up to the allure.

Fury firing her steps, Shana crossed the threshold into the workspace, hugging her terry cloth robe tighter around her.

"You're just trying to pacify me?"

"Hold on, I need to sign off." Chuck looked back at the computer screen. "Conrad, Broderick, let me get back to you later." Closing the laptop, Chuck pushed up from the desk. "I'm not sure how much you over-heard, but—"

"I heard enough to know you only asked me to help this investigation because you want to keep me busy—" she paused for a breath, anger making her dizzy "—not because you truly believe I have any-thing of value to offer."

Chuck took a beat, studying her face. Those green eyes shone in the dim room, bearing down into her soul. Awakening something...

But never mind that.

She crossed her arms over her chest in a challenge. No backing down.

"You want the truth? Fine." He walked around the corner of the desk and sat on the edge of it. "I want you to rest and to devote your energy to healing, for yourself and the baby. Can you imagine how awful it was to see you pass out and not be able to revive you?"

Anger seeped from her, replaced by an image that, even though she couldn't remember the event, she could still imagine clearly, and it tugged at her heart for him. "I'm sorry you went through that. But surely it crossed your mind that pregnant women pass out sometimes."

He stayed silent, his face sanitized of expression.

He was hiding something. God, she hated the inequality of him knowing *everything* while she stood in a void.

What would it have been like to meet him on even footing? The attraction between them was so intense.

And it was distracting her from reading the signs.

Something was off between them, and she needed to get to the bottom of it.

Her sleuthing skills screamed, an alarm walloping through her head. *Deep breaths.* She could figure this out. She had to, for the sake of her future here with this man. For the sake of her unborn child.

"You knew I was pregnant, didn't you? Or did you?" Her legs folded and she sat on the armchair near him as the truth became all too evident. "You didn't know about the baby. Why didn't I tell you?"

He scrubbed a hand along the back of his neck. "I suspect because of failed in vitro attempts and three miscarriages. You didn't want to get my hopes up."

"That makes sense." Yet it still felt like there was more to the picture when it came to why she would keep such news from him, from her husband.

"You sound skeptical."

"I sound like someone who doesn't know you well

enough to form an opinion on whether you're trust-worthy or not," she blurted out, head tilting as if to better take him in amid the books and flowers. She'd dreamed of a space like this when she was younger. Of course, younger felt like only a year or two ago—not six or seven years ago.

His jaw flexed, his lips thinning.

"You're angry." She stated the obvious, curious about why he'd had that reaction.

"I don't like my honor being called into question," he said tightly. "I just want what's best for you, for us."

Her own irritation was fanning back to life. "And that includes pacifying your baby's mother with busy-work."

"I respect your professional instincts. I always have." He sounded sincere.

Still, she felt the need to press. "So I've been work-ing during our marriage? Where's my business office?"

"You worked for the first year, until we decided to start a family."

She'd completely stepped away from the career she loved? Another twist, a blow she hadn't even consid-ered. "I haven't worked in three years?"

"You did some consulting on occasion. And you organized incredible fund-raisers for the family." He gave her a roguish smile. "I have to tell you that if you dismiss the importance of that, there are women in our family who'll come after you."

"Your mother the business executive? Your sister the CFO? Or your stepsister the lawyer?" she retorted.

She refused to let his roguish smile throw her off the scent. She'd found a sensitivity and she needed to follow it.

He stood from the desk and knelt on one knee in front of her. "Are you trying to provoke me into an argument?"

"Is that what we used to do? Fight a lot?"

She wanted to spark some memory free, something tangible to hold on to from the past five years with this man she'd cared for—enough to marry him, to give up her career to try having children together.

He took her hand in his, his clasp steady, launching tingles up her arm. "I realize that losing your memory has to be…untenable. Finding out you're married, you gave up your job, must be so hard. Finding out you're carrying a child you don't recall conceiving is more than unfair." He palmed her stomach possessively. "But let me reassure you, I remember well when we made this baby."

Sliding his hand from her still-flat belly, he lifted her hand and pressed his mouth to her wrist. Her whole body flushed with a heat that rivaled the intensity she'd felt outside the shower. The sizzle of an almost-kiss, inhaling one another's breaths, their scent.

There was no question.

They shared a connection that had nothing to do with her pregnancy.

Chuck rocked back on his heels, stood and walked away, leaving her with more questions than answers.

Chuck had a sneaking suspicion he'd find Shana in the barn.

When they'd started dating, his parents' barn had been her favorite place. He recalled how she'd taken solace in the quiet caring of the horses, a natural horsewoman. He'd gotten her a fiery filly soon after they'd tied the knot, a bay Tennessee walking horse with a feathery mane. Her name was Sedna, after the Inuit goddess of sea animals.

Over the past four years, they'd spent time breaking the horse, transforming the leggy colt into a beautifully disciplined mare.

Unlike the barn of his professional enemy turned family, the Mikkelson family barn operated for business as well as for family recreation. The sleek steel fifteen-stall structure featured small turnout paddocks and a climate-controlled tack room.

He walked down the spine of the building until he reached the last stall on the right side. Sedna's stall.

Realizing the fight last night would not win Shana over, Chuck knew he had to do better. He had to romance her. Because he'd been given a second chance to regain the marriage he'd almost lost. And because he needed to taste her lips and feel her body again.

So he'd gathered a bouquet of irises from their hothouse. He held the flowers behind his back and swept off his Stetson, hooking it on the back of a post.

Biting wind whipped through the open door to the small paddock behind Sedna's stall. Shana's honeyed hair fanned around her, her cheeks chapped from the cold.

It had taken all his willpower not to kiss her lips last night. The velvety softness of her wrist had nearly undone him.

She held a soft brush in her hand and seemed to absently brush the horse. While the memory of Sedna might not be available to her, his wife's ease around horses remained.

An ease that had once allowed them to take a weekend-long camping trek through the woods on horseback during the summer. He'd always been mesmerized by how Shana looked just as elegant in jeans and boots as in an evening gown and jewels.

In the chill of the night, they'd warmed themselves with lovemaking. He could still hear the echo of her sighs, still feel the glide of her body. He'd held her in his arms afterward as the sun rose early in the summer months.

As if she could read his thoughts, Shana glanced over her shoulder. A question already formed in the tension of her brow.

He brought his arm from behind his back, his fist around the paper-wrapped irises from the greenhouse. Year-round flowers had been his first anniversary gift to her. "You wanted to know more about the past five years. These always made you smile."

A smile spread across her face now, her eyes lighting with pleasure as she took the flowers from him.

"Thank you. This is so thoughtful, but you don't have to buy me things." Still, she buried her face in the blossoms and inhaled.

"Consider it a first-date gift." Except this wasn't a date. "Or a first-full-day-home gift."

"They're gorgeous." She smiled over the bouquet, her blue eyes deepening with joy to a near purple echoed in the flowers. "Thank you."

"They're from the greenhouse."

Her eyebrows shot up. "We have a greenhouse?"

"I like the way you say 'we.'" He rested an elbow on the horse stall, his shoulder brushing hers.

Her smile faded. "That was presumptuous of me."

"Not at all." He angled closer, their knees grazing,

his back blocking the wind rolling through the open barn door. "This is our home. This is where we've built our life together."

Her hands clenched in the paper, crackles echoing along with horse's whinnying. "Chuck—"

"No need to say anything." He toyed with a lock of her hair. How long had it been since he'd flirted with her? Too long. "I realize this is all new to you. Let me know how I can help."

"I want to know—I want to remember. I feel at such loose ends." She glanced up at him. "If you're still interested in my helping out in researching the missing employee, I *could* use something to occupy my time, especially until my mother arrives."

"I would very much appreciate your expertise in digging into Milla Jones's disappearance."

"Okay then. I'm all in. Even after my mom arrives." She looked down, their boots almost touching on the dusty barn floor. She shuffled her feet. "Do you and my mother get along?"

"Sure." He took the flowers from her and set them along the stall ledge.

"Care to elaborate?" She leaned back, arms across her chest.

Were her breasts swollen from pregnancy or was it his awareness that made them so appealing? Either way, he burned to test their weight in his hands.

His eyes grazed her chest before sliding up to her face. "Your mother and I don't argue."

"I guess I was looking for details on what you two talk about, or what you enjoy about each other."

He searched for something to share that wouldn't bring up her father. He knew she didn't like to talk about him. "Your mom makes my favorite cookies when she visits."

"What are your favorite cookies?" She went back to brushing Sedna. The horse shivered, swishing her tail lazily.

"Macadamia nut."

"Sounds delicious. Now I'm craving some."

"Craving?" His chest went tight.

She nodded, dropping her arm from brushing. "I guess that's a pregnancy thing."

He smiled and draped an arm around her shoulders.

She stiffened but didn't pull away.

"Do you mind my touching you?" He squeezed her shoulder lightly.

"I don't think so." She swayed toward him ever so slightly.

"A resounding endorsement," he said drily.

She let out a low laugh. A real, genuine one.

A surge of hope—and desire—filled him.

Laughing with her, teasing, felt good. But he was all too aware of how that laughter would stop if she remembered their more recent past before he had a chance to wrangle his way back into her bed again. Before he could reestablish the connection they had lost.

He was walking a tightrope, balancing savvy timing with racing against the clock.

One week and…nothing.

Not one memory bubbled to the surface. Nothing. Nada. Zilch.

Shana had tried holding items throughout the house. Smelling them. And still not one memory came.

She trudged forward on her daily walk, snowshoes crunching the packed surface. The crisp air teased her lungs and senses, but she couldn't shake the frustration of still feeling like an interloper in her own life.

The Mikkelson and Steele families were all visiting today. Not one person in the sea of faces managed to dislodge a memory from its hiding place.

Closing the last few steps to the house, she puffed free a cloud of air. She knelt and removed her snowshoes, one, then the other. Holding them, she opened the side porch door into the mudroom, relishing the quiet before descending into the chaos that was her new normal. So many people—relative strangers—hovered over her, staring at her with expectant eyes.

Her mom had never made it. After having had her flight canceled multiple times for weather, she'd decided to wait until later to visit rather than risk using up all her vacation days for a trip that might not happen.

Shana was on her own to sort through her convoluted life.

Glenna, Chuck's elegant sister, had invited Shana on a snowshoe walk through the grounds. His eldest sister seemed warm and thoughtful. She'd married the eldest Steele brother, Broderick. So many names still.

Glenna had popped back inside to check on her child, leaving Shana in the mudroom between the family inside the house and outside. Hand on her stomach, Shana let her eyes flutter closed.

She'd worked off some of her tension from being in close quarters with her sexy husband, who'd been Prince Charming personified every minute of every day. He hadn't been pushy, and that made him somehow all the more alluring. Every accidental touch and thoughtful gift had her tied up in knots.

He'd made dinner himself the other night. Chuck dug up her mother's Alfredo recipe and served it complete with a dark chocolate mousse cake—which he didn't bake, but had special ordered for her. So kind. And yet so strange.

He'd finished off the meal with the gift of a bracelet holding a studded diamond charm.

Her eyes fluttered back open, away from recent, accessible memories to the unfolding present. She looked for her husband through the mudroom window. A combination of snowmobiles and horses disrupted the snow-covered land, white-capped mountains in the distance.

There was a pristine beauty around the five acres of property. Chuck had told her his stable was small compared to the Steele spread, and his family kept things more understated. Somehow, as if by practice, she immediately located Chuck on his stallion Nanook—a buckskin quarter horse.

Chuck looked natural. Rugged. Familiar and strange.

She'd made it through the first week under the same roof as her husband. Although that didn't stop her from thinking about him all the time.

Of course, that could be in part because the pillows carried a hint of his scent. She hadn't been able to resist inhaling, wondering if the smell would bring memories of him or memories of when they'd conceived the baby she carried.

How surreal to be pregnant. She didn't feel different other than her breasts were a little tender. Yet the ultrasound was real, as was the follow-up appointment with her doctor yesterday. She was responsible for caring for the life growing inside her.

Chuck had mentioned several miscarriages and unsuccessful fertility treatments. Her pregnancy, combined with the amnesia, had to be all the more difficult for him.

How long would it take for her to remember?

Desperately needing to connect with something familiar, she reached into her coat pocket for her cell phone to call her mother. She craved stability. She clicked the phone on Speaker as she made her way into the kitchen.

No, *her* kitchen. The kitchen she clearly had a hand in decorating.

She listened to the ringing phone, eyes investigating the three suspended lamps that illuminated a white marble counter free of any clutter. Her actual dream.

Or rather, her lived reality.

Walking to the island, she smelled the bouquet of irises, another endearing gesture from Chuck. Turning, she opened the freezer and pulled out a tub of home-churned berry ice cream, a craving she'd had that Chuck made sure stayed in good supply, along with extra berries to spread on top.

After what felt like an eternity of ringing, the phone clicked on just as she pulled a spoon out from the drawer.

"Hello there, sweetie. I'm so sorry not to have made it. I'm going to save up all my vacation days to get there as soon as I can. But it could be a month or so."

Shana stifled the urge to beg her mom to come anyway. But she needed to be strong and learn to stand

on her own in case things didn't work out with Chuck.
"I'm okay, Mom. Really. Chuck's whole family is
watching out for us."

"But I'm your mama." Evident pain passed through
the phone. Shana scooped up a bite of berry ice cream
before she answered, savoring the bitter notes of the
blackberries.

Shana wanted to agree with her mother, but guilt-
ing her mom wouldn't help. "I understand, truly I do."

"I worry about you being there with them all feeling like strangers to you."

True enough. Her whole life felt surreal. "It's awkward at times, but they're being sensitive."

"And Chuck? How is he?"

Sexy. Unreadable. But thoughtful. And… "Careful."

He treated her like she was fragile and could break
at any moment. She hated that.

"Careful doesn't tell me much."

"He's walking on eggshells trying to make me
happy."

"That should be a good thing."

Except when someone had an agenda.

Pressing her palms into the countertop, Shana drew
in a breath, then let it out. She scanned the pristine
kitchen as if it held a clue.

Maybe it did.

The words smoked through her mind and under her
defenses. Her imagination ran wild from her days as a
private eye. Days on the job had showed her the dark
secrets people like her father hid, people who many
would think were everyday, regular folks.

Goose bumps prickled. Shana searched for a way to
end the call. Her mother had suffered too much. Shana

didn't want to add more worries, especially when there might well be nothing to be concerned about.

If there was ever a need for superior detective skills, it was now. Shana needed to piece together what had happened over the past five years. Fast.

"Hmm." She wasn't ready to tell her mother about the baby. Her life already felt so alien and unsure. She would tell her mom in person once she arrived. "Hey, I hear someone calling for me, so I'll let you go."

"Call me anytime. Love you, sweetie."

"Love you, too, Mom." She ended the call, no closer to finding answers, and only filled with more burning questions.

She scooped more ice cream into her mouth and shut her eyes again. In the movies, characters were always shutting their eyes to remember long-forgotten secrets. More than a week without any hint of her past and she found herself ready and willing to try anything.

An arm slid around her shoulders. Instant heat tingled in her skin from that strong weight.

How quickly she'd come to recognize his touch.

Chuck. Her husband.

She looked over her shoulder to smile and offer him a spoonful. "Want some?"

"Hmm." He grinned and opened his mouth.

She fed him the ice cream, shivers running up her arm. She hadn't thought about how sexy sharing food would be, but now? Her body melted faster than the serving in her bowl.

She cleared the lump in her throat—easier said than done. "How was your ride?"

He swept off his Stetson and set it on the granite counter. "Mind-clearing."

"Did we ride together often?"

He stroked back her hair, strands catching along his calluses. "We did. And we will again."

The words hung between them with the promise of a future she couldn't quite envision. Living in the present with a chunk of the past gone was tough enough.

His smile faded into a frown and she realized he was looking over her shoulder.

She touched his arm lightly. "Is something wrong?"

"I'm not sure." He leaned forward, hands on the counter, looking through the window. "But it sure seems like my baby sister is getting cozy with the youngest Steele kid."

"Kid? They look like adults to me."

"Freshmen in college." He swept his hat off the counter. "And since my and Alayna's mom married Aiden Steele's dad, those two freshmen are living under the same roof."

He jammed his Stetson back on his head and stalked out the door.

As she watched Chuck storm across the yard, leaving a trail of footprints in the snow, she fought back the unsettling feeling that this man bore little resemblance to her careful husband of the past week.

Alayna Mikkelson hugged Aiden Steele as he powered the snowmobile across the pristine stretch of ice left after the storm. She wrapped her arms tighter around one of the hottest college freshmen on campus and her brand-new stepbrother.

Even through the puffy snow gear, she could smell Aiden's clove aftershave, a rich scent, as dark and mysterious as his hair and eyes. The kind of eyes that induced blushes on even the most popular freshman girls. But here she was, perched on the back of a snowmobile with him.

They weren't blood-related. And her mom hadn't even been married to his dad for a year. So there was nothing creepy about her feelings for him. He probably wouldn't have noticed her on campus. But living in the same house with her over the past months, somehow he'd *seen* the real her.

When so many others didn't.

Being the quiet one in her family had its downsides, like when she went unnoticed or got steamrolled. But being quiet also had its perks, like hearing all the juiciest gossip because people tended to overlook wallpaper personalities.

And the best perk right now? No one seemed to realize she was on her way to being majorly noticed by Aiden Steele.

She swallowed, eyes looking past his broad shoulders and to the distant horse-filled pastures. A thump in the ground pushed her forward, closer to Aiden. Her stomach did a somersault.

Life was so surreal these days with all the past family rivalries disappearing. Who would have thought they'd be having all these get-togethers after so many years of outright warfare?

She hadn't always been the kind of person to fade into the background. As a kid, she'd demanded her rights in a big family. Sometimes loudly.

How ironic that one event had changed her so radically, silenced her so completely.

She hadn't even started school when she'd overheard Uncle Lyle—her mom's brother—talking to some strange men. To this day she couldn't recall exactly what she'd heard. She only knew it had been bad enough for him to threaten her. He'd said if she talked he would throw her through the ice and everyone would think she'd drowned. Once she'd gotten old enough to realize she should have told someone, he'd already disappeared from their lives. So there was nothing to be gained from sharing something that was now only a fuzzy memory.

Maybe she should be more proactive in digging up those memories. If she didn't, she might be forever stuck in the role of a wallflower. That kind of anonymity wasn't as comforting as it had once been.

Especially not when she wanted Aiden to see her.

Hanging around with Shana could be helpful on a number of levels. Seeing how professionals helped her regain her memories could provide tips on how to root around in Alayna's own buried recollections. Shana also happened to be a private detective and might have tips for finding out the truth of the past.

Nobody talked about Shana's career much since it seemed like everyone else either worked for the family oil business or planned fund-raisers.

There was no room for anything in between.

Even if Alayna decided to work for her family's empire someday, she needed that to be her decision.

She needed to find her voice again first.

And she needed to find a way to tell them what she knew, something deep down inside she'd feared would turn her family inside out.

Was this what Shana felt like without her memory? Afraid?

Alayna clutched Aiden harder. He would probably think it was because they'd shot over a pile of packed snow.

She knew her world had felt unsteady for a lot longer than just today.

Five

Anger coursed through Chuck's veins.

When he'd seen Alayna and Aiden together, instinct had fired his feet into motion. He hadn't even bothered to grab a jacket from the entry hallway of his home. Luckily, he hadn't yet removed his snow boots.

He heard Shana following after him. Worried she might slip on the ice, he slowed his pace and glanced over his shoulder to see her chasing him.

That chest-tightening feeling came back as he looked at her. Her puffed steel-gray jacket still managed to hug her curves and call attention to her hot figure. Her honeyed hair fell in waves, contrasting with her wind-chapped cheeks and lips. Genuine concern welled in those soft eyes.

Damn. A helluva mess.

Chuck knew full well he was channeling a week's

worth of frustration into the moment. But damn it, his shy baby sister didn't need to get tangled up with one of the Steele men.

"Chuck? Take a breath." Shana's urgent voice floated over his shoulder. "Think about what you're doing." She leaned forward, hands pressing into her thighs.

"I'm putting a stop to this before it's out of hand." He eyeballed the snowmobile in the distance where Alayna was still plastered against Aiden Steele's back.

Shana drew closer and clutched his arm. "It could be a harmless flirtation."

"I beg to differ." He rested his hand over hers because, what the hell, he wasn't ever so far gone as to miss out on a chance to touch her. "My baby sister—my shy, innocent baby sister—is all over that hellion Steele kid."

"Seriously? You're worried because they're riding a snowmobile together?" She patted his arm. "And who says the guy's a hellion?"

"She doesn't need to sit that close, he doesn't need to let her, and he looks like trouble." His protective urges kicked into overdrive. While the family companies might have merged, while their families might be blended by marriage, none of that did much to alleviate years' worth of mistrust. Not even close.

She took both of his hands, clasping them in that calming way she'd done over the years of their marriage, like when his father had died.

"Chuck, you may be right on every point, but do you think confronting them will accomplish anything positive?"

Damn it, he hated that she was right. But he also couldn't deny an easing of his tension thanks to her perspective. He appreciated how kind she'd been to come after him when she didn't even remember any of them in the first place.

"What do you suggest?" he asked. "I can't just ignore what I see and send them both on their merry way to live under the same roof. What if he takes advantage of my little sister?"

"Maybe she plans to take advantage of him." She grinned, squeezing his hands.

"You're not helping."

"Fair enough. How about let me talk to her?" She nudged his shoulder.

A familiar gesture that should feel so damn normal. Except it had been a long time since he'd had a positive connection with his wife.

Was this a sign of life in their marriage?

"And you'll tell me what she says?"

Shana hesitated, then said, "I'll tell you if I think there's cause for concern."

She arched up on her toes and kissed him. A slight brush of her lips to his, but a kiss that lingered for a moment too much to be anything platonic. The chemistry between them sparked like static popping in the air. He ached to haul her to him, her body flush against his. Yet patience would gain him so much more.

As she eased away, her eyes went wide. "I'm not sure why, um, I wasn't thinking, I, well…"

He pressed a finger to her soft lips. "No explanation needed."

Savoring the progress, he backed away, the taste of her filling him with victory.

* * *

Several days may have passed, but it didn't dull this particular memory.

She'd kissed Chuck.

On impulse but not by accident.

As much as she tried to keep her mind on the present and her conversation with Alayna, Shana found her mind wandering. Not that the teen seemed to notice as she chattered on about the gala next month. The event would gather the Alaska Oil Barons, Inc., shareholders and board members in a show of solidarity and celebration. The massive event was being planned by a Mikkelson distant cousin—Sage Hammond. Until now, Sage had been solely a personal assistant. She'd been given the event to prove herself and possibly advance in the company. So far, her work looked promising.

The gala had a steampunk theme blending Old West fashion with a technology aesthetic, the perfect showcase for an oil company with Alaskan roots.

This was as good a way as any to learn how to navigate among the Mikkelsons. Or rather, *re*learn, as they seemed quite comfortable coming and going in her home. Chuck's sister Glenna sat off to the side on a blanket with her daughter, while his youngest sister, Alayna, curled up in a wing chair by the fire.

Seeing Chuck grow so tense earlier in the week over his sister's possible love life felt oddly endearing. He cared so much. But Shana remembered being a teenager, too. She knew that explosions and sharp decrees didn't necessarily assuage puppy love. No, affairs of the heart demanded a more tender touch.

Besides, Alayna's troubles could provide some diversion from Shana's own missing memory. Something about jumping in full force to the family dynamic appealed to her.

Shana touched the marble mantel, mindlessly arranging the large group of flowers in front of the towering mirror. She loved the opulent arrangement of ferns and gardenias. The brightness contrasted well with the white room. Greens, particularly ferns, always seemed hopeful and tenacious.

When Shana had been a child, her mother had read her a book about a magical princess who rekindled the land by restoring life to a resurrection fern. Her mom told her resurrection ferns were real. They really could survive and come back after great lengths of time without sustenance. Even as a small child, Shana had felt a kinship to the plant. She liked to care for the miracle ferns in her home.

Chuck's home.

Her sexy husband, Chuck.

The man who was both familiar to her and intoxicatingly new. A man she'd impulsively kissed.

Before her accident, would that kiss have rocked through her just as much? Were they a couple who stole intimate moments like that?

She had so many unanswered questions. She needed to touch him again, to feel him press into her body. She had to go back for more. Maybe, just maybe, another kiss could unleash more than the electricity that hummed in her bones every time they locked eyes.

Alayna cleared her throat after glancing over her shoulder as if to determine if her elder sister, Glenna, would be able to hear them—but Glenna was still engrossed with her baby daughter, who was playing with a jingling ball.

Shana shifted her attention back to Alayna.

One crisis at a time. That lingering kiss with Chuck would have to wait.

Forcing the memory of his lips from her mind, Shana tilted her head to the side. Alayna again looked back at her older sister. Glenna's blond hair was gathered into a high ponytail as she played with her baby girl. An array of stuffed animals and teething toys speckled the light lavender blanket.

Shana saw an opportunity. Her memory and the specifics of this family might be gone, but her sleuthing skills were as sharp as ever. She still knew how to read people. Alayna clearly had something she wanted to share, and something she didn't want her older sister to know.

"Alayna, thank you for coming by the hospital to see me and spending time with me here."

Alayna shrugged, her oversize sweatshirt falling slightly off her shoulder. "You've been a sister to me for years. You helped me with picking makeup and dating. We were close."

"So we talked about boys."

Alayna blushed. "We did. Or rather the lack of boys in my life. I'm so shy, dating is tough for me."

A twinge went through Shana's heart. "Dating is tough for anyone in their teens and twenties... Honestly, relationships are tough when you're an adult, too."

"I'm sure amnesia doesn't help," Alayna said with eyes full of sympathy.

"I have so many questions."

"I'm glad to help how I can." Alayna paused, staring off in the distance. "Maybe you can help me with something, too."

"What would that be?"

Alayna chewed at her bottom lip, her eyes full of shadows. Whatever she wanted to talk about seemed to be weighing heavily on her. She looked away for a moment, then back with an overbright smile.

"Will you help me with my fashion sense?"

That wasn't the sort of request Shana had been expecting. It felt like a dodge. "I thought you already had a gown chosen for the gala."

"I do, but that's more of a costume since it's got the whole steampunk theme. I'm talking about the day-to-day kind of stuff. And regular special events, like a rodeo."

Intrigued, Shana sensed Alayna was circling closer to her deeper concern. The rodeo sounded specific, like a place she planned to see someone she wanted to impress.

"Of course, I'm happy to help. But are you sure there's not something else you want to talk about?"

Alayna shook her head quickly. "Nope. It's just tough stepping out of the shadow of my mom and older sister. You're not quite as…um, well…pushy."

"I think you're lovely."

Alayna crossed her arms over her body, swimming in the oversize sweatshirt. The young woman looked down at her feet, shaking her head from side to side. "I want to be a knockout."

"Is there a guy in the picture?"

"I'm nineteen. Guys are all I think about."

"I do remember that time of life very well." Shana

angled closer, their bodies effectively turned away from Glenna. "Now tell me about you and Aiden Steele."

A rush of scarlet colored Alayna's cheeks.

Here.

This was the opportunity she'd been waiting for.

Only, the window for sharing evaporated before her eyes. Alayna opened her mouth to reply but inhaled sharply as her mother, Jeannie, approached from the hall.

Shana felt her sister-in-law turn rigid as she mumbled, "I'm going to help Glenna change the baby's diaper. She deserves a break."

Just like that, Alayna moved as quickly as an Alaskan dogsled team cutting through the ice.

Jeannie's silvery-blond hair feathered around her face as she walked closer. "Teenagers," she laughed lightly. "It's hit or miss on when she wants my attention." Jeannie patted a pillow on the sofa. "You should take it easy. Put up your feet."

"I'm following the doctor's orders to the letter."

"That doesn't stop me from worrying."

"I understand." Shana paused, wondering if there was a way to help the mother and the daughter. Clothes shopping had a way of soothing a teenage soul. "Alayna asked me to go shopping with her for something to wear to the rodeo. Would you like to come along? We could all have lunch together."

"That sounds delightful." Her mother-in-law smoothed her hair before continuing, "Are you sure my daughter won't mind?"

"Why should she?"

"Asserting her independence has made things prickly between us."

Even from the brief time she'd known this family, Shana could see how tight the Mikkelsons were. They were there for each other. And yes, that felt a little claustrophobic to her at times, especially growing up as an only child, but she also couldn't deny she'd once wanted something like this. "I can tell she loves you."

"I don't doubt that. It's just a stage of life, and I'm trying not to push it. Certainly my remarriage didn't help ease the path."

Now that the subject of Jeannie's marriage to Jack Steele had come up, it seemed a good time to mention the budding romance between the two teens living under the same roof. While Shana had initially been reticent to share details with Chuck, upon further reflection, it seemed wise to bring up the matter with Jeannie.

Shana placed the throw pillow on the glass coffee table and propped up her feet. Maybe if she focused on the teen's love life, she could stop thinking about her own convoluted relationship.

Even after supper, long past when his family had left, Chuck couldn't shake the memory of the tender fullness of Shana's lips on his, which was crazy. She was his wife of four years. They'd kissed more times than he could count.

But that brief brush—at her instigation—had moved him like no kiss he could remember.

He'd tried to put it out of his mind all day. To no use. Shana's touch burned deep into him, reawakening all of their years together—the good years when their love had been flame-hot.

Chuck pulled two antique bowls from the cabinet.

They'd been his grandmother's. Shana always admired the divots in the purple Depression glass. He'd secured them from Glenna for a Valentine's Day gift for his wife three years ago.

Passing a bowl to Shana now, he wondered what item would tip her memory. When would they open the Pandora's box of their past, their complications?

But for now, she looked at the bowl only with admiration, like she was taking it in for the first time. Those light fingers touched the rim gingerly.

Shana glanced up at him through those thick lashes.

God, she looked gorgeous in leggings and a silky blouse, one hip leaning against the counter. Casual or glammed up, she always took his breath away.

He caught himself and moved toward the freezer. A few hours ago, he'd ordered more fresh-churned ice cream, this time lemon, determined to keep her as satisfied as possible.

He set the ice-cream container on the kitchen island adjacent to the blueberries, raspberries and blackberries. Shana fished spoons out from the nearby drawer and handed one to him, their fingers brushing ever so slightly.

Reminding him again of the sensation of her lips. The curve of her back.

As if that memory had, in fact, wound its way to the forefront of Shana's mind, too, he noticed a faint blush rise and spread in her cheeks. There was something oddly comforting in her reaction.

He scooped lemon ice cream into her bowl, then his. Cradling his bowl in his hand, he leaned by her still-thriving bouquet, his knee brushing Shana's leg.

She spooned an extra helping of berries on her ice

cream. "I wanted to reassure you about your sister. The opportunity arose to talk about the situation with your mother."

"What did Mom have to say?" He was still edgy and worried about Alayna. Of all of them, she'd been especially lost since their father died.

Shana looked down at her bowl. "Your mother said that Alayna and Aiden are both over eighteen, but since they're living under her roof, she'll keep watch and make sure they understand the ground rules of her house."

Some of the tension eased from him. He wasn't completely reassured, but at least his mother could keep an eye out. "That sounds like my mom."

Shana swallowed the spoonful of ice cream, the tip of her tongue swiping at the corner of her mouth in a tempting sweep. "So you approve of how I handled it?"

"I trust you." He'd always trusted her. It was Shana who'd come to the marriage with deep issues about trust, issues that had driven a wedge deeper between them with each passing year.

She stared into her bowl, quiet for too long.

Ah, that damn *trust* word.

Even without her remembering their marriage, this was still a sticking point between them. "I understand that trust is difficult for you because of your father."

Clutching the bowl with both hands, she adjusted her weight. He noted the tension in her jaw. Pain seemed to paint her slender face as a forced smile dusted her lips. "That's putting it mildly."

Maybe with the clean slate of her lost memories he could make some headway on this subject, handle it better than they had in the past. He covered her hand with his. "Your father is one person."

Her lips thinned. "One amoral person who completely fooled my mother and me for so long."

He linked his fingers with hers, and she didn't pull away. Promising. "I want to be understanding."

"Because I'm pregnant. You don't want me to leave with your child."

Damn, she was sharp. And too close to the truth for comfort.

He chose his words carefully. "So let me get this straight. Your father was dishonorable. And I'm in trouble for being honorable."

She pulled her hand away. "I would never take your child from you or keep you from seeing each other. If this pregnancy comes to term and we find we can't live together, I would work with you to put a plan in place for coparenting."

He could see her agitation in the way she mashed the berries in the bowl. The last thing he wanted was to put stress on her. He couldn't take another health scare like the one they'd just been through. "Fair enough."

Tension faded from her body. "Thank you. Let's focus on my helping you find the employee from your company who went missing. You want me to look into things, but you keep delaying the start of my investigation."

"I just want to make sure you've recovered."

"The doctors say I'm fine. I feel fine. You should know. You were at my checkup." She smiled, her blue eyes sparkling more than the most valuable jewels. "Now, let's talk."

"The missing employee—"

"Milla Jones," she verified, "who disappeared somewhere in Canada—"

"Yes, her. Before she disappeared, she made it clear she was against the merger going through. She also said she wasn't the only one spilling secrets. There was a traitor in our family—on the Mikkelson side." The sweet taste of ice cream palled on his tongue at the thought of that accusation being in any way true. "This traitor supposedly played a part in the plane crash that killed Jack Steele's first wife and his daughter Breanna. What's worse, the Jones woman intimated that Breanna Steele was actually still alive."

She gasped. "What a horrible thing to say if it's not true. How awful to give the Steeles hope that way."

"After the crash, the Steeles ran DNA tests from teeth found at the wreckage. The tests came back a match to Breanna's. Additional tests were run since she had a twin—Naomi Steele Miller." He thought of how much he and Shana wanted a child and how devastating a loss like that would be, a wreckage so fiery that identification came down to teeth.

Protectiveness surged through him. He would move heaven and earth to keep his wife—his family—safe.

She rubbed her forehead. "What would lead this Milla person to make up something like that, then?"

He fought the urge to massage her shoulders. Or ease the tension in a more pleasurable way.

"There are any number of reasons she could manufacture a story like that. To cause trouble. To drive a wedge between the families so the merger falls through. My first guess would be she was paid by a rival who stands to benefit."

"Such as?" she pressed, shifting against the counter, drawing his eyes to the slim length of her legs.

"Johnson Oil." The obvious answer. Johnson Oil was their main competitor in Alaska. "Before the merger, we were all on even footing competitively. Johnson is no match to the merged Alaska Oil Barons, Inc., though. If we pull this off, it's going to be a boon."

"Big business." She crinkled her nose.

"No need to sound so disdainful. It's not like we're the only game in town. But this edge will give us the capital for innovation—such as Royce Miller's eco-friendly upgrades to the pipeline."

They'd brought on premier research scientist Royce Miller to implement new safety measures. In the process, he'd fallen in love with Naomi Steele. They had twin girls now. Apparently, twins ran in the Steele family.

"I get that your family and the Steeles are good people. And I'm working on trust, but it's tough flying blind here. I wish my mother hadn't been stuck in the airport so long for weather."

As much as he regretted seeing Shana's frustration, he couldn't deny he'd been relieved that her mother couldn't make the trip. Having Shana all to himself gave him the time he needed to pursue his quest to get her back into his bed, and secure a place in her life. Secure their future as a family.

He didn't intend to waste an instant.

The time for waiting to make a move was over.

He spooned up some lemon ice cream and offered it to her. "Try mine."

And before the night was out, he intended to taste *her*.

Six

Shana opened her mouth for the spoon, anticipation humming through her body at the intimacy of Chuck feeding her. His green eyes glimmered with promise as his gaze held hers.

What was it about this man that drew her so? Had the attraction between them always been this intense? Or was this a phantom memory due to the longevity of their relationship?

She tasted the ice cream, her senses on overdrive. The cream and berries burst along her taste buds, saturating her craving yet somehow leaving her yearning for more. More of this moment. More of him.

She wanted to accept the promise of a kiss in his eyes. To follow wherever it led with no worry or regrets.

Chuck dipped the spoon back into his bowl. "This is like when we were dating."

She watched him take a taste from the silverware

he'd just fed her with, unable to remove her gaze from him. "I wish I remembered."

"You will," he said confidently.

She wished she shared his certainty. She wasn't sure how she would trust in the future with such a gaping hole in her past. "And if I don't?"

"Let's work on new memories, here and now." Chuck angled closer, whispering in her ear. "I have an inside track here, knowing what you like."

He pressed his mouth against her neck, just over her leaping pulse. The heat of his breath fanned an answering warmth to life in her. His lips traveled to her collarbone. He nudged aside the neckline of her sweater for fuller access, each brush of his lips more tantalizing than the one before. Her hands clenched into fists as she held back the urge to grab him.

Instead, she lost herself in the sensations he stirred. His mouth grazed back to her neck, then up further to nip her earlobe. He kissed her ear, taking his time. Her head lolled to the side, giving him space.

Finally, thank goodness, his lips moved to hers. Except he didn't make contact. He just stayed a whisper away, his mouth hovering over hers.

Hunger gnawed at her.

Just as she swayed forward, he pulled away.

"That's not fair," she protested, her words riding a sigh of desire.

But maybe pulling back was what she needed. She wanted to trust he wasn't like her father. Getting to know Chuck better was a step in the right direction.

"You know just how to kiss me to turn me inside out. Yet I don't know much about you."

He spread his arms wide. "I'll willingly donate my body for your research."

She took in the leanly muscular length of him. "I just feel we're on uneven ground because of my amnesia."

He angled back, stroking aside her hair but also giving her space. "Judging by the way you kissed me, it felt like you know me, too, on some level."

"But on so many others, I don't." She stirred her spoon through the ice cream. "There's a part of me that wonders what you would do if I gave in to the temptation to kiss you now. Would we simply kiss while you respected my need for space, or would we both throw caution to the wind?"

"As much as I want to make love to you, I hear your reservation. I respect it. We're going to take our time." His voice held a promise echoed in his eyes.

"How much time?"

She wasn't sure what she wanted his answer to be. Part of her longed to find out what it would be like to spend the night in his arms. In his bed.

What if passion unlocked her memories?

But the rational side of her knew that giving in now, before she knew everything she needed to know, probably wasn't wise.

"As much time as you need." He kissed her lips lightly, nudging the bowl of ice cream toward her. "Good night, Shana."

Alayna kept her eyes on her bowl of caribou stew and off Aiden across the dinner table from her. And she feared her mother and her stepfather might notice her nerves, or worse yet, notice her interest. They had some convoluted notion of making them all a family, as if that was miraculously achieved by just sitting in the kitchen together for a meal rather than in the formal dining room.

Sighing, she stirred her stew in hopes no one would question her silence. She wasn't ready to share her feelings for Aiden with them yet, and maybe that had something to do with the fact she knew they wouldn't approve. Her brother sure didn't. She could tell.

Picking apart her yeast roll, she half listened to the drone of her mom and Jack talking about visiting Shana and Chuck. Aiden was just as quiet, although she was in tune to every clink of his spoon against the bowl. She snuck a look at him through her eyelashes.

No one else sat at the lengthy kitchen table even though it seemed half the world lived under this roof. Jack Steele had built this huge place with private suites for his kids, the size of luxury apartments. Her sister, Glenna, lived here now, married to Jack's son.

Which made it all the more ironic she was getting flack over hanging out with Aiden. She felt his eyes on hers.

He grinned at her wryly.

She struggled to keep from blushing as she grinned back. He jerked his head toward the door. Could he really be asking her to leave with him?

Her heart leaped into her throat. She nodded quickly. He held up a finger, indicating she should wait. Aiden pushed back his chair, placed his dishes in the sink, and made a beeline for the mudroom.

Conversation at the table stopped and Alayna's breath hitched in her throat. Her stepfather scraped his chair back, standing and following his son.

Disappointment stung. It shouldn't be this tough getting time alone together, given they lived in the same house. Frustrated, she pulled her linen napkin from her lap and tossed it beside her bowl to leave.

Jeannie rested a hand on her wrist. "Hold on a minute. Let's talk."

Something in her mother's voice set off alarms. She eyed her mom warily. "About what?"

"You and Aiden."

Her stomach knotted. "There's no me and Aiden." She felt compelled to ask, though, "But what if there were? How's that any different from Glenna and Broderick?"

Her mother rubbed between Alayna's shoulder blades. "No need to get defensive. I simply want to make sure no one's heart gets hurt…and that no one ends up with a pregnancy before they're ready."

"Mom," she growled, shooting to her feet. "I get that you have to go all adult on me, but I'm nineteen. Trust me."

Heat rushed to her face. She wasn't used to speaking out this way and it made her uncomfortable. Not enough to take back the words.

In fact, as she raced back to her room, she was more determined than ever to find a chance to meet with Aiden. Alone.

Walking away from Shana the day before had been tough, but Chuck knew waiting for the right moment to make his move was crucial. He didn't want her to run. The stakes were too high.

He wasn't going to risk her walking out of his life. For a second time.

Although the waiting was damn near killing him. Would tonight—their fourth anniversary—be that perfect moment?

He hoped so.

He had spent the day working on plans while she stayed at the computer, pensive. He'd given her space, easy enough since he'd had his hands full pulling off the perfect evening to go with the gift he'd bought for the occasion. She'd seemed pleased with the diamond heart bracelet he'd given her, so he'd decided to contact one of his mother's favorite jewelry designers, a Texas-based company called Diamonds in the Rough. They specialized in rustic, eclectic pieces. He was also having a special piece designed just for her for the gala celebrating the completion of the merger forming Alaska Oil Barons, Inc. She'd been a fan of their jewelry before the accident so he felt confident in his choice to shower her with pieces now.

After jogging down the stairs, he made his way to their home office, taking a beat outside the door to pat his suit jacket over where he'd tucked the gift. Shana sat at the desk, typing away on the keyboard while classical guitar music played softly through the sound system. She'd crossed her legs on the chair, a nearly empty glass of milk on the table reminding him of the child she carried. Their child.

Her fuzzy, soft sweater hugged the curves of her breasts, making his hands ache to touch her. But he'd told her he would respect her need for space and he would honor that.

A lot of bad had happened between them over the years, but he was determined to shield her from a repeat of their arguments. He would devote the same drive he had at the office to winning his way back into her bed and into her life.

As if she felt his gaze, she glanced up from the computer. "You look nice. Do you have a business meeting?" She glanced back at the screen. "It's pretty late, though. A dinner meeting, maybe?"

"A date, actually, with my wife."

"Well, since I'm craving burgers and a milkshake, you're a bit overdressed." She laughed, combing her fingers through her loose, honey-blond hair. Her bare ring finger served as a reminder she still hadn't totally embraced their marriage. "What's the special occasion?"

He strode into the room, his cowboy boots thudding softly on the brick floor. "It's our anniversary."

She straightened behind the desk, blinking fast. "Wedding anniversary?"

"Our fourth." He sat on the edge of the desk, his leg brushing her knee.

"Fourth," she said in a shaky voice. "Isn't it the husband who's supposed to forget?"

He knew her well enough to recognize she was attempting a joke to cover nerves. He wanted—needed—for her to be at ease, so he chuckled and teased her back. "You're off the hook for a gift, though."

He withdrew the present from inside his jacket, a flat box with a blue ribbon sporting sparkly horseshoes and the logo for the maker—Diamonds in the Rough.

She took the present tentatively, resting it on the desk in front of her. "You're so generous."

"I want you to be happy."

She tugged the bow carefully, slow in opening the gift as she always was on holidays. She lifted the lid to reveal a pounded pewter necklace with diamonds and a large teardrop Peruvian opal. Shana traced the details reverently. "This is lovely."

"It's a jeweler my mother and sisters use. Diamonds in the Rough is based out of Texas. They make unusual pieces."

"Thank you. This is really thoughtful. Again." Standing, she rested a hand over his and pressed her lips to his.

Her mouth was soft and familiar. The light touch of her tongue to his sent a bolt of desire spearing through him. The kiss wasn't over the top. Their bodies weren't even touching except for their mouths. But this woman had always turned him inside out in a way no other ever had. She held the kiss for another moment before easing back, her eyes blue flames.

He didn't push her for more. They had the whole night ahead of them. "I have a date planned to go with the necklace."

"A date, tonight?"

"Yes, an anniversary celebration. A first for you, and hopefully one worth remembering. Is there a problem?"

Her smile faded. "I have other plans, actually." She tapped the computer. "My work today paid off. A lead came through about the case."

"A lead?" He'd all but forgotten he'd asked her to do this. He certainly hadn't expected results so soon.

"Cross-referencing Milla Jones's emails and bank statements, there's a name that came up frequently, strangely so, given she hadn't lived here long."

"Interesting. Bank records?" He worked to keep his

focus on her words, tough to do with the distracting scent of her teasing his every breath.

"Bank card transactions from him to her, shuffling money around. That can be iffy, of course, since shell corporations can make it too easy to hide who's really behind the money." She picked up a printout. "Anyway, I've got a lead that the guy's living at a local motel. If I can confirm that, I'll be able to trace more of his movements."

"Confirm it how?" Suddenly this job was starting to sound more complicated than he'd expected. He didn't want her digging into the backgrounds of people who might hold a grudge later.

"I'm going on a stakeout."

Alone? Like hell.

He shrugged out of his suit coat, more determined than ever to spend the evening with her. "Then I guess our anniversary plans have changed, because I'm going with you."

The decadence of this home—her home?—still caught Shana off guard sometimes. Even this closet was larger than her old apartment bedroom.

She stood in the threshold, gripping the door frame, her mind wandering back to her old cramped studio—the last place she actually remembered living. So different, with its exposed brick and water heater haphazardly placed next to the stove in her kitchen. A cheap countertop and a room with nonexistent closet space. She'd stuffed organized boxes under the bed for extra storage.

Now, before her, she took in a whole wall of shelves for shoes and sweaters, two walls with rows of clothes on hangers. And in the middle, a built-in island with drawers of jewelry and other accessories.

Her studio had been small, sure. But she knew its idiosyncrasies, knew everything in that tiny space followed rules of order because she had complete autonomy and authority. And yet, somewhere in the past five years, she'd learned to trust, to rely on another person. A man.

How had that transpired? Stress broiled in her stomach as she grasped for the truth. So she did what she'd often done as a young girl. She dialed her mom.

Shana clicked the phone onto Speaker as she stripped out of her oversize T-shirt and fluffy pajama pants. The cold air made her hair stand on end as she fidgeted with her plain white bra.

Opening the drawer of bras, she opted for a lacier number. Delicate and coy. Not that she planned on anything happening during a stakeout. But just for confidence's sake.

"Hey, Mom." Shana hooked the bra clasp, fingers moving for the Diamonds in the Rough necklace. The handcrafted piece laid flush against her breastbone, the cool metal somehow relaxing her.

"Hello, sweetheart. How are you feeling?"

Shana had told her mother about the pregnancy right after the last doctor checkup. She just hadn't been able to keep the news to herself any longer.

"I feel great. Not at all nauseous. Appetite is well and I'm full of energy." In the center of the walk-in closet, a fat, off-white ottoman flanked a mirror. She sat, shoving her legs into dark-wash denim leggings.

"And your memory?" her mother asked with subdued but persistent urgency.

Shana buttoned her jeans, a long sigh heavy on her exhale. "Still nothing."

"I wish I could be there with you."

"I understand. Chuck's family is spoiling me. Chuck too." After pulling an oversize white sweater over her body, she moved to the mirror, adjusting the way it fell, fluffing her hair.

"I'm glad to hear you two are getting along."

The comment caught Shana off guard. She should have known better than to get too complacent.

She was almost scared to ask—and come to think of it, why hadn't she quizzed her mother more deeply on this? "Did Chuck and I have problems in our marriage?"

"You had arguments like any couple. He rushed through the romance so fast at first, I wasn't sure if I liked him. But with time, I could see he's a good man, and you two were very much in love."

Shana wanted to believe her mom, but would she have confided in her mother about marital problems? Maybe, but most likely not.

"Oh," her mother said, "happy anniversary."

And there was the answer to her question. It really was her anniversary. How paranoid to have thought he would make up something so easy to prove either way.

She really was overthinking things. She should just go on the stakeout with him and lose herself in the magnetism of her sexy husband.

When he'd made his anniversary plans, Chuck hadn't expected to end up going parking with his wife outside a seedy motel.

His five-star plans for the evening had been foiled by Shana's stakeout. No way in hell was he letting her do this alone.

Years in the boardroom had taught him how to improvise on the fly. He'd brought some of the luxury to her in his black SUV. Flipping on the seat heaters, he'd made the interior of the car as comfortable as possible while they did surveillance on the Snowdrop Inn—an old-school cheap motel with peeling paint and a weak light outside. Snow filtered down from the sky in a dusting on top of the snowplowed piles. A moose ambled slowly through the parking lot.

Even without the flash of luxurious romance, the interior of his SUV seemed to have an ambience all its own tonight, jazz tunes playing softly from the radio. The casual dinner of burgers, fries and milkshakes had a first-date quality, a feeling he wanted to capitalize on even after they'd already finished their burgers. Chuck knew he had to win over his wife if he was going to get her back to his bed.

Despite the cold weather outside, the SUV hummed with promise. He'd provided the exact meal she craved, determined to pull out all the unconventional romance stops to make this work. And he couldn't deny that Shana was relaxed, happy, in her element.

God, she was mesmerizing in jeans, the new necklace he'd given her glittering against the simple white sweater. A camera rested in her lap, along with a small tablet. While this wasn't the evening he'd planned, he had high hopes it could still culminate in a satisfying end.

He draped his arm over the back of her seat, heat blasting through the vents. "How's the shake?"

"Amazing," she said blissfully, placing the cup back in the holder. "Funny how I never liked strawberry milkshakes or ice cream in the past and now I can't get enough."

He thought of prior pregnancies and how she'd craved berries then, too. But she wouldn't remember that, and he didn't see the need to bring up the heartbreak of those days.

"Glad you're enjoying it." He toyed with a strand of blond hair that had eased loose from her messy topknot. "I still want us to have a real anniversary celebration, though."

She angled her head to the side, smiling pensively. "Where did we go for our honeymoon?"

"We flew to Paris. We went to the Eiffel Tower and the Louvre." They'd been in love—or thought they were. Full of dreams for the future, no notion of how it could all implode under the stress of everyday life.

"Paris sounds romantic." She leaned her head back into his touch.

On purpose or by instinct? Either way, he was glad for the opportunity to be closer to her. He cupped her shoulder.

"We were there for two weeks. We only left our room twice to sightsee."

"Oh." Her eyes went wide, and her tongue touched her top lip, making him ache to kiss her.

Clearing his dry throat, he said, "We decided to come back another time for more sightseeing."

"Did we?" she asked, her voice breathy. "Go back, I mean."

"Yes, six months later." They'd had so much hope for the future then before real life hadn't turned out as blissfully as they'd expected. They'd had nowhere near the perfect marriage, nothing like his parents' union. "We planned to start trying for a baby soon and wanted to get traveling under our belt."

Except somehow most of those trips—other than on their first two anniversaries—were canceled at the last minute because of a crisis at the office, which led to more arguments about his workaholic ways.

She touched his chest lightly, bringing him back to the present. "Where did we spend our first anniversary?"

"We went to Australia."

"That sounds incredible."

"It was." Sensual memories scrolled through his mind, making him ache from wanting her.

"Details?" she prodded.

He shot her a heated look, then said, "We went hiking, took a serious walkabout."

"Where are the photos? I would love to see them." She stirred the straw through the cup. "In fact, I can't believe I haven't asked to see more albums before now."

"Everything is on discs. I'll find them for you." Later. Delving too deeply into the past was dangerous territory.

"Thanks." Drinking her milkshake, she looked at him through her lashes. "I appreciate how open you are about discussing all of this, but I think it would be helpful to review parts of this on my own. Videos would be incredible."

"Duly noted," he said simply.

She set aside her shake and picked up her camera, snapping a photo of him. "So we never went to a cheap motel."

"This is a first. Should we check in?" he teased, half hoping she would say yes.

"I'm on the clock." She clicked more photos of him. "What about our second anniversary?"

"We went to a cabin and unplugged from the digital world." He tapped her arm to stop the photo session so he could see her eyes again.

"And our third?"

"For number three, we planned to go to Colorado, skiing."

"I know how to ski?" She laughed, smiling. "It sounds incredible. I wish I could remember."

The levity evaporated with the memory he wished he could forget. "We canceled our plans."

"Because?"

For once, his workaholic drive hadn't been the cause. "You had an early miscarriage. Neither of us felt much like partying." He scratched his chest over the tightness that never went away when he discussed that time, when it had really dawned on them that having a baby together might not happen for them.

Shana's hand slid over her stomach protectively. "Glenna said we discussed adoption."

"We did."

"Why didn't we follow through on that?"

He hesitated a beat too long, thinking about their rocky marriage over the past months. Would she notice his hesitation?

"Family issues with Mom's engagement put things on hold, then Jack was in a riding accident, then their wedding. There just wasn't a right time before you had the aneurysm."

"I hear your words—" she chewed her bottom lip "—but I also heard your silence."

"Nothing is ever clear-cut." Certainly not when it came to their relationship.

She tipped her head to the side, studying him through narrowed eyes. "Were we having marital troubles?"

That question posed a serious risk. He needed to be honest with her, but selectively so. If she found out they were separating, she could well bolt altogether—an unacceptable outcome.

"All marriages have bumps in the road. Fertility treatments took their toll. We'd decided to stop trying for a while."

"And that's everything?" Her forehead furrowed.

He needed to tread warily in case her memory returned. "It's difficult to share everything. We had arguments. No marriage is perfect." He scratched the back of his neck, weighing his words. "You have enough to deal with. How do I tell you about arguments without it sounding like I'm trying to excuse myself or without condemning myself?"

"Did you cheat on me?" she blurted out.

"No. Never," he said without hesitation.

No one compared to Shana. While their love had faded, the physical attraction had always burned intensely between them.

"I want to believe you." Her eyes were so earnest, blue flames in the glow of the dashboard light.

"I want that as well." He reached to stroke her cheek, his fingers sliding into her silky hair.

She swayed toward him, firing the barely banked heat inside him back to life. The attraction between them was an undeniable constant. Four years ago at this time, they'd been finishing their wedding reception, anticipating being alone together on his private jet, starting their honeymoon.

Memories of that night stirred his desire higher. He urged her forward ever so carefully. Her hands flattened on his chest and he wondered for a moment if she intended to push him away. But then her fingers clenched in the flannel of his shirt and she pulled him forward.

Close. So close.

And then, yes. His mouth covered hers, her lips parting in welcome. Her hands slid up his chest and she looped her arms around his neck.

No hesitation. No doubt. She wanted this kiss, too. Wanted *him*.

Heat seared his veins, throbbing and gathering until he was hard from wanting her. Somehow, no matter what problems they faced, he could never get enough of this woman. Being inside her surpassed anything he'd felt before—and was all he could think about now.

His hand tunneled up beneath her sweater and he found the sweet curve of her breast encased in lace. She arched into his touch with a breathy sigh that caressed his cheek. Her head fell back and he pressed his lips to the vulnerable curve of her neck, right where he knew she liked best. He damn well would make the best use of his knowledge of what made her writhe with pleasure.

He needed every advantage he could get Shana.

He nipped her earlobe on the way back up to her lips—

Only to be stopped short as he caught sight of movement over her shoulder. A man and woman heading to the room Chuck and Shana had been watching all night.

The target had arrived.

Disappointment stung deep. As much as Chuck would have liked to ignore the world outside the SUV, he couldn't. They were here for a reason, an important one.

He would have to wait to finish that kiss—and to claim Shana as his once again.

Seven

Never before had Shana been disappointed that her job went well, but she couldn't deny she would have liked another moment to follow through on the attraction to Chuck.

But he'd given her this case, and she wanted to prove her independence, her business savvy. She owed it to him and to his family to help how she could.

A woman on a mission couldn't be stopped.

Shana pulled up her camera and started snapping photos. Better too many than not enough. She adjusted the lens, anchoring her focus on the man in the long, sleek black coat. Even in the dim lighting, she managed to capture a few images of his face. She zoomed in more on his features, the weathered lines on his face. As for the woman, she seemed more guarded. For one, the woman had her back to them. Might this woman actually be Milla Jones? Could they be that lucky right away?

Maybe, it was certainly possible from the photos Shana had seen. The long blond hair and height were right.

Her pulse echoed in her ears with a jagged heartbeat, and her limbs sang with anticipation. She needed this to be right. Needed to prove something to herself. That she still had her sleuthing skills. That she could take revelatory photos and discern clues from the mundane breath of daily life.

And she'd be lying if she said she didn't want to impress her sexy, broad-shouldered husband.

Her fingers worked quickly, adjusting the camera as needed to obtain the clearest images.

She snapped a quick photo of the license plate, then shifted back to the couple.

He worked the key card, and Shana snagged additional photos of the man she suspected had sent the bank transactions. Time slipping by now. Shana trained her camera on the female suspect. Sending up a silent plea, Shana wished the woman would just glance over her shoulder. All she needed was a moment.

The female in question turned to get her overnight bag, the light shining on her face, a cigarette dangling out of the corner of her mouth, the tip glowing brighter in the night with a long drag.

There. The reveal.

Clicks like rapid fire, she captured the woman's face. Heart pounding. The thrill of her work coursing through her.

Chuck growled in frustration. "It's not Milla Jones."

"Are you sure?"

"Absolutely. About ten years older, and I never once saw Milla smoke."

Disappointment churned. It really would have been too simple for things to have worked out this quickly. Regardless, Shana had a lead on the guy, photos to track and his current vehicle.

"If you're certain, then I guess that's it for tonight."

Resting the camera in her lap, she snapped the lens cover back in place. As she moved, her fingers brushed against Chuck's jeans-clad leg. Butterflies took flight in her stomach.

Heat flared in his eyes. He ran a hand down the back of her neck. Subtle. Sexy as hell. "Sorry your stakeout was a bust."

Her neck still tingled from the casual touch. "Not a total bust. I got some photos and a license plate number. Those may still provide new leads. I just need to keep gathering the pieces." She drew in the last sip of her milkshake before tossing the cup in the trash sack. "So, what do you want to do for the rest of our anniversary?"

The question had sounded more innocent when she'd thought it. Now it filled the air between them, words loaded with a double meaning.

Her mind went back to the feel of his mouth on hers, his kiss, the familiar connection. It was a day to commemorate, and she desperately wanted to remember a part of that.

Which didn't seem to be happening.

After a night charged with tension, and romance all around them in the most unlikely of places, she craved some of that for herself.

"The question should be, what do you want, Shana?"

She licked her dry lips, unable to miss the way his eyes followed the movements. She looked at him through her lashes, then…hell, straight on. Direct. No coyness. "I want you to kiss me."

"I can definitely accommodate."

Hand cupping her chin, he breathed new life into her. The kiss was as intoxicating as wine to a parched palate.

The confines of the SUV proved tight. He guided her over the bucket seats onto the back bench, then climbed over to join her.

Like high schoolers on a date, they stretched out on the seat, him on top of her, kissing. And kissing. Luxuriating in the pleasure of connecting. Their bodies knew each other well, even though Shana's memory of their past had been wiped away.

He slid his hand under the hem of her sweater again, his palm to her back. She groaned with pleasure, grabbing his wrist and guiding it upward, higher and higher until he cupped her breast. One, then the other, he stroked until her nipples beaded in response.

Her hands were just as busy, curiously exploring his chest, down his back as she met him kiss for kiss, touch for touch.

His knee nestled between her legs, pressing against the core of her. She rolled her hips, husky sighs slipping between her lips as she worked against him.

"I want more than a kiss. I want you."

Chuck had driven home as fast as safely possible, his body on fire with the prospect of having his wife in his bed again.

Naked.

Under him.

Over him.

This wasn't an invitation he intended to turn down. Who would have thought a stakeout would be more of a turn-on than his plans of a dinner at a five-star restaurant with live music? His mind raced with plan B—places to make love to her…and the perfect solution came to mind.

Not in the bed.

But in the greenhouse.

Her favorite place on their property. Something damn special for this second chance to have Shana in his arms.

He steered the car past their home, the four-wheel drive managing the narrower path to the hothouse with no difficulty.

"Chuck, um, where are we going?" She glanced over at the barn as they passed by.

"I think every woman should be showered with flowers on her anniversary, and that's just what I intend for you. An abundance of them."

Already he could envision her wearing nothing but the necklace and flower petals in the warmth of the greenhouse.

Her gaze shifted forward as they approached the domed glass structure. Her mouth bowed in an "oh." He reveled in the pleased surprise on her face.

"I like the way you think, husband."

Husband.

That word seared through him. Her acknowledgment that she was his.

Hell yes, it was a primal thing. He couldn't deny it. Didn't want to.

She was his wife. Carrying his child. They were linked. The searing chemistry between them was their right to enjoy.

And he intended for them both to indulge to the max.

As they made their way from the SUV, he draped an arm around her shoulders to keep her warm and make sure she didn't slip on the ice. Her curves fit against him in a way he remembered well and had missed lately.

He opened the greenhouse, a blast of humid warmth wafting out, carrying the floral perfume in the air. He drew her inside and swept the hood of her parka down, angling to seal his mouth to hers. She tasted of snowflakes and passion. Her hands gripped his jacket, urging him closer, but not nearly close enough.

With restless hands, he tugged off her parka and shucked his jacket, winter gear falling to the floor. With his hands bare, he stroked her back and lower, lifting her against him and deepening the kiss. Desire hummed through his veins, pulsing faster, harder. So much so, he considered setting her on the counter behind them and burying himself inside her now.

But that hadn't been his plan in coming here.

He eased back a step. She reached for him, and he kissed the tip of her nose. "Patience. I promise it will be worth the wait."

"I look forward to your delivering." Smiling, she leaned back against the wooden counter and watched him through sultry, narrowed eyes.

He strode to the reading nook in the back corner, an addition Shana had added for herself. Moonbeams streamed through the roof, illuminating the room along with the warm glow of heat lamps over seedlings. He pulled an afghan off the chaise and spread it on the floor, ever aware of her watchful gaze. Walking the length of the hothouse, he gathered irises and roses, plucking the petals and spreading them on the blanket. He turned to face her, his arms open.

She slipped off the counter and headed toward him without hesitation, her body a sultry glide of beauty that still left him breathless.

Sealing his mouth to hers again, he lost himself in the feel of her in his arms. Barely breaking contact, he peeled the sweater from her, sweeping it upward as she extended her arms to help him go all the faster.

"Shana," he said, eyeing her with reverence. "I want to take my time with you."

"That can absolutely happen, because we will be doing this more than once tonight." She tugged his belt loose. "Now let's get rid of these clothes so I can see you."

Her boldness surprised him, pleased him. He'd expected more hesitancy because of her amnesia. But he should have known. At the core, she was still his Shana. Bold. Unique. Ready to take what she wanted from the world.

At times he struggled with how that conflicted with her distrust of that same world, giving her a vulnerability he'd never quite grasped how to handle.

None of which he wanted to ponder right now with his beautiful wife shimmying out of her jeans in front of him.

He made haste to ditch his own clothes, his boots landing with a thud on top of her sweater. Until finally—*finally*—they were both bare. The appreciation in her eyes notched up his need for her as it dawned on him that—to her—this was their first time.

Slowly, carefully, he lowered her onto the afghan, the press of her body against the flower petals releasing a hint of perfume. He lifted a rose and trailed it along her skin, teasing whispers of pleasure from her lips. With each stroke of the rose, he traced the path with his mouth until her body writhed under his touch.

Her fingers gripped into his shoulders and she urged him upward over her, her legs parting to welcome him, her feet sliding up the backs of his calves. The warmth of her around him threatened to send him over the edge. It had been too long since they'd been together without a host of angry words placing a barrier between them.

Except he didn't want to think about the past now.

He just wanted to move, to thrust into his wife again and again, her hips arching up to meet him. Perspiration slicked their bodies, sealing flesh to flesh. Right now, he couldn't think of a better anniversary they'd shared.

His senses homed in to the here and now. The whoosh of the mister—the rustle of the leaves—the steam of the heated space—it was like a tropical haven in the middle of their storm-tossed landscape.

He rolled onto his back, and she purred her pleasure as she sat astride him. His fingers dug into the soft flesh of her hips, guiding her. Not that she seemed to need any assistance in knowing just how to move to drive him to the edge of completion. He gritted his teeth to hold back, determined to make this last as long as humanly possible—and to make sure she found her release.

Snow gathered on the clear glass roof, moonlight whispering through to cast honeyed beams along her creamy skin. Why had he never thought to do this with her here before? They'd made love countless times in the past, but there was a newness to this moment, to his wife.

His hands grazed upward to cup the sweet weight of her breasts, a perfect fit. He circled her nipples with his thumbs, teasing each into a hard bead of passion. All the while he watched her face, the way her eyes closed, how her nose flared with breathy sighs.

Then her spine arched and her head flung back. This, her body, he knew so well. She was close, and so was he. Restraint fell away and he guided her onto her back again, plunging inside her, savoring her husky cries of bliss that sent him plummeting into an explosion of sensation.

As aftershocks rippled through them, he grasped the edge of the blanket and draped the other half over them, petals whispering around them. He shifted, gathering her close to his side.

Shana rested her head on his chest. "Was it always like this between us?"

Such a complex question.

In some ways yes, but there had also been the tension of sex on a schedule to conceive, then the stress of their marriage crumbling. The attraction had always been intense, yet the pressures of life took away the abandon of living purely in the moment.

She tipped her head to look at him. "Did I say something wrong?"

Nothing slipped past her. Every misstep, pause, eye movement seemed to betray him.

"Not at all. Everything's right. And yes, we've always been this intensely attracted to each other."

That was true, at least.

"Hmm, I wish I could remember." Those alert, showstopping blue eyes fluttered shut, as if she was trying to conjure up the past.

A past he knew to be fraught with pain and complications.

A past he didn't want to burden her with now.

"Shhh." He kissed her temple. "Let's just enjoy the *now*."

So much easier said than done.

Stretching in her bed the next morning, Shana luxuriated in the flannel sheets against her well-loved flesh. Having sex with Chuck had been everything she'd imagined—and more. She couldn't imagine having forgotten a man like him, but she didn't intend to let regrets steal the pleasure of what they'd shared.

She vaguely remembered Chuck getting dressed in the greenhouse, then wrapping her in a blanket and carrying her to bed. He'd started to leave for the guest suite and she'd sleepily reached out a hand for him to stay.

And he did.

Beside her through the night, asleep still now.

She took the moment to study him at her leisure. He slept on his back, sprawling. He was a bed hog, and somehow knowing that intimate detail about him made her smile.

He was so in control in day-to-day life, the abandon during sleep touched her heart. He was such a strong man, but in sleep he seemed more…real. Less perfect. Which made him all the more endearing somehow.

More approachable?

An ease had settled between them during their love-making, as real and as corporeal as the light streaming through the oversize windows. Last night, she hadn't fought tooth and nail for a scrap of her past to come bounding back to her. Instead, she'd moved in the present.

Although last night, her body had certainly seemed to remember his well. She could still smell the sweet scent of flowers clinging to their bodies.

They'd certainly been in sync on a sensual level even if she had no recall of being with him before. Her flesh hummed with awareness of having been well loved.

The moment would have been perfect. Except she kept remembering his hesitation when she'd asked if things had always been this way between them.

What was he keeping from her?

A pinprick.

That's what his hesitation felt like. Small, but deep. Capable of drawing both blood and infection. Shana believed him when he said he didn't cheat. That'd been her greatest fear, an unfortunate assumption that came from growing up with a wildly unfaithful father, a man who'd strung her mother along for years while he had a secret family on the side.

If not cheating, then what would cause the misstep? Something clearly made Chuck squirm in discomfort. Tapping her temple lightly, she again tried to will the knowledge.

And… Nothing.

Again, she felt like a spinning top, circling end-lessly.

She wanted to believe in him, to have more nights

like the one they'd just shared. There had to be something between them that she remembered on a subconscious level because she'd never been the sort to fall into bed with a man she barely knew.

Her fingers itched to stroke back the sweep of hair from across his forehead, but she feared waking him. She wanted to study him awhile longer as if gathering these minutes to herself could somehow make up for the deficit of losing five years. As if she could bring the balance to at least a hint more of equality.

So many questions piled up in her mind, and not just about the time she was missing. Would their child look like him? What kind of parents would they make? Would she ever remember the night they'd made this child?

Her hand slid over her stomach, still flat. If it weren't for the ultrasound, she wouldn't have believed she was pregnant at all.

The amnesia had robbed her of so many things. But she wouldn't let it stop her from sleeping with him again.

She pressed her palm to the hard-muscled plane of his shoulders and stroked lower, lower still, until his eyes opened—groggy, sure, but a smile creased his face.

"Good morning, beautiful," he said, his voice early-morning hoarse.

"Good morning to you, too." She slung her leg over his, sliding closer just as—

The doorbell pealed through the house once, twice, then a voice called out, "Hello?"

Chuck's mother.

Again, his family was making themselves right at home. And their timing couldn't be any worse.

Eight

Yanking a thick cable-knit sweater over his head, Chuck charged down the stairs, toward his mother, who was still in the entryway. He didn't think she would actually come up to the second floor. Still, Jeannie and Shana had shared an ease and familiarity in the past. His wife had given his mom a key with Shana's blessing to use it.

But that was then.

Now things were so very different. His progress with Shana was hard-won. He couldn't take any risks that might upset the tenuous balance.

The heat of their night together was burned in his memory. Being with Shana had always been incredible, beyond anything he'd experienced with other women. But last night had surpassed even what had come before between them. He wanted to see where that connection could lead, but...

Jeannie leaned against the off-white couch. As always, his mother looked perfectly arranged. From the great window, sunlight glinted off her pearls. A staple of her wardrobe. Pearls that had been in the family for generations.

Moving farther into the living room, he feigned nonchalance as he pulled back the curtains. A light dusting of snow softened the horizon view, an elk leaving a trail of hoofprints on the pristine lawn.

"I'm sorry if I disrupted your morning," Jeannie apologized, nodding toward his bare feet. "I brought food—a simple chicken-and-rice dish that always settled my stomach when I was pregnant." She lifted a casserole dish, her smile genuine but concerned.

Growing up, food was what had woven together his family. Though lack of money had never plagued their family life, Jeannie refused to employ a cook. She'd preferred to prepare meals herself. Chuck's earliest memories always seemed to place him back in the grand Mikkelson kitchen and his mother moving between island countertop and stove, the scent of spices heavy in the air. She'd made sure they'd built traditions. They all ate in the kitchen, no formal dining room stuffiness. She made it clear to her children that values were more important than money.

Which made him itch now, thinking about how he was skirting the truth with Shana.

"Thanks, Mom. Luckily Shana hasn't been suffering from morning sickness yet, but we always welcome your cooking."

Taking the still-warm plate from his mother's manicured hands, he tilted his head, nodding toward the kitchen. A concerned smile still painted her lips as she smoothed her cream-colored cardigan before following him.

Toes touching the kitchen tile, Chuck tried to shake last night from his mind. He needed to focus on the present. He appreciated the support from his mother, but he ached to return to his bed, to Shana. He was anxious about the fragile rekindled connection. Hell, he wanted to bury his fingers in her honeyed hair.

Clearing her throat, his mother cut through Chuck's thoughts. "Will you be joining us at the rodeo tomorrow afternoon? We've got a ringside box to cheer on Marshall."

Chuck hadn't given it much thought, with his life in so much turmoil. But it sounded like a good possibility for a date night with Shana, while also further acclimating her to his new extended family.

Marshall Steele had run the rodeo circuit for years. He'd retired after a string of injuries. While he popped out of retirement on occasion, he now managed the Steele ranch about an hour away from their family mansion—which also sported a barn as big as some farms. The Steeles did nothing on a small scale.

Chuck took the glass casserole dish from his mother and opened the fridge. Tension knotted in his shoulders. In spite of trying to accommodate thoughts of family plans, memories of Shana and their hot night together fogged his mind.

Jeannie let out a little laugh, fidgeting around the room, strangely distracted. "It's not like you to sleep in."

"I took a couple of days off," he said carefully. His mom was intuitive when it came to her kids and he didn't want to risk her censure over him being selective in what he shared with Shana about their marital troubles. His mother didn't know about their plans to separate and he wanted to keep it that way.

"Like that ever made a difference to you before." She turned to face him again and took a seat. "You've always been an early bird."

Now he saw it in her eyes, the reason for her distractibility. She was concerned. As much as he wanted to rush her out the door and get back to Shana, he could spare a few moments to set her mind at ease.

Pulling a smile, Chuck nodded as his arm extended to the crisp white cabinets. His thumbs grazed the top of the glass as he pulled down a cut crystal tumbler. And then another. "Late night."

"That's right." She smiled knowingly. "Yesterday was your anniversary."

Opening the fridge again, he put space between her question and his answer, knowing how he responded would determine the remainder of the conversation. Snagging a bottle of sparkling water with a hint of lemon, he tilted the bottle to his mother in a silent question. And yeah, maybe he was stalling, too, because he felt guilty for not telling Shana the truth.

Jeannie's gracious smile brightened her face as she nodded yes. But it was clear she waited for a different kind of response.

Ah, now they were at the crux of why she'd shown up today. She was curious as well as concerned. "We went on a stakeout to follow a lead on Milla Jones."

Jeannie sat up straighter, her smile replaced by keen interest. "And?"

"It didn't work out." Well, the lead hadn't played out,

but it had certainly borne fruit for him on a personal level. "I'll go wake Shana so you can visit."

"Don't bother her. Pregnant women sleep more."

Unscrewing the sparkling water's cap, he carefully poured the water before extending a glass to his mother. He knew that, about the extra sleep, but he didn't want to dwell on the painful past, or what might or might not be in their future, especially not after last night.

"I'm very excited about my next grandchild." She thumbed the band on her right hand, her ring from her first husband, who'd died. She wore Jack Steele's ring on her left hand now.

"Cautiously so, I hope. We've been down this road so many times and it didn't work out."

The pain of those losses stayed with him still. Although he intended to do everything in his power to keep his child safe. To keep Shana safe.

Except even a perfectionist like himself knew his best might not be enough.

"I'm happy today about the baby." She took his hands in hers and squeezed. "Joyful today. Let's enjoy the moment."

He picked through her words, searching for the takeaway. "Are you telling me I should stop worrying?"

"I wouldn't presume." She squeezed his hands again before letting go. "I know that's impossible given Shana's history with fertility issues, her amnesia and the pregnancy."

He sagged back to rest against the granite counter, the weight of concern tugging at him. And he couldn't deny the need to confide at least part of his worry to his mother. "If the doctor could give us a concrete reason why we keep having trouble… If there was something we could try that we hadn't already. It's not like bedrest would even make a difference. You probably aren't surprised to hear I have a problem with accepting things I can't change."

"We would give our own lives for our children. That's natural." She cupped his face with one hand and patted. "I'm here for you anytime, and I don't just mean with casseroles."

He realized that. His whole family was there for him. They were tight that way, and he felt guilty for not holding up his end of things lately. "I'm sorry not to be as present at work these days."

"Focus on what's important," she said without hesitation. "Everyone understands you've got a lot on your plate right now."

"You and Jack deserve to enjoy retirement—and being newlyweds." Saying that still felt strange. Blending families—especially large, powerful families like the Steeles and the Mikkelsons—had been tougher than expected, even taking into consideration the two families' business feud. Thinking about it gave him new insight into how painful Shana's life must have been after her father's betrayal.

"Don't worry about the office, son. We have plenty of children between us to share the workload. You'll end up owing someone something for helping you. Perhaps naming rights."

He hadn't even dared think about baby names. He and Shana had done that far too often only to be crushingly disappointed. But unloading those fears onto his mom might well open the floodgates to sharing others.

He'd built a careful house of cards here trying to win Shana back so they could have a life together and he wasn't risking it.

He didn't fail.

He settled on a lighthearted answer. "Letting the family pick names could go way wrong."

She rolled her eyes. "Especially if Aiden gets a say."

Which brought up a whole other concern. Chuck was too damn distractible these days, which was ironic since he spent most of his time working to distract Shana. Keeping her off the scent of his deception wasn't easy, but he needed to forge ahead with the only strategy he had to win back his wife.

"Are Aiden and Alayna still flirting with each other?"

"It's a crush," Jeannie said dismissively. "He's leaving for Juneau in the fall, transferring colleges."

"A lot can happen between now and then."

"Like I told Shana, they're both over eighteen—"

"Adults living under your roof."

"True enough." She nodded without conceding. But she meant well, and her love was unquestionable. "I know your life feels chaotic right now, and that can make a person search for other things to control. But trust me, son. Jack and I have got this."

There was nothing more he could do other than keep watch. His mother wasn't the only stubborn one. "Fair enough."

She eyed him for a few moments as if she might press him further. Then she sighed, picking up her sparkling water and sitting at the kitchen island. "Now tell me about the progress Shana's making looking for Milla Jones."

Chuck embraced the subject change, grateful for the distraction from talk of Shana. He needed time to get his head in order before facing his sexy, irresistible wife again.

Shana was scared to trust that all this joy could be real, holding Chuck's hand as he led her through the rodeo crowd to their private section of the enclosed arena. The warmth and familiarity of his grip sent tingles through her, stirring memories of making love.

She had an attentive husband with chemistry off the charts. They had a baby on the way. And he was doing his best to romance her whether they were on a date for dinner or a stakeout or with family at a rodeo.

A high-pitched whinny cut through the cold Alaskan air, echoing in her chest. Something about the sheer excitement of it all also knitted rough-hewn anticipation into her very bones. Even the wind whipping across her cheeks caught her off guard, making her wonder if she was, in fact, dreaming.

Chuck opened a wooden bar, waving her toward their section of bleachers, which was already packed with Steeles and Mikkelsons. A bombardment of greetings swirled around her just before she and Chuck were separated by Jack dragging Chuck into a discussion. Her husband dropped a kiss on her lips with a quick apology before joining his stepfather.

She didn't protest, and actually welcomed a bit of distance to regain her footing. Truth be told, the events of her life these past few weeks felt surreal. Hard to trust. Hard to believe, even though she moved through a seemingly perfect setup. The kind of life she'd never dared imagine to be hers.

Therein lay some of Shana's cellular-level hesitation, a sixth sense of something amiss sounding a dull, constant warning in her head.

She shook off the premonition and looked around her. She'd never attended a rodeo before. Everything she knew about them had been gleaned from television shows. The real-life experience was so much more intense. The scent of hay and leather. The loudspeaker piping country tunes, the whinny of horses echoing in the background. And people, so many people gathered in the arena, an audience decked out in different colors of boots, flannel and fringed shirts. Bright lights glistened off an array of the biggest buckles she'd ever seen.

Shifting in her seat, she couldn't deny how normal this felt. How natural. Catching a quick glimpse of Chuck, her stomach fluttered as she fully recognized the previously unnamed awareness. She could feel herself being drawn into this large family, the sort of family she'd dreamed of having while growing up as an only child with a distant father. Discovering her father had built that large family with another woman had been devastating to both Shana and her mom.

Again, she found her thoughts running to the past. But the distant past, not the past five years. Fidgeting in her seat, she picked at the ends of her hair. In some way, this repetitive motion grounded her to the present, to the sights and sounds of the here and now.

Though she sat beside Naomi, her eyes traced the muscular outline of Chuck's broad shoulders. She appreciated the hint of his back muscles in that tight gray shirt. The deep rumble of masculine laughter drew her eyes to his seat mates—Jack Steele and Jack Steele's much younger brother, Conrad. The trio appeared immersed in light conversation, judging by the way Conrad kept chuckling.

Her gaze fell away from the sights and sounds of her immediate vicinity and turned to her curiosity about the arena and the explosion of energy in the ring. A paint horse turned on a hairpin around one of the barrels. The young woman in a pink Stetson hat with silver embellishments seemed like a shooting star. Around the second barrel, the crowd gave an audible gasp as the rider lifted from her deep seat, nearly falling off the side.

Tension mounted in Shana's throat. Seconds felt like years. Somehow, the girl managed to recover, throwing herself back into the saddle. Silently, Shana hoped this girl would make the best time. She felt a kinship to that tenacity.

As the horse and rider effortlessly curled around the third barrel, Shana felt the anxiety in her shoulders release as she relaxed into the teeming box filled with both Mikkelson and Steele family members.

Jack, the patriarch of the Steele clan, held a beer bottle in his left hand as he laughed and chatted with other family members. Ice Cap Beer, the family brewery, was one of the corporate sponsors for the rodeo. Banners featuring a scenic glacial lake, the immediately recognizable Ice Cap Beer logo, lined the arena between other banner-sized advertisements for feed stores and Western wear.

Naomi let out a gentle sigh beside her, bobbing her head, that dark, signature ponytail revealing the sharp, beautiful angles of her face. One of the twins slept soundly in her arms, seemingly unbothered by the chaos.

Shana's hand slid over her stomach and she thought

of her own child. This time next year, would she and Chuck be sitting here with their baby?

Chuck said there had been other pregnancies. She didn't remember them, but even contemplating the loss was difficult.

Shana swallowed deep, feeling her throat clog with bubbling emotions. Forcing herself to the present, she leaned over to Naomi, softly brushing the woman's shoulder in a cream sweater. "I can't believe the twins are sleeping through all of this noise."

Naomi smiled, her dark eyes dancing. "Any opportunity to wear them out, and the fact that they're both tired at the same time is nothing short of a miracle."

"They're beautiful." Shana skimmed her fingers lightly over the infant's feathery-soft dark hair.

"Thank you," Naomi said with unmistakable pride. "There are days I wonder how I'll make it until bedtime, but truly they are good babies. So far, it's doable to take them to the office with me, although I imagine that will change as soon as they're walking."

"I don't know how you juggle it all."

"Royce is amazing." Naomi beamed with love as she looked at her husband for a moment before turning her attention back to Shana. "I heard the stakeout was a bust."

As far as work, it was. Personally? It had netted pleasurable results.

"I haven't given up on that lead. It just didn't pan out this time. Surveillance operations require patience and persistence."

"I've always been in awe of your career. You're so daring."

Daring? The adjective disarmed her. How had she

given up that part of her identity? Shana couldn't imagine not working. Giving up her job felt like an alien
concept, like someone else's decision. But she didn't
have the passage of time that had eased her into that
decision.

"You're a legal eagle." Shana had dreamed of being
a lawyer but there hadn't been the money to attend law
school. "That's plenty impressive. And you manage it
all while juggling twins."

"Shana, hon, you may not remember me, but I know
you well. You'll manage the working mother routine
with ease, if returning to your job again is the path
you choose."

She hoped so. Life felt so overwhelming, so much to
process at once, like she was riding one of those bulls
and had nothing familiar to hold on to.

A roar from the crowd cut her thoughts short as
Marshall burst into the ring on the back of a bucking
horse. The Steeles and Mikkelsons shot to their feet,
whooping and whistling their support.

The vibration of her phone with an incoming message distracted her. The subject line kicked her heart
rate up a notch. Familiar nodes of anticipation worked
through her nervous system as she read.

A tip that Milla had been spotted coming and going
from the hotel they'd staked out earlier.

Could this be another false lead? Or was this legit?

She should be focused on the job, and yet her first
thought was elation over the possibility of a sexy repeat of her last stakeout with Chuck.

Alayna had been going to rodeos all her life.

Rodeos brimmed with heart-pounding moments,

though Alayna had previously believed such moments were mostly reserved for the riders. But as she stood in her brand-new cowgirl boots, boot-cut jeans and a formfitting turquoise plaid shirt, she realized the fallibility of her previous assessment.

Because she was here with Aiden.

She couldn't have dreamed up being ringside with Aiden Steele, down by the chutes where all the action happened.

But here she was anyway.

Aiden had invited her to come with him to help his older brother Marshall tack up his horse. Like the Steeles, she'd grown up around horses. But rodeo show life required a whole new set of rules, down to how the mane and tail were groomed and shined. Aiden had explained that the fancy polish that made the horse's coat gleam was part of the theatrics of the whole thing.

It wasn't enough to be good. Anyone could be good. Stars were made with these extra touches. Apparently, Marshall had been the best before injury forced him to take a slower pace.

Alayna toyed with a lock of her hair. "You know a lot about the rodeo circuit."

Aiden adjusted his black Stetson, looking like a natural part of this landscape in his worn jeans and flannel. "We supported my brother. I've been going to these since I was in elementary school."

"Did you ever think of trying your hand at it?" Just the thought of him in the arena in chaps sounded hot.

"Nah," he said, nudging his Stetson back. "It's my brother's gig. In a family as big as mine, it's tough to find a niche that hasn't already been mastered by someone else."

She understood about struggling to step out of the shadow of overachieving siblings. "That doesn't mean you couldn't be just as good, or even better."

"Easy for you to say." Aiden climbed on the second rung of the fence and leaned forward, looking wistfully at the current horse and rider. Exhaling hard, he hopped down. Leaning heavily against a beat-up barrel, he kicked dirt. "You're a straight-A student with a natural seat on a horse."

Heat rose in her cheeks, but she did her best to school her features into neutrality. The giddiness at his compliment still entered her voice, though. "You've watched me riding?"

He gave her that grin that sent her stomach turning barrel rolls. "We do live together."

"But we're not related," she reminded him, and herself. "Not really."

He snorted on a dry laugh. "Tell that to our parents. They're really over the top with the whole blended family thing."

"No kidding. I wish they would stop forcing the issue and just let us find our own pace." But no one had asked for her opinion. Apparently, since she didn't work for the corporation, she didn't count. "My mom's always been crazy big on family, though. She even put up with her sister giving her son away to us."

"I forget sometimes that Trystan isn't your biological brother, that he's actually your cousin."

"Aunt Willa and their brother—Uncle Lyle—had drug problems. Mom never gave up on them." Alayna stared out at a horse that flat-out refused to do anything but a working trot, despite the desperation on the rider's face. "I think if they showed up today, Mom would still throw them a banquet and start searching for rehab facilities."

"Is that such a bad thing?"

"If they're going to hurt my mom?" She shot upright, fired up. "Then yes, that's a bad thing. And our cousin—second cousin—Sage Hammond is related to them, too. She's been embarrassed and hurt enough by the grief they've brought on the family."

His eyebrows raised as he looked at her in surprise. "You're fiercer than I would have expected."

"Right, I'm the family mouse," she said with distaste.

"More like a kitten." He lifted her hands, his thumb stroking along her fingers. "With surprise claws."

His light caress sent shivers through her. She could hardly believe he was finally noticing her—touching her. "I'm glad you think so."

She was already anticipating the feel of his hands on her again.

"I'm leaving here, you know. I'm not sticking around home forever."

"Juneau isn't the end of the earth. We'll still see you."

"Um, it's not that simple."

She stepped closer, near enough to catch the scent of soap on him.

"Kitten, this isn't a good idea."

His words nicked her, reopening a wound. She leaned against the fence, eyes fixed on the next barrel racer. She did her best to seem normal and steady as she turned to look at him, letting her hair pool over her shoulder.

"What isn't a good idea?" she asked innocently. She wasn't giving up, but she sure wasn't going to look like an idiot, especially since they sat at the same dinner table every day.

A different kind of heart pounding took over her still-ragged chest. She turned away from Aiden, needing to collect herself, to look anywhere but at him. She scanned the crowd, trying to draw a full breath against the sting of disappointment.

Her eyes snagged on a face.

A face she remembered from somewhere.

Fear and adrenaline coursed through her as she forced air into her lungs. Had she really seen the profile of a person who had lied to her family?

There was no way to prove today that what she'd heard as a child was true. She wasn't even completely sure of what she'd heard.

She just knew there were faces that still gave her nightmares.

One face she could swear was, against all odds, right here in this arena, right now.

Fear had her digging her kitten claws into Aiden's steady arm. "You have to help me."

Chuck hadn't expected their rodeo date to end quite this way, but he had Shana alone and that was his top priority. They would end the night going to bed together. He needed to be patient.

She had received a tip that the man she was surveilling would be back at the same seedy motel tonight, an odd pattern that did bear checking out.

And Chuck certainly didn't want her to be out here alone. His sharp eyes followed the people that passed by, entering and exiting the various rooms.

Shana shifted in the seat next to him, her camera

and tablet in her lap. "Are you sure you want to stay, too? This isn't a risky stakeout and it could go late."

"I'm spending time with you." He stroked her hair, testing the silky texture between his fingers. Even as he remained patient—for the moment—he still couldn't deny the need to move faster with winning her over.

His mother's visit had reminded him too well that anyone in his family could accidentally let something slip around Shana that would blow up his world.

"Yes, I am exactly where I want to be," he said.

"You could work rather than simply watching me."

He grinned. "I could."

"But you're not." She passed him her tablet. "Here. I can make handwritten notes."

"No thank you." He passed the tablet back to her. He wasn't taking his eyes off her or the motel until he had her safely home. Then he intended to have his *hands* all over her. "We've established I'm a workaholic."

She tipped her head to the side, her arms crossed under her full breasts. "And I'm supposed to believe you've magically morphed into a footloose and fancy-free sort?"

God, he enjoyed her spunk. The urge to claim her, to move faster toward their reunion, nearly overwhelmed him.

"That would be overstating things. Let's say I'm working on delegating when appropriate." He lifted her hand. "And I know when it's time for recreation."

He pressed a kiss to the inside of her wrist, then angled up to her neck.

She sighed for an instant before easing away. "I'm a one-person shop. Delegating isn't an option. Now stop distracting me, you tempting man."

"I'm not going to argue with you."

A deep-throated laugh accompanied a pop of berries into her mouth. Her tongue teased his fingertips ever so slightly.

Damn. This woman drove him up a wall. Awareness ramping up, he did his best to draw his attention back to the movement outside.

An elderly couple hobbled by. Not them.

But from the corner, he spotted a woman with a blond ponytail. Could this be Ms. Milla Jones at last? He felt the urge to run out and see the woman up close. To know for certain. But they'd made the mistake of thinking it might be Milla before.

Shana reached for the door handle. "I can't get the angle I need with the camera."

He clasped her elbow. "You're not going alone."

She glanced over her shoulder. "Then be inconspicuous."

"I'll keep you close like any loving husband escorting his wife in for a tryst." He ducked outside into the light shower of snow, walking around the front of the SUV to her side. "Wife—"

He slid his arm around her shoulders, holding her close. Her curves pressed to him even through their parkas. He ached for this stakeout to bear fruit so they could—

No sooner had he finished the thought than the couple at the door seemed to catch sight of them. The pair took off, picking their way through the icy parking lot at a fast clip.

Chuck gripped Shana's shoulders. "I do not want you running on the ice. Period. It's too risky. I've got this."

She nodded tightly. "Go. Please."

As he took off, her words, "Be careful," carried on the snowy wind. Every footfall pushed him through the snow-covered lot, weaving between cars. He heard the chirp of a car door being unlocked remotely, lights flashing ahead. He made a beeline for the sedan, his boots gaining solid traction.

He reached the car just as the couple slid to a stop against the hood. The headlights illuminated their faces.

Their familiar, young faces.

Anger boiled to the surface, fast and furious.

"Aiden Steele, what the hell are you doing here with my sister?"

Nine

Shana bolted from the SUV at a sprint after Chuck.

She scrambled through the mix of snow and dirt that threatened to sidetrack her booted feet and upend her balance. Not fast enough for Chuck's rage, it seemed.

His anger was unmistakable and unsettling. If he charged up to the teens in this frame of mind, no good could come of the confrontation.

She remembered too many arguments between her parents. Her mother's suspicions, met with cold anger, then silence from Shana's father. Conflict still made Shana's chest go tight, but she couldn't back down from this.

Something about Alayna reminded her of herself at that age.

There'd been no one to intervene in Shana's life during those moments of vulnerability, though she certainly prayed for someone to come along. She'd wished on every evening star. But now, Shana could make a difference. A deep gulp of night air temporarily assuaged the thumping and squeezing sensation in her chest.

"Chuck," she called out. "Chuck, wait. Think about your frame of mind."

He didn't so much as glance back at her over his shoulder. He strode toward the young couple under the Snowdrop Inn sign, the last two *N*s flickering as the bulbs gasped their last breaths.

If Shana had been three steps faster, she could have caught up, but there was no stopping him.

Chuck's arm shot out and he grabbed Aiden by the back of his jacket. "What the hell do you think you're doing here with my sister?"

Alayna squeaked in surprise.

Aiden turned, his jaw jutting with defiance. "Trying to keep her out of trouble."

"You have a funny way of showing it." Chuck's tone was less a statement, more of an accusing bark.

Shana touched her husband's elbow, praying for restraint. "Careful, Chuck, he's a kid."

From across the parking lot, a beat-up SUV sputtered to life, cutting the stillness of the night. And somehow the lurching sound of the engine only heightened the bubbling tension between the Steele youth and the Mikkelson man.

For a moment, Shana averted her gaze, focused on the dull twinkle of the icicles on the roof of the Snowdrop Inn.

Aiden's shoulders braced in defiance. "I'm nineteen."

Great. Just what she needed. More testosterone in play. Shana held her calm. "Chuck, take a breath. Think."

Chuck's fist fell away from the teen's jacket. "Talk, boy. And don't try to BS me."

Alayna stepped between them. "Stop. I'm the one who wanted to come here." She held up a mittened hand. "Don't explode. We're not here for the reason you seem to think."

Chuck rocked back on his boots, easing off, for the moment at least. "Explain then, please."

Shana breathed a sigh of relief that they were talking, not fighting. She rubbed her arms to ward off a chill that had nothing to do with the icy wind.

"Let's move to the SUV to talk. It's crazy cold out here and there are people wandering in and out."

If Milla Jones was here and saw Chuck, that could be catastrophic. All the more reason to get back in the vehicle ASAP.

Chuck nodded tightly, bracing Shana's elbow as they walked along the slick lot on their way back to the vehicle. Cars slowly moved past, dim lights temporarily illuminating the blacktop path back to the dark SUV. Shana opened the door, reveling in the lingering warmth inside.

Once they were all in the vehicle, Chuck started the engine, cranked the heat and turned to the teens in the back seat. "Okay, I'm listening."

His sister chewed her chapped lip for a moment before launching in. "I saw someone at the arena that, well," Alayna rambled softly, "it's tough to explain. But someone I thought my imagination had made up.

Seeing the person for real made me want to know for sure. Aiden didn't want me to follow all on my own."

Shana twisted to the side in her seat to get a better look at the nervous teens. Alayna tugged off her plaid scarf, toying with it. Shana could practically feel the girl's nerves.

"You're right," Chuck said drily, pulling off his Stetson and resting it on his knee. "It does make a strange sort of sense. It's so convoluted I actually believe you're telling the truth. Who did you think you saw?"

Alayna exchanged glances with Aiden before continuing, "Someone who left Alaska a long time ago and has no reason to come back." Dome light beaming overhead, Alayna's blue eyes shone with confusion and a hint of wariness. "And I haven't seen him in a long time, so I could be wrong. But it looked like Uncle Lyle."

"Uncle Lyle?" Shana asked.

Chuck shifted toward her. "Mom's loser brother. His showing up would be surprising, sure. He hasn't been around in probably ten years or so. Alayna, why would you care?"

His sister hugged herself tighter, her body language shouting insecurity, as if she expected to be discounted. "Everyone's so worried about what that woman Milla Jones said, and I wanted to do my part to help."

Chuck sighed with exasperation. "What does that have to do with Uncle Lyle?"

"Um, well…" Alayna picked through the tassels on her scarf. "He disappeared not too long after that mysterious plane crash. It just seemed like Mom's brother and sister were always wanting things, like money. And they really wanted the Steeles to fail so Mom and Dad would be more successful."

The details sparked Shana's sleuth mind with possibilities. Having amnesia gave her an objectivity she might not have had before, since she was less attached to these people. How strange to have an upside to losing her memory.

Lyle was also related to one of the company's personal assistants—Sage Hammond. Shana made a mental note to look deeper into Sage's background and interview her about this Lyle character. She also needed to review the photos from the first stakeout.

Wouldn't Chuck have recognized his uncle? A lot of time had passed, though.

Chuck's mouth thinned before he continued, "I'm still not making the connection as to why you and Aiden followed a Lyle look-alike to a seedy motel."

Headlights from a lone car washed the SUV in a sickly yellow light, illuminating Alayna's sheet-white face. She looked ghostlike in her puffed purple jacket. "I've always thought Uncle Lyle had something to do with that plane crash."

Shana held back a gasp of surprise. Clearly the girl believed what she was saying, but how?

"That's a pretty, um, substantial leap. You must have a reason."

"When I was a kid, I overheard a conversation between Uncle Lyle and some guy I didn't know. It didn't make sense then. I think I was too scared, too young, to trust what I heard. But over the years that conversation has haunted my dreams. Seeing his face tonight made me wonder if maybe…"

Chuck pinned Alayna with a laser-fierce gaze. "If

you're right, then following him was the last thing you should have done. Do you realize you could have put your life at risk?"

Her brows knitted in clear frustration as a vein surfaced on her forehead. Then Alayna visibly deflated, her hands wringing her scarf tighter, knuckles blanched. "You still don't believe me."

"I believe that you believe it, and I believe you aren't trying to hook up with Aiden."

The boy nodded with a tight smile. "Thanks."

Alayna leaned forward to grip the seat in front of her. "So, are we going to check out the lead?"

"Shana is going to drive you both home," Chuck said with a voice that brooked no argument. "I'll drive Aiden's vehicle and follow."

Alayna's shoulders braced with ire, unusual from the normally passive girl. "You have no right."

Shana rested her hand on Chuck's arm. "How about you and I just follow Aiden and Alayna to make sure they're home safe and sound?"

Muscles flexed under her touch but finally Chuck nodded. "That's acceptable."

Acceptable? Shana couldn't help but wonder who this stern man was, so different from the tender lover who showered her with ice cream and flowers.

A chilling reminder that she really didn't know him at all.

The drive to the Steele home had been strained, to say the least, but then, Chuck didn't feel much like chitchat.

His sister's strange words and erratic behavior had rattled him. That his uncle could somehow be involved with the plane crash that had killed Jack Steele's wife and daughter seemed a stretch. Uncle Lyle wasn't sharp, by a long shot. He couldn't have pulled off something of that magnitude—or that horrible.

Alayna must be wrong.

Chuck prayed she was wrong.

He shook free of those thoughts and focused on following the car ahead of him as Aiden pulled up to the rustic Steele mansion on the water.

Chuck glanced over at his silent wife in the passenger seat. Something wasn't right with Shana, but he couldn't deal with that just yet. He had another crisis at hand to settle first.

Sliding into the Steele driveway, he threw the SUV into Park so quickly, the automobile seemed to stutter and exhale a sigh that echoed his own.

He needed to get to the bottom of this situation with Alayna. A belly-deep frustration moved through his blood. The cold Alaskan night grew more and more complicated.

Of course, he couldn't deny some of his focus on his sister had to do with trying to control something in his life.

Right now, he had to focus on making sure Aiden and Alayna were safely home and not running rogue with stakeouts of their own.

Some answers about what Alayna thought she'd heard would be helpful, too.

As silent as an encroaching shadow, he followed the two teens up the stairs to the house. Absently, he held the door for Shana, whose normally bright face sported knitted brows and chapped lips in a neutral line.

The group moved into the great room, a fire crackling and popping in the massive fireplace. Their party wasn't exactly loud. In fact, no one had spoken for some time. Still, the shuffling of bodies into the living room caused Jack and Jeannie to look up from their overstuffed leather sofa.

Chuck's mother and his new stepfather had been curled up on the sofa, enjoying the evening in front of the fire, if the wineglasses and cheese spread on the coffee table were any indication.

It was strange for him still, Chuck admitted, to see them like this. For his family to now include once mortal business enemies. A blended family had its challenges, for sure, but the Steele-Mikkelson merger felt fraught with even more than potential corporate espionage and possibly murderous consequences, according to the slanderous statements made by Milla Jones.

And, if Alayna's half-formed childhood memory was to be believed, Uncle Lyle's statements, as well.

And that's what Chuck needed to focus on, not how differently he'd hoped this evening would end for him and Shana.

Jack and Jeannie were clearly startled by their entry. Chuck couldn't blame them. He hadn't called or texted. He'd simply acted on instinct, knowing he needed to be here. To talk in person. To sort out this mess. Perhaps Jack and Jeannie would have insights into Alayna's strange memories.

Chuck was less and less sure that asking Shana to take on this case was a good idea.

Jeannie touched her chest in surprise. "Chuck, Shana, what a surprise. What brings you two here tonight?"

Jack was as imposing as the antlers mounted above

the fireplace. Broad and tough as nails, Jack cocked his head to the side. Though his stature had always been imposing, the Steele patriarch was gentle in the way he put an arm around his new wife.

Chuck didn't begrudge his mother her happiness, but it felt strange to surrender control of his family to this man because of some whirlwind romance that had flipped everyone's world upside down.

Chuck ran a hand down the back of his neck, about to drop a helluva story. "Shana and I were on a stakeout after the rodeo and we found these two—" he pointed to Aiden and Alayna, standing warily to the side "— going into a motel together."

Shana moved protectively toward his sister.

Jeannie gasped.

Jack scowled.

Not a good start, but there was no easy way into this, for too many reasons.

Alayna grabbed her mother's arm. "We explained it to them already. I saw Uncle Lyle at the rodeo—"

Jeannie discarded the plaid blanket that had draped around her shoulders. "He lives down in Montana."

"Well, I thought I saw him—" Alayna sounded less certain now "—and it made me remember things, especially with all of this talk about Milla Jones. Uncle Lyle wanted to hurt the Steeles, and we're all a family now."

Neither Jack nor Jeannie looked much like they believed her. Still, the older Steele stepped up. "You should have come straight to us."

"You're looking at me like I'm crazy," Alayna cried. "I wanted proof and I had Aiden with me."

Jack glared at his youngest son. "*You* should have spoken to us."

"She was moving fast," Aiden protested lamely.

Jack glared. "You have a phone."

Aiden shrugged without meeting their eyes.

Chuck's radar went on alert again as he wondered if there was something going on between Aiden and Alayna, an attraction at the very least, which would make it all the tougher to weed through Alayna's strange behavior and supposed memories.

Memories.

A beast all the way around these days—what had been forgotten by Shana, what had been remembered by his sister. Although he was more certain than ever that his sister's recollections were faulty, the product of muddled nightmares from a tough time in their past mixing with a stressful present.

And a need to get time alone with a certain Steele teen.

Jeannie squeezed her son's arm. "Thank you for taking care of this and bringing them home. Jack and I will handle it from here."

Chuck stalled. That was it?

He was supposed to back down about Alayna and Aiden sneaking around together? He'd been in charge of the family since his father's death and now his mother was making it clear his help was no longer needed?

His family's old mortal enemy was now the de facto dad.

When the hell had the world turned so crazy?

Chuck felt the sting of his mom's dismissal, deeply. Although maybe it was just as well that he step aside, since he needed to focus on Shana, for tonight and for their future.

Then he caught the scowl on his wife's face and stopped short, remembering she wasn't the least bit happy with him anymore.

As confused as ever when it came to Shana, he sensed he was running out of time.

The echoing silence from Chuck sent Shana burrowing deep into her mind, hurt on Alayna's behalf at how Chuck had handled things tonight.

She thought about saying something to him...but then she realized the tension she'd felt from him in the car came from a different source than she'd first thought.

Chuck was radiating pain.

She'd been so focused on herself, she hadn't fully considered all he'd been through with her health scare, the miscarriages, his father dying, his mother remarrying. He'd been so attentive to her every whim—without asking for anything in return.

Perhaps the time had come to quit fighting the flow and just see where life led them. After the tense evening, Shana was more than ready to lose herself in their heated connection, so she could only imagine how he was feeling. Rather than an impulsive night of intimacy, she wanted to invite him back into their bedroom to stay while they worked through her lack of memories.

"Chuck, do you think we could put aside what happened with your sister for now? There's nothing more we can accomplish tonight."

His hands clenched around the steering wheel. "It has been a long day. You should probably rest."

She stroked a hand along his arm. "I'm not in the least tired. Are you?"

He looked at her quickly, his eyebrows lifting in surprise. Then fire lit his expression. He stroked back her hair and cupped her face. "Sleep is the last thing on my mind."

"I'm glad we're on the same page about how to spend the rest of the night."

Her fingertips quivered in anticipation, her mind filling with the promise of deep kisses and twining bodies. Chuck navigated the car into the garage, careful to avoid the other vehicles lined up in the large bay.

Mind set, she reached for her door handle, anticipation singing through her veins.

With lightning speed, Chuck moved out of the car, and positioned himself by the door to the house before Shana had a boot-covered foot on the cool pavement. He gave her a sheepish smile as he opened the side entrance to their home.

As she shimmied out of her parka, her skin reveled at the warmth of the house. After placing her jacket on a hook, she shook out her hair, feeling freer and more comfortable than she had in weeks, confident in her choice, in her desire for him. Yanking off her boots, she smiled to herself, ready for this.

Crouching, he lined up their boots on the racks along the floor of the large coatroom. "You handled things well with my sister. I shouldn't have lost my temper."

She felt the heat of his gaze as he looked up at her. Those emerald green eyes seared her to her core, making her feel aware and awake. Shana's breath hitched for a moment.

Fire danced between them.

He offered her a hand. With soft footfalls, he started down the side hallway to the back staircase. Alight with a new kind of intense desire for this man, her husband, she kept pace alongside him.

"I get that you're worried about your sister." She stroked his arm. "That's understandable. I'm just sorry I haven't unearthed more information about Milla Jones."

They climbed the stairs, moving through the hallway where Alaskan landscapes hung on the wall, mixed with family and couple photos in muted gold frames.

An image of them in hiking gear in Australia tugged at her.

The photo also reminded her of how painful this time must be for him, having his wife forget about him. This should be a gloriously happy time in their marriage, expecting a child. Instead, she was floundering her way through her feelings for him, not to mention getting to know his entire family.

"I don't expect magic from the investigation, Shana. Every piece to the puzzle will eventually get us there." He stopped outside the master suite, leaning against the door frame, his eyes distant.

"Like putting together my memory." Five years of memories with this man—her husband, the father of her child—just gone. "I wish I remembered our past."

She stroked his face, tears and longing clogging her throat.

He cupped her hand and pressed it closer to his skin. "I have the honor of making you fall in love with me all over again."

His words made her heart flip inside her chest.

She couldn't claim to be in love with him, but she understood they must have been in love before. With his devotion to recapturing that again, how could she help but be moved?

One thing was without question.

Their chemistry was off the charts.

And while she couldn't seem to reclaim the memories she'd lost, she was determined to fill the present with fresh ones.

She arched up to skim her lips against his. "Come back to our bedroom. Make love to me."

With a low, sexy growl of consent, he sealed his mouth to hers. He reached behind her to open the bedroom door. Chuck scooped her into his arms and carried her across the threshold into her bedroom.

Their bedroom.

It felt so natural, so right, to be in his strong arms. Yes, she understood that he had an advantage because he knew her body so well. But instinct seemed to lead her just as surely; she knew just how to touch him, too.

Slowly, he eased her to her feet again, sliding her down the length of his body while sprinkling kisses along her face, her neck, nipping her earlobe. Hunger grew, flaring. Their hands swept away clothes, perfectly synchronized in brushing aside all barriers between them.

The backs of her bare legs bumped the bed, and he lowered her onto the broad expanse, never taking his eyes off her. His eyes flaming with desire, he knelt beside her, the mattress shifting with his weight.

Side by side they lay, his caresses intense and reverent all at once. He was so different from the angry, overprotective brother from earlier. Back to the man she'd come to know.

The husband determined to romance her.

And she was quite happy to be wooed by his seductive caresses. To forget her concerns and grasp hope, to hold her husband.

To lose herself in long, passionate kisses.

Her restless legs kicked aside the downy comforter. Her foot glided along his calf as she met him touch for touch, stroke for stroke. She savored the feel of his hard muscled body, honed from years outdoors. He wasn't just a man behind a desk. And he wasn't a cowboy in name only.

He was all man, earthy and sexy.

And hers.

He hooked an arm behind her knee and inched her leg higher, bringing her closer until…yes…the steely heat of him pressed against her core.

His eyes met hers, as he held her, as he slowly, ever so deliberately, slid inside her.

The delicious warmth of his thickness filled her with his warmth and with a sense of how right this was. Her body knew him, remembered him in a way that her mind still wrestled to rediscover.

Awash in sensation, she surrendered to the elemental. To pleasure rippling along her every nerve. She combed her hands into his wayward hair and drew him closer for another taste, tongues meeting and mating in a thrust and caress that matched their bodies.

Bliss built, taking her higher, faster, but she didn't even consider holding back because there would be more. She would have him in her bed for many nights to come, giving her time to explore every incredible inch of him at her leisure.

The power of her release gripped her in wave after

wave of ecstasy. She arched into each pulsing tremor rocking through her. Chuck's hoarse shouts mingled with her sighs as they found their climax together.

She hadn't thought anything could top their time together in the greenhouse, but there had been something special to this moment, with its promise of more.

Sweat cooling on her body, she languished in his arms, melting in the aftermath. Her fingers drew lazy circles down her husband's strong arm, along the defined muscles.

Chuck pulled the downy comforter over her and kissed her forehead. "I'll go get us some food. The rodeo refreshments feels like forever ago."

"Don't they, though?"

So much had happened in one evening, which likely explained her exhaustion. Or maybe pregnancy symptoms were finally catching up with her. She'd been following the doctor's orders to the letter, keeping in mind past miscarriages. She touched her stomach, thinking about the baby growing there.

It seemed surreal. Chuck's child.

Rolling to her back, she flung her arm overhead, stretching before swinging her feet to the floor. She tugged on Chuck's T-shirt, breathing in the scent of him, his voice drifting from the hall and over her senses.

A call? This late?

Curiosity piqued, she padded across the room. He had his cell on speakerphone, his voice a low rumble, his words indistinguishable. And the other voice…

A woman.

Shana resisted the urge to step closer to the door and listen. It was probably just a family member or a work call. There was no reason to be suspicious.

Other than the fact that she remembered nothing about their marriage.

Her head started aching, her mind filled with other memories, of her father and how her mother hadn't suspected his deception—right up to the point when she was confronted by the other woman.

Shana pressed her fingertips to her throbbing forehead. She needed to stop her roiling thoughts before she worked herself into a total meltdown. She needed to de-stress. Maybe a shower would help. At least it would keep her from standing here eavesdropping.

She made fast tracks to the bathroom and turned on the shower jets. Peeling off the T-shirt, she squeezed her eyes shut against the headache, willing it to go away. She stepped into the steamy stall, jets hitting her from all sides and easing her tense muscles.

Still, her mind spun, and she pressed her palm against the tile wall.

Flashes of memories blazed through her mind, like bursts of electricity.

Standing at the altar with Chuck.

Their anniversary trips became real, parts of them at least.

Overwhelmed, she sagged back, her legs unsteady.

The reel of fragmented memories culminated in an image of her throwing his clothes angrily into his suitcase, of her demanding that they separate.

She heard herself asking him for a divorce.

Oh God.

She pressed her fist to her mouth to hold back a cry.

How could Chuck have kept this from her? How could he have pretended this whole time?

Because she was pregnant.

The obvious answer.

She doubled over, grief and agony wracking through her. Tears streamed down her face, mixing with the pelting water. She didn't need to remember more. She didn't want to.

This was too much. It threatened to tear her in two. The pain was so intense it felt more than emotional.

It felt...

Real.

Her stomach cramped harder, harder still. Her knees gave way as she realized.

She was losing the baby.

Ten

Heart slugging in his chest, fear shredding his gut, Chuck paced in the ER waiting area.

He considered calling his family, but just couldn't find the will to say the words out loud, words that would further end what had been a period of hope for him and for Shana.

Her panicked voice still echoed in his ears. He'd hung up on his call from work and raced to her, finding her tugging on a robe while doubled over in pain.

He hadn't needed her to tell him what was happening. They'd been through this before.

The pain. The loss. The grief.

She'd been silent for the whole drive, not that he had felt much like talking, either. Fear for her seared him, threatening his focus as he guided the SUV along the icy roads. An ambulance would have taken longer, and he couldn't bring himself to think about losing her, too.

The door to her exam room opened. His stomach lurched. The nurse gave him a sympathetic smile and waved him through. "You can see her now, Mr. Mikkelson."

Shana lay on the examination table, her face as pale as the sheet covering her. "I lost the baby."

Her voice was flat, beaten down, weary, and somehow her tone was more upsetting than outright tears.

Tears, he could handle and wipe away.

Right now, he didn't have a clue what to do for her, and that made him feel helpless as hell.

"I know. I'm so sorry."

"You don't have to try and make me feel better." Her fingers clutched the sheet, twisting it in her tight fists. "I know you're hurting over this, too."

He sank down into a chair, each drag of air stinging him with the antiseptic smell of defeat. "I knew the odds were against us. If there was anything in modern medicine left to try, we would have tried it. There isn't."

He needed to box up his own hurt over the loss, the pain no easier this time than it had been the first. If anything, it devastated him more. But somehow, he knew Shana hurt even worse.

She felt the loss even more deeply for having been the one to carry the child inside her.

"The doctor said much the same," she said in that flat voice, refusing to meet his eyes, "that we couldn't have done anything differently."

"Shana." He reached for her hand.

She pulled away. "You don't have to."

Why wasn't she looking at him?

He couldn't shake the feeling that something else was going on with her. "What do you mean?"

She shifted against the pillow, sitting up with a wince, her gaze skating to him briefly, then flicking past. "After we…uh…when I was in the shower, some of my memory returned."

Chuck swallowed hard.

The worst-case scenario ran through his head like a warning siren. From her closed-off pose, it seemed she hadn't recalled their wedding and honeymoon, but something far darker.

"What part?"

Her eyes met his solidly for the first time, and he saw more than hurt staining the blue depths. Outright anger flared.

"The part where we decided to separate."

Words froze in his throat, in his mind. He'd entertained the notion of her remembering, but he had hoped she would recall happier times.

Anything but this.

"I don't know what to say."

"Nothing. There's nothing you can say now," she retorted tightly, swaying. "The time to tell me the truth has passed."

He steadied her, gripping her shoulders. His first priority needed to be keeping her as calm as possible. "I didn't want to upset you. We can discuss this later."

"Later?" She shrugged away his touch. "There's nothing more to talk about. Ever. I realize now that you were staying with me out of a sense of duty, because I was pregnant. But I'm not now. You can go."

Like hell.

"I'm not leaving you."

"The doctor said I need to stay here overnight. But you don't have to stay."

"I'm not leaving," he repeated.

Blue fire sparked in her eyes, and her normally up-turned lips thinned into an uncompromising line. "You have no obligation to me anymore."

He understood she had to be upset—about what she'd remembered, about what he hadn't said—but this complete slicing away was a surprise.

"This isn't the time to make big decisions. You're emotional." He paused, scrubbing a hand over his jaw. "As am I, truth be told."

Her brows shot skyward. That gorgeous face tight-ened with anger. "We've already had this discussion. There's no more talking to be done. I'm sorry. But it's time for us to end things."

End things.

The second time their marriage had been declared over.

He searched for words to…what?

To not have this cold silence between them.

The ER door opened, admitting two staff members ready to move her to a room for the night.

Shana reclined back. "Chuck, you should go now. Please."

The slight crack in her voice kept him from argu-ing with her. But no way was he leaving the building.

He'd told himself he was staying with her because he couldn't let their marriage fail, especially not when they had been expecting a baby, but now he found him-self thinking of all they'd shared since her amnesia.

And he couldn't just forget about that, not like she seemed determined to do.

Chuck didn't know what the future held for them. But for tonight? He was staying close to his wife.

* * *

After a restless night in an uncomfortable hospital bed with disquieting dreams startling her awake, Shana was no closer to repairing her broken heart.

How could she have become so attached so quickly to the idea of a future with Chuck when she barely knew him? She ached for everything she had lost and what could have been.

But whatever they would have created, it would have all been built on lies.

The hospital door opened, and Shana steeled herself for the possible impact of Chuck walking through.

Except it wasn't him. And it wasn't a nurse.

"Mom," Shana said, her voice wobbling.

Her mother strode across the room and wrapped Shana in a familiar hug. Her mother smelled of lilac and orange blossom, her signature scent. Though it hadn't always been. After finding out about her husband's secret family, Shana's mother had somersaulted, understandably. But the day she regained her footing was the same day she'd started wearing this scent.

For her mom, lilacs and orange blossoms marked hope, new beginnings.

The now-familiar fragrance comforted Shana as she looked at her elegantly styled mother, whose steel-gray hair flowed down her back in a sleek ponytail. Her mother had put her life together again with poise, grit and determination.

Her mom had always been there for Shana growing up, and she'd only moved on after…

The memory flickered, like a snowy mist Shana could barely push through, the frigid haze stinging. Her mom had moved forward with her dating life once

Shana became engaged to Chuck. He'd proposed on a dinner cruise along the Alaska coast on a magnificent night with a sky full of northern lights.

Her throat clogged with tears.

She swallowed hard and said, "Mom, why are you here? How did you arrive so quickly?"

Her mother eased back. "Chuck called me last night and told me about the baby. He's worried about you. I caught a red-eye flight."

"But your vacation days—"

"Don't worry about me." Her mother smoothed back Shana's hair. "I'm here for you. I would have come sooner but I thought it was best for you and Chuck to… I thought maybe…" She shook her head. "Never mind. Let's focus on the present."

"Thank you for coming. You must be exhausted after the night flight."

The smile lines by her mother's gray eyes deepened. Squeezing Shana's hand as if to dismiss her concern, she continued, "We can rest once we get you home."

"I'm going to be fine."

Her heart was shattered but her body would recover.

For a moment, her mother's slender face—normally sunny and full of life—seemed blanched of color. She focused those storm-gray eyes on Shana, a sad smile dusting her lips. "I've been through what you're experiencing."

Shana looked up in surprise. "You miscarried? You never told me. I mean, you didn't tell me when I was growing up. Maybe you did in the past five years and I don't remember."

She'd only recovered a small portion of her memories. And she sure didn't like some of what she'd seen. Fresh hurt cramped her belly for all her losses.

"I did share when it first happened to you." Her mother sighed sadly, pressing a hand to her chest, smoothing along the collar of her orange sweater. "When you were a child, there just didn't seem to be a time or reason. Then when you were a teen, there was...so much else going on."

So much else with her father.

The wreckage of his actions had left a wake of grief and distrust that still tainted their lives. His choices had effectively made a lie of anything seemingly positive he'd done in the past, because it had all been covered in a cloak of deception.

Shana pressed her hand to her heart. How could Chuck have lied to her, too, knowing how much the truth meant to her?

She blinked back tears, wary of letting her emotions rise to the surface now. She might lose control completely. She just wanted to get home, to bed.

Except her home was Chuck's home.

Theirs together.

A shaky exhale rocked her. She had few choices for now. She needed to recover first.

"Well, Mom, I guess it's no surprise my brain defaulted to amnesia." Bitterness stung her tongue. "Our family has been good at keeping secrets."

"Or trying to put a positive spin on everything as if that covers the pain." Her mother nervously picked at her chipped polish.

"Thoughts that are too deep for me today, I'm afraid."

"Of course. Let me help you get dressed to check

out of the hospital. Chuck is at the nurses' station getting the discharge paperwork rolling."

He was still here?

"Chuck? I told him he could go."

Her mother's beautiful face scrunched in surprise. "Why would you do that?"

Chuck hadn't told her mother about the separation. And he hadn't left.

She should have known he wouldn't listen. He'd given in too easily last night. That same sense of duty and obligation that had made him stay with her after her memory loss was making him stick around now.

But having him nearby hurt too much. She would accept the ride home to keep the peace, but after that they needed to talk about how to sever ties for good.

The next day had brought no peace, but Chuck took some comfort in action, accomplishing things by rote, restoring some form of order to his chaotic world.

By the time the doctor had cleared Shana, the paperwork had been completed and they'd driven home, dark had already set in due to the shortening days in Alaska now that winter approached. But there would be no holiday celebrations together for them this year, or any other.

He believed her when she said they were over. She remembered enough, and his deception now had sealed the deal.

He'd rolled the dice and lost.

Back home, Chuck settled his mother-in-law in her suite with a light dinner, although he imagined she would be asleep on her way to the pillow. Shana had gone straight to their room without a word. Not that he suffered any delusions that he was welcome back in the bed beside her, to comfort her the way he'd done in the past.

But she needed to eat. And he wasn't going to take no for an answer.

He carried a tray of food—pesto meatballs made of lean moose alongside skewers of mozzarella, grape tomatoes and spinach. Hot tea finished out the meal, steaming the scent of spices into the air.

Shana sat on the small white sofa by the fireplace. Moonlight splayed over the mountain scape, downward and through the window. Her blond hair glowed with a honey hue that made him ache to haul her into his lap and press her head to his chest. Her pale paisley robe made him think of watching her reach for it when stepping out of a shared shower.

They'd worked so damn hard to save their marriage, to have a child, and all of that had burned away, like ashes in the grate.

He set the tray on the claw-footed coffee table in front of her. "You need to eat."

She glanced at him, her eyes shadowed. "Thank you for the food, and for calling my mother."

"I'm glad Louise is here for you." He'd held back on contacting his family, not wanting Shana to be exhausted by a flood of people. Well-meaning people, but a mass, all the same. He didn't want her to feel overwhelmed. "Can I get you anything else?"

"No thank you." Her voice was hoarse with held-back tears.

"Shana," he said, his gut clenching. "For what it's worth, I'm so damn sorry."

She studied his face for five heavy heartbeats before

saying wearily, "I wish I could believe things would be different between us. But it's so hard to trust anyone after what my father did to my mother."

Unsure how much she remembered now, he let her continue, curious to see where this conversation would lead, if it could bring either of them peace.

She shook her head, clutching the neck of her robe closed. "Never mind. I'm sure we've talked about this before."

"You don't remember those conversations between us?" he prodded, sitting in a chair on the other side of the fireplace, the flames crackling in the early evening quiet. "Maybe it will help jog more memories if you talk."

"It seems silly to repeat it when I know you know."

He didn't answer.

"Fine," she caved. "I'm not going to go through all the gory details, though. I've thought it through so many different ways and why I can't seem to get over it. Unless, maybe I did get over it while we were married?" She watched him out of the corner of her eyes as she filled a plate with dinner.

"I'm sorry he hurt you so deeply." He meant it. Wished he had more to offer her than words. "We both have our fair share of baggage."

"What's yours? Other than lying."

He winced. He couldn't deny what he'd done, and it stung like hell because he considered himself a man of impeccable honor, professionally and personally. He realized now what a mistake he'd made, but he'd been so desperate to accept the second chance for his marriage.

"I'm a perfectionist and a workaholic." He picked up a plate, not really feeling much like eating but wanting to encourage her to do so. She needed to regain her strength. "I expected too much from both of us and our marriage."

"And I kept miscarrying." Her hand went to her stomach.

"I never thought that." He took her dish from her and held her hand. "Wipe that notion out of your mind."

"I want to."

"Then trust me on this much at least." He willed her to believe him, not that willing it had ever worked in the past. "Okay? Now, please, I want to hear what you're thinking about your dad."

"All right… My father liked to give gifts. When he was on the road—which was a lot—he would send elaborate presents for missed birthdays and holidays. I pretended to like them, but I just wanted him home."

"That had to be difficult when you found out the truth of where he'd been during those absences."

"Understatement." Her blue eyes took on a far-away look. "He kept sending things afterward, too, as if nothing had changed. I think that's what bothered me most. He really expected us to pretend life was the same…that what he had done was somehow normal or justified. I threw each gift away unopened."

He leaned forward, setting aside his untouched plate. "You never told me that before." What would have happened if he'd been patient about listening before rather than just growing angry over her lack of trust? "I'm sorry if my gifts were triggers for you."

"You're always thoughtful in what you give. It's not some generic present… Not that I know if my father ever got better at his choices." She toyed with the spear of cheese and veggies. "I should have donated

the presents to charity. It was wasteful to trash them."
She popped a mozzarella square into her mouth.

He noticed she still hadn't denied his gift giving had
been counterproductive. *Meaning well* wasn't good
enough. Gifts weren't a substitute for heartfelt actions.

"You have nothing to apologize for."

"I get too wrapped up in my own pain, past and
present. I know that."

He'd always considered her to be strong, so much
so he didn't always know what he had to offer her.
"You have reasons to grieve. We both do. You lost
your father. We've lost children and we've lost our
marriage."

She set down her plate, looking as disinterested in
food as he felt. "I wish I remembered more."

"No, you shouldn't."

"That bad, was it?" A tear slid down her cheek.

"Parts," he said honestly. He clenched his fists to
keep from reaching for her, knowing she would push
him away as she'd done in the past.

"Okay then." She stared at him bleakly. "Where do
we go from here?"

"If you're going to leave me, I just ask that we wait
to tell everyone until after the big shareholders' gala
next week." Not that he gave a damn about any celebration, but he wanted an excuse to keep her here to
recover before they finalized any decisions. "Can you
promise me that, for my family?"

She nodded wearily. "Until then."

Two words.

Just two words that signified the second and final
end of their marriage.

Eleven

The week passed too quickly for Shana to process the shift in her life. Flashes of memories kept knocking her off-balance just when she thought she'd found a hint of stable ground.

Sitting in her spacious dressing room with her mother and Alayna, Shana struggled to hold back tears. Makeup and cosmetic brushes spread out in front of her, she prepped for the steampunk-themed ball, sweeping shadow on for a smoky eye effect. She blended the warm brown tone on the outer corner of her eye, letting the soft brush bristles distract her from the messier aspects of the forthcoming night. Patting a shimmery gold into her inner eye corner, she took a deep breath, debating which shade of red lipstick would best complement her saloon-girl-inspired gown. She adjusted the straps on her dress, her hair piled on top of her head in a mass of curls.

The past week had been…hell.

Staying with Chuck while the end of their marriage ticked away was like inflicting paper cuts on her already raw emotions. Having her mother on hand had offered a buffer of sorts by keeping things from imploding into a horrible argument.

Not that Chuck showed any signs of temper. He seemed to be just counting down the clock until they could both officially call things quits between them.

Their only interaction all week had been about the investigation. She'd traced the man photographed at the hotel and it wasn't the infamous Uncle Lyle.

They'd also looked into Sage Hammond, all done with computer searches in bed while Shana rested and recovered. It had been difficult to imagine Sage might be involved. The woman was a shy relative, much like Alayna. A solid worker for the company. For all appearances, she seemed to be loyal, with an unblemished record.

There was no more work to accomplish on that front. No more days left to maintain the facade of a happy marriage for the family's business reputation.

Pretending at the gala tonight would be yet another, deeper level of hell.

At least Chuck's family had stayed away for the most part, respecting Chuck's request for space. Unusual in his big family. She remembered that much from her slowly returning memories. His relatives were a caring lot, but a bit overwhelming. She didn't know how so many of the Steeles—and now Mikkelsons, too—managed to live under the same roof, even with individual apartment-style suites of their own.

Apparently, the close quarters grated on Alayna,

too, as she had shown up on Shana's doorstep tonight. The teen's makeup brushes were spread on the marble countertop, too. Shana's soon-to-be ex-sister-in-law swept bold neutrals onto her eyelids. Things had blown up at the Steele home when the teens were confronted by their parents. The argument had resulted in Aiden threatening to quit college and go work in the oil fields.

Heartbroken, Alayna had raced over to Shana's. At least the teen had already been dressed for the big gala so once she calmed down, she could still attend.

Any family member's absence would be conspicuous and a sign of dissention among the ranks.

Not good.

And for that reason, Shana was attending, even though her heart was shattered, too.

Alayna was rocking leather pants and spike-heeled boots with a cream-colored bustier, mining gear hung from her belt. The shy mouse was roaring for the steampunk gala.

Shana's mother, Louise, smiled brightly, costumed like a Victorian matron with a saucy little pillbox hat perched on top of her upswept steel-gray hair. She took over helping the teen with her makeup while Shana finished her own.

"There's no hurry to fall in love, sweetie."

Alayna rolled her eyes. "You're supposed to say that."

"If you feel that way, perhaps there's something to what I'm saying." Louise swirled a plump brush in a bright shade of fuchsia before tapping off the excess.

"I'm in love. I knew the moment I saw him."

Shana chased feathery memories of the first time she'd seen Chuck. He'd come to her office to subcontract out some security work. She'd fallen hard and fast for the sexy mogul with a rugged edge. Their wedding had been a fairy tale, her mom helping her with makeup then like tonight.

So many memories.

And no doubt so many more that would filter through and break her heart all over again.

Louise dabbed blush on Alayna's cheeks. "That's attraction. Love grows over time."

"How much time?" Alayna asked desperately, testing lipstick shades on the back of her wrist.

Shana's mother sighed, placing a hand on Alayna's shoulder, her pearl ring gleaming in the light. "There's no magic formula. But it takes time to learn about each other and to learn if you're compatible for the long haul."

Shana outlined her lips in a dusty red, satisfied with the edgier look that reflected her mood. "It takes time to figure out if someone's a smooth talker or genuine."

She'd thought Chuck was genuine. And in many ways, he had been. Memories of their time together this past week collided in her mind, reminding her how good they could be together.

Alayna dabbed her finger in sticky sequins and patted a line along one eyebrow, then the other. "And if the person's genuine, then it's love at first sight after all."

"What do your mother and Jack say?" Louise pressed wisely.

"They just keep freaking out. They're so into us being stepbrother and stepsister they seem to forget that Broderick and Glenna are married. It's like their romance doesn't count since it started before this whole big, weird family merger."

Shana adjusted her peacock feather and gear-inspired wrap bracelet. "You should be talking to your mom, Alayna."

"You can keep saying that, but it's not so easy. Everyone thinks she's, like, some kind of saint." Alayna looked up at Louise standing beside her. "Our family has secrets. You should meet Mom's sister. She actually abandoned her own son—Trystan—and let my mom and dad adopt him."

Shana put a hand on Alayna's arm. "Maybe we should table this discussion for now."

"I'm tired of how nobody talks about things. Don't you want to know all the things you've forgotten?"

One part of Shana wanted that more than air. Another part winced at the thought of any more heartache.

"That can be tricky since every person who tells me something has their own interpretation of what happened. I need to get a stronger sense of who I am now before I let people start coloring in the blank slate of the past five years." She leaned forward. "I think that's what my mother was getting at, when she said you were too young to be sure of love at first sight."

"Are you saying I'm a blank slate? Because I think that would be a little offensive." Alayna scrunched her nose.

"I'm saying you may not fully know yourself yet. You don't have as much perspective as people like our mothers. Give it time."

Yet even as Shana offered the advice, she knew the answers weren't always so simple. Especially since time had run out for her and Chuck. All she had left was a chance for one last dance with her husband, one final chance to be Mrs. Mikkelson before she said goodbye.

* * *

Savoring the new-wave folk tunes, Alayna swayed from side to side, each movement sinking her deeper into her spike-heeled boots.

The band was dressed in eclectic Victorian garb. The piano resembled a saloon upright. Alayna lost herself in the music pouring from the speaker—an oversize gramophone.

Her gaze picked its way across the room, working overtime to spot Aiden in the midst of Western memorabilia and technological gadgetry. She did her best to casually squint past the giant leathery hot air balloon in the center of the room. The open basket on the ground sported a flurry of cocktail tables with saloon girls and their pocket-watch-wearing dates.

Attempting to feign interest only in the impressive details of the ball, she let her gaze go up to the balloon's full height, admiring the twinkling lights arranged to look like faux fire.

Imagination wandering, Alayna pictured what it'd be like for Aiden to grab her hand, whisk her past that hot air balloon and to the dance floor, past steel-framed lightbulbs staggered and hanging from the ceiling connected by rust-kissed chains. A manufactured night sky of possibility that Alayna wanted to entertain. Big-time.

While not as cumbersome as finding him in a masquerade ball, the job of locating Aiden among the hat wear that made fascinators seem as boring as ball caps was proving difficult.

Normally, she would enjoy a party like this. The music, the historical riff—it sure beat the stuffy formal balls her family usually dragged her to. Her mom's assistant, Sage Hammond, had outdone herself with this edgy celebration for the Alaska Oil Barons, Inc., shareholders and board of directors.

If only Alayna and Aiden could be in the middle of the dance floor, partying…

She wanted to take the advice given to her, but it was hard being okay with the fact that Aiden was leaving, and not to a place she could follow him, like a college transfer to Juneau.

Everything was changing.

The lump in her throat threatened to return. Shoving those thoughts aside, she redoubled her search, moving through the crowd of coattails and wigs of piled curls.

"For the next few songs, we'd like to welcome to the stage Miss Ada Joy Powers," the lead singer of the band called into the microphone.

Alayna stopped on her heels, turning back to see the famous vocalist burst from behind the massive clock that featured oversize wheels and hands. Dry ice spewed fake fog as the noted soprano emerged, looking as mysterious as all get-out.

The crowd went wild.

"Thank you, thank you all," she said in a husky voice before nodding to the band to begin. "'It doesn't matter unless you give your heart to the moment. To the night…'" Ada Joy belted an original song into the microphone, bopping her hips from side to side in a tight bodice and saloon-girl-style skirt.

Just beside the stage, Alayna saw her cousin Sage. Her heart twinged as she saw Sage in a too-baggy schoolmarm dress. Sage appeared to be like part of the set, fading into the background. But she was the one responsible for overseeing every last detail of this evening.

Then finally, Alayna spotted Aiden—looking hot as always, rocking his costume. He wore a military-style jacket with leather knee boots and a bowler hat with pushed-up goggles.

Her heart pounded as she caught his dark, shining eyes. That signature wide smile spread across his face. He set down his drink on a nearby cocktail table and made strides towards her. His gaze lit as he took in her costume.

She savored this moment of him seeing her—really seeing her.

Alayna perched a hand on her hip as he stopped in front of her. "I can't believe you're really leaving college."

"I plan to go back, once I've had some time to find my way and learn the business from the ground up. I finally feel like I'm stepping out of my brothers' shadows."

She swallowed down tears. He looked so happy. And she wanted that for him.

"Be careful out there."

The oil fields could be dangerous. She'd grown up hearing about the accidents, and it chilled her to think of him putting himself at risk.

"*You* be careful chasing after crazy relatives. No going after them by yourself. Okay?"

She flipped her curled hair over her shoulder. "Sure."

"I'm not joking around. There are people who care about you who would be glad to help."

"Just not you," she couldn't resist saying.

He rested a hand on her shoulder and squeezed gently, his touch warm and tingly. "I gotta find a different path from my brothers. Different from my dad. I want to build my own future."

She wanted to lean into his hand, to see if he would pull her close.

Not that she believed he would. Especially not here.

"You know you're making me like you more."

His eyes roved up and down her once more and he smiled slowly. "You're going to be just fine, Alayna."

"Says the guy who told me to find bodyguards in my family."

He winked. "That's not what I meant."

"I know." And she did. If only he meant it enough to stick around. But he didn't. "Thanks."

He extended a hand. "Wanna dance?"

It wasn't everything she wanted. But she sure as hell wasn't going to turn him down. It would have to be enough.

For now.

Chuck pushed past the vintage locomotive at the entrance of the gala, ignoring the smile of the tux-edoed engineer with striped coattails and tall leather boots passing the party gifts to passersby who hadn't received one yet. The gifts, his cousin Sage had said a few weeks ago, would be brass pocket watches with the new Alaska Oil Barons, Inc., logo plus today's date.

He'd be damned if he wanted any additional me-mentos to mark the complete failure of his marriage.

He wanted to drink, to lose himself.

He couldn't take his eyes off Shana in that saloon girl costume, high in the front showcasing her killer legs, the back of the dress trailing longer. Her hair was piled up in a messy mass of curls that called to his hands to set them free.

Even from here, he could see her swaying to the music. She seemed to fit perfectly into the alternative history theme, the copper piping framing the thick-paned circular window behind the band a natural complement to her costume. He watched her maneuver through the crowd, toward the scaled-back nineteenth-century oil rig spewing deep red wine. And then he lost her in a sea of curls and goggle-adorned top hats.

He snagged a beer from a passing waiter dressed as a mechanic and moved toward Marshall. The middle Steele brother leaned against the high cocktail table. A plate sporting a picked-at chocolate top hat and mini savory meat pies was pushed against the vintage clock centerpiece.

Marshall brought his water glass—a vintage Mason jar—back to his lips, annoyance painting his face. He had one arm in a cast and sling, the result of a nasty horse accident last week at the close of the rodeo.

Chuck stood across from Marshall at the small cocktail table. "You don't look like you're having much fun. Can I get you a beer?"

"Nah, I'm good with this." Marshall lifted his water glass, lemon wedges mixed with ice, then gestured to the space around him. "Getting dressed up for a party isn't my gig. If I don't hold strong, the next thing I know the family will be hiring some image consultant to give me a makeover like they did to your poor brother."

Chuck laughed softly, his eyes skating to his brother, Trystan, happily dancing with that same image consultant who was just showing signs of pregnancy.

A fresh wave of pain, of loss, stabbed through him.

He shifted his focus back to Marshall before his gaze went searching for Shana for the hundredth time that night. No doubt she was still standing with her mom, his wife looking so damn beautiful it hurt.

"You're wearing what you wore to the rodeo last week."

The night Chuck's marriage had ended for good.

"Exactly," Marshall retorted. "I don't like costumes."

So he'd worn rodeo gear.

Chuck had to chuckle. "Wish I had thought of it."

He'd chosen black leather, a mix of miner and biker.

They both took swigs of their drinks. Marshall lowered his glass, his expression going somber. "Hey, I'm really sorry to hear about your wife's miscarriage."

"Thank you." Chuck couldn't say anything more. The loss had hit him hard. There was no getting used to grief. But losing Shana too made the pain cut even deeper.

Marshall's father, Jack, sporting a long black duster and a top hat, moved across the room, heading straight for their table.

"Chuck, how're you holding up?"

How was he supposed to answer that? "Shana's recovered."

A flat, stark answer. Sure. But there was nothing else he could hope to say.

Jack looked like he was going to press further, but then he simply clapped Chuck on the back. "Glad you're here. Nice costume."

Marshall swirled his glass until the ice clinked, looking sidelong at his father. "Is that a dig at me, Dad?"

"We're just happy you're here, son. That was quite a tumble you took at the end of the rodeo."

"Putting my horse away." He shook his head. "I feel like a damn idiot."

"We all make mistakes. It's called being human. You'll be saddled up again before you know it."

If only life was that simple.

Make a mistake. Saddle up again.

Marshall looked into his empty glass. "I'll go see about some refills for us. Be right back."

Chuck started to leave, too—he needed to schmooze with the guests—but he just couldn't scrounge much of a party spirit in spite of the country and western tunes being belted out by Miss Powers.

"Chuck? Something on your mind?" Jack waited, and when Chuck didn't answer, he continued, "I'm not trying to pry, and even though I'm married to your mother, I don't consider myself some kind of father figure to you. You had a great one. But we are family now, and it's clear something's weighing on you."

Chuck considered blowing off the discussion, but it wouldn't do any good. "Everyone will know soon enough. Shana's starting to recover her memory, including the problems we had. She's decided to leave me."

Jack's face tightened, his dark blue eyes wild like an Alaskan blizzard. "I'm sorry to hear that."

A bark of laughter fueled by regret escaped Chuck. "What? No advice on how I should fight for my marriage?"

"Best as I can tell, you both fought to save it for a while." Jack stroked his chin.

"We did."

"What's changed?"

He'd worked too much, demanded perfection of himself...of their marriage.

But all of that was old news.

"She doesn't trust me."

"Well, you did lie to her—a lie by hedging, but still, not telling her how bad things had been between the two of you maybe wasn't the right way to go."

Had their problems been that obvious to others even though they hadn't announced their separation?

Apparently they had.

"This little talk isn't making me feel much better."

Jack Steele turned to face Chuck, shoulders square, looking every bit as powerful and commanding as a king. "Do you want me to soft-soap things or do you want to keep your wife?"

Put that simply, the answer was obvious. "I want to keep my wife."

Jack shrugged. "Sounds like you have some groveling to do."

Chuck's eyes lingered on Shana, taking in the attentive way she listened to the couple chatting with her. She had a way of making people feel valued as she took in their every word. It made her a great detective—and a wonderful person.

"That simple?"

"If you mean it. Say it, live it, walk the walk and earn her trust back. Marriage isn't easy and it sure as hell isn't perfect. Call me an old romantic, but you two have a lot of love between you."

Love.

Hearing the word from the gruff Steele patriarch brought things into focus.

Hell yes, he loved his wife. Always had.

She'd loved him, too. Even when they were separating, she'd cried over how much she still loved him even as they couldn't see their way through.

He regretted lying to her to keep her.

He regretted a whole lot of things.

But had he told her how much? Had he ever really committed to being the kind of man she needed?

The answer shamed him. Especially when he could see things from her viewpoint now.

He recognized now how he'd never made a full-scale commitment to compromise. He'd spent the past two years devoted to filling his father's shoes. Sure, Chuck had taken time off and scaled back a few meetings periodically to appease Shana, but he hadn't made a legitimate effort to change his workaholic ways.

To be there for her.

He'd chosen unbridled ambition over his wife.

Was it any wonder she didn't trust in his love for her?

Now he stood at a crossroads.

Make a real change or lose his wife forever. And looked at so succinctly, the decision was the easiest of his life.

He wanted his wife back at any cost.

Shana had spent most of the party trying to break free of people so she could corner Chuck. She knew it shouldn't make any difference if she bided her time until after the gala to say goodbye, but the pain of waiting was just too much to bear.

She needed to speak with him.

Parked by an oversize metal globe near a food

table, Shana struggled to steady her pulse, anticipation mounting in her chest as she again searched for her broad-shouldered husband.

Standing on her tiptoes, she looked over the heads dressed in Victorian garb, past goblets of wine held by the who's who of Alaska. She peered over the saloon girl in front of her, looking past the miniature top hat made of clock cogs and feathers. The live music had ended for now, a deejay taking over between sets.

Any other time, Shana might have struck up conversations with the people around her. But her body and soul hummed with urgency.

She needed to see Chuck.

Except every time she located him, by the time she made it across the crowded venue, he was out of sight once again. The event was a packed, unbridled success. And she couldn't find the will to celebrate anything.

She just wanted her husband.

Finally surrendering to waiting, she stepped out into the night air, flipping up the hood on her red velvet cape. She picked her way across the night to the steam locomotive positioned out front. Music echoed softly from the large hall. Flashes went off periodically as partiers took photos by the train car. She stuffed her gloved hands into her sleeves and perched on the train car's platform, her breath puffing clouds into the night air. Each cleansing breath should have ordered her thoughts, but the stakes were so high and she wasn't sure she had any more answers now than the times they'd failed before.

Just when she was ready to give up and go home, her eyes lit on the unmistakable form of her husband.

His broad shoulders filled out the leather duster, his black Stetson catching snow on the brim.

"Chuck…" His name came out on a whisper.

One he must have somehow heard.

He turned toward her, his eyes lasering to her from across the walkway. He strode closer, as if he'd been looking for her, which couldn't be true, but still her heart leaped at the possibility.

Each step nearer made her heart speed in her chest as she searched for the right words to begin.

Grabbing hold of the railing, Chuck swung up onto the platform in a smooth, athletic move. Before she could speak, he locked an arm around her, pulling her flush against him. His eyes met hers. Words dried up in her throat, because she *knew* he was about to…

Kiss her.

His mouth slanted over hers, gently, teasing and tasting, giving her every opportunity to pull back if she wished. But the only thing she wanted right now was more of him.

Her hands clenched in the lapels of his coat, the heat of him searing her through the cape.

He swept her hair back from her face. "I know it's too soon for more," he said hoarsely. "I just wanted you to know how special you are to me. Would you step inside so we can talk?"

Why would she deny him when she wanted that very thing and his words made her heart light with a wary hope?

"I would like that."

It had been a long, sad week of distance between them. She couldn't imagine a lifetime of that.

Inside, the train compartment was finished in plush

royal blues with gold fixtures. He gestured for her to sit on the lengthy sofa and took her hand in his, kneeling.

"I owe you an apology."

She listened, curious.

He squeezed her fingertips lightly. "I should have been honest with you when you first lost your memory. I didn't earn your trust, and just as bad, I didn't trust you."

"I did ask you for a divorce."

Even the partial memory of that day filled her with pain.

"And I didn't listen to what you needed now or then." He looked down at the floor for three thudding heartbeats before continuing, "I thought having a baby would somehow magically turn us into a family. But even just the two of us, together, we are—we should have always been—a family."

His words helped ease the grief of the other miscarriages she was starting to remember. She didn't know if she wanted to try again, not yet, but she knew for certain she didn't want children with any other man.

"Keep talking." Hope fanned higher, warmer.

"I was very lucky to have an easy childhood. I didn't fully realize how much of a mark your father's betrayal had left on you. I should have, and for that I'm so very sorry. Sorrier than I can say."

Surprise whispered through her, soothing old hurts. "Thank you—"

"I'm still not done. I love you, Shana Mikkelson." His words rang with conviction. "I love you more than any job, more than anyone else, more than life. And if you'll let me, I want to spend the rest of our days being a family, with you."

She peeled off her gloves and cupped his face in her hands. "Oh, Chuck, I love you, too, and I'm so sorry for the pain I caused you. We should have been comforting each other—you tried to comfort me—and I lashed out. I pushed you away at a time when your heart was hurting."

"You don't need to apologize to me."

"I do. I'm as much a part of this breakup as you are."

His forehead furrowed. "Did the rest of your memories return?"

"Not everything. But I remember the day we were married and other happy times, the way we felt. It's how I feel about you now. We have a love and marriage worth fighting for."

His eyes closed, and a heavy sigh of relief visibly wracked through him. "I'm so damn glad to hear you say that."

"I should have believed in you. It's clear to me now that you're a good man." She angled forward, resting her forehead against his. "We had love before. We didn't have trust. Now we have both. And I want to be your wife. Not just in name from my previous life, but now. Forever."

She nudged forward, knocking him back until they both stretched on the train car sofa. Kissing him as fully as he'd kissed her.

He palmed her waist, staring up at her, his heart in his eyes. "I'm happy and relieved to hear that because I love you so damn much. I can't imagine my life without you."

She had to know. "What if we never have children?"

"Then we don't. I can face anything as long I have you by my side." He kissed her slowly, reverently before saying, "I have ideas for our future and I want to hear yours, ways that we can make a new start."

A smile rose from her heart to her face. "I look forward to hearing them."

"Let's go home."

Home.

Here in his arms, she was already there.

Epilogue

One month later

Chuck pulled the satin coverlet over him and his wife, the railcar swaying ever so slightly as the train ate up the miles along the Canadian countryside.

He and Shana had enjoyed many romantic trips in their marriage, but this topped them all. Of course, trains would always hold a special place in his heart after they had found their way back to each other at the steampunk gala a month ago.

A lot had happened in the past few weeks as they worked to make good on their promises to build a new life together. Chuck's decision to back away from working long hours had been met by similar announcements from other Steele and Mikkelson siblings. Broderick and Glenna were expecting a baby. Trystan wasn't interested in taking more on his plate, in spite of his makeover. He wanted to focus on his family.

Marshall had made it damn clear he wasn't stepping into the void, even though he'd agreed to host a fundraiser. He was chomping at the bit to get rid of his cast so he could resume ranching duties.

So the search had begun outside the families for a CEO for the Alaska Oil Barons, Inc.

Chuck had proposed a job change for himself. He would soon assume duties overseeing the pipeline operations on the North Dakota end—an offer accepted by the board of directors even though it was a step down for him. He and Shana had chosen this mode of land travel for a romantic getaway on their trip to house hunt for the impending move. While the North Dakota office didn't come with as much prestige or as many divisions to manage, he found himself excited for the change.

They were both revaluating their priorities these days.

And focusing on their marriage topped the list.

Relocating would also give them more privacy. No question, Chuck loved his family. But as a whole, they could be overwhelming. There would still be visits, and a corporate jet afforded the easy option of attending important family functions.

But they would have their own home, their own space.

"I can hardly believe you're making this change for me," Shana murmured, nuzzling his neck.

"For us."

"I'll never get tired of hearing that."

"Good to know." He slipped his hand around to the

small of her back, her skin like silk. "How about this? I love everything about you and look forward to telling you every day."

"Hmm…" She sighed, sliding her bare leg between his. "And I love you and the life we're building together."

She was resuming her work part-time, having accepted a job in North Dakota to freelance for an established private detective agency once she moved. She wanted to keep her professional skills up to date, while also having time to travel. She was still looking into Milla Jones's disappearance and investigating the pasts of Jeannie Steele's siblings.

Shana and Chuck were both adjusting, perhaps in a way they should have before.

But they were also lucky.

They'd been given a second chance—by each other—and they were both committed to making the most of it.

Shana was remembering the past, slowly. Chuck was filling in the blanks for her as she asked. No holds barred. Some of the discussions were tough, but that also assured her of his honesty.

They didn't shy away from anything anymore.

They were building a future on a firm foundation.

Shana traced small circles on his shoulder, her wedding rings glinting, the set complete on her finger again. "This trip has been idyllic. I've been thinking we should do this more often."

"What do you have in mind?" He watched the play of shadows along her body as moonbeams shone through the slight part in the velvet curtains of the luxury suite.

"Let's revisit some of our anniversary celebrations by taking train rides through the Outback and through Europe." She rested her head on his chest, her blond hair splaying over him in a shimmering spread.

"Except we won't wait until a year has passed." He pressed a kiss to her forehead, breathing in the scent of her shampoo.

She sighed, her breath warm along his skin. "Perfection."

"Like you," he responded, meaning every word.

She grinned up at him. "You're such a romantic."

He hadn't been, not before, but that was another thing he was working on for his wife. Because she deserved it.

She deserved everything, because she was *his* everything.

He reached for a rose from the vase by their bed. "How about I shower you with more of that romance, Mrs. Mikkelson?"

Shana plucked the flower from his hand and traced the bud down his chest. "How about I romance you, Mr. Mikkelson?"

She nudged him to his back, and he took her up on her oh-so-tempting offer, looking forward to paying her back in kind.

Luckily, they had a lifetime for romance ahead of them.

* * * * *

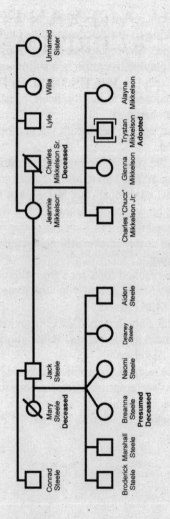

ALASKAN OIL BARONS - STEELE MIKKELSON FAMILY TREE

Conrad Steele

Mary Steele
Deceased

Jack Steele

Jeannie Mikkelson

Charles Mikkelson Sr.
Deceased

Lyle

Willa

Unnamed Sister

Broderick Steele

Marshall Steele

Breanna Steele
Presumed Deceased

Naomi Steele

Delaney Steele

Aiden Steele

Charles "Chuck" Mikkelson Jr.

Glenna Mikkelson

Trystan Mikkelson
Adopted

Alayna Mikkelson

A TEXAN FOR CHRISTMAS

JULES BENNETT

One

Scarlett Patterson clutched the handle of her small suit-case and waited.

And waited.

She'd knocked twice on the door, but still no answer. She knew this was the address she'd been given—a small cabin nestled in the back of the sprawling, pic-turesque Pebblebrook Ranch. She'd been told exactly who she'd be working for and her belly did flips just thinking of Beau Elliott—deemed Hollywood's Bad Boy, the Maverick of Movies, Cowboy Casanova…the titles were endless.

One thing was certain, if the tabloids were correct—he made no apologies about his affection for women. Scarlett wasn't sure she'd ever seen an image of him with the same woman.

That is, until his lover turned up pregnant. Then the

two were spotted out together, but by then the rumors had begun—of drugs found in his lover's carry-on, of affairs started…or maybe they'd never stopped.

Why he'd come back home now, to this quiet town in Texas and his family's sprawling ranch, was none of her concern.

With a hand blocking her eyes from a rare glimpse of winter sun, Scarlett glanced around the open fields. Not a soul in sight. In the distance, a green field dotted with cattle stretched all the way to the horizon. This could easily be a postcard.

The Elliott land was vast. She'd heard there were several homes on the property and a portion of the place would soon become a dude ranch. In fact, this cabin would eventually be housing for guests of said dude ranch.

So why was Beau Elliott staying here instead of one of the main houses, with his brothers? Was he even planning to stick around?

So many mysteries…

But she wasn't here to inquire about his personal life and she certainly wouldn't be divulging any extra information about hers.

She was here to help his baby.

Even if that meant she had to come face-to-face with one of the sexiest men on the planet.

The snick of a lock had her turning her attention back around. When the door swung wide, it was all Scarlett could do to hold back her gasp.

Beau Elliott, Hollywood's baddest boy, stood before her sans shirt and wearing a pair of low-slung shorts. Scrolling ink went up one side of his waist, curling around well-defined pecs and disappearing over his shoulder.

Don't stare at the tattoos. Don't stare at the tattoos.
And, whatever you do, don't reach out to touch one.

"Who are you?"

The gravelly voice startled her back into reality. Scarlett realized she'd been staring.

Beau's broad frame filled the doorway, his stubbled jaw and bedhead indicating he hadn't had the best night. Apparently, according to the information she'd received, his last nanny had left last evening because of a family emergency.

Well, Scarlett wasn't having the best of days, either, so they were at least on a level playing field—other than the whole billionaire-peasant thing.

But she could use the extra money, so caring for an adorable five-month-old baby girl shouldn't be a problem, right?

Tamping down past hurts that threatened to creep up at the thought of caring for a child, Scarlett squared her shoulders and smiled. "I'm Scarlett Patterson. Your new nanny."

Beau blinked and gave her body a visual lick. "You're not old or frumpy," he growled.

Great. He'd already had some visual image in his head of who she should be. Maggie, the original nanny, was sweet as peach pie, but she *could* be best described as old and frumpy. Obviously, that was what Hollywood's Golden Child had thought he would be getting this morning, as well.

Beau Elliott, raised a rancher and then turned star of the screen, was going to be high maintenance. She could already tell.

Why would she expect anything less from someone who appeared to thrive on stardom and power?

Unfortunately, she knew that type all too well. Knew the type and ran like hell to avoid it.

She'd grown up with a man obsessed with money and getting what he wanted. Just when she thought she'd eliminated him from her life, he went on and became the governor. Scarlett was so over the power trip. Her stepfather and her mother weren't happy with her choices in life and had practically shunned her when they realized they couldn't control her. Which was fine. She'd rather do life on her own than be controlled… by anybody.

"Not old and frumpy. Is that a compliment or an observation?" She waved her hand to dismiss his answer before he could give her one. "Forget it. My looks and age are irrelevant. I am Maggie's replacement for the next three weeks."

"I requested someone like Maggie."

He still didn't make any attempt to move or to invite her inside. Even though this was Texas, the morning air chilled her.

Scarlett wasn't in the mood to deal with whatever hang-ups he had about nannies. Coming here after a year away from nanny duties was difficult enough. If she'd had her way, she would've found someone else to take this assignment, but the agency was short staffed.

This job was only for three weeks. Which meant she'd spend Christmas here, but the day after, she'd be heading to her new life in Dallas.

After the New Year, she'd start over fresh.

She could do this.

So why did she already feel the stirrings of a headache?

Oh, right. Because the once-dubbed "Sexiest Man Alive" was clearly used to getting his own way.

A bundle of nerves curled tightly in her belly. He might be sexy, but that didn't mean she had to put up with his attitude. Maybe he needed to remember that he was in a bind. He'd hired a nanny and Scarlett was it.

"Maggie, and everyone else at Nanny Poppins, is unavailable during the time frame you need."

Scarlett tried like hell to keep her professional smile in place—she did need this money, and she'd never leave a child without care. Plus, she wouldn't do a thing to tarnish the reputation of the company she'd worked for over the past several years.

She tipped her head and quirked a brow. "You do still need help, correct?"

Maggie had told Scarlett that Beau was brooding, that he kept to himself and only really came out of his shell when he interacted with his baby girl. That was all fine and good. Scarlett wasn't here to make friends or ogle the superstar, no matter how delicious he looked early in the morning.

A baby's cry pierced the awkward silence. With a muttered curse, Beau spun around and disappeared. Scarlett slowly stepped through the open door and shut it behind her.

Clearly the invitation wasn't going to happen.

"I feel so welcome," she muttered.

Scarlett leaned her suitcase against the wall and propped her small purse on top of it. The sounds of a fussy baby and Beau's deep, calming voice came from the bedroom to the right of the entryway.

As she took in the open floor plan of the cabin, she noted several things at once. Beau was either neat and tidy or he didn't have a lot of stuff. A pair of shiny new cowboy boots sat by the door and a black hat hung on a hook above the boots. The small kitchen had a drying rack with bottles on the counter and on the tiny table was a pink-and-white polka-dot bib.

She glanced to the left and noted another bedroom, the one she assumed would be hers, but she wasn't going to put her stuff in there just yet. Across the way, at the back of the cabin, was a set of patio doors that led to another porch. The area was cozy and perfect for the soon-to-be dude ranch.

The lack of Christmas decorations disturbed her, though. No tree, no stockings over the little fireplace, not even a wreath on the door. Who didn't want to celebrate Christmas? The most giving, joyous time of the year?

Christmas was absolutely her favorite holiday. Over the years she'd shared many Christmases with various families…all of which had been more loving and fulfilling than those of her stuffy, controlled childhood.

Scarlett continued to wait in the entryway, all while judging the Grinch's home. She didn't want to venture too far from the front door since he hadn't invited her in. It was obvious she wasn't what he'd expected, and he might ask her to leave.

Hopefully he wouldn't because she needed to work these three weeks. Those extra funds would go a long way toward helping her afford housing when she left Stone River to start her new life.

Even so, the next twenty-one days couldn't pass by fast enough.

Beau came back down the hall and Scarlett's heart tightened as a lump formed in her throat. A full assault on her emotions took over as knots in her stomach formed.

She couldn't do this. No matter how short the time span, she couldn't stay with this man, in this confined space, caring for his daughter for three weeks and not come out unscathed.

She wasn't sure which sight hit her hardest—the well-sculpted shirtless man or the baby he was holding.

Being this close to the little girl nearly brought her to her knees. Scarlett knew coming back as a hands-on nanny would be difficult, but she hadn't fully prepared herself for just how hard a hit her heart would take.

She'd purposely given up working in homes only a year ago. She'd requested work in the office, even though the administrative side paid less than round-the-clock nanny services. She'd been Nanny Poppins's most sought-after employee for eight years, but after everything that had happened, her boss completely understood Scarlett's need to distance herself from babies and families.

Fate had been cruel, stealing her chance of having kids of her own. She wasn't sure she was ready to see another parent have what she wanted. Working for Beau Elliott would be difficult to say the least, but Scarlett would push through and then she could move on. One last job. She could do this…she hoped.

The sweet baby continued to fuss, rubbing her eyes and sniffling. No doubt she was tired. From the looks of both of them, they'd had a long night.

Instinct had Scarlett reaching out and taking the baby, careful not to brush her fingertips against the hard planes of Beau's bare chest.

Well, she had to assume they were hard because she'd stared at them for a solid two minutes.

The second that sweet baby smell hit Scarlett, she nearly lost it. Her eyes burned, her throat tightened. But the baby's needs had to come first. That's why Scarlett was here. Well, that and to get double the pay so she could finally move to Dallas.

She could've turned down this job, but Maggie was in a bind, the company was in a bind, and they'd been so good to Scarlett since she'd started working there.

Scarlett simply couldn't say no.

"Oh, sweetheart, it's okay."

She patted the little girl's back and swayed slowly. Maggie had told her the baby was a joy to be around.

"Madelyn."

Scarlett blinked. "Excuse me?"

"Her name is Madelyn."

Well, at least they were getting somewhere and he wasn't ready to push her out the door. Scarlett already knew Madelyn's name and had read all the pertinent information regarding this job, but it was nice that Beau wasn't growling at her anymore.

Still, she wished he'd go put a shirt on. She couldn't keep her eyes completely off him, not when he was on display like that. Damn man probably thought he could charm her or distract her by flexing all those glorious, delicious muscles. Muscles that would no doubt feel taut beneath her touch.

Scarlett swallowed and blinked away the erotic image before she could take it too far. At least she had something else to think of other than her own gut-clenching angst and baby fever. Hunky heartthrob to the rescue.

Scarlett turned away from the distracting view of

her temporary boss and walked toward the tiny living area. The room seemed a little larger thanks to the patio doors leading onto the covered porch, which was decorated with a cute table and chair set.

The whole cabin was rather small, but it wasn't her place to ask why a billionaire film star lived in this cramped space on his family's estate. None of her business. This would just be a quick three weeks in December—in and out—in the most un-festive place ever.

Maybe she could sneak in some Christmas here and there. Every child deserved some twinkle lights or a stocking, for heaven's sake. Definitely a tree. Without it, where would Santa put the presents?

"She's been cranky all night," Beau said behind her. "I've tried everything, but I can't make her happy. I've never had that happen before."

The frustration in his voice softened Scarlett a bit. Beau might be a womanizer and a party animal, if the tabloids were right—which would explain his comfort level with wearing no shirt—but he obviously cared for his daughter.

Scarlett couldn't help but wonder where the mother was, but again, it was none of her concern. She'd seen enough tabloid stories to figure the mother was likely in rehab or desperately needing to be there.

Madelyn let out a wail, complete with tears and everything. The poor baby was miserable, which now made three of them, all under the same roof.

Let the countdown to her move begin.

How the hell had his nanny situation gone from Mrs. Doubtfire to Miss December?

The sultry vixen with rich skin, deep brown eyes, and silky black hair was too striking. But it was those curves in all the right places that had definitely woken him up this morning. His entire body had been ready to stand at attention, so perhaps he'd come across a little gruff.

But, damn it, he had good reason.

He'd been assured a replacement nanny would arrive bright and early, but he'd expected the agency to send another grandmother type.

Where was the one with a thick middle, elastic pants, sensible shoes and a gray bun? Where the hell did he order up another one of those? Warts would help, too. False teeth, even.

Beau stood back as he watched Scarlett comfort his daughter.

Scarlett. Of course she'd have a sultry name to match everything else sultry about her.

Not too long ago she would've been exactly his type. He would've wasted no time in charming and seducing her. But now his entire life had changed and the only woman he had time for was the sweet five-month-old he'd saved from the clutches of her partying, strung-out mother.

Money wasn't something he cared about—perhaps because he'd always had it—but it sure as hell came in handy. Like when he needed to pay off his ex so he could have Madelyn. Jennifer had selfishly taken the money, signed over the rights, and had nearly skipped out of their lives and onto the next star she thought would catapult her career.

The fact that he'd been used by her wasn't even relevant. He could care less about how he'd been treated, but he would not have their baby act as a pawn for Jennifer's own vindictive nature.

Beau couldn't get Madelyn out of Hollywood fast enough. His daughter was not going to be brought up in the lifestyle that too many fell into—himself included.

He'd overcome his past and the ugliness that surrounded his life when he'd first gotten into LA. He'd worked damn hard and was proud of the life he had built, but now his focus had to shift and changes needed to be made.

Coming home hadn't been ideal because he knew exactly the type of welcome he'd get. But there was nowhere else he wanted to be right now. He needed his family, even if he took hell from Colt, Hayes and Nolan for showing up after years of being away…with a kid in tow.

Thankfully, his brothers and their women all doted over Madelyn. That's all he wanted. No matter how people treated him or ignored him, Beau wanted his daughter to be surrounded with love.

His life was a mess, his future unknown. Hell, he couldn't think past today. He had a movie premiere two days before Christmas and he'd have to go, but other than that, he had no clue.

All that mattered was Madelyn, making sure she had a solid foundation and family that loved her. The calls from his new agent didn't matter, the movie premiere didn't matter, all the press he was expected to do to promote the film sure as hell didn't matter. To say he was burned out would be a vast understatement.

Beau needed some space to think and the calming serenity of Pebblebrook Ranch provided just that.

Unfortunately, concentrating would be rather difficult with a centerfold look-alike staying under his roof. Well, not his roof exactly. He was only using one of the small cabins on the land until the dude ranch officially opened in a few months. His father's dream was finally coming to fruition.

Beau wondered how he'd come to this moment of needing someone. He prided himself on never needing anyone. He had homes around the globe, cars that would make any man weep with envy, even his own private island, but the one place he wanted and needed to be was right here with his family—whether they wanted him here or not.

Beau had turned his back on this land and his family years ago. That was the absolute last thing he'd intended to do, but he'd gotten swept away into the fortune and fame. Eventually days had rolled into months, then into years, and the time had passed too quickly.

But now he was back home, and as angry as his brothers were, they'd given him a place to stay. Temporary, but at least it was something. He knew it was only because he had Madelyn, but he'd take it.

"She's teething."

Beau pulled his thoughts from his family drama and focused on the nanny. "Teething? She's only five months old."

Scarlett continued to sway back and forth with Madelyn in her arms. His sweet girl sucked on her fist and alternated between sniffles and cries. At least the screaming wasn't so constant like last night. Having his daughter so upset and him feeling so helpless had absolutely gutted him. He would've done anything to help her, but he'd been clueless. He'd spent the night questioning just how good of a father he really was.

Madelyn's wide, dark eyes stared up at the new nanny as if trying to figure out where the stranger had come from.

He was having a difficult time not staring, as well, and he knew full well where she came from—every single one of his erotic fantasies.

"Her gums are swollen and she's drooling quite a bit," Scarlett stated. "All perfectly normal. Do you happen to have any cold teething rings in your fridge?"

Cold teething rings? What the hell was that? He was well stocked with formula and bottles, diapers and wipes, but rings in the fridge? Nope.

He had an app that told him what babies should be doing and what they needed at different stages, but the rings hadn't been mentioned yet.

"I'm guessing no from the look on your face." Scarlett went into the kitchen area and opened the freezer. "Can you get me a napkin or towel?"

Beau wasn't used to taking orders, but he'd do anything to bring his daughter some comfort. He grabbed a clean dishcloth from the counter and handed it to her. He watched as she held on to the ice through the cloth and rubbed it on his daughter's gums. After a few minutes the fussing grew quieter until she finally stopped.

"I'll get some teething rings today," Scarlett murmured as if talking to herself more than him. "They are wonderful for instant relief. If you have any children's pain reliever, we can also rub that on her gums, but I try natural approaches before I go to medicine."

Okay, so maybe Miss December was going to be an asset. He liked that she offered natural options for Madelyn's care. He also liked that she seemed to be completely unimpressed with his celebrity status. Something about that was so refreshing and even more attractive.

Watch it. You already got in trouble with one sexy woman. She's the nanny, not the next bedmate.

He told himself he didn't need the silent warning that rang in his head. Scarlett Patterson would only be here until the day after Christmas. Surely he could keep his libido in control for that long. It wasn't like he had the time anyway. He couldn't smooth the ruffled feathers of his family, care for his child and seduce a woman all before December 26.

No matter how sexy the new nanny was.

Besides, he thought, it couldn't get more clichéd than that—the movie star and the nanny. How many of those stories had he read in the tabloids of late?

No, there was no way he was going to make a move on the woman who was saving his sanity and calming his baby. Besides, he respected women; his mother had raised Southern gentlemen, after all. The media liked to report that he rolled out of one woman's bed and right into another, but he wasn't quite that popular. Not to mention, any woman he'd ever been with had known he wasn't looking for long-term—and agreed with it.

Beau had a feeling Scarlett would be a long-term type of girl. She likely had a family—or maybe she didn't. If this was her full-time job, she probably didn't have time to take care of a family.

Honestly, he shouldn't be letting his mind wander into the territory of Scarlett's personal life. She was his nanny, nothing more.

But damn it, did she have to look so good in her little pink capris and white sleeveless button-up? Didn't she have a uniform? Something up to her neck, down to her ankles and with sleeves? Even if she was completely covered up, she still had those expressive, doe-like eyes, a perfectly shaped mouth and adorable dimples.

Damn it. He should not be noticing each little detail of his new nanny.

"Why don't you go rest?" Scarlett suggested, breaking into his erotic thoughts. "I can take care of her. You look like hell."

Beau stared across the narrow space for a half second before he found his voice. Nobody talked to him like that except his brothers, and even that had been years ago.

"Are you always that blunt with your clients?"

"I try to be honest at all times," she replied sweetly. "I can't be much help to you if you just want me here to boost your ego and lie to your face."

Well, that was a rarity…if she was even telling the truth now. Beau hadn't met a woman who was honest and genuine. Nearly everyone he'd met was out for herself and to hell with anyone around them. And money. They always wanted money.

Another reason he needed the simplicity of Pebblebrook. He just wanted to come back to his roots, to decompress and figure out what the hell to do with his life now. He wanted the open spaces, wanted to see the blue skies without buildings blocking the view. And he needed to mend the relationships he'd left behind. What better time than Christmas?

"I'm Beau." When she drew her brows in, he went on. "I didn't introduce myself before."

"I'm aware of who you are."

He waited for her to say something else, but clearly she'd formed an opinion of him and didn't want to share.

Fine. So long as she kept his daughter comfortable and helped him until Maggie returned, he could care less what she thought.

But she'd have to get in line because his brothers had already dubbed him the prodigal son and were eager to put him in his place. Nothing less than he deserved, he reasoned.

As he watched Scarlett take over the care of Madelyn, Beau knew this was what he deserved, too. A sexy-as-hell woman as his nanny. This was his penance for the bastard he'd been over the past several years.

He'd do well to remember he was a new man now. He'd do well to remember she was here for his daughter, not for his personal pleasure. He'd also do well to remember he had more important things to do than drop Scarlett Patterson into each and every one of his fantasies…even if she would make the perfect lead.

Two

Madelyn had calmed down and was now settled in her crib napping. There was a crib in each of the two bedrooms, but Scarlett opted to put Madelyn in the room Maggie had vacated. This would be Scarlett's room now and she simply didn't think going into Beau's was a smart idea.

After she'd put her luggage and purse in her room, Beau had given her a very brief tour of the cabin, so she'd gotten a glimpse into his personal space. The crib in his room had been nestled next to the king-size bed. Scarlett tried not to, but the second she recalled those messed sheets, she procured an image of him lying there in a pair of snug boxer briefs…or nothing at all.

Scarlett groaned and gently shut the bedroom door, careful not to let the latch snick. She wasn't sure how light of a sleeper Madelyn was, so until she got to know the sweet bundle a little better—

But she couldn't get to know her too much, could she? There wasn't going to be time, and for Scarlett's sanity and heart, she had to keep an emotional distance. Giving herself that pep talk and actually doing it were two totally different things.

Before her surgery, she'd thrown herself into each and every job. Before her surgery, she'd always felt like one unit with the families she worked with.

Before her surgery, she'd had dreams.

The hard knot in her chest never eased. Whether she thought of what she'd lost or was just doing day-to-day things, the ache remained a constant reminder.

Scarlett stepped back into the living area and found Beau standing at the patio doors, his back to her. At least he'd put a T-shirt on. Even so, he filled it out, stretching the material over those chiseled muscles she'd seen firsthand. Clothes or no clothes, the image had been burned into her memory bank and there was no erasing it.

"Madelyn's asleep," she stated.

Beau threw her a glance over his shoulder, then turned his attention back to the view of the open field.

Okay. Clearly he wasn't chatty. Fine by her. He must be a lonely, miserable man. She'd always wondered if celebrities were happy. After all, money certainly couldn't buy everything. Her stepfather was proof of that. He'd been a state representative for years before moving up to governor. He'd wanted his children—he included her in that mix—to all enter the political arena so they would be seen as a powerhouse family.

Thanks, but no thanks. She preferred a simpler life—or at least one without lies, deceit, fake smiles and cheesy campaign slogans.

"If there's something you need to go do, I'll be here," she told Beau. Not surprisingly, he didn't answer. Maybe he gave a grunt, but she couldn't tell if that was a response or just indigestion.

Scarlett turned toward the kitchen to take stock of what type of formula and baby things Madelyn used. Being here a short time, she wanted to make sure the transitions between Maggie and her then back to Maggie went smoothly. Regardless of what Scarlett thought of Beau, Madelyn was the only one here who mattered.

Before Scarlett could step into the kitchen, a knock sounded on the front door.

Beau shifted, his gaze landing on the closed door. He looked like he'd rather run in the opposite direction than face whoever was on the other side. Given that they were on private property, likely the guest was just his family, so what was the issue? Wasn't that why he'd come home? To be with his family for the holidays?

When he made no attempt to move, Scarlett asked, "Should I get that?"

He gave a curt nod and Scarlett reached for the knob. The second she opened the door, she gasped.

Sweet mercy. There were two of them. Another Beau stood before her, only this one was clean shaven and didn't have the scowl. But those shoulders and dark eyes were dead on and just as potent to her heart rate.

"Ma'am," the Beau look-alike said with a drawl and a tip of his black cowboy hat. "I'm Colt Elliott, Beau's twin. You must be the replacement nanny."

Another Elliott and a *twin*. Mercy sakes, this job was not going to be a hardship whatsoever if she had to look at these men each day.

She knew there were four Elliott sons, but wow. Nobody warned her they were clones. Now she wondered if the other two would stop by soon. One could hope.

"Yes," she said when she realized he was waiting on her to respond to his question. "I'm Scarlett."

Colt's dark eyes went from her to Beau. "Is this a bad time?"

Scarlett stepped back. "Not at all. I just got the baby to sleep. I can wait outside while you two talk. It's a beautiful day."

She turned and caught Beau's gaze on her. Did he always have that dramatic, heavy-lidded, movie-star stare? Did he ever turn off the act or was that mysterious, sexy persona natural?

"If you'll excuse me." She turned to Colt. "It was a pleasure meeting you."

"Pleasure was mine, ma'am."

Somehow Scarlett managed to get out the front door without tripping over her own two feet, because that sexy, low Southern drawl those Elliott boys had was rather knee-weakening.

Once she made it to the porch, she walked to the wooden swing on the end in front of her bedroom window. She sank down onto the seat and let the gentle breeze cool off her heated body. December in Texas wasn't too hot, wasn't too cold. In this part of the state, the holiday weather was always perfect. Though the evenings and nights could get chilly.

Good thing there were fireplaces in this cabin. Fireplaces that could lead one to instantly think of romantic talks and shedding of clothes, being wrapped in a blanket in the arms of a strong man.

Scarlett shut her eyes as she rested her feet on the porch and stopped the swaying swing. There would

be no romance and no fires…at least not the passionate kind.

Raised voices filtered from inside. Clearly the Elliott twins were not happy with each other. Two sexy-
as-hell alphas going at it sounded like every woman's
fantasy, but she couldn't exactly barge in and interrupt.

Then she heard it. The faint cry from her bedroom,
right on the other side of the window from where she
sat. Well, damn it.

Scarlett pushed off the swing and jerked open the
front door. Hot men or not, powerful men or not, she
didn't take kindly to anyone disturbing a sleeping baby.

As she marched toward her bedroom, she shot a
warning glare in the direction of the guys, who were
now practically chest to chest. She didn't have time to
worry about their issues, not when Madelyn had barely
been asleep twenty minutes.

Scarlett crossed to the crib and gently picked up the
sweet girl. After grabbing her fuzzy yellow blanket,
Scarlett sank into the nearby rocking chair and patted
Madelyn's bottom to calm her.

Madelyn's little sniffles and heavy lids were Scarlett's main focus right now. She eased the chair into a
gentle motion with her foot and started humming "You
Are My Sunshine." Madelyn didn't take long to nestle
back into sleep and Scarlett's heart clenched. She'd just
hold her a tad longer… It had been so long since she'd
rocked a little one.

She had no idea what happened with Beau and the
baby's mother, but the tabloids and social media had
been abuzz with a variety of rumors over the past few
weeks.

Well, actually, the couple had been quite the fodder

for gossip a lot longer. It was over a year ago when they were first spotted half naked on a beach in Belize. Then the pregnancy seemed to send shock waves through the media. Of course, after the baby was born, there was all that speculation on the state of the mother and she was seen less and less.

Chatter swirled about her cheating, then her rehab, then the breakup.

Then there was talk of Beau. One online source stated he'd been passed over for a part in an epic upcoming blockbuster. One said he'd had a fight with his new agent. Another reported that he and his ex had been spotted arguing at a party and one or both had been inebriated.

Honestly, Beau Elliott was a complication she didn't want to get tangled with, so whatever happened to send him rushing home was his problem. That didn't mean, however, that a child should have to suffer for the sins of the parents.

Once Madelyn was good and asleep, Scarlett put her down in the crib. There was a light tap on the door moments before it eased open.

Scarlett turned from the sleeping baby to see Beau filling the doorway.

"Is she asleep again?" he whispered.

Stepping away from the crib, Scarlett nodded. "Next time you want to have a family fight, take it outside."

His eyes darkened. "This isn't your house," he stated, taking a step closer to her.

Scarlett stood at the edge of the bed and crossed her arms. "It isn't exactly your house, either," she retorted. "But Madelyn is my job now and I won't have her disturbed when she's been fussy and obviously needs sleep. Maybe if you put her needs first—"

In a second, Beau had closed the gap and was all but leaning over her, so close that she had to hold on to the bedpost to stay upright.

"Every single thing I do is putting her needs first," he growled through gritted teeth. "You've been here less than two hours, so don't even presume to know what's going on."

Scarlett placed her hand on his chest to get him to ease back, but the heat from his body warmed her in a way she couldn't explain…and shouldn't dwell on.

She jerked her hand back and glanced away, only to have her eyes land on the pile of lacy panties she'd thrown on her bed when she'd started unpacking earlier.

There went more of that warmth spreading through her. What were the odds Beau hadn't noticed?

She risked glancing back at him, but…nope. He'd noticed all right. His eyes were fixed on her unmentionables.

Beau cleared his throat and raked a hand over the back of his neck before glancing to where his baby slept peacefully in the crib on the other side of the room.

When his dark eyes darted back to her, they pinned her in place. "We need to talk." Then he turned and marched out, likely expecting her to follow.

Scarlett closed her eyes and pulled in a breath as she attempted to count backward from ten. This was only the first day. She knew there would be some bumps in the road, right?

She just didn't expect those bumps to be the chills rushing over her skin from the brief yet toe-curling contact she'd just had with her employer.

* * *

Beau ground his molars and clenched his fists at his sides. It had been quite a while since he'd been with a woman and the one currently staying under his roof was driving him absolutely insane...and it wasn't even lunchtime on her first day of employment.

Those damn panties. All that lace, satin...strings. Mercy, he couldn't get the image out of his head. Never once did he think his nanny's underwear would cause his brain to fry, but here he was with a silent seductress helping to take care of his daughter and he couldn't focus. Likely she didn't even have a clue how she was messing with his hormones.

Scarlett honestly did have Madelyn's best interest in mind. She was none too happy with him and Colt earlier and he wasn't too thrilled with the situation, either. Of all the people angry with him for his actions and for being away from home so long, Colt was by far the most furious. Ironic, he thought. He'd figure his own twin would try to have a little compassion.

Unfortunately, there was so much more contention between them than just the missing years. Coming home at Christmas and thinking things would be magical and easily patched up had been completely naive on his part. But damn it, he'd been hopeful. They'd been the best of friends once, with a twin bond that was stronger than anything he'd ever known.

Delicate footsteps slid across the hardwood floor, interrupting his thoughts. Beau shored up his mental strength and turned to face Scarlett. Why did she have to look like a walking dream? That curvy body, the dark eyes, her flawless dark skin and black hair that gave the illusion of silk sliding down her back.

Damn those panties. Now when he saw her he wondered what she wore underneath her clothes. Lace or satin? Pink or yellow?

"What do you want to talk about?" she asked, making no move to come farther into the living area.

Beau gestured toward the oversize sectional sofa. "Have a seat."

She eyed him for a moment before finally crossing the room and sitting down on the end of the couch. She crossed her ankles and clasped her hands as if she were in some business meeting with a CEO.

Beau stood next to her. "Relax."

"I'd relax more if you weren't looming over me."

Part of him wanted to laugh. Most women would love for him to "loom" over them. Hell, most women would love him under them, as well. Perhaps that's why he found Scarlett of the silky panties so intriguing. She truly didn't care that he was an A-list actor with more money than he could ever spend and the power to obtain nearly anything he ever wanted.

Beau didn't want to make her uncomfortable and it certainly wasn't his intention to be a jerk. It pained him to admit it, but he needed her. He was only a few weeks out on his own with Madelyn and he really didn't want to screw up this full-time parenting job. This would be the most important job he'd ever have.

"We probably need to set some rules here," he started.

Rules like keeping all underwear hidden in a drawer at all times. Oh, and maybe if she could get some long pants and high-neck shirts, that would certainly help. Wouldn't it?

Maggie sat straighter. "I work for you, Mr. Elliott. Just tell me the rules you had for Maggie."

Beau nearly snorted. Rules for Maggie were simple: help with Madelyn while Beau was out working on the ranch and trying to figure his life out. The rules for Scarlett? They'd go beyond not leaving your lingerie out. He mentally added a few more: stop looking so damn innocent and sexy at the same time, stop with the defiant chin that he wanted to nip at and work his way down.

But of course he couldn't voice those rules. He cleared his throat and instead of enumerating his expectations, he took a different approach.

"I'm a hands-on dad." He started with that because that was the most important. "Madelyn is my life. I'm only going to be at Pebblebrook for a short time, but while I'm here, I plan on getting back to my roots and helping to get this dude ranch up and running."

That is, if his brothers would let him in on realizing their father's dream. That was still a heated debate, especially since Beau hadn't been to see Grant Elliott yet.

His father had been residing in an assisted-living facility for the past few years. The bad blood between them couldn't be erased just because Beau had made a deathbed promise to the one man who had been more like a father to him than his real one.

Still, Beau was man enough to admit that he was afraid to see his dad. What if his dad didn't recognize him? Grant had been diagnosed with dementia and lately, more often than not, he didn't know his own children. Even the sons who'd been around the past few years. Beau wasn't sure he was strong enough to face that reality just yet.

"Beau?"

Scarlett's soft tone pulled him out of his thoughts. Where was he? Right, the rules.

"Yeah, um. I can get up with Madelyn during the night. I didn't hire a nanny so I could be lazy and just pass her care off. I prefer a live-in nanny more because I'm still…"

"Nervous?" she finished with raised brows. "It's understandable. Most first-time parents are. Babies are pretty easy, though. They'll pretty much tell you what's wrong, you know, just not with actual words."

No, he actually didn't know. He just knew when Madelyn cried he wanted her to stop because he didn't want her unhappy.

Beau had spent the past five months fighting with his ex, but she'd only wanted Madelyn as a bargaining chip. He'd finally gotten his lawyer to really tighten the screws and ultimately, Jennifer James—wannabe actress and worthless mother—signed away her parental rights.

As much as he hated the idea of Madelyn not having a mother around, his daughter was better off.

Beau studied his new, refreshing nanny. "I assume you don't have children since you're a nanny full-time."

Some emotion slid right over her, taking away that sweet, calm look she'd had since she'd arrived. He could swear an invisible shield slid right between them. Her lips thinned, her head tipped up a notch and her eyes were completely unblinking.

"No children," she said succinctly.

There was backstory behind that simple statement. He knew that for sure. And he was curious.

"Yet you know so much about them," he went on. "Do you want a family of your own one day?"

"My personal life is none of your concern. That's my number-one rule that you can add to your list."

Why the hell had he even asked? He didn't need to know her on a deeper level, but now that she'd flat-out refused to go there, he wanted to find out every last secret she kept hidden. He hadn't asked Maggie personal questions, but then Maggie hadn't pulled up emotions in him like this, either.

Even though he'd just vowed to stay out of Scarlett's personal business, well, he couldn't help himself. If she was just standoffish, that would be one thing, but hurt and vulnerability had laced her tone. He was a sucker for a woman in need.

Scarlett, though, clearly didn't want to be the topic of conversation, something he not only understood but respected. He told himself he should focus on his purpose for being back home and not worry about what his temporary nanny did in her off time.

Beau nodded in affirmation at her demand. "Very well. These three weeks shouldn't be a problem, then."

He came to his feet, most likely to get away from the lie he'd just settled between them. Truthfully, everything about having her here was a problem, but that was on him. Apparently she didn't care that his hormones had chosen now to stand up and pay attention to her. She also didn't seem to care who he was. He was just another client and his celebrity status didn't do a damn thing for her.

While he appreciated her not throwing herself at him, his ego wasn't so quick to accept the hit. This was all new territory for him where a beautiful woman was concerned.

"I'm going to change and head to the main stable

for a bit." He pulled his cell from his pocket. "Give me your cell number and I'll text you so you have my number. If you need anything at all, message me and I'll be right back."

Once the numbers were exchanged, Beau picked up his boots by the front door and went to his room to change. He slipped on a pair of comfortable old jeans, but the boots were new and needed to be broken in. He'd had to buy another pair when he came back. The moment he'd left Pebblebrook years ago, he'd ditched any semblance of home.

Odd how he couldn't wait to dig right back in. The moment he'd turned into the long white-fence-lined drive, he'd gotten that kick of nostalgia as memories of working side by side with his brothers and his father came flooding back.

Right now he needed to muck some stalls to clear his head and take his mind off the most appealing woman he'd encountered in a long time…maybe ever.

But he doubted even grunt work would help. Because at the end of the day, he'd still come back here where she would be wearing her lacy lingerie…and where they would be spending their nights all alone with only an infant as their chaperone.

Three

"You're going to get your pretty new boots scuffed."

Beau turned toward the open end of the stable. His older brother Hayes stood with his arms crossed over his chest, his tattoos peeking from beneath the hems of the sleeves on his biceps.

"I need to break them in," Beau replied, instinctively glancing down to the shiny steel across the point on the toe.

If anyone knew about coming home, it was Hayes. Beau's ex-soldier brother had been overseas fighting in Afghanistan and had seen some serious action that had turned Hayes into an entirely different man than the one Beau remembered.

Whatever had happened to his brother had hardened him, but he was back at the ranch with the love of his life and raising a little boy that he'd taken in as his own. He'd found a happy ending. Beau wasn't so sure that would ever happen for him—or even if he wanted it to.

"So, what? You're going to try to get back into the ranching life?" Hayes asked as he moved to grab a pitchfork hanging on the inside of the tack room. "Or are we just a stepping stone?"

Beau didn't know what the hell he was going to do. He knew in less than three weeks he had a movie debut he had to attend, but beyond that, he'd been dodging his new agent's calls because there was no way Beau was ready to look at another script just yet. His focus was needed elsewhere.

Like on his daughter.

On his future.

"Right now I'm just trying to figure out where the hell to go." Beau gripped his own pitchfork and glanced to the stall with Doc inside. "Nolan ever come and help?"

Hayes headed toward the other end of the row. "When he can. He stays busy at the hospital, but he's cut his hours since marrying and having a kid of his own. His priorities have shifted."

Not just Nolan's priorities, but also Colt's and Hayes's. All three of his brothers had fallen in love and were enjoying their ready-made families.

Beau had been shocked when he'd pulled into the drive and seen his brothers standing on Colt's sprawling front porch with three ladies he didn't know and four children. The ranch had apparently exploded into the next generation while he'd been gone.

Beau worked around Nolan's stallion and put fresh straw in the stall before moving to the next one. For the next hour he and Hayes worked together just like when they'd been kids. Teamwork on the ranch had been important to their father. He'd instilled a set of ethics in his boys that no formal education could match.

Of course they had ranch hands, but there was something about getting back to your roots, Beau knew, that did some sort of reset to your mental health. At this point he needed to try anything to help him figure out what his next move should be.

He actually enjoyed manual labor. Even as a kid and a teen, he'd liked working alongside his father and brothers. But over time, Beau had gotten the urge to see the world, to find out if there was more to life than ranching, and learning how to turn one of the toughest professions into a billion-dollar lifestyle. The idea of being in charge of Pebblebrook once his father retired held no shred of interest to Beau. He knew Colt had always wanted that position so why would Beau even attempt to share it?

"So you all live here on the estate?" Beau asked when he and Hayes had completed their stalls and met in the middle of the barn.

Hayes rested his hand on the top of the pitchfork handle and swiped his other forearm across his damp forehead. "Yeah. I renovated Granddad's old house back by the fork in the river and the creek. I've always loved that place and it just seemed logical when I came back."

The original farmhouse for Pebblebrook would be the perfect home for Hayes and his family, providing privacy, but still remaining on Elliott land.

When they'd all been boys thcy'd ventured to the back of the property on their horses or ATVs and used it as a giant getaway or a man cave. They'd had the ultimate fort and pretended to be soldiers or cowboys in the Old West.

Once upon a time the Elliott brothers were all close, inseparable. But now…

Beau was virtually starting over with his own family. That deathbed promise to his former agent was so much more difficult to execute than he'd originally thought. But Hector had made Beau vow he'd go home and mend fences. At the time Beau had agreed, but now he knew saying the words had been the easy part.

He leaned back against Doc's stall and stared blankly.

"Hey." Hayes studied Beau before slapping a large hand over his shoulder. "It's going to take some time. Nolan is hurt, but he's not pissed. Me? I'm just glad you're here, though I wonder if you'll stay. So I guess that makes me cautious. But Colt, well, he's pissed and hurt, so that's the one you need to be careful with."

Beau snorted and shook his head. "Yeah, we've already had words."

Like when Colt swung by earlier to talk, but ended up going off because of the new nanny. Colt claimed Beau was still a wild child and a player, hiring a nanny looking like that. Beau had prayed Scarlett hadn't heard Colt's accusations. She was a professional and he didn't want her disrespected or made to feel unwelcome. Not that his brother was disrespecting Scarlett. No, he was aiming that all at Beau.

Even if the choice had been his, Beau sure as hell wouldn't have chosen a woman who looked like Scarlett to spend twenty-four hours a day with inside that small cabin. Even he wasn't that much of a masochist.

Beau had no idea what had originally brought Colt

over to see him, but he had a feeling their morning talk wasn't the last of their heated debates.

"You'd think my twin would be the most understanding," Beau muttered.

"Not when he's the one who held this place together once Dad couldn't," Hayes retorted. "I was overseas, Nolan was married to his surgery schedule and you were gone. Colt's always wanted this life. Ranching was it for him, so I guess the fact you wanted nothing to do with it only made the hurt worse. Especially when you rarely called or came back to visit."

Beau knew coming back would rip his heart open, but he'd had no clue his brother would just continually pour salt into the wound. But he had nobody to blame but himself. He was man enough to take it, though. He would push through the hard times and reconnect with his family. If losing Hector had taught him anything, it was that time was fleeting.

"I can't make up for the past," Beau started. "And I can't guarantee I'll stay forever. I just needed somewhere to bring Madelyn, and home seemed like the most logical place. I don't care how I'm treated, just as long as she's loved. I can work on Colt and hopefully mend that relationship."

"Maybe you should start with seeing Dad if you want to try to make amends with anyone."

The heavy dose of guilt he'd been carrying around for some time grew weightier at Hayes's statement. His older brother was absolutely right, yet fear had kept Beau from reaching out to his father since he'd been home.

"Will he even know me?" Beau asked, almost afraid of the answer.

Hayes shrugged. "Maybe not, but what matters is that you're there."

Beau swallowed the lump of emotions. Everything he'd heard over the past year was that their father barely knew anything anymore. The Alzheimer's had trapped him inside his mind. He and Beau may have had major differences in the past, but Grant Elliott was still his father and Beau respected the hell out of that man... though he hadn't done a great job of showing it over the years.

His father had been a second-generation rancher and took pride in his work. He'd wanted his sons to follow in that same path of devotion. Beau, though, had been a rebellious teen with wandering feet and a chip on his shoulder. Pebblebrook hadn't been enough to contain him and he'd moved away. On his own for the first time, he'd wanted to experience everything that had been denied him back home, and ended up in trouble. Then he was discovered and dubbed "a natural" after a ridiculous commercial he wanted to forget.

Beau threw himself into the acting scene hard. His career had seemed to skyrocket overnight.

At first he'd been on a path to destruction, then a path to stardom. And through it all, he hadn't even thought of coming home. He'd been too wrapped up in himself. No excuses.

Then one day he'd realized how much time had passed. He had come home but the cold welcome he'd received had sent him straight back to LA.

But this time was different. This time he was going to stay, at least through the holidays, no matter how difficult it might be.

"I'll go see him," Beau promised, finally meeting Hayes's eyes. "I'm just not ready."

"Always making excuses."

Beau and Hayes turned to the sound of Colt's angry voice. Just what he needed, another round with his pissed brother.

Colt glanced to the pitchfork in Beau's hand. "Are you practicing for a part or actually attempting to help?"

"Colt—"

"No." Beau held out his hand, cutting Hayes off. "It's not your fight."

Hayes nodded and took Beau's pitchfork and his own back to the tack room, giving Beau and Colt some privacy.

"I came home because I needed somewhere safe to bring my daughter," Beau stated, that chip on his shoulder more evident than ever. "I came home because it was time and I'd hoped we could put aside our differences for Christmas."

Did he think he could just waltz back onto the ranch and sing carols around the Christmas tree and all would be well? Had he been gone so long that he could just ignore the tension and the hurt that resided here?

"You won't find a red-carpet welcome here," Colt grunted. "We've gotten along just fine without you for years. So if you're just going to turn around and leave again, don't bother with all this show now. Christmas is a busy time for Annabelle at the B and B. I don't have time to figure out what the hell you're doing or not doing."

Seeing his twin back here where they'd shared so many memories…

Every part of Colt wished this was a warm family reunion, but the reality was quite different.

Beau had chosen to stay away, to make a new family, a new life amidst all the Hollywood hoopla, the parties, the women, the money and jet-setting.

Bitterness had settled into Colt long ago and showed no sign of leaving.

"What did you want when you came by this morning?" Beau asked. "Other than to berate me."

Hayes carried a blanket and saddle down the stable and passed them, obviously trying to get the hell out of here and not intervene.

Colt hooked his thumbs through his belt loops. "I was going to give you a chance to explain. Annabelle told me I should hear your side, but then I saw your replacement nanny and realized nothing about you has changed."

Of course Beau would have a stunning woman living under his roof with the guise of being a nanny. Was his brother ever going to mature and just own up to his responsibilities?

"Replacement nanny?" Hayes chimed up.

Beau's eyes narrowed—apparently Colt had hit a nerve. But they both ignored Hayes's question.

The resentment and turmoil that had been bubbling and brewing over the years was best left between him and his twin. Colt didn't want to drag anybody else into this mix.

Though his wife had already wedged herself into the drama. He knew she meant well, he knew she wanted one big happy family, especially considering she lost her only sibling too early in life. But still, there was so much pain in the past that had only grown like a tumor over the years. Some things simply couldn't be fixed.

Beau kept his gaze straight ahead to Colt. "Who I have helping with Madelyn is none of your concern and I didn't decide who the agency sent to replace Maggie. Her husband fell and broke his hip so she had to go care for him for a few weeks until their daughter can come help. If you have a problem, maybe you'd like to apply for the job."

"Maybe you could worry more about your daughter and less about your dick—"

Beau didn't think before his fist planted in the side of Colt's jaw. He simply reacted. But before he could land a second shot, a restraining hand stopped him. Hayes stood between the brothers, his hands on each of their chests.

"All right, we're not doing this," Hayes told them both.

"Looks like I missed the official work reunion."

At the sound of the new voice, Beau turned to see Nolan come striding in. No fancy doctor clothes for his oldest brother. Nolan looked like the rest of them with his jeans and Western shirt and boots and black hat.

There was no mistaking they were brothers. Years and lifestyles may have kept them apart, but the Elliott genetics were strong. Just the sight of his three brothers had something shifting in Beau's chest. Perhaps he was supposed to be here now, for more than Madelyn.

"Throwing punches took longer than I thought," Nolan growled, closing the distance. "You've been here a whole week."

Beau ignored the comment and glared back at Colt. "You know nothing about me anymore, so don't presume you know what type of man I am."

"Whose fault is that?" Colt shouted. "You didn't let us get to know the man you grew into. We had to watch it on the damn movie screen."

Guilt…such a bitter pill to swallow.

"Why don't we just calm down?" Hayes suggested as he stepped back. "Beau is home now and Dad wouldn't want us going at each other. This is all he ever wanted, us together, working on the ranch."

"You haven't even been to see him," Colt shot at Beau, his dark eyes still judgmental.

"I will."

Colt shook his head in disgust, but Beau didn't owe him an explanation. Beau didn't owe him anything. They may be twins, but the physical appearance was where their similarities ended. They were different men, with different goals. Why should Beau be sorry for the life he'd created for himself?

Nolan reached them then and diverted his attention. "Pepper wanted me to invite you and Madelyn for dinner," he stated in that calm voice of his. "Are you free this evening?"

Beau blew out the stress he'd been feeling and raked a hand along the back of his neck. "Yeah. I'm free. Madelyn's been a little cranky. Scarlett thinks she's cutting teeth, but we should be able to make it."

"Scarlett?" Nolan asked.

"His new nanny," Colt interjected. "She's petite, curvy, stunning. Just Beau's type."

Beau wasn't going to take the bait, not again. Besides, already he knew that Scarlett was so much more than that simple description. She was vibrant and strong and determined…and she'd had his fantasies working overtime.

"You're married," he said instead to his twin. "So my nanny is none of your concern."

"Just stating the facts." Colt held his hands out and took a step back. "I'm happily married with two babies of my own, so don't worry about me trying to lay claim. I'm loyal to my wife."

"Scarlett can come, too, if you want," Nolan added, clearly ignoring his brother's argument. "Pepper won't mind."

Scarlett joining him? Hell no. That would be too familial and definitely not the approach he wanted to take on day one with his temporary help. Not the approach he'd want to take on any day with her, actually.

Not that long ago he would've jumped at the excuse to spend more time with a gorgeous woman, but his hormones were just going to have to take a back seat because he had to face reality. The good times that he was used to were in the past. His good times now consisted of a peaceful night's sleep and a happy baby.

Damn, he was either getting old or finally acting like an adult.

He'd always tried to keep himself grounded over the years, but now that he was home, he realized just how shallow Hollywood had made him. Shallow and jaded. Yet another reason he needed to keep himself and his daughter away from that lifestyle.

"It will just be Madelyn and me," he informed his brother. Then he shifted his attention back to Colt. "Do you want my help around here or not?"

"From the prodigal son?" Colt's jaw clenched, and Beau could see a bruise was already forming there. Colt finally nodded. "I've got most of the guys on the west side of the property mending fences. I'll take your free labor here."

Well, that was something. Maybe there was hope for them after all. Beau decided since they weren't yelling or throwing more punches, now would be as good a time as any to pitch his thoughts out there.

"I want in on the dude ranch, too."

Beau didn't realize he'd wanted that until they all stood here together. But there was no denying his wishes now. Whether he stayed on the ranch or not, he wanted to be part of his father's legacy with his brothers.

Colt's brows shot up, but before he could refuse, Beau went on. "I'm part of this family whether you like it or not and Dad's wish was to see this through. Now, I know you plan to open in just a few months and a good bit of the hard work is done, but that doesn't mean you couldn't use me."

Hayes shrugged. "Wouldn't be a bad idea to have him do some marketing. He'd have some great connections."

Colt's gaze darted to Hayes. "Are you serious?"

"Hayes is right," Nolan added. "I know none of us needs the extra income, but we want Dad's dream to be a success."

Colt took off his hat, raked a hand over his hair and settled the hat back in place. "Well, hell. Whatever. We'll use you until you take off again, because we all know you won't stick."

Beau didn't say a word. What could he say? He knew full well he likely wasn't staying here long-term. He'd returned because of a deathbed promise and to figure out where to take his daughter. Pebblebrook was likely a stepping stone…nothing more. Just like Hayes had said.

Four

Scarlett swiped another stroke of Cherry Cherry Bang Bang on her toes. Beau had taken Madelyn to dinner at his brother's house and told her she didn't need to come.

So she'd finished unpacking—getting all of her panties put away properly. Then she'd caught up on social media, and now she was giving herself an overdue pedicure with her new polish. She wasn't a red type of girl, but she figured with the new move coming and another chapter in her life starting, why not go all in and have some fun? Now that she was admiring it against her dark skin, she actually loved the festive shade.

And that's about as wild as she got. Red polish.

Could she be any more boring?

She never dreamed she'd be in this position at nearly thirty-five years of age: no husband, no children and a changing career.

She was fine without the husband—she could get by on her own, thank you very much. But the lack of children would always be a tender spot and the career change hurt just as much. Not that her career or lack of a family of her own defined her, but there were still dreams she'd had, dreams she'd had to let go of. These days she tried to focus on finding a new goal, but she still scrambled for something obtainable.

Scarlett adored being a nanny, but she simply couldn't continue in that job. Seeing all that she could've had but never would was just too painful.

Ultimately, she knew she had no choice but to walk away from that career. And because she had no family, no ties to this town of Stone River, she'd decided to move away, as well. In a large city like Dallas, surely there would be opportunities she didn't even realize she wanted.

As she stretched her legs out in front of her on the bed, Scarlett admired her toes. If Christmas wasn't the perfect time to paint her toes bright red, she didn't know when would be.

She settled back against her thick, propped pillows and reached for her laptop. In three weeks she'd be starting her new job as assistant director of activities at a nursing home in Dallas. While she was thrilled about the job and the prospect of meeting new people, she had yet to find proper housing. The one condo she'd hoped to rent had fallen through, so now she was back to the drawing board. Her Realtor in the area kept sending listings, but most were too expensive even with her pay raise.

While her toes dried, she scrolled through page after page of listings. She preferred to be closer to the city so she could have some social life, but then the costs just kept going up. She also preferred a small home instead of a condo or apartment, since privacy was important to her. But there was no way her paycheck would stretch enough to make a mortgage payment on a house. The condo she'd wanted to rent had an elderly lady living on the other side, so Scarlett had been comfortable with that setup.

She was switching to a new website when she heard the cabin door open and close. She eased her laptop aside and, after checking that her toes were nice and dry, she padded barefoot toward the living room.

As soon as she stepped through the door, Beau held his finger up to his lips and Scarlett noticed the sleeping baby cradled in his arm…against one very flexed, very taut biceps.

Down, girl.

She'd seen him on-screen plenty of times, but seeing him in person was quite a different image. She didn't know how he managed it, but the infuriating man was even sexier.

Wasn't there some crazy rule that the camera added ten pounds? Because from her vantage point, she thought maybe he'd bulked up since being on-screen because those arms and shoulders were quite something.

Scarlett clenched her hands, rubbing her fingertips against her palms at the thought of how those shoulders would feel beneath her touch.

She seriously needed to get control of her thoughts and focus. The only person she needed to be gripping, touching or even thinking about was Madelyn.

Scarlett motioned toward her room and whispered, "Let her sleep in here tonight since you didn't sleep last night."

He looked like he wanted to argue, but Scarlett quirked a brow, silently daring him to say one word. He may be the big, bad billionaire, but she wasn't backing down. Part of being a good nanny was to not only look after the child, but also take note of the parent's needs.

When Beau took a step toward her room, Scarlett ushered ahead and pulled the blinds to darken the space over the crib. The moon shone bright and beautiful tonight, but she wanted Madelyn to rest peacefully.

Scarlett took her laptop and tiptoed out of the room while Beau settled Madelyn in her crib. After taking a seat on the leather sofa in the living room, Scarlett pulled up those listings again. The sleeping baby didn't need her right now and she figured Beau had things to do. So, until he told her differently, she wouldn't get in the way.

Moments later, he eased from her room and closed the door behind him.

"I have food for you."

His comment caught her off guard. "Excuse me?"

Beau came around the couch and stood in front of her. That black T-shirt and those well-worn jeans may look casual, but the way they fit him made all her girly parts stand up and take note of just how perfectly built he truly was. Not that she hadn't noticed every other time she'd ever looked at him.

"Pepper, Nolan's wife, insisted I bring you food and she was angry I didn't invite you."

Scarlett smiled, but waved a hand. "No reason to be angry. You didn't need me."

Something flared bright and hot in his eyes, but before she could identify what she'd seen, he asked, "Have you eaten?"

"I had a granola bar, but I'm not really that hungry."
She was too concerned with being homeless when she
moved to Dallas.

Beau muttered something about needing more meat
on her bones before he headed back out the front door.
An instant later he came back in with containers and
headed toward the open kitchen.

Scarlett set her laptop on the raw-edged coffee table
and figured it would be rude if she didn't acknowledge
the gesture.

"I could eat a little more," she commented just as
her belly let out a low grumble. "What do you have?"

He gestured to the stool opposite the island where he
stood. "Have a seat and I'll get you a plate before your
stomach wakes my daughter."

As Scarlett eased onto the wooden stool, she couldn't
believe her eyes. Hollywood heartthrob Beau Elliott was
essentially making her dinner. There wasn't a woman
alive who wouldn't want to be in her shoes right now.

Beau pried lids off the plastic storage containers and
Scarlett's mouth watered at the sight of mashed potatoes with gravy, green beans, and meatloaf he heaped
onto a plate. Mercy sakes, a real home-cooked meal.
There was no way she could eat all of that and still button her pants.

"Don't tell me you're one of those women who count
every carb," he growled as he spooned a hearty dose of
potatoes onto a plate.

"Not every carb, but I can't exactly afford to buy
bigger clothes."

He shook his head as he once he filled the plate he
placed it in front of her. He pulled open a drawer and
grabbed a fork, passing it across, too.

"What would you like to drink? I haven't been the best at keeping food in here for me," he stated as he walked to the fridge. "I have formula, cereal, organic baby juice or water."

Wasn't it adorable that everything in the kitchen was for a five-month-old? But, seriously, what on earth was the man going to live on? Because someone as broad and strong as Beau needed to keep up his stamina... er, energy.

Do not think about his stamina—or his broad shoulders. Or tracing those tattoos with your tongue.

"Water is fine, thanks."

She decided the best thing to do was just shovel the food in. She may regret overeating later, but at least her mouth would be occupied and she couldn't speak her lascivious thoughts.

"I'll take Madelyn and make a grocery run tomorrow," she offered as she scooped up another bite of whipped potatoes.

Beau opened one cabinet after another, clearly looking for something. "I don't expect you to do the work of a maid."

"Then who will do it?" she countered before she thought better of it. But then she opened her mouth again and charged forward. "Either you have to go or I have to, unless you want the media to chase you through aisle seven and see what type of toilet paper you buy."

Beau stopped his search and turned to face her. He flattened his palms on the island and leaned in.

Maybe she'd gone too far, but seriously, who would do the shopping? Surely not his brothers, who were obviously not taking Beau's homecoming very well, for reasons that were none of her concern but still inspired her curiosity. Still, she probably should've left that last part off, but she'd never had a proper filter.

"Are you always this bold and honest?" he asked.

Oh, he didn't want her complete honesty. Was this a bad time to tell him she'd been holding back?

Scarlett set her fork down and scooted her plate back. Resting her arms on the counter, she cocked her head.

"I believe in honesty at all times, especially in this line of work. But I really am just trying to make things easier for you."

He stared at her another minute and she worried that she had a glob of gravy in the corner of her mouth or something, but he finally shook his head and pushed off the counter.

"You don't have to go," he told her. "I can ask one of my sister-in-laws to pick some things up for me."

As much as she wanted to call him out on his bull-headedness, she opted to see a different side. She may not know the dynamics of his family or the stormy past they'd obviously had, but she recognized a hurt soul when she saw one.

"I'm perfectly capable of grocery shopping," she stated, softening her tone. "I've lived on my own for some time now and besides, you wouldn't be the first client I've shopped for."

Beau folded his arms across his broad chest and leaned back against the opposite counter. "And where do you live?"

Her appetite vanished, pushed out by nerves as she pondered her upcoming move.

"Currently here."

"Obviously." His dry tone left no room for humor. "When you're not taking care of children, where do you call home?"

Between his intense stare and the simple question that set her on edge, Scarlett slid off the bar stool and came to her feet.

"I have no home at the moment," she explained, sliding her hands in the pockets of her jeans. "I'm still looking for a place."

Beau's dark brows drew in, a familiar look she'd seen on-screen, but in person… Wow. That sultry gaze made her stomach do flips and her mouth water. She didn't care if that sounded cliché, there was no other way to describe what happened when he looked at her that way.

"You're only here three weeks," he stated, as if she'd forgotten the countdown.

Scarlett picked up her plate and circled the island. She covered the dish up and put it inside the fridge. She needed to do something to try to ignore the fact that she wasn't only under the same roof as Beau Elliott, she was literally standing within touching distance and he was staring at her as if he could see into her soul.

No, that wasn't accurate at all. He was staring at her as if she stood before him with no clothes.

Maybe she should've kept that island between them.

"I'm moving to Dallas," she explained, trying to stay on topic. "This is my final job with the Nanny Poppins agency."

The harsh reality that this was it for her never got any easier to say. But, hey, if she had to leave, at least she was going out on the highest note of her nanny career. Staying with Hollywood Bad Boy Beau Elliott and taking care of his precious baby girl.

"Why the change?" he asked. "You seem to love your job."

The burn started in her throat and she quickly swallowed the emotions back. This was the way things had to be, so getting upset over it would change absolutely nothing. She might as well enjoy her time here, with the baby and the hunk, and move on to the new chapter in her life.

New year, new start, and all that mumbo jumbo. This was the second time in her life she'd started over on her own. If she did it when she was younger, she could certainly do it now.

"Why don't you get me a grocery list and I'll take Madelyn when she wakes in the morning," she said.

Scarlett started to turn, but a warm, strong hand curled around her bare biceps. She stilled, her entire body going on high alert and responding to the simplest of touches.

But this wasn't a simple touch. This was Beau Elliott, actor, playboy, rancher, father. Could he be more complex?

When he tugged her to turn her around, Scarlett came face-to-face with a sexy, stubbled jawline, firm mouth, hard eyes.

No, not hard, more like…intense. That was by far the best adjective to describe her boss. There was an intensity that seemed to radiate from him at all times, and that powerful stare, that strong, arousing grip, had her heart pounding.

"Women don't walk away from me."

No, she'd bet not. Most likely he gave them one heavy-lidded stare or a flash of that cocky grin and their panties melted off as they begged him for anything he was willing to give.

"I'm not walking away from you," she defended. "I'm walking away from this conversation."

"That's not fair." He still held on to her arm and took a half step closer until his torso brushed against hers. "I guarantee you know more about me than I know about you."

Scarlett laughed, more out of nerves than humor. "That's not my fault you parade your life in front of the camera. You know all you need in order for me to do my job."

The hold he had on her eased, but he still didn't let go. No, now he started running that thumb along the inside of her elbow.

What the hell?

She'd say the words aloud, but then he might stop and she wanted to take this thrill and save it deep inside her memory. So what if this was all wrong and warning flags were waving in her head?

"You don't look like a nanny," he murmured, studying her face. "Maggie looked like a nanny. You…"

Her entire body heated. With each stroke of that thumb she felt the zings down to her toes.

"What do I look like?" she asked. Why did that come out as a whisper?

"Like trouble."

Scarlett wanted to laugh. Truly she did. Of all the words used to describe her, *trouble* certainly had never been a contender.

This had to stop before she crossed the professional boundary. She'd never had an issue like this before, and by issue she meant a client as potent and as sexy as Beau Elliott. No wonder women flocked to him and wanted to be draped over his arm. If she were shallower and had no ambitions, she'd probably beg to be his next piece of arm candy.

But she wasn't shallow and she most definitely had goals...goals that did not include sleeping with a client.

"Make me that grocery list and text it to me," she told him as she took a step back. "Madelyn and I will head out in the morning."

She didn't wait on him to reply. Scarlett turned and fled to her room. She didn't exactly run, but she didn't walk, either. There was no way he wasn't watching her. She could practically feel that heavy gaze of his on her backside.

No doubt Beau knew just how powerful one of his long looks were. He'd gotten two big awards for his convincing performances and she couldn't help but wonder just how sincere he was with his affection or if he was just trying to find another bedmate.

Scarlett gently closed the door behind her and leaned against it. Over in the corner Madelyn slept. That little girl was the only reason Scarlett was here. There was no room for tingles or touching or...well, arousal.

There, she'd admitted it. She was so turned on by that featherlight touch of Beau's she didn't know how she'd get any sleep. Surely if she so much as closed her eyes, she'd dream of him doing delicious things to her body. That was the last image she needed on this final nanny assignment.

Scarlett moved away from the door and started changing for bed.

One day down, she told herself. Only twenty more to go.

Five

What the hell had he been thinking touching her like that?

Beau slid his cowboy boot into the stirrup and swung his other leg over the back of Starlight, the newest mare to Pebblebrook.

He'd gotten up and out of that house this morning before seeing Scarlett. A niggle of guilt had hit him when he'd slunk out like he was doing some walk of shame, but damn it. He couldn't see her this morning, especially not all snuggly with Madelyn.

He hated not kissing his daughter good morning, but one day would be all right. Perhaps when he got back to the cabin he'd have a little more control over his hormones and unwelcome desires.

Damn it. He'd been up half the night, restless and aching. Likely Scarlett had been sleeping and not giving him another thought. This was all new territory for him, wanting a woman and not being able to have her.

With a clack of his mouth and a gentle heel to the side, Beau set Starlight off toward the back of the property.

Last night, his thoughts volleyed all around. He couldn't help wondering what Scarlett planned on doing when she left the agency, or why she was even leaving in the first place, but what kept him up all night was wondering what the hell she slept in.

Maybe she had a little pair of pajamas that matched that bright red polish she'd put on her toes. Mercy, that had been sexy as hell. He was a sucker for red.

Beau gripped the reins and guided the beautiful chestnut mare toward Hayes and Alexa's house. Beau hadn't been to the old, original farmhouse nestled in the back of the ranch since coming home. It was time he ventured out there and started making amends with his brothers. So what if he was starting with the one least pissed at him?

When Hector had been diagnosed with the inoperable brain tumor, Beau had known things weren't going to end well for them. Hector had been so much more than an agent. He'd been like a father figure, pulling Beau from the mess he'd gotten himself into when he'd first hit LA. For years they'd been like one unit, and then Beau's foundation was taken away.

But Hector had made Beau promise to go home and work on the relationships with his brothers and father. So, here he was. Having a sexy woman beneath his roof was just added penance. It was like fate was mocking him by parading Scarlett around like some sweet dream that would never become reality.

Which was why he'd been scolding himself all morning.

He couldn't touch her again. First of all, he'd put her in an uncomfortable position. That wasn't professional and he probably owed her an apology…but he wasn't sorry. He wasn't sorry that he'd finally gotten to touch her, to inhale that sweet, floral scent and see the pulse at the base of her neck kick up a notch.

Second of all, he couldn't touch her again because last night he'd been about a half second from jerking that curvy body against his to see exactly how well they'd fit.

He felt his body react to that thought, and forced his mind onto something else. The weather. That was innocuous enough. He looked around. The morning sun was warming up and already burning off the fog over the ranch.

He hoped the ice around Colt's heart would burn off just as easily. Granted, the cold welcome Beau had received was his own fault. Still, Colt acted like he didn't even want to try to forgive. Maybe that was just years of anger and resentment that had all built up and now that Beau was home Colt felt justified to unload.

But Christmas was only a few weeks away, and Beau wondered if he'd even be welcome at the table with the rest of the family. Hopefully by then, the angry words would be out of the way and they could start moving forward to a more positive future.

Beau had a movie premiere just two days before Christmas, but he planned on being gone only two days and returning. There was nothing he wanted more than to have his daughter at the ranch during the holiday and with the rest of the family.

Beau's cell vibrated in his pocket, but he ignored it. Instead, he kept Starlight at a steady pace and let himself relax as they headed to the back of the estate. He'd ridden horses for movie roles, but nothing was like this. No set could compare to being on his own land, without worrying about what direction to look or how to tip his hat at just the right angle for the camera, but not to block his eyes.

Being out here all alone, breathing in the fresh air and hoping to sew up the busted seams of his relationships kept Beau hopeful.

And really, his future depended on how things went over the next few weeks. Apologizing and crawling home with his proverbial tail between his legs wasn't easy. Beau had his pride, damn it, but he also had a family that he missed and loved.

If Christmas came and there was still no further progress made with Colt, Beau would go. He'd take Madelyn and they would go…somewhere. Hell, he had enough homes to choose from: a mansion in the Hollywood Hills, a cabin in Montana, a villa in France, his private island off the coast of Italy. Or he could just buy his own spread and build a house if that's what he chose. Maybe he'd start his own ranch and show Madelyn the way he was brought up.

But he wanted Pebblebrook.

The cell continued to vibrate. Likely his new agent, worried Beau had officially gone off-grid. Maybe he had. Maybe he wouldn't emerge until the premiere in a few weeks—maybe not even then. He didn't necessarily want to go to the premiere, but this was the most anticipated holiday movie and the buzz around it had been bigger than anything he'd ever seen.

Apparently *Holly Jolly Howards* struck a chord with people. The whole family falling apart and finding their way back together after a Christmas miracle saved one of their lives was said to be the next holiday classic. Move over *White Christmas* and *It's a Wonderful Life*.

Getting his on-screen family back together had been easy. All he'd had to do was act out the words in the script. But in real life, he was on his own.

Beau had only been back in Pebblebrook a short time, but already there was a peacefulness that calmed him at times like this. Just being out in the open on horseback helped to clear his mind of all the chaos of the job, the demands of being a celebrity, and the battle he waged with himself.

These past several months since becoming a parent had changed his entire outlook on life. He wanted the best for Madelyn, and not just the best material things. Beneath the tailor-made suits, the flashy cars and extravagant parties, he was still a simple man from a Texas ranch. He'd always had money, so that wasn't anything overly important to him.

He wanted stability. He knew it was vital in shaping the future of a child. The simplicity of routine may sound ridiculous, but he'd found out that having a schedule made his life and Madelyn's so much easier. She needed to have a life that wasn't rushing from one movie set, photo shoot, television interview or extravagant party to another. That whirlwind lifestyle exhausted him; he couldn't imagine a baby living like that.

Beau may have a nanny now, but that's not how he wanted to live his entire life. He wasn't kidding when he said he wanted to be a hands-on father. He wouldn't be jetting off to various locales just to have someone else raise his daughter.

As Hayes's white farmhouse came into view, guilt reacquainted itself with Beau. His parents had done a remarkable job of providing security and a solid foundation for the four Elliott boys.

Once their mother passed, that foundation was shaken and everyone had to figure out their purpose. Beau had started getting that itch to see if there was something else out there for him. Since money hadn't been an issue, he'd taken a chunk out of his college fund and headed to Hollywood, despite his father's demands to stay.

The cell in Beau's pocket vibrated once again as he pulled his horse up to Hayes's stable. He dismounted and hooked the rein around the post. When he turned toward the house, Alexa stepped out the back door and her son, Mason, came barreling out past her.

Beau smiled, loving how his brother had found this happiness. They'd even decorated the house for the holidays. Sprigs of evergreen seemed to be bursting from the old wagon in the yard, a festive wreath hung on the back door, and red ribbons were tied on the white posts of the back porch.

"Hope you don't mind me stopping by," Beau said as he approached the steps. "I figured I should get to know my new family members a little better."

Alexa crossed her arms and offered a welcoming grin. "Never in my life did I think I'd meet a movie star, let alone have one for a soon-to-be brother-in-law."

Mason stopped right in front of Beau and stared up at him. "Hi."

Beau tipped his hat back and squatted down to the little guy. "Hey, buddy," he greeted. "How old are you?"

Mason held up one finger and smiled. Beau had already been educated on the ages of his nieces and nephews. This was just another reason he wanted Madelyn here. This new generation of Elliotts should be close, because when your life went to hell and got flipped upside down, family was invaluable.

Beau thought of his brother Colt's reaction yesterday. Part of him knew that if Colt didn't care, he wouldn't be acting like a wounded animal right now. The ones you loved most had the ability to cause the most pain.

"Why don't you come on in," Alexa invited. "Mason and I were just about to make some muffins to take to Annabelle this afternoon. She's got her hands full at the B and B, so I offered to help. I'm not a great baker, but I can make muffins."

"I don't want to interrupt."

Alexa raised her brows. "Yet you rode out here without calling or texting?"

She offered a wide smile and waved her hand. "Get in here. Family doesn't interrupt."

Beau could see how Hayes hadn't stood a chance with this one. She was sassy and headstrong...pretty much like the sultry seductress down in his cabin.

Granted, Scarlett didn't have a clue how his stomach knotted up just thinking of her, how he'd been in a tangle of sheets all night because...well, the fantasies wouldn't let him sleep.

Mason lifted his arms toward Beau. Without hesitation, Beau picked up his...well, this would be his nephew. He hadn't been around children until he'd had his own. Oh, there were a few on some sets that he worked with, but they weren't his responsibility or they were a little older and so professional, they didn't act like regular kids.

But this little guy didn't care that Beau had two shiny acting awards back at his Hollywood Hills mansion. He didn't even know who Beau was or why he was here. Mason wanted affection and he was open and trusting and ready to accept the comfort of a stranger.

If only the rest of the family could be as welcoming as a child.

"Hayes actually just ran into town to get more supplies at the store," Alexa stated as she stepped into the house and held the door open for him. "I offered, but he keeps saying he needs to get out more."

Which was a huge accomplishment in itself. Suffering from PTSD had kept Hayes hidden away and everyone shut out for too long. Alexa had pulled him out of the rubble he'd buried himself in. The love of a good woman, Beau reckoned, was clearly invaluable. All of his brothers had found their perfect soul mate and secured a happy future.

There was clearly something in the water on Pebblebrook Ranch. No way in hell was he drinking from the well. The last thing he needed was more commitment or a relationship to worry about. Maybe one day—maybe—but not now.

Beau stepped into the kitchen and stilled. "Wow."

Alexa smiled. "I know. Hayes did an amazing job of renovating this place, though he did take my advice on the kitchen and use some of my Latino heritage as inspiration."

Judging by the bold colors from the blue backsplash to the yellow and orange details in random tiles on the floor, there was no doubt Hayes had made his fiancée feel part of this renovation.

"I haven't been back," he murmured as he held on to Mason and stepped farther into the room. "I'm going to need a tour."

Alexa reached for an apron on the hook by the pantry doors. "I'm going to let Hayes do that," she stated. "I'd say you two need some time alone."

The back door opened and Beau spun around to see his brother step in carrying bags of groceries.

"That place was pure hell," he growled as he set everything on the raw-edge kitchen table. "Remind me never to go in the morning again. Every senior citizen from town was there, all wanting to talk or shake my hand."

Beau knew his brother was grateful for the people who appreciated his service to their country, but Hayes had never been one for accolades.

"That's because they're thankful for your service." Alexa laughed and crossed to Beau. She lifted Mason from his hands. "Your brother wants a tour of the house. Now, go do that and let me work on these muffins so Annabelle doesn't have to do everything for her guests."

Annabelle, Colt's wife and owner of the bed-and-breakfast next door, was not only the mother of nearly two-year-old twin girls, rumor had it she was also a phenomenal chef. Beau had the utmost respect for her because he could barely make a bowl of cereal and care for Madelyn at the same time.

Hayes eyed his brother and Beau slid off his cowboy hat and hooked it on the top of a kitchen chair. "Care to show me what you did to the place?"

"Are we rebuilding the brotherly bond?" Hayes asked.

"Something like that."

Hayes stared another minute before giving a curt nod. "Let's go, then."

Beau followed Hayes out of the kitchen and caught Alexa's warm smile and wink as he left.

They stepped into the living room, and Beau noticed the old carpet had been replaced with wide-plank wood flooring. The fireplace and mantel had been given a facelift. The room glowed with new paint, new furniture.

The fireplace had garland and lights draped across it, as well as three knitted stockings. A festively decorated Christmas tree sat in the front window. Presents were spread all beneath and Beau figured Hayes may have gone a bit overboard with the gifts for Mason.

Everything before him, from the renovations to the holiday decor, was the sign of a new chapter in his brother's life.

Beau wanted to start a new chapter, but he couldn't even find the right book for his life.

"We'll start upstairs," Hayes said over his shoulder. "That way I can grill you without Alexa overhearing."

Beau mounted the steps. "Why do you think I came here instead of Colt's? I'm easing into this re-bonding process."

Hayes reached the landing before making the turn to the second story. "Heard you went to Nolan's last night. Does that mean Colt is tomorrow?"

Beau shrugged. "We'll see."

"And Dad?"

Beau stood on the narrow strip with his brother and stared into familiar dark eyes. "I'll get there," he promised.

Hayes seemed as if he wanted to say more, but he

turned and continued on upstairs. "Then we can discuss your nanny while I show you what I did with
the place."

Great. As if she hadn't been on his mind already. She
actually hadn't gotten *off* his mind since she'd showed
up at his door looking like she'd just stepped off a cal-
endar for every male fantasy. The fake women in LA
didn't even compare to the natural beauty of Scarlett
Patterson.

"There's nothing to know about her," Beau stated,
hoping that would end the conversation, but knowing
better.

"Here's the guest bath." Hayes motioned toward the
open doorway, but remained in the hall. "We gutted it
and started from scratch. So, Scarlett replaced Maggie.
That was quite a change."

"That wasn't a very smooth transition from the bath
to the nanny."

Hayes merely shrugged and leaned against the door
frame, clearly waiting for an answer.

Returning his attention to the renovated bath, Beau
glanced around at the classy white and brushed nickel
decor. He was impressed with all the work that went
into the restoration, but he couldn't focus. Just hearing Scarlett's name had his body stirring. It had simply been too long since he'd been with a woman, that's
all. It wasn't like he had some horny hang-up over his
nanny. For pity's sake, he was Beau Elliott. He could
have any woman he wanted.

Yet he wanted the one with a killer body, doe-like
eyes, a layer of kickass barely covering a heavy dose
of vulnerability. The fact that she cared for his daughter above all else and wasn't throwing herself at him

was just another piece in the puzzle that made up this mystery of emotions.

His cell buzzed again and this time Beau pulled his phone out, grateful for the interruption so he could stop the interrogation.

The second he glanced at the screen, though, he barely suppressed a groan at the sight of four voice mails and three texts. The texts, all from his new agent, were frantic, if the wording in all caps was any indicator.

"Problem?" Hayes asked.

Beau read the messages, but ignored the voice mails. "The movie I have coming out is getting in the way of my sabbatical."

Hayes crossed his arms and leaned against the wall. "Is that what this is? You're just passing through until something or someone better comes along?"

Beau muttered a curse and raked his hand through his hair. "Hell, that didn't come out right. I just… I have no clue what I'm doing and it's making me grouchy. My agent and publicist have scheduled so many media slots for me to promote this movie, but I've told them I need to cancel. I'll do call-ins, but I'm not going to LA or New York right now to appear on talk shows."

He simply couldn't handle it. First, he wasn't dragging Madelyn to every event because they lasted from early morning until late at night. Second, well, he needed a damn break.

"You're a good dad."

Beau jerked his attention to Hayes, surprised by his brother's statement. "Thanks. My agent, he tried to get me to take Madelyn and basically use her for more publicity. I won't do that. Jennifer tried and I won't have it. I want Madelyn as far away from the limelight as possible."

Hayes nodded, whether in understanding or approval Beau didn't know. Perhaps a little of both.

"Maybe now you can see a little where Dad was coming from."

Hayes muttered the statement before moving on down the hall like he hadn't just delivered a jab straight to the heart of the entire matter.

Beau respected the hell out of his brothers and his father. Perhaps because they all had chosen one path and been happy with their lives. Beau had thought he'd been happy and on the right path, until he became a father and his ex had decided drugs and wild parties and a future as a star were much more important.

"Show me what else you've done with the house," Beau said, shoving his cell back in his pocket.

"Don't you need to call someone?"

"This is more important."

Hayes offered a half grin, which was saying something for his quiet, reserved brother. "There's hope for you yet. But we're still going to circle back to Scarlett."

Of course they were, because why not? He'd left the house to dodge her for a bit, but now he was forced to discuss her. There was no end in sight with that woman.

Well, in less than three weeks there would be an end.

But he had a feeling she'd haunt his thoughts for some time.

Six

Scarlett handed Madelyn another fruit puff while she sat in her high chair. She wasn't surprised Beau wasn't here when she'd gotten home from the store.

Home. No. Pebblebrook wasn't her home by any means.

Yet she'd gone a tad overboard purchasing Christmas items to decorate the place. But she couldn't pass them by. She only hoped Beau didn't mind.

She busied herself putting together one of her favorite dishes. She'd come here in such a hurry and at the last minute, she had no clue if Beau had food allergies or what he liked.

Madelyn smacked her hands against the high chair tray and made little noises then squeals. Her little feet kicked and Scarlett smiled.

As much as being with a baby hurt her heart, Scarlett couldn't deny it was something she'd missed. Madelyn was such a sweetheart and so easy to care for. The few times she'd fussed with her swollen gums had passed quickly, thanks to cold teething rings.

Once the casserole was assembled and put into the oven, Scarlett unfastened Madelyn from the high chair. Madelyn let out high-pitched happy squeals and Scarlett's heart completely melted. Babies had their own language, no doubt about it.

"You need a bath," Scarlett crooned. "Yes, you do. You have sticky fingers and crazy hair."

The click of the front door had Scarlett shifting her focus from the baby to the sexy man who filled the doorway. The second he stepped inside, his dark eyes met hers. Even from across this space, she felt that intense stare all through her body. Those eyes were just as potent as his touch.

For a moment, Beau didn't move and she wondered what he was thinking. She really wished he'd say something to ease the invisible charge that crackled between them.

Scarlett finally broke eye contact, needing to get beyond this sexual tension because suddenly she was getting the idea that it wasn't one-sided anymore. And that could be trouble.

Big trouble.

"I just put dinner in the oven," she stated as she held on to Madelyn and circled the island. "I'm about to give Madelyn a bath."

The front door closed, then the lock clicked into place. Beau slid his black hat off his head and hung it on a peg by the door. Finally, his gaze shifted from her and roamed around the open cabin.

"What's all that?" he asked, nodding toward the sacks lining the sofa and dotting the area rug.

Madelyn reached for Scarlett's hair and tugged. "Just some Christmas decorations," she said, pulling her hair from the baby's sticky grasp.

Beau propped his hands on his hips and shook his head. "Give her to me. I'll give her a bath."

"Are you sure? I don't mind at all."

Beau stepped toward her, that long stride closing the distance between them pretty quickly. "I'll do it."

He slid Madelyn from Scarlett's arms and once he had his daughter, he lifted her in the air and a complete transformation came over him. He smiled, he made silly noises and had the craziest baby-talk voice she'd ever heard.

Well, Maggie had been right on this. Beau was completely different with Madelyn. He may be dealing with his own personal battles, but he wasn't letting that get in the way of his relationship with his baby.

When he went into his room and closed the door, Scarlett figured she might as well tidy up the kitchen. She'd put groceries away, then fed Madelyn when he brought her out, and laid her down for a nap. With time on her hands, she knew she should continue the house hunt. Each day that passed took her closer to her move and it was looking more and more like she'd be in a hotel for longer than she'd anticipated.

But she pushed those worries aside for now, eschewing the laptop for the bags of decorations. She got to work taking the holiday items out of the sacks and figuring where to put them. Considering she was watching every penny, she hadn't bought too much, but now that she was looking at everything in this small space, maybe it was a good thing she'd limited her impromptu spree. But there had been sales and, well, she was a savvy woman who couldn't turn down a bargain—or those little rustic cowboy boot ornaments.

Live garland nestled perfectly on the thick wood mantel. Once the two plaid stockings were in place, Scarlett stood back and smiled. This was already starting to look like home. Not for her, but for the little family in the other room.

She tried to take into consideration Beau's tastes, though she didn't know him well. At least she'd kept the decor more toward the masculine side. Though it had been difficult to leave behind the clearance garland with kissing reindeer and red sparkly snowflakes.

For reasons she couldn't explain, there wasn't a tacky Christmas decoration she didn't love.

Before Scarlett could go through the other bags, the oven timer went off.

She'd just set the steaming casserole dish on the stovetop when Beau stepped from his bedroom. He had Madelyn in a red sleeper with little reindeer heads on the feet. The baby looked so cute, but it was the man who drew her eyes like a magnet. Beau looked so sexy, his chest bare and his jeans indecently low on his narrow hips.

She licked her lips, then realized that wasn't the smartest move when his eyes dropped to her mouth. There went that tug on the invisible string pulling them together.

Why did he have to put those tattoos on display? The image of wild horses obviously paid homage to his roots, but she couldn't help it they also encompassed his true spirit of wanting to be wild and free…or maybe he used to be.

Either way, the ink was a distraction she didn't need, yet she desperately wanted to explore. Along with the lean muscles and six-pack abs.

Scarlett cleared her throat. "Dinner is ready."

Beau moved closer, his eyes locked on hers as if he could read her thoughts. "Is that why you're staring at my chest?"

Scarlett blinked and snapped her eyes to meet his. "I was not."

"You're a liar, but I won't report that to your employer." As he handed Madelyn over, he leaned in close and inhaled right by her neck. "Dinner smells good."

That low, gravelly tone sent shivers throughout her body and she nearly gave in to the temptation to close the two-inch gap and touch that gorgeous chest that beckoned her. But before she could move, he turned away and went back into his bedroom. Scarlett just stood there, stock still, wondering what the hell had just happened. What was he doing and why had she almost let herself get caught up in it? Damn it. That behavior was not at all professional.

Done berating herself, she took Madelyn to the portable swing in the living area and fastened her in. Once the music and swing were on, Scarlett went back to the kitchen and started dishing up the casserole. There was no way she was knocking on Beau's door to see if he was coming out to eat. She'd simply make a plate and he could eat when he wanted.

Scarlett had just poured two glasses of sweet tea when Beau stepped from his room. With his wet hair glistening even darker than she'd seen and a fresh T-shirt stretched across his broad shoulders, it was all she could do to force her eyes away.

He eyed the two plates sitting on the island, then he glanced to her. "You don't have to cook for me."

"You're welcome." The snarky reply just came out, so she added, "I had to cook for myself anyway. Hope you like cabbage."

He didn't say a word, but came over and sank onto one of the stools on the bar side of the island. As he dug in, she watched for a moment and figured he must not hate it. Part of her was relieved, though she didn't know why. What did it matter if he liked her cooking? She wasn't here to impress him with her homey skills.

Scarlett remained on the kitchen side of the island and started eating. The cabbage, bacon and rice casserole was one of her favorites. It was simple, filling, and rather healthy.

"You can have a seat," he told her without looking up from his plate. "I only bite upon request."

Why did she have to shiver at that? Just the idea of his mouth on her heated skin was enough to have her keeping this island between them. She may only "know" Beau from what she'd read online over the years, but she knew enough to realize he was a ladies' man and an endless flirt. And she was just another female in what she was sure was a long line of forgettable ladies.

So the fact that she lit up on the inside and had those giddy nerves dancing in her belly was absolutely ridiculous. She was leaving soon and he'd go on to more women and probably more children.

"I'm fine," she told him. "I'm used to eating standing up anyway."

That wasn't a lie. In fact, when she'd worked in other homes with small children, she'd been happy simply to get her meal hot. Besides, there was no way she'd get close to him. It wasn't so much him she was afraid of but her growing attraction, and she worried if she didn't keep some distance…

Well, she'd keep her distance so they didn't find out.

"I can keep an eye on Madelyn this way," she went on.

Beau glanced over his shoulder to where his daughter continued to swing. Then he jerked around, his fork clattering to the plate.

"What the hell is all that?" he barked.

Scarlett nearly choked on her bite. She took a drink of her sweet tea and cleared her throat. "Christmas decorations. I told you earlier."

His dark eyes shifted straight to her. "I know what you said earlier, but I didn't realize you were taking over the entire cabin. I thought you were putting stuff in your room. Why the hell is it all over my living room?"

"Because it's Christmas."

Why did he keep asking the most ridiculous questions?

"I didn't ask you to do that," he grumbled.

"Well, you didn't ask me to cook for you, either, but you're clearly enjoying it."

He muttered something else before going back to his plate, but she couldn't make it out. And she didn't ask him to repeat it. Instead, they finished eating in awkward silence. Only the sound of the nursery rhyme chiming from the swing broke through the space.

"There's no reason to get cozy here."

His words sliced right through her and she pulled in a deep breath before addressing him.

Scarlett propped her hands on her hips. "Are you talking to me or yourself?"

His dark eyes darted to hers once more. "Both."

"Well, I don't know what's going on in your personal life, but this is Madelyn's first Christmas. She deserves to have a festive place, whether it's temporary or not."

Madelyn started to fuss and Scarlett ignored her plate and went to the baby.

"Eat," Beau stated as he came to stand beside her. "I can give her a bottle and get her ready for bed."

Scarlett unfastened Madelyn and turned off the swing. "I've got her. You worked all day, so finish your dinner."

She didn't wait for his reply or give him an opportunity to argue. She started to make a bottle, but Beau beat her to it.

"Lay her in my room." He kissed Madelyn's head and glanced up to Scarlett. "I'll keep her tonight."

He stood so close, too close. His arm brushed hers, those eyes held her in place. She'd thought they were dark brown, but now she could see almost golden flecks. They were nearly hypnotic, pulling her in as if in a trance she couldn't resist.

But you have to.

The silent warning broke the spell and she cleared her throat.

"You're paying me to watch her," Scarlett told him, pleased when her voice sounded strong. "If you're going to the stables early, then you need your rest."

She should take a step back, but she didn't want to. He smelled too good and looked even better.

"I also said I'm a hands-on dad." He handed over the bottle. "So leave her in my room after she eats."

Scarlett wasn't going to argue with him. She worked for him and this was his child. If he wanted to be woken up during the night, that was his call.

She clutched the bottle in one hand and held the baby in the other as she headed toward his room, leaving him in the kitchen to finish his dinner. The second she stepped into his bedroom, a full-on assault hit her senses. If she thought he smelled good a moment ago, that was nothing compared to the masculine, fresh-from-the-shower scent that filled his space.

The sheets were rumpled and she found herself transfixed by the sight. Just the thought of Beau Elliott in a tangle of dark navy sheets would fuel her nighttime fantasies for years. He was a beautiful man, all sculpted and tan, with just a little roughness about him.

Was it any wonder Hollywood had pulled him into its grasp and cast him in that first film set in the Wild West? He'd been perfect. Captivating and sexy, riding shirtless on his horse. A handsome cowboy straight from a Texas ranch. He didn't just play the part; he was the part.

Scarlett hated to admit how many times she'd watched that exact movie.

She closed her eyes and willed herself to stop the madness of these mind games. Hadn't she vowed not to focus on the man and remain dedicated to the child?

She fed Madelyn and soothed her until she was ready to be laid down. Once she had the baby in her crib, Scarlett turned to leave, but once again her eyes went to that messy king-size bed.

How many days did she have left?

Scarlett closed her eyes and pulled in a deep breath.

She would get through this and keep her lustful desires out of the picture.

She tiptoed from the room and gently shut the door behind her. When she came back into the open area, she noted the kitchen had been cleaned up and the dishes were all washed.

She was stunned. Not only at the idea of a celebrity getting dishpan hands, but a billionaire who had employees who likely did everything from his laundry to making his reservations with arm candy dates.

Scarlett nearly laughed at herself. She wasn't going to date Beau; she wasn't even going to be friends with the man. This relationship, if it could be called such, was strictly professional.

She turned from the kitchen and spotted Beau standing in front of the fireplace. With his back to her, Scarlett had a chance to study him…as if she needed another opportunity or reason to ogle. But that shirt stretched so tightly across his shoulders and that denim hugged his backside in all the perfect places.

"I used to want this."

His low words cut through her thoughts and she realized she'd been caught once again staring. He'd known she was back here.

Scarlett took a few cautious steps forward and waited for him to continue. Clearly he was working through some thoughts.

"Christmas as a kid was always a big deal," he went on as he continued to stare at the stockings. "My mom would bake and I remember coming in from the barns and smelling bread or cookies. There was always something in the oven or on the counter."

She continued to listen without interrupting. Whatever he was working through right now had nothing to do with her. But the fact she was getting a glimpse into his personal life only intrigued her more. Scarlett had a feeling not many people saw this side of Beau.

"Mom would pretend that she didn't see Colt and me sneak out a dozen cookies before dinner." He let out a low rumble of laughter. "That poor woman had a time raising four boys and being a loving wife to my dad. She never worried about anything and was so relaxed. I guess she had to be, considering she was in a house full of men."

Beau paused for a moment before he went on. "Christmas was her time to shine. She had every inch of that house covered in garland and lights. I always knew when I married and settled down I wanted my house to be all decked out. I wanted my kids to feel like I did."

Scarlett's heart did a flip and she realized she'd closed the distance and stood so close, close enough to reach out and touch him. She fisted her hands at her sides.

Beau turned to face her. The torment on his face was something she hadn't seen yet. The man standing before her wasn't an actor. Wasn't a billionaire playboy. The man before her was just a guy who felt pain and loss like anyone else.

"I appreciate what you did here for Madelyn," he told her.

Scarlett smiled. "I did it for both of you."

His lips thinned and he glanced down as if to compose himself. "You didn't have to," he said, his gaze coming back up to hers.

"I wanted to."

Before she thought twice, Scarlett reached out, her

hand cupping his cheek. She meant to console, to offer support, but his eyes went from sad to hungry in a second.

Scarlett started to pull away, but he covered her hand with his and stepped into her. Her breath caught in her throat at the brush of his torso on hers.

If she thought his stare had been intense before, it was nothing compared to what she saw now. Raw lust and pure desire.

"Beau."

He dipped his head and she knew exactly what was coming. She also knew she should move away and stop this before they crossed a line neither of them could come back from.

But she couldn't ignore the way her body tingled at his touch, at the passion in his eyes. She desperately wanted him to put that tempting mouth on hers. She didn't care if she was just another woman to him. She wasn't a virgin and she knew exactly what this was and what this wasn't.

It was just a kiss, right?

Beau feathered his lips over hers. The instant jolt of ache and need shot through every part of her body. But then he covered her mouth, coaxing her lips apart as he teased her with his tongue.

He brought their joined hands between their bodies and the back of his hand brushed her breast.

She'd been wrong. So, so wrong.

This was so much more than a kiss.

Seven

Beau had lost his damn mind, yet there was no way he could release Scarlett now. He'd wanted to taste her since she showed up at his doorstep looking like some exotic fantasy come to life.

Alarm bells went off in his head—the ones that usually went off when he was about to make a mistake. He ignored them.

Scarlett's curvy body leaned in, her nipple pebbled against the back of his hand. The way she groaned and melted into him had Beau ready to rip off this barrier of clothing and take exactly what they both wanted.

Beau took his free hand and settled it on the dip in her waist, curling his fingers and pulling her in tighter. She reached up and gripped his biceps as she angled her head just enough to take more of the kiss.

Kiss. What a simple word for a full-body experience.

Beau eased his fingertips beneath the hem of her shirt and nearly groaned when he came in contact with silky skin.

Scarlett tore her lips away and stepped back. Coolness instantly replaced the heat where her body had been. Beau had to force himself to remain still and not reach for her.

She covered her lips with her shaky hand and closed her eyes. "We can't do that."

"We just did." Like hell he'd let her regret this. They were adults with basic needs. "Did you not want me to kiss you?"

She pulled in a breath and squared her shoulders before she pinned him with that stunning stare. "I wanted it. No use in pretending I didn't, considering I nearly climbed up your body."

Beau couldn't help the twitch of a smile. "Then what's the problem?"

"The problem is that I'm your nanny," she volleyed back. "The problem is I won't be another woman in your long line of panty-droppers."

Panty-droppers? Beau laughed. Full from the belly laughter. Well, at least now he knew exactly what she thought.

Scarlett narrowed her dark eyes. "I don't see what's so funny."

"You can't believe the tabloids," he told her. Because he really wanted her to understand, he explained further. "I know everyone thinks I'm a major player, but that perception is fueled by the tabloids. They like to come to their own conclusions and then print assumptions. Just because a woman was on my arm or in my car doesn't mean she was in my bed."

"I won't be in your bed, either."

That smart mouth of hers kept him smiling. "Well, no, because Madelyn is in there. We should use your bed."

Scarlett let out an unladylike growl and turned away. "We are not discussing this."

"What? Sex? Why not?"

Beau started after her, but stopped when she spun back around. "Other than the obvious reason of me being your daughter's nanny, and I really hate clichés, I'll repeat that I won't be another girl in your bed."

Now she was just pissing him off. "You're really hung up on who's in my bed."

"Or maybe I'm just reminding myself not to get caught up in your charm." She propped her hands on her hips and tipped her head. "I realize I may be a challenge and you're not used to people saying no, but we kissed, it's over. Can we move on?"

She had to be kidding. That heat wasn't just one-sided. She'd damn well melted against him. She claimed to always be honest, but she wasn't just lying to him, she was lying to herself.

"Move on?" he asked. "Not likely."

Her dark eyes flared wide. The pulse at the base of her throat continued to beat faster than normal.

Yeah, that's right. He wasn't one to hide the truth, either. There was no way he could just move on now that he'd tasted her and felt that lithe body against his.

"I have no interest in a fling or to be bullied by someone just because they have money and power," she sneered. "I'm going to bed. I'll keep the monitor on in case you need me."

Money and power? What the hell did that have to do

with anything? Clearly she had other issues that went well beyond him, this moment and her attraction.

The second Scarlett turned from him, Beau closed the gap between them and curled his arm around her waist, pulling her side against his chest.

"I never make a woman do anything," he corrected. Above all, she had to know he wasn't like that. "We were both very involved in that kiss. If I thought for a second you weren't attracted to me, I never would've touched you, Scarlett."

She shivered beneath him when he murmured her name in her ear. His thumb eased beneath the hem of her shirt and slid over that dip in her waist.

"Tell me who hurt you," he demanded, his tone firm, yet low.

He didn't like the idea of any woman being hurt by a man, but something about Scarlett made him want to protect her, to prevent any more pain in her life.

Scarlett stiffened and turned those dark eyes up to his. There was a weakness looking back at him that he recognized. He'd seen that underlying emotion every single day in the mirror for the past year. Whatever she was battling, she was desperately trying to hide it. Damn it, he knew how difficult it was to keep everything bottled up with no one to talk to, to lean on.

Circumstances as of late had led him to that exact vulnerable point in his life.

Beau hadn't expected a layer of admiration to join the physical attraction, but slowly his take on Scarlett was evolving into something he couldn't quite figure out.

"I won't be here long enough for my personal life to matter to you," she whispered.

"So I can't care about your feelings while you're here?"

Her eyes darted away, looking in the direction of the fireplace. Maybe the holidays were difficult for her, as well. Did she have family? She hadn't mentioned being with them or buying presents or anything that came with sharing Christmas with someone special.

Everything in him screamed that he was walking a fine line with her. He had a sinking feeling she was alone or she'd lost someone. Whatever the reason, the holiday was difficult on her.

Something twitched in his chest, but Beau refused to believe his heart was getting involved here. There was nothing wrong with caring or worrying about someone, even if that person was a virtual stranger. He'd been raised to be compassionate, that's all. Just because he was concerned didn't mean he wanted a relationship.

He stroked his thumb along her bare skin again, reminding himself anything between them should and would stay physical.

Finally, her eyes darted back to his. "I don't think this is a good idea."

The goose bumps beneath his touch told a different story. He feathered another swipe across her waist.

"What part isn't a good idea?"

"The kiss, the touches." She shook her head and stepped away from him. "I'm going to my room. I still need to find housing before my move so I'm not stuck in a hotel forever...and I need some space from you."

"I'll give you space," he vowed. "That still won't make the ache go away. You know ignoring this will only make the pull even stronger."

She took another step away, as if she could escape what was happening here.

"Then we both better hope we can control ourselves until my time here is up."

Well, so far she'd managed to find eight places to rent, all over her budget, she'd done some yoga trying to calm her nerves, and she was now browsing through social media but not really focusing on the posts.

And it was one in the morning.

Scarlett kept telling herself to go to sleep because the baby would need her undivided attention tomorrow and she may even wake during the night.

Honestly, though, there was just no way she could crawl between the sheets when her body was still so revved up. She didn't even have to concentrate to feel his warm breath tickling the sensitive spot just below her ear or the way he kept that firm yet gentle touch just beneath the hem of her shirt. He tempted, teased…left her aching for more of the forbidden.

How dare Beau put her in this position?

Granted, she hadn't exactly resisted that toe-curling kiss. She'd thoroughly enjoyed Beau. She knew he would never force himself on her. No, he'd kissed her because she hadn't been able to hide her desire and that made her just as easy as all the other women he'd charmed. Damn it, she'd told herself to hold it together. It was only three weeks, for pity's sake.

The last thing she needed was a temporary, heated fling with her movie star boss. Other than the obvious working relationship that should keep them apart, she valued herself as more than someone forgettable—because she knew once she was gone, Beau wouldn't remember her.

Scarlett's heart clenched. Her family had forgotten her, as well. When she didn't bow to their wishes or aim to fulfill any political aspirations to round out the powerhouse family, they'd dismissed her as easily as a disloyal employee.

She slid off her bed and stretched until her back popped. She'd like to grab a bottle of water, but if he was out in the living room, then she really should stay put. She hadn't heard him on the monitor, so either he was incredibly stealthy or he hadn't gone to bed yet.

Scarlett eased over to her closed door and slowly turned the knob to peek out. There was a soft glow from the Christmas lights she'd strung on the mantel, but other than that, nothing. She didn't see him anywhere.

Tiptoeing barefoot, she crossed the living area and went into the kitchen. She tried her best to keep quiet as she opened the fridge and pulled out a bottle of water. When she turned, she spotted the bags of Christmas decor she hadn't done anything with yet.

She wasn't sure if she should mention a tree to Beau or just have one appear. Even if it was a small one, everyone needed a little Christmas cheer. She'd seen a tree farm in town earlier and had heard good things about the family-owned business. Maybe she'd check it out tomorrow just to see if they had something that would work in this small space.

Growing up she'd never been allowed to decorate. Her stepfather always had that professionally done. After all, what would their guests say when they showed up for parties and the tree had been thrown together with love by the children who lived there?

Not that Scarlett got along with his kids. They were just as stuffy and uptight as he was. The one time Scarlett tried to have a little fun and slide down the banister from the second floor to the entryway, her step-siblings were all too eager to tattle.

Scarlett crossed the small area and sank down onto the rug. Glancing from one shopping bag to the next, she resisted the urge to look inside. The rattling of bags would definitely make too much noise—besides, she knew exactly what she had left. Little nutcracker ornaments, a few horses, some stars. Nothing really went together, but she'd loved each item she'd seen so she'd dumped them into her cart.

Scarlett uncapped her water and took a sip.

"Can't sleep?"

She nearly choked on her drink, but managed to swallow before setting her bottle on the coffee table beside her.

Beau's footsteps brushed over the hardwood floors as he drew closer. Scarlett didn't turn. She was afraid he'd be in something like boxer briefs and all on display. Not that she was much better. She had on her shorts and a tank, sans bra and panties because that was just how she slept. At least she'd thrown on her short robe, so she was covered. Still, her body tingled all over again at the awareness of him.

She didn't answer him. The fact that she sat on the floor of the living room at one in the morning was proof enough that she couldn't sleep.

When Beau eased down beside her, Scarlett held her breath. Were they going back for round two? Because she wasn't so sure she could keep resisting him if he didn't back off a little.

Or perhaps that was his plan. To keep wearing her down until he could seduce her. Honestly, it wouldn't take much. One more tingling touch and she feared she'd strip off her own clothes and start begging for more.

There really was only so much a woman could handle.

"I still won't apologize for that kiss."

And here they went. Back at it again.

"But I also won't make this more difficult for you," he quickly added. "I need you and Madelyn needs you."

She exhaled that breath she'd been holding. That was what she'd wanted him to say, yet now that she knew he was easing off, she almost felt cheated.

Good grief. Could she be any more passive-aggressive? She just… Well, she just wanted him, but that wasn't the issue. The issue was, she *shouldn't* want him.

"I'm not sorry we kissed," she admitted. Might as well go for honesty at this point. "But I need this job, so we have to keep this professional."

Now she did risk turning to look at him. He had on running shorts, not boxers, thank God. But then she raised her eyes and saw that he wore shorts and nothing else.

Why could men get away with wearing so little? It simply wasn't fair. It sure as hell wasn't fair, either, that he looked so perfectly…well, perfect.

"You have somewhere to put all of this?" he asked, nodding toward the bags.

Scarlett nodded, pulling her attention from that bare chest to the sacks. "On the tree."

"I don't have a tree."

"I plan on fixing that very soon."

When he continued to stare at her, she didn't look

away. Scarlett stretched her legs out in front of her and rested her hands behind her, daring him to say something negative about Christmas or decorations.

"I assume you saw the Christmas tree farm down the road?" he asked.

Scarlett nodded. "I believe Madelyn and I will go back into town tomorrow and check it out. I'll just get something small to put in front of the patio doors."

"Were you going to ask?"

"Like you asked about kissing me?"

Damn it. She hadn't meant to let that slip, but the snark just came out naturally. The last thing she could afford was for him to know she was thinking of him, of that damn kiss that still had her so restless and heated.

"Forget I said that." She shook her head and looked down at her lap. "I'm—"

"Right," he finished. "I didn't ask. That's because when I see what I want, I just take it. Especially since I saw passion staring back at me."

He didn't need to say he wanted her—she'd gotten that quite clearly. Most likely she appealed to him because she hadn't thrown herself at him or because she was the only woman around, other than his brothers' women.

Beau slid his finger beneath her chin and forced her to look at him. Oh, that simple touch shouldn't affect her so, but it did. She was human, after all.

"What makes you so different?" he muttered beneath his breath, but she heard him.

Scarlett shifted fully to face him. "What?"

Beau shook his head, almost as if he'd been talking to himself. That fingertip beneath her chin slid along her jawline, gentle, featherlight, but she felt the touch in every part of her body. The stillness of the night, the soft glow of the twinkling lights just above Beau's head had her getting wrapped up in this moment. She told herself she'd move away in a second. Really, she would.

Beau didn't utter a word, but his eyes captivated her, held her right in this spot. He feathered his fingertips down the column of her neck and lower to the V of her robe. She pulled in a deep breath and tried not to stare at those tattoos on his chest that slid up and disappeared over his shoulder. If she looked at his body, then she'd want to touch his body.

Scarlett clenched her fists in her lap. The robe parted slightly, and her nipples puckered in anticipation.

"Beau," she whispered.

His eyes dropped to where his hand traveled and explored, then he glanced back up to her. "I want you to feel."

The raw statement packed a punch and Scarlett wasn't sure what he wanted to happen, but she definitely felt. Just that soft touch had her body tingling and burning up.

He dropped that same hand to the top of her bare thigh and she stilled. Those dark eyes remained locked on hers as he slid his palm up her leg and beneath the hem of her robe.

Scarlett's breath caught in her throat as she glanced down to watch his hand disappear. Beau leaned in closer, his lips grazed her jaw.

"You promised no more kissing," she whispered.

"I'm not kissing you." His warm breath across her skin wasn't helping. "Relax."

Relax? He had to be kidding. Her body was so revved up, there was no relaxing. She trembled and ached and it took every bit of her willpower not to strip her clothes off, lie down on this rug and beg him for every single thing she'd been denying them both.

His fingertips slid beneath her loose sleep shorts. If he was shocked at her lack of panties, he didn't say so and his fingers didn't even hesitate as they continued their journey to the spot where she ached most.

She shifted, easing her legs apart to grant him access…all while alarms sounded and red flags waved trying in vain to get her attention. All that mattered right now was his touch. Who they were didn't matter. They were beyond that worry and clearly didn't give a damn.

There was only so long a woman could hold out and Beau wasn't an easy man to ignore. Damn it, she'd tried.

Scarlett spread her legs wider, then before she knew it, she was lying back on that rug with Beau propped on his elbow beside her. He slid one finger over her before sliding into her. She shut her eyes and tipped her hips to get more. Did he have to move so agonizingly slow? Didn't he realize she was burning up with need?

"Look at me," he demanded.

He slid another finger into her and Scarlett opened her eyes and caught his intense gaze. The pale glow from the Christmas lights illuminated his face. This wasn't the movie star or the rancher beside her. Right at this moment, Beau Elliott was just a man with basic needs, a man who looked like he wanted to tear off her clothes, a man who was currently priming her body for release.

"Don't hold back." It was half whisper, half command.

Considering she'd had no control over her body up

until this point, let alone this moment, holding back wasn't an option.

The way he continued to watch her as he stroked her was both arousing and intimidating. What did he see when he looked at her? Was he expecting more? Would they carry this back into her room?

Scarlett's thoughts vanished as her body spiraled into release. She couldn't help but shut her eyes and arch further into his touch. He murmured something, perhaps another demand, but she couldn't make out the words.

Wave after wave rushed over her and Scarlett reached up to clutch his thick biceps. He stayed with her until the tremors ceased, and even then, he continued to stroke her with the softest touch.

How could she still be aroused when she'd just been pleasured?

After a moment, Beau eased his hand away and smoothed her shorts and robe back into place. Scarlett risked opening her eyes and found him still staring down at her.

"You're one sexy woman," he told her in that low, sultry tone that seemed to match the mood and the dark of night.

Scarlett reached for the waistband of his shorts, but he covered her hand with his. "No. Go on to bed."

Confused, she drew back and slowly sat up. "You're not—"

Beau shook his head. "I wanted to touch you. I *needed* to touch you. I'm not looking for anything in return."

What? He didn't want more? Did men like that truly exist? Never would she have guessed Beau to be so giving, so selfless.

Scarlett studied his face and realized he was completely serious.

"Why?" The question slipped through her lips before she could stop herself.

Beau answered her with a crooked grin that had her stomach doing flips. "It's not important. Go on, now. Madelyn will be ready to go early and I need you rested."

When she didn't move, Beau came to his feet and extended his hand. She slid her fingers into his palm and he helped her up, but didn't release her.

"I'll be busy all day," he told her. "I look forward to seeing that Christmas tree when you're done with it."

He let her go, but only to reach up and smooth her hair behind her ears. His eyes held hers a moment before he turned and headed back to his room and silently closed the door.

Scarlett remained in place, her body still humming, and more confused than ever.

Just who was Beau Elliott? Because he wasn't the demanding playboy she'd originally thought. He was kind and passionate, giving and self-sacrificing. There was so much to him that she never would've considered, but she wanted to explore further.

Which would only prove to be a problem in the long run. Because a man who was noble, passionate and sexy would be damn difficult to leave in a few weeks.

Eight

Colt eased back onto the patio sofa and wrapped his arm around Annabelle. Lucy and Emily were happily playing on the foam outdoor play yard he'd just put together. With the padded sides and colorful toys in the middle, the two seemed to be perfectly content.

"You're home earlier than usual," Annabelle stated, snuggling into his side. "Not that I'm complaining."

"I knew you would be in between cleaning the rooms and checking new guests in."

She rested her delicate hand on his thigh. Those gold bands on her finger glinted in the late-afternoon sunshine.

"We are actually free for the night," she replied. "The next several days are crazy, but I love it."

He knew she did. Annabelle's goal had always been to have her own B and B where she could cater to guests and showcase her amazing cooking skills.

Colt never could've imagined how much his life would change when this beauty came crashing onto his ranch...literally. She took out the fence in her haste to leave after their first meeting and he had been smitten since.

"You've not talked much about Beau."

Her statement brought him back to the moment and the obvious situation that needed to be discussed...even though he'd rather not.

"What do you want me to say?"

Lucy patted the bright yellow balls dangling on an arch on one side of the play yard. Annabelle shifted in her seat and eased up to look him directly in the eye.

He knew that look...the one of a determined woman.

"I can't imagine how difficult this is for you," she started, then patted his leg. "But think about Beau. Can you imagine how worried he was coming back, not knowing if he'd be accepted or not and having a baby?"

Colt doubted Beau had ever been worried or afraid in his life. He'd likely come home because... Hell, Colt had no idea the real reason. He hadn't actually asked.

"I can see your mind working."

Colt covered Annabelle's hand with his and gave her a slight squeeze. Lucy let out a shriek, but he glanced to see that she was laughing and nothing was actually wrong.

"This is tough," he admitted, hating the vulnerability, but he was always honest with his wife. "Having him back is all I'd ever wanted for so long. I guess that's why I'm so angry now."

"Then maybe you should talk to him about your feelings."

Colt wanted to. He played various forms of the conversation over and over in his mind, but each time he approached Beau, something snapped and the hurt that had been building inside Colt seemed to snap.

"Do you trust me?"

Colt eased forward and kissed Annabelle's forehead. "With everything."

"Then let me take care of this," she told him with that grin of hers that should scare the hell out of him. She was plotting.

Colt wasn't so far gone in his hurt that he wouldn't accept help and he trusted his wife more than anyone.

"I love you," he told her, then glanced to their twin girls. "And this life we've made."

Annabelle settled back against his side and laid her head on his shoulder.

"Let's see if we can make it just a bit better," she murmured.

If anyone could help repair the relationship between him and Beau, he knew it was Annabelle.

Maybe there was hope, because all he'd ever wanted was a close family. That was the ultimate way to honor their father.

Beau glanced over the blueprints of the dude ranch. The cabins, one of which he was using, were in perfect proportion to the river, the creek, the stables. His brothers couldn't have chosen a better spot for the guests to stay.

The mini-prints hung in raw wood frames on the wall of the office in the main stable closest to Colt's house. Beau's eyes traveled from one print to the next. The four original surveys of the land from when their grandfather purchased the ranch were drawn out in quarters.

So much was the same, yet so different since he was home last.

A lump of guilt formed in Beau's throat. His brothers had designed this and started construction while he'd been in LA living his own life and dealing with Jennifer and her pregnancy. His father's main goal for his life was to see a dude ranch one day on the Elliott Estate. Now the dream was coming to fruition, but Grant couldn't even enjoy it because he was a prisoner in his own mind. Even if Beau or his brothers managed to bring their father here to see the progress, he'd likely never realize thc sight before him, or the impact he had on his boys.

"I was hoping to find you here."

Beau glanced over his shoulder at the female voice. Annabelle, Colt's wife, stood in the doorway with a sweet smile on her face. Her long, red hair fell over both shoulders and she had a little girl on her hip.

"Which one is this?" he asked, smiling toward the toddler.

"This is Emily. Lucy is back at the house for a nap because she didn't sleep well last night."

Emily reached for him and Beau glanced to Annabelle. "May I?"

"Of course."

Beau took the child in his arms, surprised how much different she felt than his own. Granted, there was nearly a year between the two.

"I imagine having twins is quite a chore," he stated. "Do you ever get sleep?"

Annabelle laughed. "Not at first, but they're pretty good now. Lucy is getting another tooth, so she was a bit fussy during the night."

Apparently teeth were a huge deal in disrupting kids' sleep habits.

Emily smacked her hands against his cheeks and giggled. Such a sweet sound. "What brings you to the stables?" he asked Annabelle. "If you're looking for Colt, I haven't seen him today."

Likely because his brother was dodging him, but Beau wouldn't let that deter him. He was here to try to repair relationships and he couldn't give up.

"I'm actually looking for you," Annabelle stated. "I'd like you to come to dinner this evening. Well, you, Madelyn and Scarlett."

Beau stilled. Dinner with his disgruntled twin brother? Dinner with his baby and his nanny? Why the hell would he want to torture himself?

When he and Colt got a chance to speak about their past, Beau sure as hell didn't want an audience.

There was so much wrong with this dinner invitation. First of all, he wasn't quite ready to settle around a table with his brother and second, he couldn't bring Scarlett. Having her there would make things seem too familial and that would only give her the wrong impression.

Damn it. Beau could still feel her against him, still hear her soft pants and cries of passion. Last night had been a turning point, though what they'd turned to he had no idea. All he knew was they were far beyond nanny and boss—which was the reason she couldn't come to dinner.

"I can tell by your silence you're not thrilled." Annabelle smiled. "Let me rephrase. You will come to dinner and bring your daughter and your nanny."

"Why are you so determined to get me to dinner?" he asked.

Emily reached for her mother and Annabelle took the little girl back. "Because you and Colt need to keep working on this relationship. My husband is agitated and he's keeping his feelings bottled up. The more time you two can spend together, the better off you both will be."

He nodded, not necessarily in agreement, but in acknowledgment of what his sister-in-law had just said.

Beau tipped back his hat. "Why does Scarlett need to join us?"

Annabelle rolled her eyes. "Because it's rude to leave her at the cabin and I imagine she wants some female companionship."

Did she? He'd never asked. Granted, it was difficult to talk about her needs when he'd only been worried about his own—which basically involved touching her, tasting her.

Annabelle's intense stare held him in place and he wrangled in his errant thoughts and let out a deep sigh.

"Does Colt ever win an argument with you?"

A wide smile spread across her face. "Never. We'll see you all at six." Then she turned and headed out of the office.

Beau stared after her until he realized he was still staring at the open doorway. That was one strong-willed woman, which was exactly what Colt needed in his life.

The Elliott men were headstrong, always had been. A trait they'd all inherited, right along with their dark eyes and black hair. Beau figured there would never be a woman who matched him, but that was all right. He had Madelyn and she was more than enough.

He turned back to the blueprints on the opposite wall and continued to admire what would become of this property. Beau didn't know if his father would ever be able to come see this, but he couldn't help but wonder if he should take a copy of these blueprints to show him. Maybe seeing something that meant so much to him his entire life would trigger some memory.

Beau just wanted to do something, to make it possible for his dad to have some semblance of his past to hopefully trigger the present.

In all honesty, Beau wondered if his dad would even recognize him.

He did know one thing. He couldn't keep putting that visit off. He pulled his cell from his pocket and figured it was time to set up a time to see his father.

Scarlett adjusted the tree once again, but no matter how much she shifted and tilted it, the stubborn thing still leaned…and by leaned she meant appeared as if it was about to fall.

She let out the most unladylike growl, then startled when she heard chuckling behind her.

"Problem?"

Turning toward the doorway, Scarlett tried to keep her heart rate normal at the sight of Beau. First of all, she'd thought she was alone, save for Madelyn. Second, she hadn't seen him since he'd sent her to her room last night, though she'd thought of him all day.

Okay, she'd actually replayed their erotic encounter over and over, which was quite a leap ahead of just thinking of her hunky roommate. Had Beau thought about what happened? Did the intimacy mean anything to him at all or was this just one-sided?

"The damn tree is crooked," she grumbled.

Beau tilted his head to the side and narrowed his eyes. "Not if I stand like this."

She threw up her hands. "This doesn't happen in the movies. Everything looks perfect and everyone is happy. Christmas is magical and everyone has matching outfits and they go sleigh riding in some gorgeously decorated sled pulled by horses."

Beau laughed as he slid his hat off his head and hung it on the peg by the door. "That's quite a jump from worrying about a tree. Besides, everything is perfect in the movies because decorators are paid a hefty sum to make that happen. Real life isn't staged."

Scarlett turned to stare back at the tree. "It was the only one they had that would fit in this space. I thought I could make it work. Now what am I going to do?"

Beau's boots tapped across the hardwood, then silenced when he hit the rug…the very rug where she'd lain last night and on which she'd been pleasured by this man. She'd tried not to look at it today. Tried and failed.

"Decorate it."

She glanced over her shoulder at his simple, ridiculous answer, but he wasn't looking at her. He only had eyes for his little girl who sat in her swing, mesmerized by the spinning bumblebee above her head.

"How's she been today?"

"Pretty happy." Scarlett stepped around the bags of ornaments and lights she had yet to unpack. "I made some organic food for her so you have little containers in the fridge we can just grab whenever. It's better than buying jars."

Beau jerked his dark eyes to her. "You made her food?"

"I know you want to keep things simple and healthy for her." Now she felt silly with the way he seemed so stunned. "I mean, if you don't want to use it, that's fine, I just—"

"No."

He reached for her arm and Scarlett tried not to let the warmth from his touch thrust her into memories of the night before. But considering they were standing right where they'd made the memory, it was rather difficult not to think of every single detail.

"I'm glad you did that for her," he added, sliding his hand away. "I just didn't expect you to go above and beyond."

Scarlett smiled. "Taking care of children is my passion. There's nothing I wouldn't do for them."

Beau tipped his head. "Yet you're not going to be a nanny anymore when you leave here."

There was no use trying to fake a smile, so she let her face fall. In the short time she would be here, Scarlett really didn't want to spend their days rehashing her past year and the decisions that led to her leaving her most beloved job.

Scarlett stepped around him and turned the swing off. She unfastened Madelyn and lifted her up into her arms. When she spun around, Beau faced her and still wore that same worried, questioning gaze. Not what she wanted to see because he clearly was waiting on her to reply.

Also not what she wanted to see because she didn't want to think about him with those caring feelings. Things were much simpler when she assumed him to be the Playboy Prince of Hollywood.

"Let me get Madelyn settled into her high chair and

I'll start dinner." Maybe if she completely dodged the topic, then maybe he wouldn't bring it up again. "Do you like apricots? I found some at the farmer's market earlier and I want to try a new dessert."

Before she could turn toward the kitchen, Beau took a step and came to stand right before her.

"Actually, Annabelle is making dinner tonight," he told her. "She came to the stables earlier and invited me."

"Oh, well. No worries. I'll make everything tomorrow." She brushed her hand along the top of Madelyn's baby curls. "Should I put Madelyn to bed while you're gone or are you taking her?"

Beau cleared his throat and rocked back on his boot heels. "We're all going."

"Okay, then I'll just clean her up and—" Realization hit her. "Wait. We're all going. As in *all* of us?"

Beau nodded and Scarlett's heart started that double-time beat again.

Why on earth would she go to Colt and Annabelle's house? She wasn't part of this family and she wasn't going to be around long enough to form a friendship with anyone at Pebblebrook Ranch. She was trying to cut ties and move on, not create relationships.

"There's really no need," Scarlett stated, shaking her head. "I can make myself something here."

"Annabelle didn't exactly ask," he told her. "Besides, why wouldn't you want to come? The only person Colt will be grouchy with is me."

"It's not that."

Silence nestled between them. She couldn't pinpoint the exact reason she didn't want to go. There wasn't just one; there were countless.

"One meal. That's all this is."

Scarlett stared up at him as she held on to Madelyn. Beau's dark eyes showed nothing. No emotion, no insight into what he may be thinking, but his words were clear. Just dinner. Meaning there was no need to read any more into it.

Was that a blanket statement for what happened between them right here last night? Was he making sure she knew there was nothing else that could happen? Because she was pretty sure she'd already received that message. A message she needed to keep repeating to herself.

"We should discuss last night." As much as she didn't want to, she also didn't want this chunk of tension growing between them, either. "I don't know what you expect of me."

"Expect?" His dark brows drew together.

Why did he have to make this difficult? He had to know what she was talking about.

"Yes," she said through clenched teeth. "You don't think I believe you don't want...something in return."

Beau's eyes darkened as he took a half step closer, his chest brushing her arm that held his daughter. "Did I ask you for anything in return? Did I lay out ground rules?"

Scarlett shook her head and patted Madelyn when the baby let out a fuss. She swayed back and forth in a calming motion.

"Then I expect you to listen to your body," he went on in that low, whisky-smooth tone. "I expect you to take what you want and not deny the pleasure I know you crave. I expect you to come to me when you're ready for more, because we both know it will happen."

Scarlett licked her lips and attempted to keep her breathing steady. He painted an erotic, honest image. She did want him, but would she act on that need?

"You sent me away last night," she reminded him. "If you know what I want, then why did you do that?"

He reached up and slid a fingertip down Scarlett's cheek, over her jaw and around to just beneath her chin. He tipped her head up and leaned in so close his lips nearly met hers.

"Because I want you to ache just as much as I do," he murmured in a way that had her stomach tightening with need. "Because I knew if we had sex last night, you'd blame it on getting caught up in the moment. But now, when you come to me, you'll have had time to think about what you want. There will be no excuses, no regrets."

Her entire body shivered. "You're so sure I'll come to you. What if I don't?"

Beau's eyes locked onto hers and he smiled. "If you weren't holding my daughter right now, I'd have you begging for me in a matter of seconds. Don't try to lie to me or yourself. You will come to me."

"And if I don't?"

She fully expected him to say he'd eventually come to her, but Beau eased back and pulled Madelyn from her arms. He flashed that high-voltage smile and winked. That man had the audacity to wink and just walk away.

That arrogant bastard. He thought he could just turn her on, give her a satisfying sample, then rev her up all over again and she'd just…what? Jump into his bed and beg him to do all the naughty things she'd imagined?

Scarlett blew out a sigh. That's exactly what she

wanted to do and he knew it. So now what? They'd go to this family dinner and come back to the cabin, put Madelyn down and…

Yeah. It was the rest of that sentence that had nerves spiraling through her.

Beau Elliott was a potent man and she had a feeling she'd barely scratched the surface.

Nine

Beau was having a difficult time focusing on the dinner set before him. Between his brother's glare at the opposite end of the table, the noise from the three kids, and Scarlett sitting right across from him, Beau wondered how much longer he'd have to stay at Colt's.

He'd left Scarlett with something to think about back at the cabin, but he hadn't counted on getting himself worked up and on edge. That flare of desire in her eyes had given him pause for a moment, but he had to be smart. Wanting a woman wasn't a new experience, but wanting a woman so unattainable was.

The temporary factor of her presence didn't bother him. After all, he wasn't looking for anything long-term. He actually hadn't been looking for anything at all…but then she showed up on his doorstep.

What bothered him was how fragile she seemed beneath her steely surface. He should leave her alone. He should, but he couldn't.

Scarlett wasn't playing hard to get or playing any other games to get his attention. No, she was guarded and cautious—traits he needed to wrap his mind around before he got swept up into another round of lust.

"Scarlett, what are you going to be doing in Dallas?"

Annabelle's question broke into Beau's thoughts. He glanced across the table as Scarlett set her fork down on the edge of her plate.

"I'll be an assistant director of recreational activities at a senior center."

She delivered the answer with a smile, one that some may find convincing. Even if Beau hadn't been an actor, he knew Scarlett enough to know the gesture was fake.

"I'm sad to leave Stone River," she went on. "But Dallas holds many opportunities, which is what I'm looking for. I'm excited. More excited as my time to leave gets closer."

"What made you decide on Dallas? Do you have family there?"

Beau was surprised Colt chimed in with his questions. But considering Beau was curious about more of her life, he turned his focus to her as well, eager to hear her answers.

Her eyes darted across the table to him, that forced smile frozen in place. "I have no family. That's one of the reasons being a nanny was so great for me. But circumstances have changed my plans and I'm looking for a fresh start."

Colt leaned back in his seat and smiled. "Well, good for you. I wondered if my brother would convince you to stick with him."

Beau clenched his teeth. Was Colt seriously going to get into this now? Did every conversation have to turn into an argument or a jab?

"There's no convincing," Scarlett said with a slight laugh. "I've already committed to the new job. Housing has turned into a bit of a chore, though. I didn't realize how expensive city living was."

"Small towns do have perks." Annabelle came to her feet and went to one of the three high chairs they'd set up. She lifted one of her twins—he still couldn't tell the difference—and wiped the child's hands. "Miss Emily is messy and I need to clean her up and get her changed. I'll be right back."

Scarlett took a drink of her tea and then scooted her chair back. "I can start taking these dishes to the kitchen. Dinner was amazing."

"Sit down." Colt motioned to her. "Annabelle wanted to make a good impression so she made everything herself, but our cook will clean up."

Scarlett didn't sit, but she went to Madelyn who played in her high chair, patting the top of the tray, then swiping her hands in the water puddles she'd made by shaking her bottle.

"Let me get her," Beau said as he rose and circled the antique farm-style table to extract her from the high chair. "I haven't seen her much today and when we get back she'll need to go to bed."

Which would leave them alone again. Night after night he struggled. Last night had barely taken the edge off. No, that was a lie. Last night only made him want her even more. She'd come to him tonight, that much he was sure of.

"Never thought I'd see you back at the ranch," Colt stated. "Let alone with a child."

Beau patted Madelyn's back as she sucked on her little fist. "I knew I'd come back sometime, but I never had intentions of having children."

When Lucy started fussing, Colt immediately jumped to get her.

"You plan on settling down anytime soon?" he asked as he picked up his daughter. "Maybe have more kids?"

Beau wasn't sure what his next move was, let alone if there was a woman somewhere in his future. "I have no idea," he answered honestly. "Believe it or not, I did love growing up here and having a large family. I'm not opposed to having more kids one day. Being a parent changes you somehow."

Scarlett cleared her throat and turned away. "Excuse me."

She fled the room and Beau glanced over his shoulder to see her heading toward the front of the house. What was wrong with her? Was it something he'd said? Was she that uncomfortable being at this family dinner?

She didn't owe him any explanations, but that wouldn't stop him from finding out what he could do to make her stay here a little easier. The pain that she kept bottled up gnawed at his gut in a way he couldn't explain, because he'd never experienced such emotions before.

"She okay?" Colt asked.

Beau stared at the empty doorway another minute before turning to his twin and lying to his face. "She's fine. We can head on out if you'd rather. I know Annabelle probably forced your hand into this dinner."

Lucy plucked at one of the buttons on Colt's shirt.

"She didn't, actually. I wanted you here and she offered to cook."

Shocked, Beau shifted Madelyn in his arms and swayed slowly back and forth as she rubbed her eyes. "So she jumped at the chance when she saw an opening?"

Colt shrugged. "Something like that. Listen, I don't want—"

"Sorry about that." Scarlett whisked back into the room and Beau didn't miss the way her eyes were red-rimmed. "Let me take Madelyn back home and put her to bed. You two can talk and maybe Colt can bring you back to the cabin later."

"I'll come with you," he offered.

She eased a very tired baby from his arms and shook her head. "I'll be fine," Scarlett said, then turned to Colt. "Please tell Annabelle everything was wonderful."

"I will, though I'm sure she'll have you over again before you leave town," Colt assured her. "I'll make sure Beau has a ride back."

Scarlett nodded and then turned to go, catching Beau's eyes before she did so. Her sad smile and that mist in her eyes undid him. She took Madelyn and left, leaving Beau torn over whether he should stay or go.

"You're really just going to let her go?" Colt asked. "She's clearly upset."

Shoving his hands in his pockets, Beau weighed his options. "She wants to be alone. I can talk to her once I'm back and Madelyn is asleep. Besides, you and I need to talk, don't we?"

Staring at his brother had Colt really taking in the moment. He loved Beau—that was never in question.

He loved him in a completely different way than Hayes or Nolan. Not more, just different. Perhaps because of the special bond from twins; he wasn't sure.

Colt knew no matter how much anger and resentment tried to push them apart, their connection could never be completely severed.

"I'm surprised you don't have plans set in place to leave the ranch," Colt stated after a moment.

Or if Beau did, Colt didn't know. And he wanted to… no, he needed to know. He had to steel his heart if his brother was just going to hightail it out of town again and not be heard from for years.

"I came back for Madelyn," Beau replied.

"You came back for you," Colt tossed back, unable to stop himself. "You may have had a change of heart from whatever you were doing in LA, but you needed to be here because something or someone has made you face us again. You didn't come back because you actually wanted to."

Beau stared at him for a minute. Silence settled heavy between them and Colt waited for his brother to deny the accusation. He didn't.

"I've wanted you home for so long." Colt softened his tone. He didn't want to be a complete prick, but he also had to be honest. "When you left, I was upset, but I understood needing to do your own thing. But then you didn't come back and… I resented you. I felt betrayed."

Beau muttered a curse and glanced down to his still-shiny boots before looking back to Colt. "I wanted to see just how far I could get," he admitted. "I knew I was good at acting. So once I did that commercial, then my agent landed that first movie, things exploded. I admit I got wrapped up in my new lifestyle. But I never forgot where I came from. Not once. It just wasn't me anymore."

Colt gritted his teeth and forced the lump of emotions down. "And now? Is this ranch life still not you?"

Beau's lips thinned as he hooked his thumbs through his belt loops. "I want a simpler life for my daughter. I don't want her growing up around pretentious people and worrying if she fits in and all the hustle and bustle. Becoming a parent changed everything I thought about life."

On that, Colt could agree one hundred percent. "Being a father does change you."

But Beau still hadn't answered the question completely.

Before Colt could dig in deeper, Annabelle came back into the room without Emily. "Well, Little Miss was happy lying in her crib in her diaper, so I left her there chatting with her stuffed elephant."

His wife stopped her chatter as she came to stand next to Colt. "What's going on?" she asked as she slid Emily from Colt's arms.

"Just talking with my brother," Colt stated.

"I'm glad to hear it." She rocked Emily back and forth and patted her back. "Where is Scarlett?"

"She took Madelyn back to the cabin for bed," Beau told her. "She wanted me to tell you thanks for everything."

Annabelle shot a glance to her husband. "And did she leave because you guys were bickering or to give you space to actually talk?"

"She really was putting Madelyn to bed," Beau added. "I'm sure she wanted to give us space, too."

"And how has the talking gone?" Annabelle asked, her gaze darting between them. "I lost my sister in a car accident not long ago. We had our differences, we said things we thought we meant at the time, but I'd give anything to have her back. I just don't want you guys to have regrets."

Colt's heart clenched as Annabelle's eyes misted. When he stepped toward her, she eased back and shook her head. Such a strong woman, his Annabelle. He admired her strength and her determination to repair this relationship between brothers.

"You're getting another chance, so work on it," she added. "It's Christmas, guys. Just start a new chapter. Isn't that what your parents would've wanted?"

Beau stepped forward and wrapped an arm around her shoulders. "They would've," Beau agreed before releasing her.

Annabelle sniffed and swiped a hand beneath her eye.

"Babe, don't cry." Colt placed his hand on her shoulder and looked to his twin. "We're making progress. It's slow, but it's coming. Right, Beau?"

He nodded. "We're better than we were, but we're working on years of animosity, so it might take a bit."

Something settled deep within Colt—something akin to hope. For the first time in, well, years, Colt had a hope for the future with his brother.

Did Beau ultimately want that? Colt truly believed fatherhood had changed him, but they'd have to see because words were easy…it was the actions that were difficult to execute.

"I'll let you guys finish your chat," Annabelle said with a soft smile and left the room.

Colt nodded toward the hallway and Beau followed him to the living room. They truly had taken a giant leap in their relationship.

Once they were in the spacious room with a high-beamed ceiling and a stone fireplace that stretched up to those vaulted beams, Beau took a seat on the dark leather sofa.

They had a full, tall Christmas tree in this room, as well. He couldn't help but laugh. As beautiful as the perfectly decorated tree was, he suddenly found himself longing for the tiny cabin with the crooked, naked tree.

If he were honest with himself, he longed more for the woman in the cabin who was determined to give his daughter a nice first Christmas.

How could he not feel a pull toward Scarlett? Sexual, yes, but there was more. He couldn't put his finger on it…or maybe he didn't want to. Either way, Scarlett was more than Madelyn's nanny.

"Are you planning on leaving Hollywood?" Colt asked as he stood next to the fireplace.

Beau eyed the four stockings and shrugged. "No idea, honestly. I know I don't want that lifestyle for Madelyn. There's too much in my world there that could harm her. I couldn't even take her to a park without the paparazzi attacking us. I just want a normal life for her."

"You gave up the normal life when you chose to pursue acting," Colt sneered. "You had a life here, on the ranch."

Beau shook his head and rested his elbows on his knees. "I'm not rehashing the past or defending myself again. I'm moving on. I won't stay at Pebblebrook, though. There's clearly no room and I'm still not sure what my place is."

"What the hell does that mean?" Colt demanded.

"Your place is as an Elliott. You're still a rancher whether you want to be or not. It's in our roots."

Yes, it was. Being back here had been like a balm on his tattered heart and soul. But even with coming home and diving right back into the life he'd dodged for years, something was still missing. His world still seemed as if there was a void, a huge hole he'd never fully be able to close.

Perhaps it was Hector's death. Losing his best friend, his father figure, his agent, was hell. But Beau wondered if being home and not seeing his actual father riding the perimeters or herding cattle was the main reason he felt so empty.

"I'm just trying to figure things out," Beau admitted. "I have a movie premiere a few days before Christmas. I'll have to attend that, and then I'd like to be here for the holidays. I'll go after that."

"And when will you fit a visit to Dad in there?" Colt propped his hands on his hips.

"I'm hoping to go see him tomorrow."

That shut Colt up. Beau knew his brother hadn't expected that comeback and Beau would be lying if he didn't admit he was scared as hell to see his dad. He didn't know how he would feel if he walked into the room and Grant Elliott had no clue who he was.

Ironic, really. He was an award-winning movie star, but the one person in the world he wanted to recognize him was his own father.

"Do you want me to come with you?"

Colt's question shocked him. Beau never expected his twin to offer. Maybe this was the olive branch that Beau wondered if he'd ever see.

He swallowed the lump of emotions clogging his throat and nodded. "Yeah, sure."

Colt gave a curt nod, as well. They may not be hugging it out and proclaiming their brotherly love, but this was a huge step in what Beau hoped was just the first phase in repairing their relationship. Because this process wouldn't be quick and it wouldn't be easy. But it was a start.

Ten

Scarlett continued to stare at the tree mocking her in the corner. The one in Colt and Annabelle's house had looked just like the perfect ones she'd described to Beau. There had even been ornaments on the tree of twin babies with a gold ribbon across that said "Babies' First Christmas."

Scarlett hadn't been able to handle another moment. As much as she wanted to be the woman for Beau, she also knew she could never fully be the woman he wanted…not if he wanted more children and a family.

And this little cabin may not be her home, but Scarlett was determined to give Beau and Madelyn a nice Christmas. Too bad she felt she was failing miserably.

Madelyn had taken a bottle and gone right to sleep, leaving Scarlett alone with her thoughts…thoughts that drifted toward the man who would walk through that door any minute.

So she'd opted to try to decorate this tree. Once the lights went on and she plugged them in, she decided to stop. Maybe this was the best this poor thing would look. The crooked trunk didn't look so bad on the tree lot, but now that it was in the small cabin the imperfection was quite noticeable.

Maybe if she turned it slightly so the leaning part faced the patio doors?

Scarlett groaned. Perhaps she should bake some cookies instead. That would help liven up her holiday spirit, plus the house would smell better than any potpourri or candle she could've bought.

But it was late, so she decided to postpone that until tomorrow. Now she headed to her room to change her clothes, figuring on making some tea with honey to help her relax. She really should make it quickly and get back to her room before Beau came home.

Beau...

He'd tempted her in ways that she'd never been tempted before. Never had a man had her so torn up and achy and...damn it, confused.

She shouldn't want him. There was no good ending to this entire ordeal. They clearly led different lives and he was so used to getting what he wanted, yet another reason why they couldn't work. If she stayed and tried at a relationship, even if he was ready for that, she couldn't ultimately give him what he wanted.

But there were so many turn-ons—so, so many.

Scarlett pulled on a tank and a pair of cotton shorts as she mentally argued with herself. She could either continue to dodge the pull toward Beau or she could just give in to this promised fling. After all, she was leaving in a few weeks. She could have the fling and then move, start her new life and not look back.

He'd already pleasured her, so she knew what awaited her if she surrendered to him. And she knew it would be even better when they actually made love, when his body was taking her to those heights instead of just his hand.

Just thinking about that orgasm caused her cheeks to flush. Yes, that was an even bigger reason to want to agree to everything he'd been ready to give. If that had been part of his master plan the entire time, well then, he'd won this battle.

Fanning her heated cheeks, Scarlett opened her bedroom door…and froze. Beau stood just on the other side, his raised fist poised to knock.

She gripped the doorknob in one hand and tried to catch her breath. Between the surprise of seeing him here and the intense look in his eyes, Scarlett couldn't find a reason to ignore her needs any longer.

Not that she could ignore them even if she wanted to. Not with this gorgeous, sexy, intense man looking at her like he was.

She did the only thing she could do at that moment. She took a step toward him and closed the gap between them.

She kept her eyes locked onto his as she framed his face with her hands. That dark stubble along his jaw tickled her palms, the simple touch sending waves of arousal and anticipation through her, fanning the flames her fantasies had ignited.

"Scarlett—"

She slid her thumb along his bottom lip, cutting off his words. "Do you still want me?"

She had to take charge. She had to know the power belonged to her or he wouldn't just win the battle between them…he'd win the war.

Beau's tongue darted out and slid across her skin as he gripped her hips and pulled her to him, aligning their bodies. There was no mistake how much he wanted her, no mistake in what was about to happen.

She needed this distraction, needed to forget how much she'd hurt earlier seeing all those babies and the happy family. Maybe she shouldn't use him for her need to escape, but she'd wanted him all along and why shouldn't she take what she wanted?

"Why now?" he asked, studying her face. "What changed?"

Scarlett's heart thumped against her chest as she swallowed and went for total honesty…well, as much as she was willing to share about her pain.

"Sometimes I want to forget," she murmured. "Make me forget, Beau."

The muscle clenched in his jaw and for a moment she wondered if he'd turn her down and leave this room. But then he covered her mouth with his and walked her backward until her back came in contact with the post of the bed.

His denim rubbed her bare thighs, only adding to the build of the anticipation. As much as she loved how he looked in his cowboy wardrobe, she desperately wanted to see him wearing nothing but her.

Beau's hands were instantly all over her, stripping her of her shorts, then her tank. He only broke the kiss long enough to peel away the unwanted material and then he wrapped her back in his strong arms and made love to her mouth.

That was the only way to describe his kisses. He didn't just meet her lips with his; he caressed them, stroked them, laved them, plundered them. And she felt every one of those touches not only on her mouth but in the very core of her femininity.

Needing to touch him the same way, Scarlett reached between them for the hem of his T-shirt. She'd lifted it slightly when his hands covered hers and he eased back.

"In a hurry?" he asked.

She nodded. "I'm the only one ready for this."

"Baby, I've been ready since you walked in my door."

She shivered at his husky tone and glanced down to their joined hands. Her dark skin beneath his rough, tanned hands had her wondering why this looked so… right. Was it just because she hadn't been with someone in so long? Was it because this was *the* Beau Elliott?

She didn't think so, but now wasn't the time to get into why she had these unexplainable stirrings at just the sight of them coming together.

"Someone is thinking too hard. Maybe this will keep your thoughts at bay."

Beau stepped back and pulled off his shirt, tossing it aside. He was playing dirty and he damn well knew it.

As if to drive the point home, he quirked his dark brows as a menacing, sexy smile spread across his face.

"What did you want when you came to my room?" she asked, surprised she even had the wherewithal to speak.

He went to the snap of his pants and shoved them off as he continued to stare at her. He stood before her in only his black boxer briefs and she couldn't keep her eyes from roaming every inch of muscle and sinew on display before her. His body was pure perfection. The sprinkling of dark chest hair and the dark tattoos over his side, pec and shoulder were so sexy. Who knew she was a tattoo girl?

"I wanted to talk," he replied.

"That look in your eye doesn't look like you wanted to talk."

His lips thinned. "Maybe I needed to forget, too."

She crossed her arms and glanced down, suddenly feeling too vulnerable standing before him completely naked as he let a crack open so she could glimpse into his soul.

Beau reached out, unhooking her arms. "Don't hide from me. I've been waiting to see you."

Scarlett swallowed and looked up at him. "You saw me last night."

"Not enough."

His fingertips grazed down the slope of her breasts and around to her sides. She shivered when his hands slid down the dip in her waist, then over the flare of her hips.

"Not nearly enough."

He lifted her by her waist and wrapped his arms around her. Scarlett wrapped her legs around his waist as he carried her to the bed. She slid her mouth along his as she tipped back, then found herself pressed firmly into the thick comforter, Beau's weight on her. She welcomed the heaviness of this man.

The frantic way his hands and mouth roamed over her made her wonder if he was chasing away some demon in his own mind.

Maybe for tonight, they were just using each other. But right now she didn't care. She wanted him. She needed him. Right now.

When Beau sat up, Scarlett instinctively reached for him to pull him back to her.

"I need to get protection," he told her as he grasped his jeans.

Scarlett hadn't even thought of that. Of course pregnancy wasn't an issue for her, but she didn't know his history and he didn't know hers. Safety had to override hormones right now. She was just glad one of them was thinking straight.

She watched as he removed his boxer briefs and sheathed himself, relishing the sight of his arousal. Nothing could make her turn away or deny this need that burned through her. Well...if Madelyn started crying, but other than that, nothing.

Beau eased his knee down onto the bed next to her thigh. Scarlett rose up to her elbows, her heart beating so fast as desire curled all through her.

He trailed his fingertips up her thigh, teasing her as he went right past the spot she ached most, and on up her abdomen.

"You're one sexy woman," he growled. "It was all I could do to hold back last night."

Which only made him even more remarkable. He wasn't demanding and selfish. Even now, he was taking his time and touching, kissing, enjoying...all while driving her out of her mind.

Those fingertips circled her nipples and Scarlett nearly came off the bed.

"Beau."

"Right here," he murmured as he leaned down and captured her lips.

She opened to him and shifted her legs restlessly. Beau settled between her thighs and she lifted her knees to accommodate him. He hooked one hand behind her thigh and lifted her leg at the same time he joined their bodies.

Scarlett cried out against his mouth as she tilted her hips to meet his. He seemed to move so slow in comparison to the frantic need she felt. The man was maddeningly arousing.

She clutched at his shoulders and arched against him, pulling her mouth from his as she tipped her head back. Beau's lips traveled a path down her neck to her breast and Scarlett wrapped her legs around his waist, locking her ankles behind his back.

Beau never once removed his lips from her skin. He moved all over her, around her, in her, and in minutes that familiar coiling sensation built up within her and Scarlett bit her lip to keep from crying out again.

But Beau gripped her backside, his large powerful hand pulling her to him as he quickened the pace and Scarlett couldn't stop the release from taking over, nor could she stop the cry.

Beau's body tightened against hers as he surged inside her, taking his own pleasure. After a moment, that grip loosened and he eased down onto the bed, shifting his weight so he wasn't completely on top of her.

When the pulsing stopped and her heartbeat slowed, and she was able to think once again, Scarlett realized she was in new territory. She wasn't sure what she was supposed to say or do here. Anyone she'd ever slept with had been someone she was committed to. What did she do now, naked, sated and plastered against a man who was nothing more—could be nothing more—than a fling?

"Someone is thinking too hard again," he said, trailing his finger over her stomach and up the valley between her breasts. "Maybe I didn't do my job well enough."

Scarlett laughed. "You more than did your job. I'm just confused what to do now."

Beau sat up and rested his head in his hand as he stared down at her. The entire moment seemed so intimate, more than the act of sex itself.

"This doesn't have to be anything more than what it was," he told her. "You needed to escape something and so did I. Besides, this was bound to happen."

His words seemed so straightforward and matter-of-fact. They were all true, but she wished he'd...

What? What did she wish? That they'd start a relationship and see where things went? She knew full well where they'd go. She'd be in Dallas and he'd be back in LA. There was nothing for them other than a brief physical connection.

Scarlett shifted from the bed and came to her feet. Being completely naked now made her feel too vulnerable, too exposed emotionally.

She started putting her sleep clothes back on, trying to ignore the confident cowboy stretched out on her bed.

"Care to tell me what had you running from Colt's house?"

Scarlett pushed her hair away from her face and turned to face him. "I told you. Madelyn was tired and I was letting you guys talk."

He lifted one dark brow and stared, silently calling her out on her lie.

"Could you cover up?" she asked. "I can't concentrate with you on display like that."

Beau laughed and slowly came to his feet...which

maybe was worse because now he was closing in on her with that naughty grin. "I like the idea of you not concentrating."

Scarlett put her hands up and shook her head. "Don't touch me. We're done for the night."

He nodded. "Fine, but I still want to know what had you scared or upset."

From his soft tone, she knew he truly meant every word. He didn't care that they weren't diving back in for round two and he genuinely wanted to know what had bothered her.

Scarlett didn't want to get into her emotional issues. Dredging them all up wouldn't change anything, and the last thing she wanted was pity from Beau. Besides, he'd said he was dealing with his own issues.

"I think it's best if we don't get too personal," she told him and nearly laughed. This was Beau Elliott and women all around the world would give anything to trade places with Scarlett right now.

"We're already personal," he countered, reaching for her. When she tried to back away, he cupped her elbow. "You're taking care of my daughter, living with me and we just had sex. Not to mention my sisters-in-law have all taken to you. We're temporarily bonded, so stop trying to push me away. I can listen and be a friend right now."

Scarlett raked her eyes over him. "With no clothes on?"

He cursed beneath his breath as he spun around and grabbed those black boxer briefs. As if putting on that hip-hugging underwear helped.

The second he turned his focus back to her, she

crossed her arms and decided to give the interrogation right back at him.

"Do you want to tell me what's got you so torn up here?" she asked. "Other than your brothers?"

He stared at her for a moment before he shrugged. "I'm not sure what future I have to offer my daughter because I have no clue what I want to do. I'm mending relationships with my brothers, hopefully my father, and figuring out if I even want to go back to LA."

Scarlett couldn't believe he'd said anything, let alone all of that.

"My life is a mess," he went on. "My former agent was more like a father figure and best friend. He recently passed away."

Scarlett put her hand over her heart. "Oh, Beau, I'm sorry."

"Thank you. It's been difficult without him, but each day is a little easier than the last. But the next step is so unclear." He pursed his lips for a moment before continuing. "I have a feeling someone with her new life laid out before her isn't so worried about the future."

"Not when I'm constantly haunted by my past," she murmured.

She rubbed her arms, hating how he was somehow managing to break down her walls. He'd easily opened and didn't seem to care that she saw his vulnerability. Could she do the same?

"I could guess and I bet I'd be right."

She shook her head. "You don't know me."

Beau stepped into her and reached up, smoothing her hair from her face. "You love Christmas and more decorations than anyone needs. You chose the most hideous tree I've ever seen, yet you're determined to make this a good holiday. You're passionate in bed and let yourself lose all control, which is the sexiest thing I've ever seen, by the way."

She stared at him, listening as he dissected her from the nuggets of information he'd gathered over the past few days. Beau was much more perceptive than she gave him credit for. No selfish man would've taken every moment into consideration and parsed each portion of their time together to understand her better.

"I also know that my daughter and I are lucky you're here," he went on, inching even closer until she had to tip her head to look up at him. "And I know too much discussion on babies or families makes you shut down and get all misty-eyed, yet you're a nanny."

Scarlett tightened her lips together and tried to ignore that burn in her throat and eyes.

Beau slid his finger beneath her chin and tipped her head up. "Shall I keep going?" he asked. "Or maybe you could just tell me what you're running from."

Scarlett pulled in a shaky breath and closed her eyes. "I can't have children."

Eleven

Beau's suspicions were right. He wished like hell he'd been wrong because he could see the pain in her eyes, hear it in her voice.

Just as he started to reach for her again, she opened her eyes and held up one hand. "No. I don't need to be consoled and please, don't look at me like that."

He didn't know what she saw in his eyes, but how could he not comfort her? He may have the reputation of a playboy, and perhaps he didn't do anything to rectify that with the media, but he did care.

Even though he'd only known Scarlett a short time, it was impossible to ignore the way he felt. Attraction was one thing, but there was more to this complex relationship.

Unfortunately, he had to ignore the pull and remain closed off from tapping into those unwanted, untimely feelings. He had a future to figure out and he'd already screwed up with one woman.

"I love being a nanny," she went on, her voice still laced with sadness and remorse. "But my life changed about a year ago, and I just can't do this job anymore."

"That's why you're leaving."

Beau crossed to the bed and sat down. Maybe she'd feel more apt to talk if he wasn't looming over her in only his underwear. He never wanted her to feel intimidated or insecure. He doubted she really had anyone she could talk to and the fact that she chose him—after he'd somewhat forced her hand—proved she was more vulnerable than he'd first thought.

But he actually wanted to listen and he wanted to know how he could help...even if that only came in the form of making her forget.

"I can't be in Stone River." Scarlett's words cut through his thoughts. "There are too many memories here of my life, my hopes and dreams. Starting over somewhere fresh will be the best healer for me."

He understood all too well about needing to start over. The need to find a place that would be comforting and not pull you down further. Her reasons for leaving Stone River were the exact reasons he'd left LA. They both needed something new, something that promised hope for an unknown future.

"I'm sure that wasn't an easy decision to make," he stated.

She turned to face him and shrugged one slender shoulder. "There wasn't much else I could do. After my surgery, I took a position out of the field, in the office. I love the people I work with. I just couldn't be a nanny anymore. I thought working in the office would be easier, but it wasn't. I was still dealing with families and listening to the stories of my coworkers. Then Maggie asked me to fill in for these few weeks before I leave and I couldn't tell her no."

"I'm glad you didn't."

Scarlett stared at him for a minute. The lamp on her bedside table set a soft glow on her mocha skin. Skin he ached to touch again. Scarlett was one of the sexiest, most passionate women he'd ever known, and after hearing a bit of her story, he knew she was also one of the strongest.

"Me, too," she whispered.

He did reach for her now and when her hand closed in his, he pulled her toward him. Scarlett came to stand between his legs and she rested her hands on his shoulders.

"What surgery did you have to have?" he asked.

When she pulled in a shaky breath, he placed his hands on her waist and offered a comforting squeeze.

"I had a hysterectomy," she explained. "The short version of my story is I had a routine checkup. The test results came back showing I had some abnormal cells and the surgery was necessary. Unfortunately, that took away any chance I had at my own family, but in the end, the threat of uterine cancer was gone."

He couldn't imagine wanting something, dreaming of having it your whole life and then not obtaining it. There was nothing Beau didn't covet that he couldn't get through money or power. That's how he'd been raised. Yes, his parents had instilled in him a strong work ethic, but he also knew that at any given time he could reach for anything and make it his.

Yet with all his money, power and fame, he couldn't

make his own future stable when he was so confused where he should land. And if he had the ability, he'd sure as hell do something to make Scarlett's life easier.

With a gentle tug, Beau had Scarlett tumbling onto his chest. He gripped her thighs and helped her straddle his lap. As he looked up into her eyes, he realized that if there was any woman who could make him lose his heart, it could be her.

Which was absolutely crazy. Why was he even having such thoughts? He'd screwed things up before when he'd let his heart get involved. Wanting a woman physically and thinking of deeper emotions were two totally different things and he needed to refocus before he found himself even further from where he needed to be.

Between all of this with his family and now his mixed feelings for Scarlett, he needed to remain in control before he completely lost himself.

"Let's keep our painful pasts out of this room, out of this bed," he suggested as he nipped at her chin. "For as long as you're here, stay with me."

Her eyes widened as she eased slightly away. "You want to continue this fling?"

"'Fling'? That's such a crass word." He let his hands cover her backside and pull her tighter where he needed her most. "We don't need a title for this. Just know I want you, for however long you're here."

Scarlett laced her hands behind his neck and touched her forehead to his. "I swore I wouldn't do this with you," she murmured.

"Yet here we are."

She laughed, just as he'd hoped. "I guess I'm wearing too many clothes."

He stripped her shirt off, sliding his hands and eyes over her bare torso, her breasts. "Let's make each other forget."

Scarlett pushed Madelyn in the child swing that had been hung on the back patio. Even though winter had settled in and they were closing in on Christmas, the sun was shining bright in the cloudless sky and with a light jacket and pants, the day was absolutely beautiful.

Madelyn cooed and grinned as the swing went back and forth. Scarlett couldn't help but return the smile. It was impossible to be unhappy around Madelyn. Even when she'd fussed about her sore gums, Scarlett cherished the time. Madelyn was such a special little girl and having a father who cared so deeply made her very fortunate.

Beau had made a difficult decision to leave his Hollywood home and find out what life he and his daughter should lead.

Maybe he'd go back to his home in LA, but for now he seemed to be in no hurry. After spending the past several nights in his bed—well, hers—Scarlett wasn't in too big of a hurry to leave, either.

But she had to. She couldn't stay here forever playing house. There was no happily-ever-after for them, no little family. No, Scarlett wasn't going to get that family…at least not with Beau.

Maybe one day she'd meet a man and he might have kids already or maybe they'd adopt. She still couldn't let go of that dream. A new dream had replaced the old one and Scarlett had a blossom of hope.

Strong arms wrapped around her from behind, pulling her out of her thoughts, and Scarlett squealed.

"It's just me," Beau growled in her ear. "Unless you were expecting someone else."

Scarlett eyed him over her shoulder. "My other lover was supposed to come by because I thought you were out."

He smacked her butt. "There are no other lovers as long as I'm in your bed," he said with a smile.

Which would only be for another two weeks.

Scarlett didn't want to think of the end coming so soon. Only a few days ago she was counting down until she could hightail it out of town, but now...

Well, falling into bed with Beau had changed everything.

"I thought you were with Colt and Hayes looking over résumés for guides for the dude ranch."

The new business venture of the Elliott brothers was due to start in early spring. Scarlett had heard Beau discussing how much still needed to be done, she was only sorry she wouldn't be around to see how magnificent all of this would be. Pebblebrook was a gorgeous, picturesque spread and no doubt they would draw in thousands of people a year.

Scarlett wondered if Beau and Colt had told their dad about the ranch, about the way they were closing in on making his dream a full reality, when they'd gone to see him yesterday morning. But Beau had been closed off when he'd returned. Scarlett hadn't wanted to press him on a topic that was obviously so sensitive. She couldn't imagine that bond father and son had shared growing up and how much this must be hurting Beau.

Growing up, she did everything to avoid her stepfather and mom. They'd been so caught up in their own worlds anyway, so she went unnoticed.

"We finished early," Beau told her. "I told my brothers I needed to get back home to see Madelyn."

Scarlett gave the swing another gentle push and turned to face Beau. Those dark eyes, framed by thick lashes, all beneath a black brim only made him seem all the more mysterious. Over the last week she'd found out that there were several sides to him, and she had to admit she liked this Beau.

The man before her wasn't the actor she'd seen on-screen or the playboy the media portrayed. This Beau Elliott was a small-town rancher.

Albeit a billionaire.

She glanced over at Madelyn. "She woke from a nap about twenty minutes ago, so you're just in time."

Beau slid his hands up her arms, over the slope of her shoulders, and framed her face. "I may have wanted to see you, too."

Scarlett couldn't help the flutter in her chest. The more time she spent with him and his daughter, the more she realized how difficult leaving would be. But she'd be fine. She had to be.

"I also left because I have a surprise planned for you."

"A surprise?" she repeated, shocked he'd think to do anything for her. "What is it?"

Beau slid his lips softly over hers, then stroked her cheeks with the pad of his thumbs. "If I tell you then it won't be a surprise."

"Oh, come on," she begged. "You can't tease me like that."

He thrust his pelvis toward hers and smiled. "You weren't complaining about being teased last night, or the night before, or the night before that."

Scarlett slapped him on the chest. "Fine. But you'll pay for that."

Beau grazed his mouth along her jaw and up to the sensitive area just behind her ear. "I'm counting on it."

Madelyn let out a fuss, which quickly turned into a cry. Before Scarlett could get the baby from the swing, Beau had moved around her and was unbuckling her.

Scarlett stepped away and watched as he cooed and offered sweet words and patted her back. Something stirred inside her. An unfamiliar feeling. An undeniable feeling.

She was falling for Beau.

How ridiculous that sounded even inside her own mind. But there was no denying the fact. Beau Elliott had worked his way past her defenses and into her personal space, quite possibly her heart. There was no future here and she was a fool for allowing this to happen.

Of course she didn't *allow* anything. There had been no stopping these feelings. From the second Beau showed her just how selfless he was, how caring, Scarlett couldn't help but fall for him.

Beau lifted Madelyn over his head and spun in a circle. With the sun off in the distance and the soft rolling hills of the ranch as the backdrop, Scarlett had to tamp down her emotions. The father/daughter duo was picture perfect and maybe neither of them realized how lucky they were to have each other.

Scarlett let them have their moment as she slipped inside the tiny cabin. As silly as it was, she'd come to think of this little place like home. This was nothing like the massive home she'd grown up in. The place might as well have been a museum with the expensive furniture, priceless art and cold atmosphere.

Maybe that's why this cozy cabin touched her so much. There was life here, fun, a family. All the things she'd craved as a child and all the things she wanted as an adult.

But they weren't hers…and she needed to remember that.

Instead of dwelling on those thoughts, Scarlett moved to the kitchen where she'd baked sugar cookies earlier. They were ready to be iced and taken to Annabelle, Alexa and Pepper.

Scarlett didn't proclaim to be the best baker, but she did love her sugar cookie recipe. In fact, she'd made extra just for Beau. Maybe part of her wanted to impress him still, which was silly, but she hadn't been able to help herself. She cared for him, so much. Much more than she should be allowed.

The man came through the doorway just as her thoughts turned to him once again. Of course, he was never far from her thoughts, just as he was never far from her in this tiny space.

"I thought I smelled cookies when I came in earlier." He held Madelyn with one strong arm as he came to stand on the other side of the island. "But it looks as if you have enough to feed a small army. Are we expecting company?"

Scarlett started separating the icing she'd made into smaller bowls so she could dye it in different colors. "I'm taking a dozen each to your brothers' houses later. I just… I don't know. I thought I should do something and I love to bake. I think Christmas just demands the house smell like warm sugar and comfort."

She applied two drops of yellow food coloring into the icing for the star cookies, then she put green drops into another bowl for the tree cookies. The silence had her unsettled so she glanced up to find Beau staring at her with a look on his face she'd never seen before.

"What?" she asked, screwing the lids back on the small bottles of food coloring.

"You watch my baby all day, you cook, you decorate—"

"Don't call that tree in the corner decorating," she grumbled. "Maybe I baked because I need a chance to redeem myself."

He chuckled and shifted Madelyn around to sit on the bar and lean back against his chest. He kept one firm hand on her belly.

"The mantel is beautiful and way more than I'd ever think of doing, and the front porch looks like a real home with the wreath and whatever you did to that planter by the steps." He slid his hat off and dropped it onto a bar stool. "I don't know how you do it all. Maybe women are just born with that gene that makes them superhuman."

"We are."

His smile widened. "And a modesty gene, too, I see."

"Of course," she said without hesitation.

"Regardless of how you get everything done, I'm grateful."

The sincerity of his statement just pulled back another layer of defense she'd tried to wrap herself in. Unfortunately, every time the man opened his mouth, he stripped away more and more. She was losing this fight with herself and before these next couple of weeks were up, she had serious concerns about her heart.

"How long until the cookies are ready to deliver?" he asked.

"I just need to ice three dozen." She glanced behind her to the trays lining the small counter space. "I can ice the dozen for us after I get back."

"You made cookies for us, too?"

Scarlett laughed. "You think I'm baking and not thinking of myself?"

Madelyn let out a jumble of noises as she patted her father's hand. Was there anything sexier than a hunky rancher caring for his baby? Because she was having a difficult time thinking of anything.

"Well, as soon as you get those iced, you'll get your surprise," he told her. "This will all work out quite well."

"What will?"

"The deliveries, your surprise." He leaned in just a bit as his eyes darted to her mouth. "Coming back here later and pleasuring you."

Her body heated, not that she needed his promise for such a reaction. Simply thinking of him incited her arousal. But all of the emotions swirling around inside her were so much more than sexual. Her heart had gotten involved in this short span of time. She hadn't seen that coming. She'd been so worried about not falling for his seduction, she hadn't thought of falling for the man himself.

Damn it. She was sinking fast and not even trying to stop herself. Why bother? Why not just enjoy the ride as long as this lasted?

She deserved to go after what she wanted, no matter how temporary, and she wanted Beau Elliott. Considering he wanted her just as much, there was no reason to let worry in now.

For the time they had left, she planned on enjoying every single moment of her last job as a nanny.

As for her heart, well, it had been broken before. But she hadn't experienced anything like Beau Elliott. Would she ever be able to recover?

Twelve

Scarlett put the final lid on the gold Christmas tin. She stacked the festive containers in a tote and went to get Madelyn from her swing in the living room. Thankfully, she wasn't so fussy with her swollen gums now. The teething ring had helped.

"All ready?"

She turned to see Beau. "I'm ready." Giddiness and anxiousness spiraled through her. "Just what is this surprise?"

That familiar, naughty smile spread across his face. Beau could make her giddy like a teenager with her first crush and arouse her like a woman who knew exactly what she was getting into. She'd never met a man who could elicit such emotions from her.

"You're about to find out," he promised with a wink. "Let me take the cookies out and I'll be right back."

"I can carry them," she argued.

Beau put his hand up. "No. Stay right there with Madelyn. Actually, she'll need a jacket and hat. It's cool this evening and we'll be outside for a bit."

Scarlett narrowed her eyes. "We're not driving to your brothers' houses?"

The estate had a ridiculous amount of acreage—she thought she'd heard the number of five thousand thrown out—so the only way around the place was on tractors, four-wheelers, horses or cars.

With only a smile for her answer, Beau adjusted the wide brim of his black hat before he grabbed the bag stuffed with cookie tins and headed out the front door.

Scarlett glanced to Madelyn and tapped the tip of her nose.

"Your daddy is driving me crazy."

By the time Scarlett grabbed the jacket and hat for Madelyn from the peg by the door, Beau swept back inside.

"I'll finish getting her ready," he said, taking his daughter. "Take a jacket and hat for yourself, too. I can't have you shivering or you won't appreciate the surprise."

Scarlett laughed. "You're making me nervous, Beau."

He reached up and stroked one finger down the side of her face. "Trust me."

How could she not? She trusted him with her body... and he was closing in on her heart.

Scarlett smiled, mentally running from the unfamiliar emotions curling through her. "You know I do."

She went to her room to get her things. Whatever Beau had planned, he seemed pretty excited about what he'd come up with.

Warmth spread through her at the thought of him thinking of a way to surprise her. Was this a Christmas present or just because? Or did this surprise involve something he liked, as well? The questions and the unknowns were driving her crazy.

It was difficult not to read more into this situation because they'd agreed to have just these last couple of weeks of intimacy before she left. So why was he going that extra mile? Why was he treating this like…well, like a relationship?

Scarlett groaned as she tugged on her red knit hat. Her thoughts were trying to rob her happy time here. She had one of the sexiest men in the world waiting to give her something he'd planned just for her. And she'd simply enjoy it.

She slid on her matching red jacket, perfect for the holiday season and delivering Christmas cookies. For another added bit of flair, she grabbed her black-and-white snowflake scarf and knotted it around her neck.

When she stepped back into the living room, Beau held Madelyn in one hand and extended his other toward her. He kept that sneaky grin on his face and she just knew he was loving every minute of torturing her.

Giddy with anticipation, Scarlett slid her hand in his. She had to admit, she liked the look of her darker skin against his. Her bright red nails were quite the contrast with his rough fingertips from working on the ranch.

Beau tugged her forward until she fell against his side and he covered her mouth with his. The short yet heated kiss had her blinking up at him and wondering how he kept knocking her off her feet. She never knew what he'd do next, but he continued to have her wanting more.

"Everything's ready," he told her. "Go on outside."

She couldn't wait another second. Scarlett reached around him and opened the door. The moment her eyes focused on the sight before her, she blinked, wondering if this was a dream.

"Beau," she gasped. "What did you do?"

Directly in front of the porch were two chocolate-brown horses in front of a wide wooden sled. A sled decorated with garland and lights. On the seat she saw plaid blankets. There was evergreen garland wrapped around the reins, and the horses stood stoic and stared straight ahead as they waited for their orders.

Scarlett spun back around and threw her arms around Beau, careful of how she sandwiched Madelyn in the middle.

"I can't believe you did this," she squealed. "How on earth did you manage it?"

Beau took her hand in his and led her to the sled. "I have my ways and that's all you need to know."

Scarlett didn't hesitate as she carefully climbed into the sled. Once she nestled against the cushioned seat, she reached down for Madelyn.

The sled jostled slightly as Beau stepped up into it and folded his long, lean frame next to her. He gripped the reins in hand as Scarlett pulled the cozy blanket up over their laps. She laced her hands around Madelyn and glanced to Beau as he snapped the reins to set the sled in motion.

"Why did you do all of this?" she asked.

"Why not?" he countered, shooting her that toe-curling grin and dark gaze. "You mentioned loving Christmas and sleigh rides. I'm just giving you a bit of extra cheer."

Scarlett wasn't quite sure what to say. Beau had put so much thought into this, even though he tried to brush the sweet gesture aside. This full-on reality was so much better than anything she'd ever seen in the movies.

"I'm glad I made you a dozen cookies, then," she joked as he headed in the direction of Nolan's house. "You may even get extra icing."

"Is that a euphemism?"

Scarlett's body heated, but she laughed because she didn't want to get all hot and bothered when she was in the midst of this festive family moment.

The breath in her throat caught and was instantly replaced with thick emotions. Family. This fantasy moment she was living in had thrust her deeper into her job than she'd ever been.

Feeling like part of the family was often just a perk of being a nanny. But nothing had ever prepared her for falling for the man she worked for, or for his daughter. And how could she not fall for him? He'd been attentive since day one…which really wasn't all that long ago.

Still, Beau actually listened to her. He met her needs in the bedroom and out, and she was an absolute fool if she thought she'd walk away at the end of this without a broken heart.

"So you'll be leaving at the end of next week for your movie premiere," she stated, more reminding herself and making sure this stayed out in the open. "Are you sure you'll be home Christmas Eve?"

"Positive," he assured her. "Nobody else is playing Santa to my girl but me."

"I wondered if you'd bought presents."

He shot her a side glance. "Of course I have. You

think I'd let my baby's first Christmas come and go and not have presents?"

"Well, you didn't have a tree or a stocking," she reminded him with an elbow to his side.

Beau guided the horses as Nolan's home came into view. The large log resort-type home looked like something from a magazine. Not surprising, though, since the Elliotts had the lifestyle of billionaire ranchers and Nolan was a surgeon. He and Pepper lived here with their little one and their home was beautifully decorated, with wreaths adorning every window and a larger one with a red bow on the front door.

"Maybe I didn't have a tree or stockings," Beau added. "But I'm not a complete Scrooge."

Scarlett shifted in the seat and glanced down at the baby. "I think we're putting her to sleep," she stated. "Next time her gums are bothering her, just hitch up the sled and take her for a ride."

"Sure." He snorted. "No problem."

Within another minute, Madelyn was fast asleep. There were so many questions Scarlett had for Beau regarding his future, but she wasn't sure if she had a right to ask…or if she even truly wanted to know the answers.

She decided to wait until they left Nolan's house to bring up her thoughts. Nolan and Pepper weren't home, so Beau left the tin on the porch swing and sent his brother a text.

As they took off again, this time toward Hayes and Alexa's house, Scarlett figured this was the perfect time. If he didn't want to answer, then he didn't have to, but she couldn't just keep guessing.

"When you go back for the movie premiere, do you think you'll want to stay?"

"No. I'll definitely be back here for Christmas."

Scarlett pulled the plaid blanket up a little further. "I mean, will being back there make you miss that life?"

He said nothing. Only the clomping of the horses through the lane broke the silence. Scarlett wondered if she'd gone too far, simply because he hadn't talked much about the movie and she got the impression that topic was off the table.

"Forget it," she said after waiting too long for his reply. "None of my concern. It's not like I'll be here or part of your life."

"It's okay." He shifted in his seat, his thigh rubbing against hers. "Honestly, I doubt it. I'm not looking forward to going back."

"Do you hate that world so much?"

Beau's brows dipped as he seemed to be weighing his words. "I hate how people can get so swept up in their own lives they forget there's a world around them. The selfishness runs rampant out there. Everyone is out for themselves, but they're never happy because when they get what they want, they still want more."

He pulled in a deep breath and shook his head. "I can say that because I'm that person."

Scarlett slid her left hand over Beau's denim-clad thigh. "You're not that person at all."

The muscles in his jaw clenched. "I am," he volleyed back. "I left here because I wanted more. I made it in Hollywood, had a career people would kill for and still wanted more. Then I won two big acting awards, and that wasn't enough, either. I met Jennifer and thought we might have had a future together, but that went to hell. I have a gorgeous baby, yet I'm still looking for more."

Scarlett didn't like the defeated tone in his voice. "You're not looking for more," she scolded. "You're looking for the right place to raise your daughter and trying to reconnect with your family. That's not selfish. And it sure as hell wasn't selfish that you surprised me with a horse-drawn sleigh ride."

"Oh, the sleigh ride was just so I'd get laid."

Scarlett squeezed his thigh until he yelped.

"I'm joking," he laughed. "Well, not really. I still want in your bed tonight."

"You didn't have to do this to get there," she reminded him. "I haven't been complaining, have I?"

He pulled back on the reins until the horses and sleigh came to a stop. When Beau shifted in his seat to face her, Scarlett's heart kicked up.

"I've been thinking…" He gripped the reins in one hand and slid his other beneath the blanket to cover hers. "I don't want to cheapen this to just sex or for you to ever think I'll forget you when you leave."

A burst of light filled the cracks in her heart. What exactly was he trying to say?

"I know you're moving and I have no idea where I'll be," he went on. "But I don't want to just hide in the cabin and keep you naked."

Scarlett rolled her eyes and glared. "Really?"

His lips quirked into a half grin. "Okay, that's exactly what I'd like, but I want you to know you're more important to me than Madelyn's nanny or my temporary lover."

Scarlett pulled in a breath and held his dark gaze. "So what are you saying?"

"I want to take you on a date."

"A…a date?"

Not what she thought he'd say, but she wasn't exactly opposed to the idea.

"I didn't think you wanted to be seen in town or anywhere because of privacy."

He squeezed her hand and leaned forward to graze his lips across hers. There was no chill in the December air at all when she had Beau next to her. Just one simple touch, just one promised kiss had her entire body heating up.

When Beau eased back, he stroked the back of her hand with his fingertip. "Some things are worth the risk."

Well, that sealed the deal. There was no coming back from this because her heart tumbled, flipped, flopped, did all the amazing things that had her wanting to squeal and yell that she'd fallen completely in love with Beau Elliott.

Unfortunately, there was no room in this temporary relationship for such emotions. There would be no love, no family Christmas cards and definitely no happy-ever-after.

She only had a week left with Beau and then she'd be out of his life for good.

Thirteen

Beau wasn't sure what had made Scarlett shut down after he'd asked her on a date. Honestly, he hadn't planned on that impromptu invitation, but he'd needed her to know that she wasn't just some woman he'd seduced and conquered. He'd never thought of any woman in that manner, and he sure as hell had more respect for Scarlett than that.

She was special. Not because of how she cared for Madelyn and not because she was so easy to talk to. Scarlett presented the entire package of an honest woman, one who genuinely cared.

Part of him wanted to give her the world, but what part of his world could he actually give? He couldn't even figure out his own plan. Though after being at Pebblebrook for a few weeks, he knew he wanted a ranch of his own. The hands-on approach he'd taken each day had turned something inside of him. The fact that he wasn't interested in looking at scripts now was rather telling.

Maybe one day he'd look to the screen again, but for now, Beau truly felt this was his destiny. He'd gone and explored like he'd wanted. He'd made himself one of the biggest names in Hollywood, but like he'd told Scarlett, something had still been missing.

Beau nearly laughed at himself for his *Wizard of Oz* epiphany. Everything he'd ever wanted was right here in his own backyard…literally.

He stood in front of the crazy Christmas tree in the corner of the cabin. Scarlett's soft singing voice filtered in from his bedroom as she got Madelyn to sleep for the night.

They'd delivered cookies and both Annabelle and Alexa were thrilled with the surprise. Beau loved the praise they gave Scarlett, and the fact that they treated her like family had him wanting to explore more with her. He'd never wanted someone like this before. Not just for sex, but to see if they could grow together.

But she was moving to Dallas.

Beau's mind raced in too many directions to try to keep up with, but he figured he didn't have a set place he wanted to be. He was quite literally free to do anything.

Was he even ready for something like this? He'd come back home to mend relationships, not to try to build a new one. Added to that, he hadn't known Scarlett very long. Was he honestly considering this? He'd made such a terrible judgment call with Jennifer, but Scarlett was so different than his ex. Scarlett wasn't out to gain anything for herself or trying to use him for anything other than a job before she left.

As one idea formed into another, Beau found him-

self smiling while still staring at the undecorated tree—
save for the lights.

"She's out."

Scarlett's words had him turning to face her. When
he met her gaze across the room, she stopped and set
the bottle on the kitchen island.

"What?" she asked, tipping her head. "You're smiling and you've been staring at my tree. You're plotting
something, aren't you? Are we burning it and roasting
marshmallows?"

Beau shook his head and circled the couch to head
toward the kitchen. She never glanced away and he
figured he looked like a complete moron because he
couldn't wipe the smile off his face.

If she thought the sleigh ride was nice, she'd be ut-
terly speechless when he presented her with the next
surprise.

"We aren't burning it," he told her as he drew closer.
"But in continuing your festive holiday cheer, I say we
break out our cookies and get them iced."

She narrowed her dark eyes. "Why do I have a feeling this will end with my clothes on the kitchen floor?"

Beau shrugged. "Because you're realistic."

Scarlett shook her head as she laughed. "You don't
have to talk me into getting naked, you know?"

Beau slid his hands over the dip in her waist. "Maybe
not, but I'm in the mood for dessert."

He backed her up until they circled the island. Scarlett gripped his biceps when she stumbled.

"What are you doing?" she asked, smiling up at him.

Beau planted a kiss on the tip of her nose. Her frea-
kin' nose. Now he knew he'd gone and lost his mind.
He'd never done such an endearing action before, but

he couldn't help himself. For as sexy as Scarlett was, she was also quite adorable.

"We're going to ice those cookies," he told her. "You did promise."

She jerked back, her brows shooting up. "You seriously want to ice cookies? Does this mean I'm melting Scrooge's heart?"

He smacked her on the butt before releasing her. "I'm hardly Scrooge, but I'll admit I've never iced cookies. My mom did all of that. Baking and cookie decorating was serious business at Christmastime in my house and she wanted it to be perfect."

Beau grabbed the icing from the counter next to the stove and set it on the island. Then he reached back around for the tin of cookies.

"I guess Christmas baking was the one time she wasn't about to let a bunch of boys ruin her creations." Beau glanced at the spread before him and laughed as he turned to Scarlett. "So I guess your work is cut out for you."

Scarlett went to pull off all of the lids, revealing the yellow, green and red food coloring. The instant smell of sugar hit him and he couldn't wait to take a bite.

Beau picked up a bare cookie and dipped it in the yellow icing before taking a bite. "You're right. These are good."

"Beau," she exclaimed, smacking his chest. "The icing isn't a dip."

He chewed his bite and went back in for more icing—red this time. "I think I'm onto something here."

"You're impossible." She reached into a drawer and pulled out a plastic spatula. "Let me show you how you should ice cookies."

As he continued to dip, Beau watched her expertly smooth the frosting over the tree cookie. When she was finished, she laid it aside on the wax paper and grabbed another.

"Want to try?" she asked.

"Sure."

He took the cookie and the utensil, then dipped the spatula into the red icing. With a quick move, he streaked a stripe across her shirt.

"Oops." He smiled and shrugged. "That didn't work. You might want to take your shirt off before that stains."

Scarlett propped a hand on her hip and narrowed her eyes. "That's not very original."

He gave another swipe. "Maybe not, but I bet you take that shirt off."

She kept her eyes on his as her fingers went to the top button. One slow release at a time, she revealed her dark skin and festive red bra.

Once she dropped her shirt to the floor, she reached around him and picked up another cookie. She grabbed the spatula from his hand and proceeded to decorate.

"Just because you act childish doesn't mean the lesson is over," she informed him. "Do you see how I'm using nice, even strokes?"

"I can use even strokes, too."

Scarlett rolled her eyes and laughed. "I'm talking about icing."

Beau leaned in and nipped at her ear. "Maybe I was, too."

Scarlett leaned slightly into him. "I can't concentrate when you're doing that."

Good. He slid his hand along the small of her back, around the dip in her waist, and covered her flat abdomen. She shivered beneath his touch, just as he'd expected.

"I can't concentrate when you're not wearing a shirt," he whispered in her ear.

She tipped her head back to meet his gaze. "And whose fault is that?"

"You're the one who took it off."

Beau spun her slightly and gripped her hips. He lifted her onto the counter, away from the mess. "Let's see what else we can do with this icing."

Her eyes darkened as she raised a brow. "You didn't really want to learn how to decorate cookies, did you?"

He flashed her a smile. "Not at all."

But he did make use of all of the icing and by the end of the night, Scarlett wasn't complaining.

Scarlett lifted Madelyn out of the car seat and adjusted the red knit cap. Downtown Stone River may be small, but people bustled about and businesses thrived like in a major city.

The sun was high in the sky, shining down on this picturesque square. The large tower clock in the middle struck twelve. Benches in a circle around the clock were filled with couples eating lunch. Every single lamppost had garland and lights wrapped around it. Oversize pots sat on each corner and overflowed with evergreens and bright red poinsettias.

Scarlett would miss this place.

"Hey. You okay?"

Beau came to stand beside her, his hand resting on her back. She offered him a smile and nodded.

"I'm fine," she told him. "And ready to eat. I used too much energy last night."

"We could've had more cookies for breakfast," he offered with a naughty grin and a wink.

"Considering you ate every cookie and, um...we finished the icing, that wasn't an option."

Mercy, her body still tingled just thinking about what they had done with those colors. The extra-long shower to cleanse their bodies of the sticky mess had only led to even more intimacy. And more intimacy led to Scarlett wishing she didn't have to leave.

"I think we should try that café on the corner," he said, pointing over her shoulder. "It looks like you."

"I've eaten there before," she told him, without looking to see which place he referred to. "And what do you mean it looks like me?"

Beau shrugged and looked back down at her. His wide-brim hat shielded a portion of his face from the sun. She didn't know if he wore the hat because he'd gotten used to it since he'd been back or if he'd brought it to be a little discreet. Either way, he looked like the sexy cowboy she'd come to know and love.

Fine. There it was. The big L word she'd been dancing around and not fully coming to terms with. She knew she was falling, but she could admit now that she was there.

"It's all festive with the gold-and-red Christmas signs out front," he told her, oblivious to her thoughts. "The big wreath on the doorway, the candles in the windows. It just looks like you."

She figured that was a compliment, but she wasn't quite sure.

Madelyn let out a yawn and rubbed her eyes. Scarlett patted her back and eased her head down onto her shoulder.

"We should eat so we can get this one to take a nap on the car ride home," she told him.

Beau's cell went off and he groaned. "I'm not answering that."

"You should," she retorted. "It could be about your dad."

Which he'd still never talked about. She wanted to know his feelings and help him if she could. Maybe when they got back home she'd address the topic.

Beau pulled his cell from his pocket and stared at the screen, then a wide smile spread across his face.

"I take it that's not your agent?" she asked.

He pocketed the cell and leaned in, covering her mouth with his. The kiss ended as quickly as it started, leaving her a bit unbalanced.

"What was that for?" she asked.

"I have a surprise for you."

Her heart warmed. "Another one?"

"I promise, this one is much better than the last."

Scarlett's face lit up. "Tell me."

He kissed her once again, lingering a bit longer this time. "When we get home."

"Then we're getting our food to go."

Beau laughed as he steered her toward the café. "No, we're not. I promised you a date and that's what we're doing."

Fourteen

Scarlett wasn't sure whether to be nervous or not with Beau's mysterious surprise. They stepped into the cabin and Madelyn was wide-awake now after a brief nap in the car.

Beau had only been asked about twenty times at the café for his autograph, and with each person who approached him, he took the time to talk and sign. He might be a star, but he was also humble and so far removed from the celebrity she'd originally thought him to be.

Christmas was coming quickly and he'd be leaving in just a few days for his premiere. Their time together had been rocky at first, but then it had become an absolute fantasy. She'd never, ever gotten involved with someone she worked for. Beau had made that personal ethic impossible, though, and she wasn't the least bit sorry.

"Wait right there," he told her.

Scarlett stood in the living area and obeyed. She couldn't imagine what could top the horse-drawn sleigh, but she couldn't wait.

She took Madelyn to the little play mat on the floor. Carefully, Scarlett eased down to her knees and laid Madelyn beneath the arch where random plush animals swung back and forth. At the sight of them, she started kicking her feet and making adorable cooing noises.

Scarlett stood back up and smiled. She was seriously going to miss this sweet little nugget.

"Are you ready?"

She spun around and her smile widened as Beau came back in with his laptop. "I don't know what I'm ready for, but bring it."

He took a seat on a bar stool and patted the other one for her. Once his computer was up, he clicked through several screens before pulling up a page with several images of a beautiful old white farmhouse. There was a stone path leading up to the door, four gables on each side of the house, a pond in the back. The landscaping had to have been professional and there was even a white porch swing with colorful pillows. The entire place looked straight out of a magazine.

"If you like the outside, I can move on and show you the inside," he told her.

Scarlett gasped. "Beau, did you buy this?"

He clicked on the next screen and pulled up the entryway photo. "I knew it was the one the second my real estate agent sent options."

Joy consumed her and she reached for his hand. "Beau, I'm so happy for you. I didn't know you were that close to finding a permanent home."

She glanced back to the screen and looked at the thumbnail photos. "Click on that one," she said, pointing. "I think that will make a perfect room for Madelyn. Does it overlook the pond?"

"Wait." He squeezed her hand until she shifted her focus to him. "I bought this house for you."

Scarlett jerked back. "What? For me?"

He released her hand and clicked on another tab. "See? It's just outside of Dallas and only a twenty-minute commute to your new job."

Shock and denial replaced happiness. She stared at him for a moment before looking back to the image of the route from the new house to her new job. She didn't even know where to start with the questions because there were so many swirling around in her head.

"If you don't like it, I can put this on the market and find another," he went on.

She snapped her attention back to him. "Do you hear yourself? When people give gifts they usually give a scarf or a candle, sometimes jewelry. Who buys gift houses on a whim?"

Those dark brows drew in as if he were confused. "It wasn't necessarily a whim. I mean, I knew you were having trouble finding a place to live and I wanted to help you out. Besides, you've done so much for Madelyn and me, plus it's Christmas. I thought you'd like this."

Scarlett shook her head and slid off the stool. How in the world had this last job run the gamut of every single emotion she'd ever had? Worry, anxiety, stress, giddiness, love, anger…betrayal.

"You can't do this," she snapped as she turned back around. "You can't just send me on my way with a parting gift, as if that will replace what has happened here."

Damn it. She hadn't meant to let that sliver of her feelings out. She didn't want him to know how much she'd valued and cherished every second of their time together. When it was time for her to go, she'd have to make a clean break in an attempt to keep her heart intact…if that was even possible.

"You think that's what I'm doing?" he asked. "I bought this for you to make your transition easier, because you deserve a damn break. Why are you angry?"

Maybe her anger stemmed from confusion and hurt and the loss of a hope that maybe they could've been more. Which was ridiculous considering who he was, how they met and how little they'd known each other.

But still, how could she just ignore all that had transpired up until this moment? They'd shared a bed almost every night, he took her on a sleigh ride, he asked her on a date…they'd crammed a lifetime of memories into a few short weeks.

"I can't accept this gift," she told him. "I can't live in a house that you bought when you were thinking of me. When I leave here, I need to be done with what we had, and living there would only remind me of you. Besides, I couldn't accept something so extravagant. It's just not normal, Beau."

"It's not normal to want to help?" he tossed back. "Who's to say I wouldn't come visit?"

Oh, now that was just being cruel. "For what? To extend the affair? What happens if you meet someone else or I do? What happens when one of us decides to get married? We can't drag this affair on forever."

No, because that would be a relationship and they'd

both agreed this fling was temporary. Besides, after she left, she didn't want to know who he was seeing or what was going on in his personal life. No doubt she'd see another piece of arm candy at his side. She certainly wouldn't follow him on social media, but his face would be on every tabloid at the supermarket checkout line. It would be difficult to dodge him completely.

Beau opened his mouth, but a pounding on the cabin door stopped him. Scarlett propped her hands on her hips and stared at him across the room. More pounding on the door had Beau cursing.

He went to the door and jerked it open. "What?" he barked.

Colt stood on the other side holding his cell up for Beau to see a photo. Scarlett couldn't make out exactly what it was, but Beau's shoulders went rigid and he let out a string of curses.

"Want to explain what the hell this is?" Colt demanded. "I believed you when you said she was only your nanny."

Scarlett went nearer to see the image on the phone Colt held out. An image of Beau, Madelyn and Scarlett on the street earlier when he'd leaned in to kiss her. Above it was the headline: "A New Leading Lady for Hollywood's Favorite Cowboy."

Scarlett stilled. Was nothing sacred anymore? It just took one person to snap a picture on their phone and send it to the masses.

Colt's eyes went to her, then back to Beau.

"I am his nanny," Scarlett started. "We just—"

"It's not like that," Beau said, cutting her off. He kept his back to her and his focus on his brother. "She is my nanny and when I leave for the premiere, she'll stay here and care for Madelyn. Scarlett is moving next week and we went out for lunch. I leaned in and kissed her, so what? It's nobody's business."

"Nobody's business?" Colt roared as he pushed his way inside. "You do realize we are trying to honor our father and work on the opening of this dude ranch. Now you're back in town and making headlines like this. What about two weeks from now when it's another woman, or another? We're a close family, with strong core values Dad taught us. Those are the values we want to promote in this new business."

"Calm down," Beau demanded. "Scarlett and I kissed. Don't read anything more into that. It was an innocent kiss. I didn't think anything of it. The only person who will make a big deal about this is you."

Innocent kiss? He didn't think anything of it?

The air whooshed from her lungs and her throat clogged with emotions. She turned from the dueling brothers and went to Madelyn. Blinking against the tears gathering in her eyes, Scarlett bent down and lifted Madelyn in her arms. Then she headed toward her room.

"I'll let you two talk," she said without glancing their way.

She couldn't let Beau see her hurt. She couldn't let him see just how his words had cut her down. What happened to the man she'd come to know? To pretend their kisses meant nothing was flat out a bastard move.

So she'd hide out in her room and gather her strength. Because there was going to be a showdown and there was no way in hell she'd confront him with tears in her eyes.

Fifteen

"You better get your head on straight," Colt commanded through gritted teeth. "Scarlett isn't one of your random women."

Beau glanced to the closed bedroom door and wanted to punch something. He fisted his hands at his sides to prevent decking his own twin.

"I never said she was." Beau faced Colt and pulled in a deep breath. "I said this was nobody's business. And the dude ranch won't suffer because I kissed someone in public. Don't be so dramatic."

Colt adjusted his hat and pocketed his phone. "That's not what I'm saying. You claimed you've changed, but all of the media wrapped their claws around you and what woman you'd be with on any given day. I don't want that carried over here."

"It's not."

Damn it. He didn't want to have this conversation with Colt. He wanted to be in that bedroom because he knew he'd hurt Scarlett with his careless attitude. In his defense, he hadn't wanted to let Colt in on the relationship. He'd been trying to save her reputation. Instead, he'd left her thinking what they had wasn't special.

Only a jerk would purposely hurt a woman.

"If you're done berating me like a disappointed parent, you are free to go."

Colt clenched his jaw and nodded. "If you want to prove you've changed, then start by doing right with Scarlett."

His brother turned and left the cabin, closing the door with a hard click that echoed through the tiny space. Beau muttered a string of curses and raked his hand over the back of his neck. He should've seen this coming. One of the reasons he'd been staying in the cabin was because he'd wanted to dodge the press and any outsiders while he tried to find some semblance of normalcy.

Of course then Scarlett landed on his doorstep and everything snowballed from there. Somehow he needed to fix this—all of it. Her anger toward the home he'd purchased for her, hurting her and having Colt witness everything.

This morning he'd been full of hope and the possibility of exploring a future with her. Now…hell, he didn't have a clue what lay on the other side of that door.

Beau made his way across the cabin and tapped his knuckles on Scarlett's bedroom door. Without waiting for an answer, he tried the knob, surprised she hadn't locked him out.

Easing the door open, he peeked his head through.

Scarlett sat cross-legged on her bed reading a book to Madelyn, who lay in front of her on the plaid quilt.

"What you heard out there—"

"Was the truth," Scarlett said as she closed the book and laid it on the bedside table. "You didn't say anything but the truth. There's nothing more to us than a few weeks of passion and a good time. We've made memories, but that's where it ends."

Beau slipped into her room, but remained by the open door. Her words shocked him. Her steely demeanor seemed so out of character, and he wasn't sure what to say.

Scarlett swung her legs off the side of her bed and came to her feet. She made sure to keep distance between them.

"Since we are so close to the end of our time together," she said, "it's probably best to end the intimate side of things. I'm sure you understand why. And I'm sure you can see why I cannot accept the house. I appreciate the gesture, but you should have your agent put it back on the market."

Well, wasn't her speech all neat and tidy and delivered with an iciness he never expected from someone so warm and caring.

Beau had never experienced this before. Rejection. But it wasn't the rejection that stung. No, what really sliced him deep was the fact that he had caused Scarlett so much suffering that she'd resorted to this as her defensive mechanism.

"Maybe I'm not ready to end things," he stated, folding his arms over his chest.

She stared at him across the room and finally took a step toward him. "There's no reason to prolong this,

Beau. I will continue to care for Madelyn and watch her while you're gone to your premiere. But Maggie will be back next week and I'll be gone. This had to come to an end sometime."

Beau couldn't penetrate this wall she'd put up so quickly around herself. She'd need time and he needed to respect her enough to give it to her. Unfortunately, time wasn't on their side. He could give her today, but that's all he could afford.

"Scarlett, I never want you to believe that kiss, and everything before that, meant nothing." He needed her to know this above all else. "Anything I said to Colt was to protect you. Maybe I didn't go about it the right way, but don't think that I don't care for you."

Scarlett crossed her arms over her chest and nodded. "I'm going to feed Madelyn and take her for a walk to the stables. Then I'll come back and fix dinner."

She didn't extend the invite to the stables. Beau would stay behind, to give her time to think. Because there was no way she could just turn off this switch. If she felt half of what he felt for her, she couldn't ignore such strong emotions.

"I'll make dinner," he volunteered.

"Fine." She reached down and lifted Madelyn in her arms. "If you'll take her for a minute, I need to change my clothes."

"Scarlett—"

"Please."

Her plea came out on a cracked voice and he finally saw a sheen of tears in her eyes. She was struggling to hold everything together.

Beau reached for his baby and held her tight against

his chest. Scarlett continued to stare at him, blinking against her unshed tears.

Without another word, he turned and left her alone in her room. After he shut the door firmly behind him, Beau went to his own room to contact his agent.

Not his real estate agent about the house. No, Beau had every intention on keeping that.

He laid Madelyn down in her crib and handed her a plush toy to chew on. With a deep sigh and heavy dose of guilt, he pulled his cell from his pocket and dialed his agent.

"Beau," he answered. "You're one hell of a hard man to get ahold of."

There wasn't much to say and this conversation was long, long overdue. But it was time for some changes and they were going to start right now.

Beau gripped the phone as he watched his daughter play.

"We need to talk."

Scarlett didn't know what was more difficult, having Beau in the cabin or knowing he was miles away and gearing up for a fancy movie premiere tomorrow.

The past few days had been strained, to say the least. They'd been cordial to each other, like strangers who were stranded together and forced to cohabitate.

Scarlett had just put Madelyn down for her morning nap and was heading to the sink to wash bottles when a knock sounded on the front door.

She wore only leggings and an oversize sweatshirt, and her hair was in a ponytail—compliments of insomnia, anxiety, and a broken heart. But she ignored her state of dress and went to see who the unexpected visitor was.

After glancing through the peephole, Scarlett pulled in a long, slow breath and blew it out before flicking the dead bolt and opening the door.

"Annabelle," she greeted. "What brings you by?"

His beautiful sister-in-law offered a sweet smile and held up a basket. "I brought fresh cranberry apple muffins. Can I come in?"

"I would've let you in without the bribe, but I won't turn it down." Scarlett laughed as she stepped aside to let Colt's wife in.

Annabelle set the basket down on the island. "The muffins were just an excuse," she said as she turned back to face Scarlett. "Can we talk for a minute?"

Scarlett didn't know why Annabelle wanted to talk, but she wasn't stupid. Likely this had to do with Colt and Beau, but if the woman thought Scarlett had any hold over Beau or could sway him to work on the relationship with his brother, well, that couldn't be further from the truth.

"Sure," Scarlett replied. "Have a seat."

She hadn't seen or talked to any of Beau's family since Beau had left a couple of days ago. Scarlett didn't think Beau counted their kisses as nothing, but hearing the words had hurt just the same. And hearing those words only gave her the smack of reality that she'd needed in order to see that this wasn't normal. What normal, everyday woman fell in love with a movie star and had him reciprocate those feelings? The idea was simply absurd.

Annabelle took a seat on the leather sofa and Scarlett sat on the other end. "What's up?" Scarlett asked.

"I'm going to cut out the small talk because it's pointless." Annabelle crossed her legs and leveled her gaze at Scarlett. "I know you have feelings for Beau. Don't deny it. I saw the two of you together. And I can also tell you that he has feelings, too."

Scarlett wanted to deny both statements, but she simply didn't have the energy. Maybe if she let Annabelle talk, she'd get this off her chest and then leave. Scarlett preferred to sulk in private.

"I also know my stubborn husband came down pretty hard on Beau and you, by default," Annabelle went on. "This ranch is absolutely everything to him and he sometimes speaks before he thinks."

Scarlett smiled. "You didn't have to come down here to apologize for him."

"I'm not," Annabelle corrected. "He needs to apologize on his own. I'm here to tell you that you need to ignore what Colt says, what the media speculate and what you're afraid of."

She let out a soft sigh as she scooted over a bit farther. "What I'm trying to say is, your time here is almost up and I'd hate for you to go when you have so much unresolved."

Scarlett glanced down to her clasped hands and swallowed. "How do you know what's unresolved?"

Annabelle reached over and offered a gentle squeeze of her hand. "Because Colt and Hayes commented on Beau's broodiness before he left for LA and he was so happy before that. You make him happy. When he came back here he was broken and scared. He'd never admit that, so don't tell him I said it. But he was so worried for Madelyn and how his relationships with his brothers would pan out...or even if they would."

Scarlett glanced back up. "Beau and I aren't anything. I mean, I won't lie and say things didn't progress beyond a working relationship, but that's over."

"Is it?"

Nodding, Scarlett chewed the inside of her cheek before continuing. "He hasn't fully let me in. I know about the reasons he left here when he was eighteen. I know the issues with his brothers and his dad. But when he and Colt went to see their dad the other day, Beau shut down and wouldn't let me help. I don't even know what happened."

Annabelle leaned back on the couch and released Scarlett's hands. "Grant didn't remember his sons," she stated. "Colt said Beau took it pretty hard and wouldn't even talk to him on the ride home."

Oh, Beau.

"He has let you in," Annabelle went on. "And I'm here to tell you that if you want to give it a try with him, I'm going to help. Alexa and Pepper are ready to join in, too."

Stunned, Scarlett eased back and laughed. "Excuse me?"

Annabelle's smile spread wide across her face. "We all three figured if you want to make a statement, it's going to have to be bold."

"The three of you discussed this?" Scarlett asked, still shocked. "What do you all think I should be doing?"

That smile turned positively mischievous and the gleam in her eye was a bit disconcerting. Annabelle reached for her hand once again.

"What do you say about going to your first movie premiere?"

Sixteen

This entire thing was absurd. The fact that she'd let Annabelle, Alexa and Pepper not only talk her into using the Elliotts' private jet to fly to LA, but they'd given her a makeover on top of that. Somehow, in a whirlwind of deciding she couldn't let Beau go without a fight and getting her hair curled and lips painted, she'd ended up at a Hollywood movie premiere.

Scarlett sat in the back of a limo—somehow the dynamic trio managed to get her that as well—and looked over at Madelyn in the carrier car seat. She'd guarantee this was the only limo arriving tonight with a car seat in the back.

Somehow the ladies had not only procured a dress for Scarlett, along with shoes and a fashionable bag, they'd found a red sparkly dress and matching headband for Madelyn.

As the limo slowed, Scarlett turned her attention to the tinted window. Bright lights flooded the night, cameras flashed, the roar of the crowd filtered in and nerves swirled through her belly at the sight and sound.

What was she thinking coming here? She was so far out of her element. She didn't do crowds or glam or dressing up in a fitted, sequined emerald green gown with her hair curled and in bright red lipstick. She was more of a relaxed kind of girl who made homemade baby food and decorated with clearance Christmas decor.

"Ma'am, I'm going to pull closer to the red carpet entrance," the driver informed her. "Please wait until a guard opens your door and escorts you out."

Oh, mercy. She was really going through with this. Scarlett didn't know how the incredible Elliott women managed the jet, the wardrobe, the limo and a last-minute invite to the red carpet to arrive just after Beau's car. No doubt money talked and they had tapped into some powerful resources to make all of this happen in less than twenty-four hours.

The car came to a stop and Scarlett unfastened a sleepy baby from her car seat. She cradled Madelyn against her chest and adjusted the headband, which had slipped down over one eye like a pirate's patch.

"You'll just be around the block?" she asked the driver. "I'm leaving the rest of Madelyn's things in here."

"Yes, ma'am. You call me and I'll be right back. I'm only driving for you tonight."

Scarlett's stylish clutch was just large enough for a couple of diapers, a travel pack of wipes, her cell and her wallet. She'd just fed the baby before Madelyn fell asleep so they should be good for a few hours. Besides, who's to say Beau wouldn't publicly reject her and she'd be right back in this car in just a few moments?

But what if he asked her to stay? What if he wanted to take her and Madelyn into the premiere and whatever party after?

She'd worry about that when the time came. Right now, her car had eased up and came to another stop. The lights and the screams intensified and Scarlett had to concentrate on the sweet child in her arms, still sleeping and oblivious to this milestone moment.

The door opened and the warm California air hit her. She already missed Texas and the laid-back life with cool evenings. Maybe city life wasn't for her. Maybe she hadn't only found the man—she'd found a piece of herself that clicked right into place. Perhaps the next chapter she was going to start was the wrong one. She had so many questions…and they were all about to be answered.

Scarlett laid a protective hand over Madelyn's ears to protect her from the thundering noise, but she stirred and her eyes popped open.

Questions and microphones were shot in her direction, but Scarlett looked ahead, beyond the men in black suits with mics attached to their lapels. She ignored the questions of who she was, what part she had in the film, who was the cute baby.

Scarlett spotted a flash of the wide, familiar grin then broad shoulders eased away from one set of reporters to another. Beau was flanked by those men in suits who were unsmiling and whose eyes were always scanning the area.

A hand slid over her elbow and Scarlett jerked to see who was beside her.

"Right this way, ma'am." One of the suited men clearly recognized the newbie on the red carpet and tried to usher her along. "There is extra security tonight with all the hype. I'll make sure you and your little one get to the entrance of the theater."

She had to strain to hear him over the white noise of the crowd and she didn't even bother to tell him this child wasn't hers, but rather belonged to the star of the premiere. Had she made a mistake bringing Madelyn? Would Beau be upset? She wanted to show him they could all be a family—they could be one unit and build something solid together.

One thing she knew for certain: she wasn't about to stop and talk to the different media outlets. For one thing, she had nothing to say that she'd want printed or quoted. For another, she was here for only one reason and it wasn't to be interviewed.

Scarlett shifted Madelyn in her arms, still shielding the baby's ears from the chaos. She leaned toward the security guard as she tried to keep up with the pace he'd set.

"I don't need to talk to any reporters. I'm here with Mr. Elliott," she informed him. Then she realized how stalker-like that sounded, so she quickly added, "And this is his baby."

The guard looked at her then down to Madelyn, but Scarlett smiled, hoping he'd move this process along. She had a right to be here—she assumed since Annabelle assured her this was okay—and she couldn't wait.

The man finally nodded and gripped his lapel as he talked out the side of his mouth and ordered the guards up ahead to stop Beau from moving to the next set of reporters.

Scarlett pushed through, ignoring the yells from either side of the roped-off area. If she tried to take in all the lights, all of the questions, all of the chaos around her, she would give in to the fear and the anxiety that had accompanied her all the way from Texas.

She never should have let Beau walk out of that cabin thinking he didn't mean more to her. Their time together since she'd shut down had been so strained and she'd ached for him in ways she'd never imagined possible.

In her defense, she'd been hurt and thought it best if they made a clean break since their temporary arrangement was coming to an end anyway. Unfortunately, that clean break didn't work.

Because she loved him.

There was no way to ignore such strong emotions and if she had to make a fool of herself and take the biggest risk of her life, then she was willing to try for the man she'd fallen for so helplessly.

One of the escorts next to Beau tapped on his shoulder and intervened, pulling him from a current interview. Then the man leaned in and told Beau something that had Beau darting his gaze straight in her direction and their eyes instantly locked.

Scarlett wasn't sure if it was the shock in his eyes or the wide smile on his face that had her nerves kicking in even more. She watched as he raked that sultry dark gaze over her body. Even at this distance and despite the chaos around them, the visual lick Beau gave her had her body instantly responding.

His eyes snapped back to hers and then he was taking long strides to come back down the red carpet. Scarlett didn't think she'd ever seen him smile this much.

"Scarlett."

Beau reached her and shook his head, as if still processing what she was doing here. That went for her, too. She felt as if this whole night was surreal.

"How did you… What… Annabelle texted me and asked if I could get a couple of passes and a limo. My agent pulled everything together, but I just assumed she and Colt were coming."

Well, that explained how the quick red carpet treatment happened.

"Mr. Elliott, who's the lady?"

"Beau, is that your little girl?"

"Is Jennifer James no longer part of your life?"

Reporters shot off so many questions, so prying and so demanding. Part of Scarlett wished she would've waited until he got home, but the other part was glad she'd allowed herself to be talked into coming. Standing here, supporting him, was the only way she knew to truly show him how sorry she was and how much he meant to her.

"I wanted to surprise you," Scarlett told him. "This wasn't my idea, but I needed to tell you—"

He slid his hands up her bare arms and stepped farther into her, with Madelyn nestled between them.

"Say it," he demanded. "I need to hear it."

Scarlett stared up into those dark eyes. "What do you need to hear?"

"That you love me." A corner of his mouth quirked into a grin. "That's why you're here, isn't it?"

She shifted Madelyn, but Beau ended up easing his

daughter up into his arms. He palmed her back with one large hand and held her secure against his chest.

Questions roared even louder, but his eyes never left Scarlett's. The media might as well not even exist; all his attention was on her.

How did she ever think that his words weren't genuine? That he didn't think they were something special? He'd shown her over and over again just how much she meant to him and she'd shied away in fear. She firmly believed that everything he told Colt was to save her reputation, which only added another layer of respect and love.

"Scarlett."

She smoothed her hand down her emerald beaded gown and tucked the clutch beneath her arm.

"I wanted to be the one to tell you." Scarlett smiled, though her nerves were at an all-time high. "But you stole the words from my mouth."

Beau's hand went to her hip and he leaned down. If she thought the crowd was loud before, that was nothing compared to the roar now. They were yelling so much. She couldn't make out full questions, but she did pick up on "romance" and "love." Yes, they had all of that and so much more.

"Say it," he told her again.

Her eyes darted away, but he raised his hand to cup her face, drawing her attention back to him.

"I'm right here," he stated. "They don't exist. It's just the three of us."

His sweet girl was a package deal and she absolutely loved how he always put Madelyn first. And she wanted them as a package because she couldn't think of a better present.

"I love you," she told him as she reached up to lay her hand over his. "I'm sorry I didn't have the courage to say it before, but I got scared the other day. All of this happened so fast, but everything I feel is so, so real."

He closed the distance between them and touched his lips to hers. And that set the media into a tizzy.

"Beau, is this your new leading lady from the picture?"

"Does she have a name?"

"Is this the rumored nanny?"

"Are you planning a Christmas proposal?"

Beau pressed his forehead to hers. "Are you sure you're ready for all of this tonight?"

Scarlett wasn't sure, but if this was what Beau's life consisted of, she'd find a way to make things work.

"If you love me, then I'm ready for anything," she said, easing back to glance up at him.

"I love you, Scarlett. As crazy as it is, as little time as we've known each other, I love you more than I ever thought I could love any woman."

Her heart swelled and she knew the risk she'd taken had paid off.

"I know I could've waited for you to get back to Texas, but Annabelle thought I should make a statement."

Beau chuckled as he slid an arm around her waist. "Baby, that dress is quite the statement and I plan on showing you when we get back to my place tonight."

She hadn't thought that far, but the idea of ending the night at his house in the Hollywood Hills, of seeing even more into his world had her giddy with anticipation.

Scarlett smoothed a hand over Madelyn's dark curls.

"You mentioned wanting a big family and you know that I can't give you that."

"Adoption," he said, using one simple word to put her worries at ease and further prove just how amazing he was. "We'll have that large family when the time is right."

She chewed on her bottom lip and then smiled. "Is it too late to tell you that the farmhouse you bought is perfect for us?"

Beau tapped her forehead with a quick kiss. "That place was always for us," he explained. "I just didn't get a chance to tell you before Colt showed up and then you kicked me out of your room."

He'd planned that house to be for the three of them all this time? Scarlett's eyes welled with tears, but she couldn't cry. It had taken a small army to get this makeup so perfect.

"I think we need to give the reporters something to chew on before they break the barriers."

Scarlett nodded. "Whatever you think."

Beau cradled Madelyn in one arm and kept his other firmly around Scarlett's waist. He angled them toward the front of the red carpet so both sides of the aisle could see them. As soon as they were facing forward, the crowd seemed to hush, waiting for that next golden kernel of a story.

"I'm happy to announce that Scarlett Patterson is in fact my next leading lady," Beau declared. "And my future wife."

Wife? Scarlett jerked her gaze to his, which warranted her a toe-curling wink that set butterflies fluttering in her stomach.

"Is that a proposal?" she asked, shocked her voice was strong.

Beau kept that wide grin on his face. "What do you say? Be my leading lady for life, Scarlett."

"Yes." As if any other answer was an option. "There's nobody else I'd ever want for the star in my life."

Flashes went off, one after another, causing a strobe light effect. As people started yelling more questions, Beau waved and smiled. Scarlett wasn't sure what world she'd stepped into, but the strong man at her side would help her through.

She never thought she'd have the title of leading lady, but as Beau escorted her into the venue, Scarlett realized there was no greater role she could think of—besides wife and mother, of course.

Once inside, Beau ushered her down a hallway to find some privacy.

"I'm taking a break from Hollywood," he told her when they stopped in a quiet place. "I decided that before you came, but now that I see a better future, I'm not sure I'll want to come back here at all."

She didn't know how to respond, but she didn't get a chance. Beau backed her up a step until she came in contact with the wall. He held Madelyn in one arm and reached up with his free hand to stroke the side of her face, then sifted his fingers through her hair.

"You take my breath away, Scarlett. I want you forever, so if we need to take things slow before we marry, I'll do whatever you want."

He kissed her, pouring out his promise and love. When he eased back, he kept his lips barely a whisper away.

"This is the greatest Christmas present I could have ever asked for," he told her.

Scarlett rested her hand over his on Madelyn's back. "Me, too, but I don't know what to wrap up and put beneath our crooked tree."

He nipped at her bottom lip. "How about more of that cookie dip?"

She wrapped her arm around his waist and smiled. "I think I can manage that, but first we have a movie premiere to get to."

"And then we have the rest of our lives to plan."

Epilogue

"What the hell is that?" Colt demanded.

Scarlett smiled and held up her hands in an exaggerated fashion toward the tree. "It's our Christmas tree," she exclaimed.

"Why is it crooked?"

Beau stepped into the room after putting Madclyn down for the night. "Don't ask. Just go with it."

Scarlett rolled her eyes. "He loves it, don't let him fool you."

Colt's brows drew in before he shook his head and shrugged. "Whatever makes you two happy."

Oh, she was most definitely happy. Christmas Eve was magical here at the ranch and tomorrow was Christmas where all of the Elliotts—spouses, fiancées, and children—would gather and start a new chapter.

"I just wanted to come by and let you guys know that

I spoke with the nursing home and they're okay with us bringing Dad home for the day tomorrow."

Beau's eyes went from his brother to Scarlett, then back again. "Seriously?"

Colt nodded. "They said as long as he's having a good day. They offered to send a nurse, but I truly think once he's home, he might see something that triggers some memories, and we can care for him well enough. Even if he's only there an hour. I think we all need it."

Scarlett's heart swelled as tears pricked her eyes. She crossed the room to Beau and wrapped an arm around him.

"This is great news for you guys," she stated. "I think it's exactly what this family needs for a fresh start."

"I just hope he remembers," Beau added.

Colt nodded. "I have a feeling he will. I think this is definitely a Christmas for miracles."

He drifted his gaze toward the leaning tree. "I mean, if you can call that a Christmas tree, I think anything is possible."

Beau laughed as he hugged Scarlett tighter against him. "That tree embodies our lives. We're not perfect, but we're sure as hell trying."

Scarlett smiled as she watched the twins share an unspoken message with their eyes and their matching grins.

Yes, this was a season for miracles.

* * * * *

COMING SOON!

We really hope you enjoyed reading this book. If you're looking for more romance, be sure to head to the shops when new books are available on

Thursday 15th November

To see which titles are coming soon, please visit
millsandboon.co.uk

LET'S TALK
Romance

For exclusive extracts, competitions
and special offers, find us online:

▪ facebook.com/millsandboon

🐦 @MillsandBoon

📷 @MillsandBoonUK

Get in touch on 01413 063232

For all the latest titles coming soon, visit
millsandboon.co.uk/nextmonth